Jane Costello was a newspaper journalist before she became an author, working on the *Liverpool Echo*, the *Daily Mail*, and the *Liverpool Daily Post*, where she was Editor. Jane's first novel, *Bridesmaids*, was an instant bestseller and her subsequent novels have been shortlisted for a number of prizes, including The Melissa Nathan Award for Romantic Comedy and the Romantic Novelists' Association Romantic Comedy Award, which she won in 2010 with *The Nearly Weds*. Jane lives in Liverpool with her fiancé Mark and three young sons. Find out more at www.janecostello.com, and follow her on Twitter @janecostello

Also by Jane Costello

Bridesmaids
The Nearly-Weds
My Single Friend
Girl on the Run
All the Single Ladies
The Wish List
The Time of Our Lives

The Love Shack

JANE COSTELLO

**SIMON &
SCHUSTER**

London · New York · Sydney · Toronto · New Delhi

A CBS COMPANY

First published in Great Britain by Simon & Schuster UK Ltd, 2015
A CBS COMPANY

3 5 7 9 10 8 6 4 2

Simon & Schuster UK Ltd
1st Floor
222 Gray's Inn Road
London WC1X 8HB

www.simonandschuster.co.uk

Simon & Schuster Australia, Sydney
Simon & Schuster India, New Delhi

A CIP catalogue record for this book
is available from the British Library

PB ISBN: 978-1-47112-927-8
EBOOK ISBN: 978-1-47112-928-5
TPB ISBN: 978-1-47112-926-1

Typeset by M Rules
Printed and bound by CPI Group (UK) Ltd, Croydon, CR0 4YY

For my fabulous bridesmaids,
Ali and Nina

Acknowledgments

This book was a joy to write, but I can't deny it involved the odd moment – the ones all authors know about – during which I was quietly tearing out my hair. Special thanks go to Mark O'Hanlon for the reassurance, IT support, for coming up with the title and, if that wasn't enough, for proposing marriage too. (I said yes, obviously).

Huge thanks also to my editor Clare Hey, whose insight played such a crucial role in making *The Love Shack* the book it became. It would've been a far poorer novel without her.

The entire team at Simon & Schuster remain a pleasure to work with – there are too many to lovely people there to mention them all but I must give a shout-out to Suzanne Baboneau, Sara-Jade Virtue, Ally Grant and Dawn Burnett. Thanks all!

One of the more challenging – and interesting – elements of this novel to write about was Dan's job at a homeless charity. Although the charity in this book, its staff and service users, are all entirely fictional, I did spend some time shadowing the team at The Whitechapel Centre in Liverpool before I wrote it. I found such an inspiring bunch of people there, all of whom are doing vital work to help those less fortunate than most of us. I salute you all and thank you for putting up with my (probably daft) questions.

Speaking of which, thank you also to Donna Smith for putting me straight on what might happen in an armed siege (a sentence I never thought I'd find myself writing!)

Thanks also to my agent Darley Anderson and his angels, with a special mention for Clare Wallace and Mary Darby.

Thanks, as ever, to my mum and dad, Jean and Phil Wolstenholme– and (Uncle) Colin Wolstenholme for the number crunching.

And a final mention to my gorgeous children, Otis, Lucas and Isaac – love you all <u>lots</u>. x

Chapter 1

Dan

When a man loves a woman, there are moments when she'll nudge him out of his comfort zone. Most of the time, he can live with this. He'll man up and remind himself what she is to him: his Ingrid Bergman in *Casablanca*. His Patricia Arquette in *True Romance*. His Princess Fiona in *Shrek* (though somehow she never appreciates that comparison).

However, there are times when even the most temperate of men, and I consider myself among them, approach their limit.

I am standing outside a row of small cottages, set high above the River Dee in Heswall in the Wirral Peninsula. I am clutching the estate agents' blurb that was thrust at me this morning – and which I'd shoved into the 'man bag' my mother bought me in her enduring quest to turn me into a metrosexual – and my limit currently feels dangerously close.

When, four months ago, my girlfriend suggested that we buy a place together, I was nothing less than keen. Gemma is the

1

sort of woman I never thought would come along: the girl of my most pleasant dreams, my All Time Great.

But who knew that house-hunting would turn out to be the hardest thing a man could do, outside training as a Royal Marine or venturing into Next on a Saturday?

We started our quest with the old houses we both liked in the Georgian Quarter in Liverpool. 'We could buy somewhere cheap and do it up,' I agreed. What a hopeless, naïve fool.

That was before our chips were thoroughly pissed on, along with all hopes of cracking open the Blossom Hill. The houses in that part of the city – the ones for sale anyway – were miles out of our price range.

So we widened our search to include anywhere within a forty-minute drive from Liverpool, making the rookie error of believing this would open up a cornucopia of choice. Since then, weekends have been dominated by viewings of places it was impossible to leave without wondering whether you'd contracted typhoid from the door handles.

Things came to a head last week when we were touring a semi with a pungent nursing home fragrance and a bathroom suite the colour of bile. I was invited to inspect a converted under-stairs toilet, only to come face-to-face with the owner's teenage grandson, mid-way through evacuating the by-products of the previous night's takeaway.

It wasn't just the puking teenager that did it for me. It was that there was simply nothing left that we hadn't seen. We'd already viewed a vast spectrum of houses, starting with The Dead Certs and ending with The Dregs, and one fact was now screaming at us: *WHAT WE WANT DOESN'T EXIST.*

Which I must admit, even I find hard to believe. I know we're first-time buyers with a challenging budget, but our tick-list shouldn't be insurmountable: nice area, two bedrooms, running water a bonus.

There is of course another issue, one I couldn't say out loud: some houses were deemed unsuitable by Gemma for reasons that remain as mysterious and inexplicable as the construction of Stonehenge.

I'd complete the tour, optimistically anticipating her verdict about a place I couldn't see anything wrong with, only to be told emphatically that she couldn't see anything right about it.

It's not often that I put my foot down. I'd flatter myself if I could list three occasions in the four years we've been together. But we needed a break from this, and I said so.

To my surprise, she agreed wholeheartedly. For a week and a half, life *Before Rightmove* resumed and the internet was free to exist without risk of Gemma melting it.

Then I got a phone call yesterday asking me to knock off work early to check out this place because it looks 'completely perfect on paper'.

So here I am.

'You're early. Anyone would think you were starting to enjoy all this,' she grins, clasping my hand as she stands on her tiptoes and sinks her lips into mine. She tastes of the same cherry lip balm she used to wear when we first got together. I feel a nostalgic pang of regret that this time, instead of heading back for some pleasures of the flesh, I've got to go and pretend I have an opinion on some bay windows.

She's come straight from work and is in heels, a suit and is carrying her 'statement bag' (which I've now learned simply means psychotically expensive).

'I can think of nothing more enjoyable, except perhaps plucking out my own armpit hair,' I say.

'It'll be worth it if it's *The One*. And I've got high hopes. I don't know how I missed this place. It's been on and off the market for a while, apparently. And look at the view, Dan.'

I can't argue with the view, which stretches across rooftops, fields and trees, right down to the river and across to the Welsh hills.

We look up to see the estate agent marching towards the house, his phone at his ear. 'There's one and a half per cent at stake here. I don't care if she's a little old lady – so was the Witch of the West.' He sees us and straightens up. 'Gotta go.' He slams shut the phone.

'*Hiyyy*.' He grabs me by the hand and pumps it up and down. Like Gemma, he's wearing pinstripes, though his are crooked at the top as his trousers stretch violently over a pronounced belly. 'Rich Cummins. FAB to meet you both. Day off, is it?'

'No, I ...' I glance down at my jeans and long-sleeved T-shirt, which might breach the dress code in some work-places, but not mine.

'Pah. Five years ago you'd have been sacked for not wear-ing a tie, and now look. Standards, eh?' Gemma stifles a smile. 'KIDDING! Right. This ... is Pebble Cottage.' He presents the house to us with a flourish of his arm, like a magician's assistant after sawing someone in half. Then he opens up.

The hall is small but bright and overwhelmed by the kind of junk only women buy: candle-holders, key hooks, picture frames that are battered (deliberately).

We enter a living room that's been decorated by someone who knows what they're doing. It has a cast-iron fireplace, lots of books, pale walls, a faintly ethnic rug. On the mantelpiece, there's a single picture – of three women in their late twenties in front of the Sydney Opera House – and gaps where it looks as though others once were.

It's a nice gaff. At least, I think so.

I glance at Gemma as she runs a finger along the window-frame with her Bad Cop face on. She's worn this expression at every viewing since her friend Allie confided that she had paid more than necessary for her house because she failed to hide how keen she was.

The estate agent claps his hands together. 'I should warn you that this property is *blindingly* popular.'

'Um ... why's it still for sale then?' Gemma asks. He responds with an odd little laugh, as if she's told a joke he doesn't quite get.

'There's no chain in this sale – the owners are moving out this weekend. The schools here are UH-MAZ-ING ...'

'We don't have kids,' Gemma tells him.

'The bars and restaurants in Heswall are pumping.'

'Potential for noise and drunks then?'

'It's fabulously convenient for the station ... a commuter's paradise.'

'Thought I'd heard the clatter of trains.'

He does the laugh again and shows us into the kitchen. It's another nice room. Very nice. As are the two bedrooms, with an old-fashioned radiator and antique rocking horse in the window bay, which I presume is some sort of 'feature' as there are no other signs of children living here.

More nonsense spills from Rich's mouth all the way round, while Gemma steadfastly maintains a look that says she couldn't be less impressed if he'd paused to piss on the carpet.

By the time we reach the end, he's still banging on about 'original features' as he points to a rusty door hinge, and effervescing about the 'access arrangements', while highlighting the single front step.

'We'd like to have a look round by ourselves now, if that's okay?' Gemma asks.

'Sure. I'll step outside – take as long as you want. Well, not too long: *Robocop*'s on tonight.' He winks at her and grins. I decide I don't like him very much.

We head up the stairs as Gemma takes more photos on her phone, resisting discussion of whether she likes the place until after the viewing. When we reach the room with the rocking horse, she wanders over, runs her hand along its mane.

'I had one of these when I was a little girl,' she tells me wistfully. 'Mum used to sit on it and hold me on her lap.'

'Go on, no one's looking. I dare you.' I suggest this in the full knowledge that it's never going to happen.

'What – have a go? Don't be ridiculous,' she tuts. Then she bites her lip. 'What if it breaks?'

'You've just said yours used to take the weight of both you and your mum. Although . . .' I register how old it looks . . . 'maybe you're right. It might not hold you.'

She produces a familiar look of indignation. 'Are you saying I've put weight on?'

I love this kind of logic. 'Of course not, there's nothing of you.'

She looks the horse up and down and clearly decides that proving the weight issue – the one that never *was* an issue – is of vital importance. She defiantly hoists up her skirt and climbs on.

I wince as it creaks loudly in protest, but decide not to point this out to her.

'I know what you're thinking: I look like that Khaleesi in *Game of Thrones*,' she grins, rocking backwards and forwards.

'The resemblance is uncanny, particularly with your steed's glass eye and wooden legs.'

'Oh, Dan, this brings back memories,' she sighs, gooey-eyed, as she increases in force and speed until the horse is virtually galloping through the window. 'I have no idea what happened to mine.'

She appears entirely oblivious to the cracking sound vibrating through the floorboards, the sharp pops farting themselves from the arse end of the horse.

'Erm, Gemma . . .'

'I hope my mum didn't throw it away – these things are worth a fortune.'

The horse now makes a sound I can only compare to a 300-foot redwood tree falling on a shed. Gemma's eyes inflate.

'Shit!' she shrieks, but it's too late to rein in and dismount. The horse sinks to one side, throwing her off as if she's just insulted the braid in its mane.

I help her up as she scrambles to a standing position, hoists her skirt over her knickers and stands gaping at an angry break in one of the rocking horse's legs. It's hard to avoid the conclusion that the horse has a glittering career as firewood ahead of it.

'Oh my GOD,' she hisses, hysteria wobbling in her voice. 'Don't suppose you've got any Blu Tack on you?'

Ten minutes later, Rich drives off in his snot-green Seat Ibiza with a '*Laters!*' hanging in the air.

Gemma turns to me. 'I'm going to have to phone and offer to pay for the horse,' she says, rubbing her brow. It is true that our restoration job, which involved precariously balancing the top half of the horse on the broken leg, then hurrying away – would not win either of us a job on *The Antiques Roadshow*.

'Why didn't you just confess to it there and then, like you said you were going to? I'd have said it was me if you were that worried.'

'I know,' she cringes. 'Anyway, look: what did you think of the house?'

It took a few attempts before I worked out the right answer to this question. *Small. No character. Not my cup of tea.* But she doesn't give me a chance to say anything.

'Dan, it's absolutely gorgeous. Did you see the cornices in the bedroom? And the distressed tiles in the kitchen? There's even somewhere for my shoes – that little closet in the main bedroom. Oh my God, I love *everything* about it. This one's not just perfect on paper, it's perfect in every conceivable way.'

She throws her arms around me as one word springs to my lips. *Hallebloodylujah.*

Chapter 2

Gemma

I feel like shouting it from the hilltops: I AM IN LOVE!

I am completely and utterly smitten with a two-bedroom period home boasting Edwardian-style geometric tiled splash-backs, dogtooth oak flooring, restored cast-iron radiators and a fully-functioning feature fireplace.

'Where do I sign?' Dan asks, as he threads his fingers through mine and we walk towards the beach. 'I want to get this done before you change your mind.'

'I'm not changing my mind. I want that house. I'd sell a kidney for it.'

Although I'm a southerner – I grew up just outside Brighton – I've lived in Liverpool long enough to get to know Heswall. It's small but bursting with character, and midway between my work in Cheshire, and Dan's, a hop across the River Mersey in Liverpool.

As we stroll along Thurstaston beach, I mentally replay the tour of each room in the house, trying to stop myself from breaking into song like in the opening scene of *The Sound of Music*.

I picture my beautiful Turkish kilim in front of the fire, the contrasting throws we could drape over the sofa. I imagine the wall art we could hang, the roman blinds we'd install in the kitchen, the vintage wallpaper we could choose for the hall.

'So shall we phone and make an offer?' Dan suggests.

'I thought you'd never ask!' I say. 'Right, what figure should we try? The asking price is over our budget, but in today's market, you can knock £15k off of virtually anything. We could just about do that and still have a little left over to decorate.'

'Would they accept that, when it's so *blindingly* popular?'

'We've got nowhere to sell ourselves, so there's no chain,' I remind him. 'We've already got an in-principle mortgage offer and only have to give a month's notice on our flat. Let's start with £15k less. They'd be mad not to snap it up.'

I phone the number on Rich's business card. It rings four times before someone answers.

'MI5 Central Intelligence. What's your ID code, please?' I frown. 'HA! Don't worry, it's only Rich! Ha, ha!'

When he finally composes himself, I take a deep breath,

make our offer – and sit back and listen while he sucks his teeth. 'Dunno if the sellers'll go for that, to be honest.'

I straighten my back. 'Okay, but I'd appreciate it if you could just put it to them.'

'Will do. I don't hold out much hope though.'

'That's up to them, surely.'

'Yeah, but it is blindingly popular, with the schools and the bars and the—'

'Would you just tell them that we've made an offer, please?' I interrupt.

'You wouldn't want to increase it?'

'That's as far as our budget stretches,' I say firmly.

'Ok-ay-eee,' he replies, as if we'd have more of a chance bartering in chocolate coins.

As I end the call, Dan puts his arm around me and I relax into him, breathing in the faint aroma of his aftershave (which I love) and the clean, salty scent of his skin (which I love even more).

When we first got together, I worried about Dan's looks and the baggage I feared came with them. Without a hint of exaggeration, he is jaw-droppingly gorgeous. A big man, he's physically commanding and athletic, with a tiny scar on his cheek that does nothing to detract from an incandescent smile that makes him appear younger than twenty-nine. His hair is thick, treacle brown, and short. Always short. Anything over three weeks' growth irritates the hell out of him.

If the truth be told, I worried a lot about Dan when we first got together. About what the catch could be. In my early twenties, I'd gravitated towards men you'd describe as 'bad news', having developed a perverse assumption that to be interesting, men had to be flawed, the loopier the better.

I'm about to steal a kiss when my phone rings again. I hold my breath.

'Gem? It's Rich. M'lady . . . I bring news!'

'Okay.' I can hear my heart over the seagulls. Dan raises his eyebrows expectantly.

'And . . . it's . . .' there's clearly a drum roll happening in Rich's head '. . . not good.'

'Oh. They said no?'

'Like I said, it's *blindingly* popular. And what with the schools and the—'

'Did they say what they would accept?'

'Doesn't work like that, hon. If you want to make another offer, feel free. Though, between you and me, you'll have to do a *lot* better. So. Go and have a chat with Hubbie . . .'

'We're not married.'

'. . . and once you've crunched your numbers, reviewed your situation, re-evaluated and revised, come back to Rich and we'll see what we can do.'

I end the call and Dan squeezes my hand for moral support as I fill him in despondently. 'We could go another £2k higher, couldn't we?' he says. 'At a push.'

'That'd leave us with no money to spend on decorating it how we want.'

'Yeah, but it's already lovely as it is. Obviously, I'd be devastated not to dust off my Black and Decker, but I'd cope,' he smiles.

A thought tugs at my brain. 'Dan, I think we need to go higher. I'm going to add my savings. It's not much but the more we can edge it up, the better.'

'I've got a little too – and there's some Premium Bonds I could sell that Grandma bought me years ago.'

Over the next hour, we perform such a thorough scrape-around for cash, I've virtually organised a car-boot sale to flog my knickers.

Rich is not exactly bowled over. 'You can't do any better? I'm saying this because I *like* you guys and I think this house is made for you. But that's not going to cut the mustard. At best it'll curdle the mustard. And this is blindingly popular mustard.'

He returns my call three and a half minutes later to say the answer is no.

'I can sell my car, and downgrade it to something cheaper,' I tell Dan, stifling the urge to weep.

'You could downgrade to the bus like me.'

'We need one car in the household, it wouldn't be practical otherwise,' I insist, attempting to conceal my alarm.

I phone Rich back to add five grand to our offer and wait for his return call as I drive us back to Liverpool, savouring the beautiful interior of my automobile while I can. The clock ticks painfully towards 5 p.m.

'I can't bear this. He said he'd come back to me today and it's now six minutes to five. They close then.'

'So there's still six minutes,' Dan says calmly. Dan is always calm. It drives me mad sometimes, but mostly I've found this to be a positive quality in a boyfriend – particularly, in my experience, following hairdressing crises.

'Listen, Gemma,' he goes on, 'try not to be devastated if we can't make this work. There'll be other houses.'

'Not on the evidence of what we've seen so far. I'd be uncheer-upable if it's a no.'

'Oh, I'd think of a way to cheer you up.'

'Impossible.'

'Will you marry me?'

'Bugger off,' I tut, 'I'm being serious.' The 'will you marry me' quip has been trotted out regularly ever since I confided in Dan that I'd rather chew off my own arm than end up like my parents – just for the sake of a big dress. He laughs as we turn into Liverpool city centre and the phone rings. I pull over to answer.

'Rich?'

'Nope, Spiderman.' I hesitate. 'Pah, gotcha! No, you were actually right first time. It is Rich. Rich Cummins. From Pritchards estate agents.'

'Yes, I know.'

Dan reaches over and clutches my hand. He feels warm and safe and I know that, whatever happens, the house of our dreams or not, as long as we're together we're always going to be all right.

'Before we get onto the offer, might I ask whether one of you had a go on that rocking horse while you were there?'

I hold my breath. 'Oh Rich, I'm so sorry – I meant to say earlier that I'd pay for the damage.'

'Oh no, it's okay. It was actually already broken. I was just meant to warn you about it, that's all – everyone seems to want to have a go. Anyway, the offer . . .'

A glint of light sparkles in Dan's eyes as Rich delivers the verdict.

'Sorry, Gem. Not even close. It's time to look for another house.'

Chapter 3

Dan

We tramp up the stairs to our apartment, having stopped off for a takeaway and wine – in which Gemma was fully complicit despite her recent, self-imposed mandate banning midweek drinking.

The flat is in a new block, an urban stalagmite that's joined the others on Liverpool's burgeoning skyline a few years ago. Although it only has one bedroom, I was sucked in by the slick bathroom, state-of-the-art fridge with built-in ice-maker and a burning lack of desire to traipse around dozens of other places. It was the first place I saw and it's served us well. I never imagined when I signed the lease nearly five years ago that I'd still be here, although what I thought the alternative might be I couldn't tell you.

It wasn't long before I stopped noticing the slick bathroom, of course – though the ice-maker justifiably remains a conversation piece. But I only registered how slack my flatmate Jesse and I had been with the dusters when I first thought about inviting Gemma back for a highly presumptuous coffee. Which brings me to the other reason I remain steadfastly attached to this place: it was the setting of the best date in the history of dates, anytime, ever. Our third.

As I lay in bed feeling the twists of her hair between my fingers, I couldn't recall ever feeling quite so exhilarated. Okay, that sounds a bit weird, as if I'd just had a hard session in the gym, so I'll keep things simple. Even then, after I'd known her only days, she made my chest feel like it was going to burst open every time I looked at her.

You'd think that might have augured something big right there: the fact that we'd both end up falling in love for the first time in our lives. But the only future I was planning with her at that precise moment in time involved getting overheated under the duvet again at some point in the next twenty minutes.

Despite the flat being mine to begin with, when Jesse moved out and Gemma moved in, indecently soon after we'd met, she made it feel like a home for reasons that went beyond the co-ordinated cushions that came with her.

In lots of ways, we shouldn't work together. I'm a 'bleeding heart liberal' (her words) and she's a card-carrying fascist i.e. she reads *Mail Online*, even if it's only for the sidebar of shame.

I was privately educated, went to Cambridge and had a glittering career as *A Disappointment* (at least to one parent). She went to a middle-of-the-road state school and dazzled her family. I read Louis de Bernières and *The English Patient* and go to sleep each night feeling enriched and relaxed. She reads Lee Child and Luther and goes to sleep with a bread-knife under the bed, just in case.

'This is the crappiest takeaway I've ever tasted,' Gemma says, throwing down her fork on a chicken chow mein that looks like it's been fished out of a sludge pipe.

'That cannot possibly be true,' I say, topping up her glass. 'We have had some truly crappy takeaways.'

I shove my dish on the coffee table and pull her towards me, tucking her hair behind her ear. It's only when I register the wobble in her lip that I realise just how much this house business has got to her.

'We could always do something else with the money we've saved up. Go travelling or something,' I say, though I have no idea where it came from. I'd never even thought of it before – and I already know she toured south-east Asia with two friends in her gap year after university.

'I've done all that, Dan,' she sighs. 'I'm twenty-nine now, not eighteen.'

I squeeze her closer into me, wanting to make her feel better but at a loss as to how. I decide to pay a visit to the florist tomorrow. Life became far easier the day I worked out that flowers, particularly *outside* the traditional birthdays or anniversaries, are not in fact the pointless waste of money I'd assumed they were for the last twenty-odd years.

We stay up late, watching a vacuous action film that I pretend not to enjoy, before going to bed and making passionate but mildly clumsy, wine-drunk love. She falls asleep with her head on my chest, but I can't bring myself to move her, even if I know I'll wake up with a crick in my neck. For a few hours I fall into a deep, dreamless sleep.

It's at 4.30 a.m. that, aware of a series of explosive coughs about five centimetres from my ear, my eyes spring open.

'Oh sorry, did I wake you?' The cough mysteriously disappears.

'It's okay,' I mumble, about to turn over when she props herself up on an elbow. I close my eyes.

'Well, now you're awake . . .'

'I'm not awake.'

'Clearly you are or you wouldn't be talking to me.'

'I'll be asleep again in seven seconds,' I yawn.

'Okay. But can I ask you something?'

'Is it: "Darling, why on earth can't you get to sleep?"!' I ask.

'Sorry! It's really important though.'

She reaches over to turn on the bedroom light. Her hair is mussed up on the top like Russell Brand's and she has a smudge of mascara under her eye. I suppress a smile. 'Go on.'

'It's about Pebble Cottage. I've had an idea. I reckon we're about another five grand short of making an offer they couldn't refuse.'

'Gemma, you've already planned on selling your car, my Premium Bonds and half the furniture. The only thing left is our bodies. You'd do all right, but I don't think I'd raise more than a fiver.'

I expect her to make a joke about being certain that someone would have me in the right part of town, but she doesn't. This is a worrying development.

'I'm talking about something completely different. Changing tack. I'm talking about reducing our outgoings drastically to free up a lump sum of capital. I'm talking about getting rid of the flat.'

'What?'

'If we didn't have any rent to pay, not to mention bills, we'd save up that amount in . . . I don't know, five months. Think about it.'

'Yes, but there's a vital flaw in your cunning plan, Baldrick,' I tell her. 'And it's that we need the flat. You know, to live in.'

'I was coming to that.' Only she doesn't say anything.

'Go on then.'

Her mouth starts to twitch at the side and I can tell she's gauging my reaction before she's managed to even spit it out. She sits up straight, defiant, and looks me in the eye. 'We can go and live with your mother.'

I laugh. I laugh quite a lot. In fact, I almost fall off the bed.

21

Then I realise she isn't joining in. 'You're not serious.' And when she edges closer and puts her arm on mine, leaning in to kiss me, 'Don't be trying to use your feminine wiles on me. They won't work.'

'Dan,' she fake-murmurs. 'Do it for me.'

'You can bugger right off.'

'Okay, okay,' she says, sitting up again. 'Just hear me out. I know it wouldn't be ideal. I know you vowed when you moved out when you were seventeen—'

'Sixteen.'

'Sixteen, that you'd never live there again, but it's not like you don't love your mum. She's great.'

I flash her a look. 'Well, yeah. She's my mum so she's great by default, but here's the difference – she's *not* great to live with. Whose mum is, once you're no longer a kid?'

'It wouldn't be that bad.'

'I'd prefer to live with Genghis Khan.'

'Her house is enormous . . .'

'You're not listening to me.'

'Your grandma lives there too and she's gorgeous.'

'Is my voice like a dog whistle? Inaudible to human beings?'

'It's on the right side of Cheshire, so totally commutable.'

'It takes ages to drive from there to Liverpool – and I don't even have a car.'

'With no rent to pay, you could get a cheap one. It'd only be for six months.'

'You said five.'

'Six months tops.'

'You said—'

'Oh come on, Dan. I'm not asking you to do this for me, I'm asking you to do this for *us*. You want the house, don't you?'

'Gemma, that house will not still be on the market in six months' time. You heard what the estate agent said.'

'I know, but it might be in *two*. It takes a few months for a house sale to happen – with all the surveys and legal work. So if we moved out now and started saving really hard, we could make an offer after a couple of months with a view to completing the sale a few months after that. Only then would we need to hand over the full amount of money.'

'What if it's gone by then?'

'It won't be. But if, for argument's sake, it was – we'd simply have some extra cash under our belt, which will put us in a stronger position to buy somewhere else.'

'You've hated everywhere else.'

She shakes her head. 'It's not going to happen. I've got a good feeling about it.'

'I'm sorry, Gemma,' I say assertively. 'It's absolutely out of the question. There is no way you're going to change my mind. I'm a hundred per cent against the idea.'

By 7.35 a.m. we've handed in our notice on the flat.

Chapter 4

Gemma

I drive to work with adrenalin pumping through my body for reasons that go beyond the fact that I got beeped at traffic lights while fantasizing about free-standing oak kitchen units with a Belfast sink and vintage taps.

I'm tired but wired, my head buzzing as I pull into my allotted space outside Wilburn House, the northern headquarters of Austin Blythe, the advertising agency where I work. The building is a former stately home, complete with shrubbery clipped to within an inch of its life, a Grecian-style outdoor pool (in which nobody, to my knowledge, has ever dared swim) and humungous, phallic gates, which my friend Sadie says is a convenient warning to those who enter that the place is run by pricks.

'You know that bottle of Peach Schnapps I got from a client

at Christmas?' Sadie greets me as she types feverishly at the desk opposite mine. 'It's still in my drawer and I'm currently feeling a need to stick a straw in it and suck until I'm unconscious.'

The room in which Sadie and I work isn't huge – there are just eight desks – but it's perfectly formed: they upgrade the interior here more often than I do my bikini line. At the moment, it's all Danish-designed chairs, monochrome desks and, in a bid to underline how cutting-edge we are, a selection of outlandishly-coloured bean bags arranged in a circle under the window in an area officially named the 'Think Tank' (and unofficially the 'Wank Tank').

'Good morning!' I say brightly.

'Not by anyone's definition is it a good morning,' she mutters. 'We've had a meeting sprung on us at ten, we need to chase up the visuals we should've had a week ago, and we need to complete something resembling an advertising campaign before we see Sebastian this afternoon.'

There is a peculiar way things work in advertising that is virtually unique to this profession, with the exception of police work and the writing of West End musicals: we have partners.

Sadie and I have had this conjugal arrangement for six years, since the day we started. As art director, she does the pictures; as copy writer, I do the words – although the reality is rarely that defined. Think Cagney and Lacey without the guns, Lennon and McCartney without the guitars, Ant and Dec without the six-figure salaries.

25

People assume that, because the average television advertisement is less than twenty seconds long, my bit doesn't involve much. I'm convinced my mum thinks I jot something on a fag packet, then spend the rest of the day filing my nails.

In reality, a vast amount of work goes into creating what viewers see on screen: research, brainstorming, endless fine-tuning with account managers, creative directors, motion graphics specialists – and fighting off the 'traffic managers', whose job it is to organise our workload i.e. pile as much on us as possible.

Today, we're putting the finishing touches on the ideas Sadie and I have worked up for a new condom campaign, before presenting it to Sebastian Boniface – Austin Blythe's brand new, hot-shot creative director.

'Why don't I get some coffee first,' I suggest, taking out my purse.

She looks at me like I need some strong pills and a session of electric shock therapy. 'We haven't got time for coffee!'

'Deep breaths,' I wink, heading to the staff canteen, or *The Playhouse* as they've rebranded it. I wait in the line as Shirley, our long-standing dinner lady, has her daily battle with the cappuccino machine before setting down a cup in front of me that looks very like she's pumped it out of a can of Gillette shaving foam.

I glance up into the car park and spot the man himself, Sebastian, getting out of his classic car. I couldn't tell you what it is, except that it's a convertible, expensive-looking and so vividly red that if it was a lipstick shade it'd be called 'floozie's knickers'. He clicks the lock and caresses the bonnet with his fingers in the same mildly erotic manner you see on soft porn movies or adverts for leather sofas.

I pick up the coffees, register that the clock has hit 9 a.m. and step outside to make a crucially important phone call – to Rich.

'So basically, you can't afford the house now, but you will in a couple of months?' he concludes, after I've brought him up to speed on my grand plan.

'Exactly.'

'There's absolutely *no way* this house will still be on the market then,' he tells me stoutly. 'It's *blindingly* popular and—'

'Rich,' I interrupt. 'You told me it'd been up for sale for a while. Is it *really* blindingly popular?'

'Yes! But for one reason or another things haven't progressed as we would've liked.'

My skin prickles with suspicion. 'Is there something you're not telling me?'

'Course not!'

'It hasn't got dry rot or rising damp or electrics that were rewired by a chimpanzee?'

'Don't be daft. Full disclosure these days, Gem. All I'm saying is – yes, properties take longer to sell now than a few years ago. But waiting a couple of months before you put in an offer . . . don't get your hopes up is my advice.'

27

'If we can get the money together before then, we'll act sooner. How long exactly has it been on the market? Did you say a couple of months?'

'Arhoehr,' he coughs.

'Eh?' I repeat.

He sighs. 'It first went on the market two years ago, but the seller's chain fell through, so they took it off for ages. When it went back on, it got a buyer early on, but their mortgage offer was retracted, so it came off the market again for a few months. It went back on last week.'

'So that's why I've only just seen it on Rightmove.'

'Precisely. They got totally fed up of the whole thing. But this time they're certain.'

'So am I.'

'Good luck with that saving then. Just don't take too long, will you?'

By the time I've returned to my desk, Sadie is glaring at her to-do list as if her head might cave in. I thrust a coffee in her hand and place a hazelnut cookie – her favourite – on her desk.

'Thanks, Gem,' she says. 'Oh God, sorry, I haven't even asked you about the house you went to look at yesterday. Any good?'

'We're putting in an offer.'

Her eyes widen. 'Wow. Dan must've had the shock of his life.'

'It wasn't just me who didn't like the others, you know. He felt as strongly as I did that they were all rubbish.' She picks up her biscuit. 'Anyway, it's over our budget, but the plan is to go and live with Dan's mum for a few months to save up some money. Assuming she'll have us.'

Sadie's biscuit slips out of her fingers and plops into her coffee, pebble-dashing half her desk with cappuccino foam. She gapes at me with an open mouth, as if I've just told her I'm off to run a tattoo parlour in a small village on the fringes of the Peruvian Andes.

'You must really love it if you're prepared to live with Dan's mum,' she says.

I tut. 'Dan's mum's great.'

'I couldn't live with anyone's mum, even my own. Much as I love her, that lost its appeal after I hit . . . ooh, five.'

Sadie Dass is an exiled Londoner who moved here with her then boyfriend when he got a job in Manchester. He dumped her within six weeks of the move, but having driven here in her VW Beetle on a Bank Holiday weekend, she decided she couldn't face the M6 again, so would stay for the foreseeable. Seven years later, she's still here, and in that time has got herself a far nicer man, Warren, who last year became her fiancé.

The wedding is scheduled for next year, grows more lavish by the day and it's fair to say that the planning has done nothing to instil Sadie with a sense of inner harmony.

She has a soft London accent, enviably smooth skin,

inherited from her Guyana-born great-grandmother, and hair that she insists she can't do anything with but which always looks amazing to me.

I must admit, she took a little while to grow on me after we first met. I always assumed I worked better with people who are rational, calm. Sadie is about as calm as Hurricane Katrina. But she is also thoughtful, a good listener, hilarious on a night out and the most dedicated office gossip you could hope to meet.

That afternoon, we head to the boardroom to set up before our meeting with Sebastian. Sadie battles with the flip-chart stand for our 'scamps' – the initial sketched concepts – while I lay out the product i.e. enough condoms to service an STD clinic for a year.

Then I turn my attentions to the door, which I hate with a passion in this meeting room because it doesn't close properly and, when open, bangs against the filing cabinet – something that's guaranteed to happen at the exact moment you're attempting to say something important.

'This isn't going to work,' I mutter, shoving a folded piece of paper under the door, 'and we're going to be starting in ten minutes. We need something that will buffer the handle.'

She scans the room like she's Bear Grylls trying to find some edible vegetation in the jungle. 'Wait here! I've got an idea,' she says, darting to the presentation table. She grabs a straw-berry-flavoured condom and rips open the packet.

'What the hell are you doing?' I ask.

'Improvising,' she replies. Then, holding it to her lips like some demented children's party entertainer, she starts blowing into it, until it's the size of a small beach ball.

'Please tell me you're about to turn that into a giraffe for me to take home with a party bag – and not try to fix the door with it,' I say.

'It'll be fine, watch,' she insists, as she proceeds to secure it to the door handle with an elastic band.

I glance at the clock: we have one minute before Sebastian is due to arrive. To be fair to Sadie, her contraption is completely effective – and not at all visible from where we'll be sitting.

We head back to the table, just in time for Sebastian to appear in the doorway.

'Sadie! Gemma!' He's wearing the sort of grin you'd expect to see in the closing moments of an accomplished fellatio session.

Sadie runs over and shakes his hand vigorously. Then he turns to close the door, but she leaps in front of him. 'It's very stuffy in here – do you mind if we leave it open?'

'Good idea,' he decides, heading to the desk.

His hair is thick, dark blond, a bit too long; like Severus Snape with highlights. He's in his early fifties but looks younger. And, judging by his dress sense (fitted shirt with a millimetre of breathing space; Armani chinos) is aware of it.

Everything about him is smooth: his hair, his voice, even his teeth look as though they've been polished with Mr Sheen. He invites us to sit down and insists on pouring the tea for us. I can see why clients would love him.

'So, ladies,' he says, clasping his hands together and making the twinkliest of eye-contact. '*Condoms.*' He pronounces the word animatedly. Sadie crosses her legs.

'Johnnies,' he continues, with a flourish. 'Rubbers, French letters, sheaths . . .'

Sadie visibly relaxes when he stops. But it's only a momentary intermission.

'Joy Bags, Close Combat Socks, Gentlemen's Jerkins . . .' Then he smiles benignly. Sadie and I exchange glances. 'One thing's for sure, there are a heck of a lot of euphemisms for one of *these.*'

He pulls out a *Bang* condom packet – the brand we're working on – and starts twiddling it round in his fingers. 'Question is, how can we make *Bang* Condoms the UK's diving suit of choice?'

'Would you like us to show you our thoughts so far?'

He opens his arms wide. 'Can't wait. Your reputations precede you, ladies. I'm . . . *excited.*' There's something terribly unsettling about the way he says that.

I turn over the first scamp, hopefully to blow him away with our ideas, when I am sharply interrupted.

Pthwww!

I know it's the condom deflating. Sadie knows it's the condom deflating. Sebastian, on the other hand, can only come to the conclusion that the origin of this outburst is one of the two of us.

He shifts in his seat, glancing between us, clearly trying to work out which of us has consumed an abundance of broccoli and baked beans for breakfast.

I hastily decide to move on and pray he assumes he's imagined it.

At this stage, we produce three concepts – a safe option, something more edgy and the one we like the best. I go for safe first, as always – the Volvo of condom adverts.

'We saw this one as being entirely animated,' I explain. 'It's a quirky take on boy meets girl—'

'Let me stop you there.' I do as I'm told. 'I'm going to say something . . . radical.' Sebastian opens his mouth.

Pwththhh!

I grab the sides of my seat and start jigging it about. 'Damn chair,' I apologise. 'It's always squeaking. Sorry. Carry on.'

He narrows his eyes then continues, 'We're not having a safe option.'

'Oh. Okay,' I reply, interested, while Sadie's brow furrows deeper.

'Here's my thinking. Condoms are safe, by definition, so we need to be edgy to counter-balance that. Edgy is the only way to go on this. We don't give them the usual three choices. We give them: edgy, edgier, and so edgy they're a step away from falling off a cliff.'

Sadie can't contain herself. 'But we've spent weeks—'

'We'll show you our "edgy" first then,' I interrupt, taking out the next scamp. 'In this one, the tone is different. We're at a club. We've got a Hed Kandi-type soundtrack. We've got dancers here and—'

'Ladies, this is not edgy,' he proclaims. 'This is *predictably* edgy. The twisted Utopia theme, the post-apocalyptic, narcissistic atmosphere. I bet you've even thrown in a couple of kissing lesbians, haven't you?'

The answer is no, but I don't get a chance to tell him.

Pwtthh!

He grits his teeth and just looks appalled by both of us now, but carries on regardless. 'Predictably edgy and edgy are not the same thing at all. What I want is . . . unpredictability.'

Sadie has stopped breathing. And I must admit, I'm not feeling great about having weeks' worth of work dismissed before he's even looked at them properly.

'Now. Who is the *last* person you'd expect to be advertising condoms?'

Pwthw— 'Gloria Hunniford?' Sadie blurts out, in a desperate bid to distract him. To be fair, it works.

Sebastian raises his eyebrow, puts his hand on his chin and nods thoughtfully. 'Keep going.'

Sadie swallows and looks at me for help. 'Um . . . Keith

Chegwin,' she splutters. He raises an encouraging eyebrow. 'Peter Sissons, Prince Philip . . .'

Pwthw— 'The Archbishop of Canterbury!'

He grins and looks at both of us. 'Ladies, I like your way of thinking.' He stands up, removes the scamps and flings them across the desk at us. 'Take another week on this one. You'll come up with the goods, I know it.'

I am trying my best to think of a diplomatic way to protest about this in the strongest possible terms, when something else does it for me.

PWTTHWWWTHTH!

The condom disengages itself from the door handle and performs a spectacular loop-the-loop across the floor before landing slap bang on the desk in front of Sebastian, who is so stunned he appears to have lost the motor skills in his bottom jaw.

And that, ladies and gentlemen, is how to make an impression with your new boss.

When I get back to my desk, my phone is ringing. I see that it's Dan and decide to take the call in the corridor.

'How's your day going?' he asks.

'I've had better.'

'You're not the only one.'

'Why, what's happened to you?' I ask.

'My mother's agreed to let us stay.'

'Ah, brilliant!' I gush.

'Isn't it?' he deadpans.

'Oh, come on, you know it'll be worth it.'

'I know, I'm only joking. Sort of anyway. You do realise however,' he adds teasingly, 'that before I met you, there was no woman on earth I'd have made a sacrifice like this for.'

I hesitate, suppressing a reflex action to return the sentiment and assure him that there's no man I'd have done it for either. But that wouldn't exactly be the truth.

Chapter 5

Dan

I've spent the morning getting to know a twenty-one-year-old alcoholic who's been out of prison for eleven months and has a mental-health file as long as your arm.

This might not be most people's idea of fun, but it's an average day – in that there's no such thing – in my job at a homeless charity called the Chapterhouse Centre.

My role as a supported housing worker is to keep people *off* the streets before they get there. Our team helps vulnerable people from all walks of life to climb out of their deepening hole and build something you or I might recognise as a normal life.

Not all of them have drink problems like Gary, the twenty-one-year old, although I've helped my share of alcoholics, as well as sex workers, ex-cons and drug users. They all have a different story to tell. And while in lots of cases those stories involve abuse, dysfunctional childhoods and substance misuse from a stupid age, some have simply fallen on hard times.

I'd never claim it's an easy job, but I'd never want to do anything else.

After a bus journey from Gary's temporary accommodation, I arrive at the administrative office where I'm based – a renovated Victorian school house half a mile outside the city centre. It's a beautiful building, although I can't claim it'd win design awards once you're through the door.

If ASDA Smartprice did offices, this'd be what it would look like: functional, but bright, clean and notably no frills (the day we got a microwave capable of emitting more than 400 watts was the source of significant celebration).

It's a long way from the workplace I left four years ago, when I was a stockbroker for a firm called Emerson Lisbon. I earned three times as much as I do here, and while I miss the salary, the same can't be said for the job.

I'd been volunteering at the Chapterhouse Centre since university – at our enablement centre, where rough sleepers go for a solid meal and help from a support worker – when the chance of a fulltime job came up. I couldn't bring myself to say no.

I'm in the hall, heading towards the stairs when our administrator Jade pops her head round the door.

Jade's in her early thirties and is on her own with two young daughters after her husband ran off with a nineteen year old.

Her take on this is: 'She must've found his farting and smelly feet just irresistible.' She's great fun – and pretty, if not my type – with vivid green eyes and lips she paints in a colour that looks like it's come out of a highlighter pen.

Jade is known for two things. First, she's been on a diet for the entire five years I've known her. Secondly, Pete – my colleague, good friend and long-time drinking accessory – is madly in love with her, a fact of which she is blissfully oblivious, despite him having the subtlety of a five-foot air horn.

'How was the house – any good?' she asks.

'So good Gemma wants to buy it.'

'Oh, that's great news!'

'But we can't afford it.'

She frowns. 'That's *not* great news.'

'Except she's found a way.'

'Oh brilliant!'

'But it's a terrible idea.'

She frowns. 'Oh. Then … *bad*. So what's the idea?'

I wonder if there's a way of saying this without losing every shred of professional credibility I possess. 'We're moving in with my mum.'

'HAHAHA!' Pete is on the stairs, doubled up with laughter. 'Your *mum*?'

I look beadily at him. 'What's wrong with … I won't finish that question.'

Pete, who works on our Dual Diagnosis team, is three years

older than me, five inches shorter, and has been single for six months after finally dumping his longterm girlfriend Sarah (a nightmare) to focus on his so far fruitless quest to seduce Jade. He's employed every tactic in the book: enquiring what her perfume is (her reply: 'Erm, Sure Ultra Dry'); fixing the Secret Santa so she got a book called *Why Short Men Are Better Lovers* and hanging round her desk with this pathetic doe-eyed expression that makes him look like Droopy Dog after a heavy glue-sniffing session.

He slaps my back. 'There's nothing wrong with your mum, my friend. There's definitely something wrong with a twenty-nine-year-old man still living at home though. Will she ground you if you don't finish your homework?'

'Oi! I lived with my mum when I split up with Alan,' Jade says indignantly.

'That's totally different,' Pete decides. 'You were destitute. You had nowhere to go. You were on your own with two young children and—'

'Actually, I could've rented but my mum insisted on doing the girls' ironing and sorting their tea out every night. I wasn't going to say no to that.'

'Besides,' I interrupt, 'I'm not "still living at home". This is a temporary arrangement while we save up enough for the house we want.'

Pete looks at me. 'So what time's your curfew?'

Jade laughs. Then: 'Ooh, Dan, while I remember: my

friend's over from America in a few weeks. What bars shall I take her to? You know all the trendy places.'

'Hmm . . . I'll have a think,' I reply.

'*I* know some good places,' Pete leaps in.

'Oh, okay,' she shrugs.

'I could come with you, if you like.'

'Oh. You wouldn't mind?'

For a moment he looks as though he's experiencing some sort of transcendental awakening; his eyes are virtually rolling into the back of his head with joy. 'Of course not. It'd be a pleasure.'

Then her face drops. 'Oh bugger. I forgot. I said we'd have a girls'-only night. She's just been dumped. You'd be bored stiff.'

'I wouldn't!'

'God, you would – it'd be awful for you,' she insists. 'We just want to spend the night slagging off men.'

'*I* can slag off men,' he offers.

'You'd hate it.'

'I'd love it!'

'Let's do it another time, shall we? I'm sure my mum'll agree to babysit again. Maybe some point next year.'

By the time we get upstairs to the office, he's inconsolable. 'That's it. I need tips,' he says, flopping onto his chair.

'Don't look at me for some sort of insight,' I tell him.

'Come off it. When I first met you, there wasn't a night out that didn't involve some woman thrusting her phone number into your trouser pocket.'

'You exaggerate.'

'You were a great big slag and don't deny it.'

'Am I supposed to defend myself?'

'No,' he sighs. 'You're supposed to tell me how to do it.'

To listen to Pete, you'd think I was some sort of Aldous Snow figure in my pre-Gemma days. But we're talking about a few flings, not six dancing girls and a two-litre bottle of Durex Play every week night.

I will admit though that the first time Gemma and I crossed paths, the idea that one day we'd contemplate buying a house together would have filled me with ... surprise.

The reason wasn't just because we'd have looked an unlikely couple physically, though at the time that was true, nor because I didn't fancy her (also undeniable). It was because we were both on a date – with other people.

I was nineteen, back from Cambridge for Christmas after my first term and technically living at home with Mum. In reality, I spent that break bunking in with people, including an old mate from school nicknamed 'Stringfellow', who'd quit Cardiff University to set himself up as a nightclub entrepreneur.

I'd agreed to take my date for the evening to an insalubrious bar on the edge of Duke Street because two 'contacts' had offered 'Stringfellow' the unmissable opportunity of buying a stake in it. He wanted my opinion on the place while he cut his teeth at the bar, serving Cider and Black to Goths, bikers and miscellaneous reprobates, none of whom looked overly impressed with my nice V-neck jumper and Shockwaved fringe.

My date, Terri, was small, blonde, stupendously bosomed and had the eyes of a possessed Barbie doll. I'd handed my number to her in a club the previous weekend, in such a drunken blur that I barely recognised her now. She'd brought with her this unfeasibly small handbag, from which an array of eyeliners and lipsticks kept tumbling. The solution, she decided, was getting 'her man' (that, apparently, was me) to put them in my coat pockets.

It was clear when we pushed open the door that she wasn't massively enthusiastic about the venue. In fact, she looked at the clientele as if she'd been presented with the still-beating hearts of two slaughtered lambs.

Still, Terri decided to make the best of a bad job and seduce me. Unfortunately, I couldn't dredge up a flicker of attraction to her. Besides – date from hell that this probably makes me – my interest was already diverted: to a girl with a nose ring, dreadlocks and – I swear this is what I thought – the face of an angel. Poetic, I know.

From her body language – the crossed arms, the lack of eye-contact – her evening was not going well either.

The guy she was with, a skinny, tattooed bloke with an explosion of facial hair, was pleading with her, flirting with tears one minute and rage the next. She'd clearly had a few and was tiring of his advances, though was too polite to punch him in the face, despite how tempting it must have been.

I was mesmerised by her. The defiant crook of her brow. The smart, glittering eyes. The full mouth I knew would light the place up when she smiled.

As Terri encouraged me to engage in a conversation about the merits of stockings and suspenders, I asked her to pause while I ordered more drinks. But when I turned back from the bar, the girl who'd caught my attention was gone. Her date was left standing, the only guy in the place who hadn't realised she was probably never going to return from the ladies, at least not this decade.

The next thing I knew, Terri's arms were around me and she was running her tongue along my ear, like she was trying to fish something out of it. I can't remember much after that, nor indeed the exact events that led to Terri storming out after I'd failed to ravish her.

I do remember sitting there in a haze of alcohol, giving Terri a couple of minutes' head start, before I threw on my coat and left. Outside, the weather had turned biblical, hailstones plummeting from the sky as if Someone was pelting me from up on high for being a less than gentlemanly date.

I pulled up my collar and ran to the closest taxi rank I knew, as water seeped into my boots. When I reached the end of the queue, it eased off slightly.

'Not your type of pub?' It was the girl with the dreadlocks and defiant brow. She sneezed and held the back of her hand up to her face self-consciously. Rain slid off her nose and black trails of make-up swam down her cheek. I decided there and then that she was beautiful, though I got the impression that she either didn't know it, or at least refused to acknowledge it.

'Not my type of date, if I'm honest.'

She smiled briefly, then crossed her arms and turned back to the queue. It wasn't moving. The rain was picking up again.

I assumed by the fact that I was staring at the tiny seashell tattoo on her shoulderblade that our small talk was over, until she turned and said, 'We're going to be at least fifteen minutes here. You do realise we're going to get drenched?' Her eyes flickered to my jacket.

'Oh, sorry,' I said and slipped it off my shoulders to offer it to her. She burst out laughing and I felt like the new boy at school wearing shit trainers. 'I wasn't after your coat, honestly,' she assured me.

I needed to up my game. I'd spent the last couple of years coming up with a repertoire of amusing, self-deprecating pick-up lines. I needed to say something now with a pinch of flirtation, a soupcon of irony and just the right amount of cheeky, wide-boy candour.

'Just thought you might want to stop your hair getting wet.'

Brilliant. Just brilliant. Why she didn't run a mile at these new depths of gormlessness is anyone's guess.

'I suspect you spent longer on your hair than I did,' she teased, as rain fell onto her cheekbones. I must have looked put-out. 'Sorry, I was just joking with you. Your hair's very nice.'

'That's overwhelming, thank you,' I said snarkily in a bid to regain some self-respect.

She'd have been within her rights to tell me to piss off right then, but I'm happy to say that she just smiled and said, 'Where do you live?'

'Staying at a friend's in Waterloo. Normally Cheshire.'

'Hmm, very posh,' she smirked.

'Not really.' Then her teeth started chattering. 'You sure you're okay?'

She shrugged. 'Starting to think I was a bit hasty about your coat.'

I took it off and thrust it round her shoulders, feeling a tug of self-satisfaction. It was huge on her, a big tent of fabric that swamped her frame. I liked the look of it on her bare arms.

'Are you at university here?' I asked.

'Yep. Doing English Lit. You?'

'Economics. Not here though. Cambridge,' I said.

'Ah ... definitely posh then.' And when she smiled this time, it was big and warm and her whole face shone.

As the taxi queue disappeared, I attempted to manufacture

a moment when I could ask for her number. But when that moment came, near the front of the queue, she opened her bag and gasped.

'What is it?'

'I've lost my purse! Oh, bollocks, I've lost my purse!'

A frantic minute ensued in which she persuaded half the queue to scramble through the gutter, before the car at the front got fed up and started beeping. 'Oh Gawd,' she sighed, looking at the heavens. 'Looks like I'm walking.'

This was my opportunity to do something heroic, something gallant that couldn't fail to make her want to throw herself at me, or at least consider a snog.

'Take this,' I said, thrusting my last £20 in her hand.

She opened her mouth to protest, then decided against it. She looked genuinely touched, genuinely impressed. I was quite taken aback myself.

'Have you got enough yourself? To get home, I mean,' she said, concerned.

'Ah, don't worry about me, I'll walk,' I replied coolly, as if I was at home in even the most treacherous of conditions; this wind was so strong it could have flattened my fringe with one gust.

'You can't do that – I feel terrible now,' she said.

'I insist,' I replied.

She handed back my coat, clambered into the taxi, then turned to look at me. 'Give me your number. I'll pay it back immediately.'

'Gladly.' The boy was back in business. 'Have you got a pen?'

She rustled around in her bag then looked at me, dejected. 'No.'

The taxi driver was thoroughly pissed off by now. 'Hurry up, Romeo and Juliet, shut the bloody door.'

'Sorry, mate,' I mumbled, then a flash of genius hit me. I rooted in my coat pockets and pulled out one of Terri's lip-liners.

'Here. This'll work.'

I held Gemma's hand and crayoned my number on the back of it, in bright pink digits. She looked up and blinked, clearly lost for words.

'Nice colour,' she said eventually.

The implications of this compliment hit me like a 4-ton freight train. 'The lipstick isn't mine!' I blustered.

'It's cool,' she shrugged. 'I'm very open-minded. Thanks again.' And at that, she closed the taxi door and trundled away up Mount Pleasant.

I slipped my coat back on and felt light-headed as her scent drifted around me. Then I started the four-mile walk home, which should have been the most miserable journey of my life. I was drunk, broke, soaking wet and shivering. But my head was swollen with thoughts of her.

If she phoned like she said she would, I could explain that, while I too am 'very open-minded', I am not in fact flirting with transvestitism, and if I were, I'd choose a better lip colour.

But after two days, the smell of her perfume had faded from my coat, and I couldn't remember what her face looked like. I was annoyed that I'd failed to ask for her number, and that the only new entry I'd been able to put in my contacts book was a doodle of her seashell tattoo on the front cover.

Instinct, I'm afraid, was starting to tell me that she wasn't going to phone.

And, as ever, instinct proved to be right.

Chapter 6

Gemma

Dan has been really evasive about buying a car in which to commute to work from his mum's.

Buddington, where she lives, is only a fifty-minute drive to Liverpool, but local public transport is dire, offering little more than a Noddy train that leaves approximately every six days; travelling by donkey might be easier.

I've been pointing out the increasing urgency of the situation in the four weeks since we handed in our notice to the landlord – as well as the fact that I've managed to part-exchange my own vehicle (sob) for an eight-year-old Fiat Punto, in an attempt to swell our coffers.

This afternoon, with less than twenty-four hours before we are due to leave our flat, Dan finally phones as I'm heading into a meeting to tell me he's bought one.

'Oh good!' I say brightly, as I hurry along the corridor to *The Think Bubble*, which used to be known as Meeting Room One. 'Where did you get it?'

'From a friend of a friend of Pete's. Or maybe a friend *of a friend* of a friend of Pete's.'

I feel a shiver of unease.

'Pete's coming with me first thing tomorrow,' he continues.

'But the move's tomorrow.'

'It'll only take half an hour to pick it up, I promise – then we'll load up both of our cars and make the trip to my mum's.'

I pause in front of the door as Sebastian strides past and gives me a salute. 'Okay, I'll have some last-minute packing anyway. How much did this car cost? You didn't go over budget?'

'The car more than fulfils all criteria with regards cost-control.'

My ears prick up. 'Go on, how much?'

'Honestly, not much.'

I glance into the room and realise they're waiting for me. 'The fact that you're refusing to tell me means it was either too expensive or so cheap it's falling to bits,' I hiss.

'Which would you prefer?'

'Under normal circumstances, I wouldn't do things on the cheap, but given that the object of this exercise is saving money, the latter. You could turn up in a baked bean can and I'd be pleased.'

'Great,' he replies. 'Just remember those words when you see it.'

That evening, as we sit in the living room of the flat surrounded by boxes, he shows me the advert that Pete's friend of a friend *of a friend* had listed on eBay. There's no picture, but what it lacks in photographic evidence, it makes up for in descriptive prose:

1999 ALFA ROMEO 145 T-SPARK 16V SILVER
A hero of a car.
Gutted to lose her due to shitty 12-month driving ban.
Guaranteed Fanny Magnet.
£195.

To call the monstrosity parked outside our flat the following morning 'a car' pushes every boundary of the dictionary definition. It is a rusting, backfiring, filthy lawnmower with windows – except that one of them is covered with the box from a 24-pack of Carlsberg, held on with duct tape. It possesses no passenger seat, just a gap where one once was. The other seats are brown – but not a good brown, like taupe or caramel. These seats could originally have been any colour of the rainbow, but have turned this shade due to a plethora of dubious-looking spillages. I can't even look at them without wanting to scrub myself with a wire brush.

'You asked for cheap and you've got to admit it was cheap,' says Pete triumphantly.

'This isn't going to last five minutes,' I tell Dan.

'It's not great, is it?' he concedes. 'But it *was* cheap.'

'A hundred and ninety-five quid isn't cheap if it's not drivable. How did it pass its MOT?'

'There are six months left on it, believe it or not,' Dan says. 'The seller admitted it has suffered some wear and tear since it passed.'

'*Wear and tear*? There are vehicles that have done a tour of duty in Afghanistan that look better than this.'

Dan shrugs. 'Well, it'll do for now and if I need to sell it on as scrap, I will. Although we had no problems getting here in it. You never know, Gemma,' he grins, 'we could be lucky enough to end up with this for years.'

It takes longer than expected to pack up both cars, even with Pete's help. Every inch of available space in the Fanny Magnet is taken up with bin bags of clothes, boxes of kitchen utensils and holdalls containing more stuff than I dreamed I owned. I had a clear-out before the move, but still found it difficult to throw a lot away, even the old CDs I know I'll probably never play again, the three or four diaries I've accumulated over the years (though never get the time to write in these days) and, of course, my shoes.

Dan opens the door gingerly and, as Pete and I strain to

hold back a bag of bedding, my boyfriend squeezes himself into position. He turns the key, and is rewarded with a noise like an exploding Spitfire crashing into the side of a mountain. The engine ticks over for several seconds and, deciding not to tempt fate by hanging around, I leap into my car.

I follow Dan, letting him set the pace. But the pace, it turns out when you're driving a sixteen-year-old skip, is S-L-O-W. I register the looks of grotesque astonishment on other drivers' faces as they overtake us.

We finally reach the country roads that lead to Buddington and, when forced to negotiate their narrow, winding contours and hills, it becomes very apparent that Dan's car is not over-burdened with suspension, judging by the way it's jiggling up and down like the boobs on a Las Vegas showgirl. He gets round this issue by speeding up ahead of every bump in the road, so that the Fanny Magnet actually leaps in the air in a manner that I'm convinced must have shifted several of his internal organs.

We arrive at the imposing gates of Buddington Hall in a toxic cloud of smoke and frayed tempers.

The oldest surviving part of the house was built at the end of the sixteenth century, but it's still immaculate. Timber framed with ochre-coloured plaster panels, there are ornate finials along the roof and two bays flanking a gabled porch. By my semi-detached standards, it's huge – surrounded by stunning gardens, with terraced lawns and, courtesy of its position on the edge of a sandstone cliff, dramatic views of the Cheshire plains.

It's been a few months since I was here and, as my car crunches after Dan's along the driveway, it strikes me as a hell of a big place for his mum and grandmother to be in by themselves.

Dan's car splutters to a stop and he gets out, stretching his legs and saying, 'I feel like I've been shrink-wrapped for the last hour.' He walks over and slides his arms around my waist.

He has this entirely uninhibited way of kissing me in public that caught me by surprise the first time. For all he cares, anyone can see; when the urge to claim a moment of tenderness takes him, it's as if no one else even exists. And it's impossible not to be swept along by this. Dan is unequalled as a kisser, so gently powerful that, every time, it gives me a momentary amnesia that lasts for several seconds after he lets me go.

I suddenly become aware of where we are.

'We can't smooch when your mum's around,' I object, but he pulls me closer in a way I find difficult to argue with.

'Might as well make the most of it before I lead you into the lion's den.'

My body instantly responds to him, and I feel unexpectedly and inappropriately turned on. Then a voice cascades across the lawn. '*Joyce, wait – I'll ask Daniel, he'll know.*'

Dan's mother Belinda is on the phone striding towards us

purposefully. When she's a few steps away, she covers the handset and, dispensing with formal hellos, asks: 'Daniel: can you, or can you not catch pubic lice from the seat of a jet-ski? Joyce is phoning from the Caribbean.'

Dan throws me a weary glance. 'I doubt it. Why would you think *I'd* know?'

'I thought you had an *experience?*'

His mouth drops open. 'No.' He turns to me. 'I have never, ever had pubic lice. I swear.'

'No, I mean you've been on a jet-ski,' she tuts, then returns to the phone. 'Joyce, Daniel doesn't think the jet-ski could be to blame. Who've you been sleeping with over there?' Protestations echo from the handset. 'You're going to have to see a medical professional when you get back. What about the man who did your hysterectomy? You said he was good.'

Joyce apparently protests again. 'Oh, I'd forgotten about the sexual harassment accusations.' Dan's mum rolls her eyes at us. 'At least he dropped the charges against you.'

When she finally gets rid of Joyce, she throws her arms around me. 'How's my favourite daughter-in-law?' The fact that we're not married and she doesn't have any other daughters-in-law has never mattered.

'I'm fantastic, thanks, Belinda,' I reply, squeezing her arm. 'It's incredibly good of you to let us stay.'

'Oh, it'll be a hoot!' She turns and glares at the Fanny Magnet. 'What on earth is *that?*'

'My new wheels,' Dan replies, marching to the car to remove the bouquet he bought this morning.

She pulls a face. 'I'll find a space round the back for it.' She takes the flowers and sticks her nose in them. 'Ooh, lovely. He never used to buy flowers before he met you, you know,' she tells me. 'You've got him well trained. Now, come on you . . . a kiss for Mum, please – you're not too old.' She grabs Dan by the arm and plonks a kiss on his cheek.

Belinda, who is in her late-fifties, is today dressed like Carole Middleton at Glastonbury: in sharp, slim jeans with a low-slung belt, Hunter wellies and a fur-lined gilet that appears to have sacrificed half a dead yak in the making.

She wears little make-up, but is naturally attractive, with noble bone structure and good skin. I've told Dan a few times that I hope I look like her when I'm her age, but for some reason he doesn't appreciate the sentiment.

Despite the fact that I've seen first-hand what a flirt she can be, Belinda has never really had a Significant Other since her divorce from Dan's dad Scott all those years ago.

This in itself isn't unique. But in Belinda's case – or rather, Dr Belinda Blackwood's case – it's something on which she's built her career, a philosophy and an extremely lucrative empire.

Belinda was responsible for one of the biggest publishing phenomena to have emerged from the late 1980s: *Bastards*.

She was a psychotherapist in private practice when she

started writing it, as a self-help book for women experiencing acrimonious divorces. But by the time she'd completed the first draft, she was in the throes of one herself – and it's hard to imagine a messier example.

The final book was part-anthropological analysis of human behaviour and part thinly-disguised anecdotal prose plundered from the wreckage of her own relationship.

She concluded that men are evolutionarily programmed to spread their seed as far and wide as possible, yet in the modern world, we expect them to desist when they find a mate and marry them.

In the days when marriage was invented, life expectancy struggled to top forty years, therefore this wasn't too much of an issue. Couples didn't need to put up with each other for too many decades after the first flush of romance headed toilet-wards. Today, we're living longer – and still expect couples to stick together for good. Yet those seed-spreading instincts have never disappeared, which explains why, after a few years' marriage, many men won't hesitate when they have the opportunity of mating with someone younger, prettier and more enthusiastic in the bedroom.

Not all of them are like this, of course. But the chances of finding a 'good' one – with the skills and inclination to suppress their polygamous instincts – are low.

The solution, Dr Belinda argued, is that women should shed long-held romantic notions and, rather than skip down the aisle thinking life will be one long fairytale, should regard men in more practical terms: as breeders. Then they should run.

That way they can have a lovely, simple life, raising their children in the company of their infinitely more reliable friends – and never have to pick up a pair of Y-fronts from a bathroom floor again.

The book polarised reviewers ('A must read!' – the *New York Sun*; 'Unmitigated drivel' – the *Economist*), but flew off the shelves. It was followed up in 1993 with its sequel: *Complete Bastards*, and the trilogy was concluded in 1995 with *Complete and Utter Bastards*.

She invested the substantial proceeds of all the books on the Stock Market and, judging by the house, the Porsche and the indoor swimming pool, didn't do badly.

To Belinda's credit though, she's extremely generous. Even before we started house-hunting, she tried to give Dan a lump of money that would pay for a deposit somewhere. Typically, he was having none of it. He's always found the idea of sponging off his parents – neither of whom are short of a bob or two – abhorrent. As far as Dan's concerned, if we can't stand on our own two feet and buy this house by ourselves, we're not buying it at all.

'Mum, where do you want me to put all this stuff?' Dan asks. 'We need to start unpacking if we're going to make two more trips.'

'All your clothes can go in the little bedroom at the front. Gemma can have the walk-in wardrobe and—'

'We won't be unpacking *our bags*,' Dan clarifies. 'I just meant unpacking the car.' His mum frowns. 'We won't ever be unpacking our bags. Not ever. This is a temporary arrangement.'

'All right, Mr Independent,' Belinda replies, grabbing him by the cheek and giving it a tweak. She turns to me. 'He was just the same when he was three and insisted on wiping his own bottom.'

Chapter 7

Dan

As I head into the house, I remind myself that I spent sixteen years living with my mum, so a few months isn't going to kill me. It's not like I don't love her – plus, I'm hardly alone. If I believe what I read, loads of people in their twenties and thirties are doing this to get on the housing ladder.

I enter the hall and cross the big oak floor that my friends and I would fight on as kids – not usually to the death, it was more your average rough and tumble. I breathe in a dozen childhood smells: furniture polish and old wood, cut grass and my mother's freshly-cremated biscuits. The house was always full when I was a kid: of her friends, my friends, the sound of scraped knees and laughter, usually after we'd done something we weren't allowed to. The list – from burying the contents of Mum's entire cutlery drawer in the garden to taking a selection of her bras to school to attempt to trade them for football cards – was endless. My eight-year-old self was an arsehole, I'm afraid.

I abandon my bag and enter the kitchen, as a magnetic force pulls me to the fridge. I bypass a couple of ambiguous, home-made lumps and grab a Kit Kat, which is an undeniable improvement on the underwhelming 'treats' I'm used to when Gemma's on a healthy-eating kick (pro-biotic yoghurts, I'm talking to you).

I look up as Gemma and Mum walk in chatting – and experience a bolt of optimism that makes me wonder if this set-up might be tolerable.

'While I remember,' Mum says, 'we need to talk about the birds and the bees.' I splutter asthmatically as a piece of chocolate becomes lodged in my windpipe. 'Obviously, I'll expect both of you *not* to partake in any conjugal relations under my roof.'

I let out a sigh as Gemma's mouth forms a perfect O.

'PAH! GOTCHA!' Mum hoots, wiping tears of mirth from her eyes. 'Seriously, Gemma. You can go at it like rabbits for all I care.'

I just love this sort of thing, as you can imagine.

'Dan knows,' she continues to my girlfriend, 'that I have a very relaxed attitude towards anything like that. And despite the circumstances, it's important to keep your sex-life active and interesting. You've been together four years – if you don't make the effort now, you risk things becoming stale.'

'I think that's enough, Mum,' I say calmly, turning to Gemma. 'She hasn't taken her happy pills yet today.'

'Don't be cheeky,' Mum says, swatting me over the head. 'Besides, I'm serious. If you want to experiment with some alternative locations, Dan's grandma and I will go out and give you free run of the place. The pool might be nice. Just make sure you check the *pH* balance afterwards. Of the water, obviously. Ha!'

'Mum, stop. Please.'

She nudges Gemma conspiratorially. 'He's so old-fashioned. It was like the time I told him about the lesbian affair I'd had at school . . .'

'MOTHER!'

'Oh God, it only lasted a week,' she tuts. 'I don't think that even made me bi-curious. More *bi-couldn't-be-bothered*.'

We have been on the premises for nine minutes. It already feels like nine weeks.

'Where's Flossie?' asks Gemma, diplomatically changing the subject.

'Good question.' Mum strides to the side window and thrusts out her head in the direction of the converted stable block where my grandmother lives.

'MUMMM!' Mum shrieks.

'Why don't I go and get her?' I offer.

'She'll have her hearing aid off again,' Mum tuts. 'We'll all go. It'll be a nice surprise.'

We trail after her through the hall and I reach for Gemma's hand. 'We'll say hello to Grandma then start unloading, is that okay?'

'Course – we're in no rush. The landlord said as long as everything's out by tomorrow morning, it'll be fine.'

We head around the side of the house to the granny flat which, when Gemma first saw it, she said was enough to make her want to become a granny herself. It's small and self-contained, with a chalky blue front door flanked by pots of Ferrari-red geraniums. At the front is a bright patio, where Grandma spends summer days reading on the sweetheart bench my grandad made for her fortieth birthday.

Mum starts banging on the door. 'MUMMM!'

'Don't you have a spare key?' I ask.

'I wanted one, but she seems to think it'd be compromising her independence,' Mum says, rolling her eyes. 'I don't know what she thinks I want to do – break in and do her washing up for her?'

She bangs again, with no response. 'I can't imagine what she could be doing.' Her hand shoots to her mouth. 'Oh God, what if something's happened?'

This tends to be my mum's default position. If the cleaning lady's late, she won't assume it's because there are roadworks in the village, but that she's been kidnapped, held at knife-point and sold to a human trafficking gang.

'Something won't have happened,' I say reasonably. 'She'll

be playing online Boggle, or have her hearing aid switched off, like you said.'

'She'd have still heard that knocking,' Mum says. 'I don't like this. I don't like it one bit.'

'Dan,' Gemma turns to me, 'I think you should climb through a window.'

'What?'

'We'll give you a leg up,' Mum offers.

'I don't *need* a leg up. She won't want someone climbing through the window. Look, let me go and see if she's gone for a walk first. I'll be five minutes.'

'Five minutes might be too late,' Mum protests.

'What if poor Flossie has fallen and can't get to the door?' Gemma says, her eyes heavy with disappointment in me.

'She won't have,' I assure her.

'I can't believe you'd be so heartless,' Mum responds.

'I'm not being—'

Gemma tuts. She's only been here twenty-three minutes and she actually tuts.

'Okay.' I hold up my hands. 'You win.'

We march round to the kitchen window, which is the biggest, and find that it is open, but with no sign of Grandma. I examine the available space and estimate that a fifteen-year-old ballet dancer couldn't squeeze her hips through without surgical intervention. 'I'll never get through there.'

'Just breathe in,' Gemma declares, as if this is an issue that could be solved with a pair of Spanx. 'Here, stand on my hands.'

'Gemma, I'm too heavy.' I give her my most authoritative glare, to ensure my point is made.

'We'll both do it,' Mum says, shuffling into place with her usual bulldozer subtlety.

This is very obviously a bad idea.

Yet there's some perverse sense of macho pride digging at me, refusing to let me walk away. So, with the *Mission Impossible* soundtrack running through my ears, I shove one size 11.5 shoe on Mum's hands and another on Gemma's, pulling myself up as they make these monstrous sounds, like a pair of labouring hippos.

I get halfway through, my legs out of the window, when I become aware of something.

There is nothing like knowing that your mother and girl-friend are standing by supportively, watching your heroics in concern and awe, as you face any number of dangers (splinters mainly) without a thought for your own wellbeing.

And this is nothing like that.

Both are near incontinent with laughter at the sight of my arse in the air.

Ignoring their cackles, and the fact that they've apparently overcome their concern that this is a life-or-death situation, I shunt through the top window and press my hands on the edge of the sink. Then I straighten my legs and end up recreating a human version of that *Mousetrap* game – as if someone only need drop a silver ball on my shins to catapult my head into the ceiling.

Gemma and my mother are now hysterical. I edge through, sweating and panting as I realise there is literally no way down without rupturing a kidney.

'Are you okay, darling?' asks Gemma, failing to stifle her laughter entirely.

'Thank you for your concern, Munchkin,' I reply sarcastically, shifting my hands across onto the top of the dishwasher, and landing on a cheese grater, which makes parmesan of my hand. I eventually pull up my knees and by some miracle end up in the kitchen sink, rather than with a cracked skull.

I climb out and examine my shredded hands as I hear voices outside. I open the window fully, only to discover Grandma outside, chatting to Gemma and Mum.

'Grandma had just been for a walk,' Mum announces cheerfully. 'She'd locked up. That was why we couldn't get in.'

Grandma narrows her eyes and looks at me. 'You don't want to go in that way, Danny. You might end up hurting yourself.'

I defy anyone in the world to tell me they have a better grandparent than Flossie Blackwood. My grandma rocks for reasons that go beyond the usual qualities of unconditional love, patience and wisdom. She is as fearless as she is energetic, as cynical as she is a boundless optimist. And she's always had the ability to make me laugh – something that was the case when I was ten and which still applies now I'm nearly thirty.

She met my grandad, Tom, in the village shop where she worked in Buxton shortly after the war. He'd gone in to buy some potatoes, a story to which she adds every time: 'Our eyes met over the King Edwards.' She adored him until the day he died, sixteen years ago. In fact, I don't think she's ever stopped adoring him.

'Can you not stop for a cup of tea?' she asks, now we're all assembled in her kitchen.

'We'll have to be quick,' I reply. 'We've got a mountain of stuff to drive over.'

Her creased hands reach out for the kettle and she walks with it to the sink. Her movements seem slower than even six weeks ago, when I was last here. She is eighty this year, I suppose, although that still seems impossible to believe.

It was Grandma who introduced me to one of my passions – open water swimming – and, although she mainly sticks to swimming pools these days, she still loves the water as much as when she was a young woman.

Unlike Mum, who's on the skinny side, Grandma is a solid-looking woman, whose life revolves around simple pleasures: the great outdoors, church, good food (and Rioja) and her iPad, on which she plays Boggle obsessively.

'Where's all your stuff going?' she asks.

'There's plenty of room in the garage,' Mum says, 'and

they can always unpack some of it. *If* they choose. You never know, they might like it here so much they want to stay for good.'

'I wouldn't count on it,' Grandma says, winking at me. 'Anyway, I'm not convinced there is a lot of room. I was in there this morning looking for some varnish and it was a complete tip.'

'What did you want varnish for?' Mum asks.

'Your father's sweetheart bench is starting to look weather-beaten. I was going to give it a touch up.'

'I'll do that for you, Grandma,' I offer. 'You just need to ask, you know. It's no problem.'

'I'm perfectly capable of putting a bit of varnish on a bench, Danny. But on this occasion,' she continues, 'I'll think about letting you do it.'

'Thank you,' I laugh.

'That's what they call reverse psychology,' she grins. 'Though I am giving in for a reason.'

'Which is?'

'I'm getting rid of the bench. Giving it away.'

I find it hard to hide my disbelief. 'But why? Grandad made that for you. I thought it was one of the most precious things you own.'

'It is. Which is why I'm giving it to you and Gemma. It's going to be my housewarming present when you move into your new love shack.'

I am momentarily lost for words. 'Grandma, we couldn't accept it.'

'But you must,' she insists. 'Your grandad would've wanted it. *I* want it. It was meant for lovebirds, not old ladies.'

'Flossie, this is so kind of you,' Gemma pipes up. 'I don't know what to say. The bench is beautiful.'

'Thank you, Grandma.' The words catch in my throat as I think about sitting with Gemma looking out at the view from Pebble Cottage.

'Oh, don't get all soppy on me, Danny,' she chides as the kettle boils and Mum steps in to pour water into the tea pot. Grandma looks up at her. 'Has your mother told you about her new venture?' she asks me.

Mum bites the inside of her mouth. 'Not yet.'

'She's writing another book,' Grandma announces.

I look at Mum. 'Seriously?'

Mum straightens her back. 'There's a lot of demand for it these days. Feminism's back in fashion, thanks to that woman Caitlin Moran.'

'Your books weren't about feminism,' I argue. 'Just what a tosser every man is, whoever walked the earth. It's a wonder I never ended up on a psychiatric ward from the emotional strain.'

'You do exaggerate sometimes, Daniel.'

'What's your new book about, Belinda?' Gemma asks, appearing – worryingly – to be interested.

Mum clasps her hands together. 'It's called *Beyond Bastards*.

It's kind of a twenty-first-century take on my previous work. Revisited in the light of the last twenty-five years.'

'Are we all still tossers?'

'I never said *all* men were incapable of long-term commitment,' she reproaches. 'Perhaps you'd realise that if you actually read it.'

Gemma looks at me in the same way she did during the conversation about the number of times the average single man washes his bedsheets per year. 'You've *never* read it?'

'I've told you this,' I lie.

'You have not!'

'I was only four when it came out,' I defend myself. 'And anyway, why would any man read a book that advocates the theory that all men are – to use the title phrase – *bastards*.'

'I never said *all* men—'

'Because your mum wrote it,' Gemma replies, killing dead the discussion. Mum glances at me with an expression so smug she's nearly cross-eyed.

Today is feeling very long already.

Mum has a get-together with her Pilates mates to go to, leaving us free to spend the day chugging up and down the M53 with belongings stuffed in our cars. Each time we arrive at Buddington, we work in a tag team: I carry stuff from the car to the house and garage while Gemma does the run upstairs to our room.

When we've finally made the last trip, locked up the old flat, delivered the key to the landlord and driven to Mum's, it's past dinnertime and all we're capable of is demolishing a takeaway pizza, washing it down with an uninspiring bottle of 7-11 red and preparing to collapse into bed.

I'd failed to check which room Mum was putting us in, having assumed – and hoped – it would be the small spare room, which she decorated last summer and, more importantly, is on the opposite side of the house from her bedroom.

But, apparently overcome by a wave of nostalgia, she decided we'd sleep in my old room, which to be fair is the second largest in the house. I throw the pizza box in the recycling bin, before Gemma and I head to the stairs.

I can see the front door opening as I have my foot on the first step – but we're just not quick enough. I hold my breath as Mum and her five friends – all of whom classify themselves as Aunty Someone – stumble in. A cacophony of coo-ing ensues as I'm cuddled and kissed and Gemma is paraded before the crowd like a Roman virgin.

We finally extricate ourselves from their grip and announce that we're heading to bed, prompting a flurry of knowing looks and seaside-postcard innuendo.

'They were nice,' Gemma says, apparently seriously. 'It's great that your mum has such an active social life.'

It strikes me that she's probably right as I push open the bedroom door ... and am lost for words. Gemma glances at me, gauging my reaction with an impish smile. 'I think your mum wanted to make you feel at home again.'

I have not lived in this house for thirteen full years. A week after I moved out, the walls were stripped and whitewashed, the bed fumigated and the place transformed into something sufficiently pastel and pleasant to be used as a guest room.

Yet, for a reason I cannot explain, my mother has taken it upon herself to restore this room to the original and produce a weird, quasi-historical recreation of it, circa 1999.

I haven't seen the posters she's plastered up since the days when I'd while away hours dousing my forehead in Clearasil and experimenting with activities that risked hairy hands and blindness.

I gaze at the walls, noting how schizophrenic my tastes were when I was fifteen: there's a massive image of Che Guevara and another of Bob Marley next to a marijuana leaf. Underneath are movie posters – X-Men, *The Matrix* and, to prove my intellectual credentials, *Betty Blue* (which I'd never actually seen).

Directly in front of us is a shrine to the leading ladies of late 1990s showbusiness: Marisa Tomei, Cameron Diaz, Cerys Matthews, Jennifer Lopez and – in the centre, in glorious, bootylicious Technicolor – Kylie. Although to say Kylie is misleading: this is simply Kylie's rear end, a close up of her hot-panted bum, as featured in the *Spinning Around* video. I'm trying to work out whether these went up before or after I took out a subscription to *New Socialist* magazine and developed a passionate disapproval of the objectification of women – a firmly-held principle that I struggled with daily, I recall.

'My mother is insane,' I decide, sitting on the edge of the bed.

Gemma doesn't answer. 'Sorry, I was just distracted by J-Lo's hair. I never remember it being quite so . . . nineties.'

'I wasn't interested in her hair.'

'Clearly.'

She sits next to me and slides her arms round my neck, kissing me on the lips. I experience a rush of what you'd politely call well-being. More kissing ensues, as we fall backwards on the bed in a tangle of hot limbs.

'God, I fancy you tonight,' she whispers. It's not an especially poetic string of words but they have a positively magical effect on re-diverting my blood supply. With my face against her neck, I slip my hand between her legs and pull back to get a proper look at her. She's breathtaking: all pink skin and soft breasts and parted mouth and . . .

She stops and glares at me. I lean in to kiss her, pretending not to notice, but she closes her legs on my hand like a trap door.

'What's the matter?'

She hesitates. 'Nothing.' I've learned over the years that the accurate interpretation of this is, in fact, 'something'.

'Go on, tell me,' I insist. The idea that I'd rather Talk – with a capital T – than get down to any kind of conjugal business is of paramount importance in situations such as these.

'Honestly, it's nothing.' I slide my hand across her skin, when she pauses again and says, 'Now you mention it . . .'

I pull away. 'What?'

'It's Kylie's arse,' she splutters. 'How am I meant to do this with Kylie's arse looking over us.'

'It's not looking over us. Arses can't look.'

'Well, whatever. I can't.'

'I'll just tear Kylie down then,' I decide, standing up. 'If it's Kylie or you, then you win, hands down. I never wanted her up there in the first place. Not since 1998 anyway.'

Gemma props herself up on her elbows and watches as I peel away one corner, before starting on the adjacent one.

'You're being very careful, considering you were going to "tear it down",' Gemma points out.

I shrug. 'Oh, come on. This *is* Kylie we're talking about.'

She kicks me in the leg and I chuck away the poster, before sinking into the warm, soft pleasure-zone that is my woman's arms.

Only she seems distracted. 'Don't tell me,' I sigh. 'Reese Witherspoon's cleavage?'

'Course not,' she lies, glancing resentfully across the wall. 'I'll just turn off the light.'

She flicks the switch and presses her lips against mine . . . then lets out a small gasp. I'm fairly sure it has little to do with any dexterity in my right hand.

'What was that?' she asks.

The wail of half a dozen drunken women reverberates through the house. 'Oh God . . . it's that lot downstairs,' I groan.

'They're right below us,' she hisses.

'They must've moved into the living room. Why couldn't they just stay in the kitchen?'

'We can just do it quietly,' she whispers.

I nod. 'They're too busy talking anyw—' She has her lips on mine before I can finish my sentence and is manoeuvring into position underneath me.

But as blood thunders in my ears, I become aware of something. The bed has a squeak. Under normal circumstances, this would not be a big deal. But now, with the Golden Girls downstairs, it is catastrophic, comparable in volume to an eighty-piece orchestra of primary-school violinists.

Every movement I make on the mattress involves the entire frame shifting with me. I realise that I am holding my breath, which does nothing for a sensuous approach.

'They're making a lot of noise down there,' Gemma breathes. 'They won't hear us.' She grabs my behind and pulls me forwards; by the time I'm inside her, frankly, I wouldn't give a toss if the Pope could hear.

That's what I think at first anyway.

After a minute or so, it is very apparent that this is not the moment of tender intimacy that it should be, largely because each thrust sounds like I'm riding a rusty Penny Farthing across a defective bridge. Eventually, I slow down and can see the outline of Gemma's expression. It is not a look of sexual rapture – rather the look you'd wear if you had one ear on a tumbler glass and were trying to hear what your neighbours were discussing through the door.

'Why are they suddenly not making any noise?' she says in my ear.

'I have no idea,' I mutter, determined to plough on.

But above their silence, the soundtrack to this seduction consists of one note: squeak, squeak, squeak.

'Let's do it on the floor,' Gemma suggests, so we haul ourselves off the bed and onto the sanded floorboards, just under my *Fast and Furious* poster.

I offer to go underneath, wincing as several splinters harpoon my bum. 'The chair would be better,' I decide, as we scramble into the tub seat by the window and, as the laughter starts again, Gemma attempts to climb on top.

Chairs and sex *can* be a nice combination. But not this chair. This is the kind that was meant for nursing babies or sewing tapestries. But FHM's *Positions To Please a Woman* number 27, absolutely not.

It's too small, too round, too squashed, and no matter how many attempts Gemma makes at wrapping her legs round me in various positions, the closest we get to success results in her big toe tickling my ear canal.

'This is the least sexy sex position ever invented,' Gemma

sighs, clambering down. 'And I am bloody determined to have a shag tonight. Determined.'

Under normal circumstances, these are not words I'd be unhappy to hear. But over the course of the next forty minutes we try the no-pants dance on top of a suitcase, a stack of pillows on the floor, a bin bag full of handbags (yes, a whole bin bag), before finally attempting it against the chest of drawers.

'This is just no good,' Gemma sobs, defeated. 'There's a knob between my legs and I don't mean in a good way.'

I stop myself from laughing and kiss her as I note that it's gone quiet again downstairs.

'DON'T STOP ON OUR ACCOUNT!' someone shrieks. Gemma's mouth falls open in silent horror as she makes it clear from her expression that she is now too mortally ashamed to (a) have sex ever again (b) leave this room ever again or (c) make any form of human contact ever again.

We lie in bed, listening to what sounds like a cackle of hyenas pissed on Malibu Screwdrivers, and I ask, 'Remind me how long you reckoned it'd be before we can put in an offer?'

'Two months,' Gemma replies grimly. 'Assuming we stick to the budget.'

'And the house remains on sale.'

She looks at me anxiously. 'I'll phone the estate agent first thing, shall I?'

Chapter 8

Gemma

I wake up feeling disorientated, unrested and vaguely turned-on, though the latter sensation disintegrates when I open my eyes and am surrounded by Supermodels and actresses of the early 2000s. Dan is stirring, snuggling into his duvet – a jet black and silver striped affair that belongs in an advert for an aftershave called 'Bloke'.

His eyelashes flutter open. 'Why are you smiling?' he asks.

I shrug. 'Nothing. I just love you, that's all.' And it's true.

It's hard to believe that there was a time when I was utterly convinced that I'd never find someone like Dan. I suppose that's one of the downsides of discovering love too early.

I was fifteen when I lost my heart the first time, to a boy called Alex Monroe.

I barely think about him these days, but even now, more than a decade on, I'll get an occasional pang of recollection, of the delirium of falling so hard for someone. Which makes me all the more thankful that I went on to find a man who lived up to it. A man who's with me forever.

I'm about to lean in to kiss him when he frowns, as if he's just remembered something.

'Did you get up to go to the loo last night, then come back and . . .'

'What?'

'Start messing with the duvet?'

I frown. 'What are you on about?'

He shakes his head. 'Nothing, must've dreamed it.'

I wriggle over and lock my body into his, kissing his lips as the fact that it's Sunday morning drifts to the front of my consciousness. There's one thing we do before anything else on a Sunday morning – and it doesn't involve a shave or fry-up.

There's a sharp knock on the door.

He freezes and a low groan escapes from his lips.

'I've got your brekkie on! It'll be on the table in five minutes.'

Dan clears his throat. 'It's okay, Mum, we're going to pass on the breakfast.'

There's a silence. He rolls over and kisses me.

'Well, I've made it now.'

'Let's just go. It's fine,' I whisper.

'It seems a terrible waste to have to throw those eggs out,' Belinda continues. 'And the bacon's on now. *Right now*. I can hear it sizzling, I'm going to have to go. Fine, if you're not coming, then fine. Just fine. But—'

'We're on our way,' Dan shouts, and covers his head with the Man Duvet.

We enter the kitchen to find a cooked breakfast that could fill the buffet area of a decent-sized B&B. Sadly, size and quality do not equate. There are scrambled eggs speckled with unidentifiable brown lumps, bits of bacon that have either been incinerated or are effectively raw. She's even managed to burn the baked beans, which I'd thought was a chemical impossibility.

We sit down.

'Dan – I got your favourite,' she says, thrusting a pack of Cheerios at him. I've literally never, in the four years we've been together, seen him eat Cheerios. He grabs a bowl enthusiastically as my eyes dart around the cooked offerings, attempting to identify something edible.

'I hope this isn't all for me?' I laugh nervously, eyeing up a bowl of goo.

'It won't do you any harm to fatten yourself up a bit,' Belinda says. 'Or you for that matter, Dan. When I tucked you in last night, I was thinking how skinny you'd become.'

I attempt to suppress any visible horror, but it's extremely difficult. Fortunately, her attention is diverted to Dan, who echoes my thoughts entirely. 'You *tucked me in*?' he growls.

She bites her lip. 'Oh, I couldn't resist,' she confesses with a grin. 'I always tucked you in, when you were living here. You used to look so cute when you were asleep. Less so now, it has to be said.' She scrunches up her nose.

'Mum, I'm twenty-nine years old so hadn't thought this needed saying – but just to be clear, I don't need to be tucked in. Thanks.'

'Oh, talk about Mr Grumpy!' she exclaims. 'Gemma, have some black pudding.' I attempt to stick my fork in a piece but it's as hard as the Kray Twins.

'Mum, look,' he adds, far more patiently than I'd be if my mum pulled something like this, 'you know how grateful we are to be here. I'm just saying, we'd appreciate a bit of privacy. That's all.'

She purses her lips. 'If you're referring to yesterday evening, it was Sabrina who shouted up to you while you were –you know, *at it.*' She winks pointedly and I study my plate, my neck flushing a similar colour to the streaky bacon. 'I told her off immediately, then turned the volume up on Kool and The Gang so you could do whatever took your fancy.'

Dan puts his head in his hands. I tentatively reach out for the beans and try, with several hard thrusts, to spoon some on my plate. Then I add eggs and a blackened mass that I *think* are baked tomatoes.

Dan starts munching his Cheerios as I struggle with the burnt offerings. 'Wouldn't you prefer Cheerios, Gemma?' he suggests diplomatically. 'I know how much you love them. Gemma loves cereal,' he adds.

I perk up. 'Oh, that'd be lov—'

'Of course she wouldn't,' Belinda interrupts, picking up the box, standing and putting it back into the cupboard.

'Er, I'll help you out,' Dan says, and starts piling his plate up. He picks up a piece of under-cooked sausage on his fork and examines it. We make eye-contact but say nothing.

'Everything okay?' Belinda asks.

Dan swallows. 'Lovely. Thanks for this, Mum.' He takes a bite of some bacon and chews it slowly. It has the consistency of a mummified flip-flop.

'So this book,' he begins. 'When are they publishing it?'

'November,' she says. 'There's still lots to do but the publishers are already thinking about covers and the publicity plan. I'm going to have an intensive schedule – interviews, photo shoots . . . ooh, you could be in one if you fancy it? *Hello!* would definitely go for it.'

'Do you still actually believe all that stuff?' he asks, putting down his fork.

She frowns. 'Why do you talk about my work as if it's some nonsense? It's highly respected in some quarters. And it's helped empower women all over the world.'

A few minutes later, when Dan stands up to clear away the

dishes, Belinda looks at my plate and gasps, 'Don't tell me that's all you're eating!'

'I'm absolutely stuffed,' I lie. 'But thanks, Belinda – it was lovely. You didn't need to go to all that effort.'

'Oh, we'll do this every weekend,' she promises. 'Make it a new Sunday-morning tradition.' Dan's jaw twitches. I'm fairly convinced he'd have preferred to stick to the sex.

The grounds of Buddington Hall are like something out of a nineteenth-century romance, with swirling pathways, lush lawns, terraces, a strawberry patch behind the house and a small rose garden abundant with scent. But Dan's favourite part is the small lake at the furthest point from the house, reached via ivy-clad steps and flanked by a curtain of greenery.

'Fancy a dip?' It's a warm, sunny spring morning, but I'm still not tempted.

'Not my cup of tea,' I reply. 'You, on the other hand, are very welcome to go in.'

'You'll do anything to see me naked,' he smirks, peeling off his top.

I refuse to react to the sight of his torso as he strides to the lake's edge, in the aussieBum undies I bought him for Christmas. He slips in and powers through the water to the willow tree that draps along the opposite bank, before turning round and swimming to the middle.

'You don't know what you're missing,' he shouts, treading water.

'I'd prefer to spectate than get plankton in my knickers, thanks.'

I lie back on the grass, resting my head in my hands as I look up at the sky, luxuriating in the feel of sunshine against my skin. My eyes dance in and out of focus onto a wisp of white clouds – until I realise that the sensation is making me feel queasy. I close my lids, but that only exacerbates the feeling. My stomach lurches and saliva gathers at the sides of my mouth.

'GEMMA!' Dan shouts.

I push myself up and shade my eyes from the sun. 'Yeah?'

'How are your guts?'

A wave of nausea washes over me. 'A bit ... unsettled, if I'm honest.'

I watch as he wades towards me, his expression shifting from mild concern to panic. 'What's up?' I ask.

'Oh God ...' he replies, hobbling out of the lake. Dan's complexion has drained of colour and he's staggering towards me like a dying Gladiator in a bad B-movie.

We link arms and stumble – him near-naked, me fully-clothed but in increasing discomfort – towards the main house. He pauses halfway and looks around in desperation. 'God, I think I'm going to be sick.'

By the time we reach the house, my insides feel as though they're about to explode, and Dan is clutching his stomach.

'Take the downstairs loo,' I splutter, deciding that he looks the most desperate. 'I'll go upstairs.'

We prepare to sprint Marine-style, to our respective targets, when Belinda twirls into the hall as if she's hosting a cocktail party.

'There you are! Dan, Gemma – I'd like you to meet James Shuttlemore, our new neighbour.' She ushers him forward, apparently oblivious of my knotted brow, and the fact that Dan is doubled up and dripping wet.

'James moved into The Stables several weeks ago, but this is the first time we've met. He's an architect.'

James looks to be in his early sixties, but with all his own hair and only a slightly rounded belly he is, as my mum would say, *well preserved* – like a good piccalilli. He stretches out his arm to shake hands. 'Lovely to meet you.'

I can virtually hear the contents of my boyfriend's stomach climbing up his foodpipe as he turns and darts to the downstairs bathroom, almost concussing himself against the banister. I stand, swaying, as Belinda seems determined to act as though nothing untoward is happening.

'Gemma works for a big advertising agency. She writes all the scripts. That's right, isn't it?'

I nod frantically.

'I considered a career in advertising myself after I'd left the Army,' he replies. 'But I decided to make life hard for myself and train to be an architect instead.'

A conversation ensues that would be perfectly engaging were it not for the soundtrack emanating from the lavatory.

'Were you familiar with Buddington before you moved here?' asks Belinda coolly, as an explosion of coughing reverberates through the house.

James's eyes shift to the bathroom door, then he refocuses. 'I'd grown up in Cheshire as a boy, but it was only when my company relocated from Manchester that I decided to move back.'

Belinda smiles. Dan sounds like he's slaughtering a warthog with a plastic picnic knife.

Every time I think I'll make a getaway, Belinda yanks me back by asking about my earrings, my mother, my job, or any other number of subjects to which I'm unable to respond with anything other than a grunt. We run out of conversation at the exact moment that Dan's latrine emergency draws to a close and the door opens.

'Chuck my trousers in will you, Gemma?' he groans and I hand them over silently as another hideous crunch hits my stomach.

Belinda claps her hands together. 'How about a snack, everyone? I made some prune turnovers yesterday.' At this, the only reaction I'm capable of is turning and stumbling up the stairs on all fours as Belinda cries after me: 'I'll save you one, shall I, Gemma?'

Chapter 9

Dan

After three and a half weeks, Mum has driven me to near distraction. I barely know where to start, but I'll focus on last Saturday, just for the hell of it.

She's taken to responding with quiet martyrdom whenever Gemma and I go upstairs to watch TV, as though we're abandoning her to face a lonely, rat-infested death surrounded by her copies of *New Therapist* magazine. Gemma is very conscious of not hurting her feelings and therefore we've tended to spend at least half our evenings in the living room with her.

'Janice Bozhkov, who worked in the same clinic as me when I started out in London, recommended this DVD when she was on the phone this week,' she announced, just after dinner. 'It was nominated for an Oscar. She raved about it.'

I was flicking through my phone, while Gemma scrutinised

some home decorating magazines and therefore neither of us were paying much attention. Then I looked up and recognised the opening credits of *The Wolf of Wall Street*. I was immediately on edge: I'd never seen the film, but I knew it wasn't classed family viewing.

This turned out to be a glorious under-estimation.

The next twenty minutes represented, without question, the most excruciating in my life. If I was mortified by *Carry On Camping* aged ten (when my mother rocked with laughter as Barbara Windsor's bra flew off), that was nothing compared with this.

I won't bore you with the full, earth-shattering horror of what Gemma and I had to sit through, pretending *not* to watch. But I will say that the nipple-count couldn't have been higher if I'd spent a year painting the window sills of a brothel.

I can't claim to be a prude, or indeed deny that if we'd been viewing a similar display of debauchery without a parent in the room, there's every possibility I'd have enjoyed it. As it was, my eyes were bleeding.

The worst moment involved a scene with Leonardo DiCaprio's character, a prostitute and the most pornographically outlandish variation of cocaine ingestion that the human imagination has ever conjured up.

As the hooker removed her underwear and manoeuvred into the sort of pose you'd strike while looking under the skirting boards for a lost pound coin, Gemma and I quietly died inside.

At this point, most mothers would be sufficiently rattled to pick up the remote and switch over to *Casualty*. Not my mum.

She put her glasses on, leaned in, and commented: 'What a strange thing to do!' as if we were watching someone do the crossword upside down, rather than rectal drug abuse. 'Is *that* what people do these days?'

'I don't know,' I muttered.

'Have you two ever done it?'

At which point Gemma and I announced we were getting a couple of hot chocolates and turning in.

The last weeks have been dotted with occasions like this, for there is no subject-matter Mum considers to be out of bounds – from menstruation to depilation, IUDs to STDs, we've had to listen to it all. Worse, despite our best efforts to maintain a semblance of having our own space, she is *always there*. Just . . . there.

She seems to be attempting to form some sort of bond with Gemma too. Not that I have a problem with that *per se* – I'm glad they get on. I just wish that didn't involve flicking through old photos of me in an array of Superman pyjamas or the time when I starred as the arse end of a cow in a nativity play. I know we've been together for four years, but I'd like to retain some mystique in front of my girlfriend – and that's very difficult when she's constantly being told that I was still wetting the bed at six.

Plus . . . I don't want to give the impression that I'm

obsessed with this subject, but I need to get it off my chest. I have had conjugal relations with my infinitely desirable girl-friend, the woman I will love until my dying day, just *twice* since we arrived.

I know some men wouldn't think this was too bad; if we were in our early sixties and had enough romance under our belt to last a lifetime, I'm sure I'd consider this to be passable. But I am twenty-nine years old. I have needs. She has needs. Not to put too poetic a point on it, we want to *get jiggy*.

Yet, despite attempting more positions than a rhythmic gymnastics team, we have exhausted every spot in the bed-room, bar the inside of the wardrobe, and can confirm that there is quite simply nowhere that doesn't squeak. So we have to wait until Mum's out.

And, for a reason I can only put down to the fact that she'll never get a man after writing that bloody book (to which I resigned myself years ago), SHE IS NEVER OUT.

In amongst this is my growing concern that we are going out on a limb with Pebble Cottage. Although it's still up for sale, I can't see how it won't already have sold by the time we're in a position to put in an offer.

The prospect of where this would leave us (i.e. still here) does not bear thinking about. We need a Plan B.

It has also struck me that if that Plan B happened to involve us finding a cheaper house we could move into sooner, then all the better. Obviously, I don't want to buy somewhere for the wrong reasons, but even a slim chance of precipitating our departure from Buddington Hall is worth investigating.

Gemma, to my surprise, agrees – something I can only attribute to her crumbling belief about my mum's awesomeness. 'Have you seen this?' she asks as we pull up outside our first of five houses. She's reading a story on the *Guardian* app on her phone.

'"Dr Belinda Blackwood, the controversial figure behind the hit book *Bastards* is to pen another tome, updated for the twenty-first century, named *Beyond Bastards*",' Gemma reads out. '"Publishers are tipping it as one of the most hotly-awaited books of the year, and the announcement that Dr Blackwood was writing again sparked a bidding war that resulted in a six-figure advance for the manuscript. It remains to be seen whether the book will prove as big a success as it was twenty-five years ago – when one in five women in the USA owned a copy".'

'Hotly awaited?' I mutter. 'Not by me it isn't.'

Gemma drops the paper in the footwell and opens the car door.

The terrace house we've come to see is £20k cheaper than Pebble Cottage, with a pleasant, if modest front garden. The area isn't quite as nice, the front of the house not quite as quaint – but it's still more than passable in my book.

'Looks like it's got potential,' Gemma smiles. I try not to get my hopes up.

We'd agreed to meet the estate agent at 1 p.m. because the

couple who own the house work in hospitality and are both hard at it every Saturday. It's a couple of minutes past now.

'Maybe we should ring the bell – perhaps the estate agent's inside,' I suggest.

Gemma presses the buzzer, but there's no response. 'I could've sworn I heard someone,' she frowns, before the noisy clatter of high heels diverts our attention. Their owner is a woman in her early fifties, who has either had a lot of Botox or a head transplant from one of the dummies in the window of House of Fraser. She's out of breath when she reaches us.

'I'm Hannah Bailey,' she pants, flipping a shawl over her shoulder. Gemma holds out her hand.

'Pleased to meet you, I'm Gemma.'

But Hannah Bailey barely notices Gemma. Instead, she turns and focuses her gaze on me.

'*Hellooo*,' she says, shaking my hand. I smile and try to pull it away, but she's like a Cocker Spaniel with a novelty rubber turkey and refuses to let me go.

I glance at the door. 'Shall we go in?' I suggest. She releases me and grins.

'Why not? Lovely property this one,' she begins, pushing a key into the door. 'Nice young couple like yourselves own it. They're moving to Bristol. Chefs. Must be an interesting job. Long hours though. Go on in, Gorgeous,' she winks at me.

I glance at Gemma to see if I can detect any jealousy, but she's too busy examining the double glazing.

'Here we've got a beautiful inglenook-style fireplace with a spacious, newly-carpeted lounge area,' Hannah says in the living room. 'The windows are recently double glazed, the décor is contemporary yet homely. The radiators are all less than ten years old and there's an efficient combi-boiler upstairs. Any questions?'

'Not so far, thanks,' Gemma says. She doesn't look massively impressed but, as I've come to learn, that means nothing.

'Follow me,' Hannah instructs as she leads us to the kitchen. There, she announces: 'Here we are in the kitchen!' which is the kind of technical detail we've come to expect on these tours. 'And what a lovely room this is. Practical but stylish, lots of cupboard space. A large, bright window, more generous space under the sink for your cleaning items.' She turns to me and softens her eyes. 'I bet you're good with a feather-duster . . .'

She grabs me by the arm and leads me to the stairs. We've viewed the spare bedroom, the bathroom and are heading for the main bedroom when I'm sure I hear a thud. 'What was that?'

Gemma shrugs. 'I didn't hear anything.'

'Go on in,' says Hannah, opening the door. We shuffle in and my eyes are drawn to a grim fitted wardrobe with a gold trim that clearly hasn't been updated since *The Professionals* was on television. Gemma gasps.

'Not great, is it?' I have to agree. 'But we could tear the fittings out.'

Then I look up and realise that the source of her horror is not the wardrobes. She is gazing at a pair of legs. And feet. And tangled sheets with the outline of a hairy bum underneath, frantically pumping up and down like the piston in a 9,000 horsepower steam locomotive.

Mr and Mrs Withers, it appears, are not out. They are very much in. And out.

'Oh God!' cries Hannah. 'Let's get out of here.'

The three of us trip over ourselves to try to leave, which in our haste creates enough of a pantomime to prompt a temporary cessation in between-sheets activity.

'What the—'

The refrain comes from the owner of the hairy bum, who sits up, fumbles with his glasses and, once in position, gapes at us as sweat glistens on his brow.

'Mrs Withers, there appears to have been a mix-up,' Hannah babbles, as the woman starboard side of hairy bum bloke attempts to hoist up the sheet to her chin. 'I'd been told that nobody was in and therefore I was to do the viewing.'

Mrs Withers's face is ashen. 'The viewing's tomorrow – Saturday. That's tomorrow.'

'No, it's today, I'm afraid.'

'But it can't be.'

'It is.'

'No, no, it really can't.'

'Ask these two,' she says, exasperated, at which point Gemma nods. 'Sorry.'

Mrs Withers takes a deep breath. 'Right. Bugger. What a fiasco.'

'Not to worry,' says Hannah conciliatorily. 'They've had a good look around the house. Perhaps I can update you later.' At which point, she ushers us out of the room, before adding to Mrs Withers, 'Do carry on.'

She's about to close the door when Mrs Withers calls out, 'Oh, Hannah?'

'Yes?'

'You won't mention any of this to Mr Withers, will you?'

Chapter 10

Gemma

Busting Mrs Withers is only the start of it. We spend the whole, futile weekend looking at heroically awful houses and all it does is underline my belief that there isn't a suitable place within a twenty-five-mile radius. Not that beats Pebble Cottage anyway. Yet, still we continue, tirelessly, ceaselessly, determined and – in my opinion – completely deluded. No matter how many *Benefits Street*-style houses we view, it's apparent that nothing will satisfy Dan that there's no hope until he's seen every one with his own eyes.

So we go to the house with the dog the size of a radioactive donkey, the one that's dribbled on every piece of furniture and masticated through half the wallpaper. Then we go to *The House with The Teenager* and open a bedroom door into a dark vortex – a portal into another, terrifying world in which the drawn curtains cannot detract from the pungent aroma of cheesy turnips, maze of dirty pants on the floor and crusty toes poking out from under the duvet. I couldn't tell you if he was asleep or dead; it could easily have been either.

There's a house with effulgent purple walls in every room, and another in which the owner proudly informs us that there's a ghost in the airing cupboard which occasionally strays to her knicker drawer – a feature she seems to think should carry a premium.

By 4 p.m., despite being on an austerity drive, there's only one place for us: the pub. 'I can think of more satisfying ways to spend an afternoon,' I grumble as we pull up in the car park of the Jug.

'Like picking someone else's nose,' Dan agrees as he checks an email on his phone. 'Bloody hell, I'm honoured,' he says, perking up. 'I've actually had some correspondence from my father.'

'Oh,' I reply, never knowing quite how to react to news about Dan's dad. 'What's he got to say?'

Dan slows his walk as he begins reading out loud. '"Hi Son, been meaning to respond for a while – sorry it's taken so long. Things are mad busy. I'm tying up a deal in the UK shortly so might be over at some point. I'll let you know if I am. Hope all is well. Dad".'

Dan looks at me, significantly less perky than when he'd only read the subject line. 'Wow – it's from the heart, that one, isn't it?' he mutters sarcastically. 'That's his response to an email I sent three weeks ago.'

'He sounds pretty busy to be fair,' I shrug. 'Anyway, if he's in the UK soon, I might finally get to meet him.'

He raises his eyebrows. 'I wouldn't hold your breath.'

Dan's dad runs a property conglomerate in New York, which partly explains why I've never met him. Though, in Dan's head, this is more likely attributed to his father's general lack of interest in anything he does. Dan suspects that the existence of a girlfriend – me – for the last four years will have gone entirely unnoticed.

Still, they email each other intermittently and sometimes get together for a drink when he's in the UK. But the picture Belinda's books painted of Scott Bushnell – as a man whose focus is work, women and more women – is remarkably similar to Dan's view, whether he's read her book or not.

Despite this conclusion, I can't help wondering if there's more to Scott than that. He might not make an effort with Dan, but the same is patently true the other way around these days, justified or not. Not that this is an opinion I express, obviously.

Dan pushes open the door to the Jug and we look around for a free table. It's one of those great pubs that you want to tell the world about, but simultaneously keep a secret in case the world turns up. It's a cask-ale and posh Ploughman's kind of place, which gets things just right without trying too hard.

'No lunch, just a drink, okay?' I say firmly, eyeing up a bowl of twice-cooked chips that I could happily devour in seconds.

'Fine. We are professional cheapskates,' he agrees. 'I can ask for two glasses of tapwater and a glacé cherry if you like?'

'Let's go wild and get a couple of halves of lager. Make sure you get some little umbrellas though.'

Dan goes to the bar as I flick through my phone at the photos I took today of some of the houses. Even with an Instagram filter, there's little improvement – it's like applying lip gloss to a blowfish. I gaze out of the window at the cloud-speckled sky as I think about what I've seen this afternoon.

It isn't just that everything compares so unfavourably with Pebble Cottage. It's a feeling in my gut, a warmth spreading through me that makes me determined about one fact: *we have to have that house.*

As Dan walks towards me with two drinks – complete with brollies – I can barely wait until he's sat down before I speak. 'Dan, I've got something to say about the house situation.'

He glances up. 'Me too.'

He hands me my drink as I tell myself calmly that if he says we need to persevere with the house-hunting, I must not under any circumstances throw it over him.

'We've *got* to have Pebble Cottage.'

I gasp. 'That's what I was going to say.'

'Well, after today, I agree.'

I am unable to stop myself from reaching over the table,

grabbing his face in my hands and pressing my lips against his. 'I thought you thought I was being fussy. That I should consider making do with one of the others.'

'Yes, because they were all so enticing,' he laughs. 'Who'd have thought Not-Mr-Withers's arse-crack would be the highlight of the afternoon?'

'I was afraid you'd thought a few others were okay.'

'Okay isn't good enough for a place we're going to invest our every last penny in and where – hopefully – we'll be for a very long time.'

I sip my drink. 'I think I should phone Rich and see if there's anything we can do.'

'Like what?'

'I honestly don't know. Until we've got the extra money together we're a bit stuck.'

Dan clears his throat. 'Mum offered to give us some again the other day again.'

I bite my lip. 'Oh . . .'

'You understand why I don't want to take it, don't you?' I obviously don't answer this question quickly enough. 'Gemma, I work in a job that involves being surrounded by people who have *nothing*. I couldn't look myself in the mirror if I just took a few grand from my mother like she was giving me my pocket money.'

'Okay, of course I understand,' I say feebly. 'Look, let's not go down that route. Let me phone Rich.'

I dial the number and Rich picks up after a few rings.

'Gemma Johnston, what can I bedobee for you today?'

'How did you know it was me?' I ask.

'It's always you.'

I frown. 'It can't always be me – I only phone twice a week. Three times at a push.'

'Is that all? I could've sworn it was more. What did you think of the house I sent you to today?'

'You mean the one with crumbling ceilings, a filthy back yard and walls that were crawling with rising damp?'

'Yes. The Project.'

'It's a project we won't be taking on,' I reply.

'I had a feeling you were going to say that. My Spidey Sense was tingling.'

I meet Dan's eyes and continue talking: 'What this has underlined is how much we want Pebble Cottage. There's no other option for us.'

And it's then, at that very moment, that I decide I've had quite enough of all this messing about. It's time to take matters into our own hands. Not a couple of months down the line, but now.

'Rich, what about this: we make a firm offer today and exchange contracts as soon as possible, so that neither party can back out, but defer completion on the sale until, say, September, when we will have all the money.'

'You want to drag out a house purchase for four months?

This is the opposite of what everyone else wants, you do realise? They all want to move in, like, yesterday.'

'By the time the survey and legal work are done, we wouldn't be far off that anyway. Plus, the summer is a quiet period for the housing market, or so I keep reading. Will you ask them? Please, Rich? I know we can't complete on this fast, but we're first-time buyers with no chain and we'll sign the contract literally as soon as the survey and legal work is done – so they are guaranteed the sale.'

He sighs. 'I'll see what I can do.'

I put away the phone and turn to Dan. 'He'll see what he can do.'

Dan reaches over to take my hand, running his fingertips gently over my skin as the tension in my spine drifts away.

'You're beautiful, by the way,' he says.

A self-conscious laugh escapes my mouth. 'Where did that come from?'

'It's just the truth.' And he smiles his self-effacing smile before standing up and heading in the direction of the gents.

A barman comes over to clear my glass, when my phone rings. Rich's number flashes up.

'Rich! Aren't they in?'

'Very pessimistic of you, Gemma,' he comments. 'You ought to read that book *The Secret*. It's all about the power of positive thinking. Think positively and abundance will come to you.'

'Does that mean they've said yes?'

'No.'

'Oh.'

'It's not quite that simple anyway. If you add four grand to your offer, you've got a deal. I must admit, I'm surprised they said this though. Two other couples have been to see it this week. It's an amazing offer. Must be your lucky day.'

My mouth opens silently as I look to the door of the gents to see if Dan is any closer to returning. Because, frankly, I wasn't expecting this response. Not in a million years. Deep down, all I was expecting was a no that couldn't have been bigger or fatter had it left its vegetables and binged on chocolate all week.

'So if I say yes, we'll start the legal work and exchange contracts as soon as possible?'

'That's what they said. It's the fact that you haven't got a house to sell that made them agree to it.'

I'm virtually speechless. We could exchange contracts – and guarantee the house will be ours – as early as next month if Dan and I agree to this. And although it's not entirely clear . . . okay, not at all clear . . . where we'd get another four grand, in the scheme of things it feels like a small sum. Certainly not a show-stopper.

'I'll obviously have to discuss it with Dan, but—'

'They need an answer now. Mrs Deaver works in the UAE a few times a year and she's at the airport and about to get on a flight. This is a one time only offer.'

'I can phone you back in an hour.'

'Our office closes in two and a half minutes.'

I look in the direction of the loo, willing the door to open.

'Do you want to phone me back?' he asks.

'No!' I shriek, panicking that the office will close, along with this opportunity, if I let him go. 'Just hang on the line until I can get him.'

He sighs again. 'Have it your way. Fancy a game of *Name That Tune?*'

Chapter 11

Dan

I'd put the boy standing at the toilet door at five, maybe six. He has blond hair, glasses and ears that stick out a little, like my grandad's used to. He's also wearing a huge, bright blue woolly cardigan, despite the fact that it's about 25 degrees in here.

'Excuse me,' he announces as I'm washing my hands.

'Hi there,' I reply, glancing round.

'I think the toilet might be broken.' He looks at me with big, helpless Malteser eyes. 'And I don't know what to do because I still need to get rid of these.'

He turns out the pockets of his cardigan and produces what appears to be two pork sausages.

'What are those?'

'They're from my dinner. My mum said if I didn't finish it

I wouldn't get an ice cream or a sticker for my sticker chart. But I'm not hungry.'

'So you flushed your dinner down the loo?' I suppress a smile and resist the urge to congratulate him on his ingenuity.

'I tried to,' he begins, pushing open the toilet door.

I am confronted by what I can only describe as a lavatorial apocalypse. The kid has stuffed his entire dinner – complete with chips, about sixteen napkins and a sachet of ketchup – down the bog and attempted to flush it.

Unfortunately, this master of deception's plan has gone awry and instead of a sticker and a Knickerbocker Glory, he's been left with a blockage of Hoover Dam-style proportions.

'We need to get a member of staff,' I say, turning to the door.

'DON'T!' he shrieks, grabbing me by the arm. 'MY MUM WILL KILL ME! *AND I WON'T GET A STICKER!*'

As the water level edges treacherously up towards the top of the bowl, the kid bursts into tears.

'Will you help me, *please*?' he bawls, clutching my leg.

I look at the door and hesitate. Then I roll up my sleeves.

Chapter 12

Gemma

Dan finally emerges from the gents about ten minutes after he went in. It might be more, it might be less – I couldn't tell you because all I can think of is how I'm going to tell him our news.

'Rich phoned back,' I say as he sits down. 'The buyers had a proposition . . . why are your trousers soggy?'

He looks down. 'I was diverted.'

'What happened?'

'This little boy . . .' he begins then: 'What's the matter? Why do you look so shifty?'

I straighten my back. 'I don't. As a matter of fact, I've got some good news.'

His eyes widen. 'They didn't say yes?'

Clearly, the answer is a complicated one, so I decide for the moment to stick with the headline. 'Well . . . yes!'

He looks as though he's gone into shock. 'Oh, Gemma, that's brilliant.' He throws his arms round me and gives me a big, demonstrative kiss on the lips.

'So, what next? We appoint a solicitor? Get a survey?' The words tumble from his mouth. 'This is *amazing* news, Gemma. I feel as though the end is in sight. In four months' time, we'll be starting a new life in a new home, away from my mother.'

I nod and grin.

'I can't believe how excited I am,' he babbles on. 'I'm actually surprising myself!' Then he stops and looks at me. 'Are you not telling me something?'

'Hmm?'

'Come off it. There's something else. You're an open book, Gemma.'

I frown. 'You said I was mysterious when you first met me.'

'I was trying to pull you,' he replies. 'Come on. Spit it out.'

I think about going to buy him a drink first, but his eyes are now boring into mine. 'It's a small thing in the scheme of things,' I start.

'Okay.'

'Totally worth it.'

'Okay.'

'And the fact is, they weren't going to go for our original offer.'

He pauses. 'Oh. *Kay*.'

I take a deep breath. 'They asked for another £4k and I said yes.'

'What?' There is little evidence of joy in his voice.

'When you're dealing in these sorts of sums, £4k is nothing. Not really, is it?'

He looks obstinately unmoved by this assertion. 'It is when you haven't got it and have no prospect of getting it.'

'We'll get it.' I feel actual, bona fide confidence in this, despite the slight deficiency in logic.

He picks up his drink and downs a mouthful silently. Then he looks in my eyes with the peculiar intensity he usually reserves for grand declarations: the first time he said he loved me, when he asked me to go on our first ever holiday together, or when he suggested I should move into his flat.

Somehow, I suspect he's not about to suggest Paris now. 'Gemma, where are we going to get that from?' The quiet exasperation in his voice makes me clench my teeth. 'We've already sold everything we own to get to the figure we offered them. Another four grand is just not possible.'

'I don't think we should be so defeatist,' I say weakly.

'You mean realistic.'

'We've got four months to come up with the money, Dan. This is do-able,' I say. 'I'm absolutely convinced of it.'

Chapter 13

Gemma

I met Dan for the second time six full years after the night our paths first collided at that taxi rank in Liverpool. It was September 2010, on an achingly beautiful autumn day on the banks of Lake Windermere. We were in the throes of an Indian summer, with weekends filled with boozy barbecues, hazy days in the park, cycle rides through the city with the dying rays of the year's sunshine on our shoulders.

I was in the Lake District because my friend Allie asked if I'd cheer her on in an open water swimming competition. I was happy to oblige as long as the most energetic thing I had to do was flip open my sun cream.

Allie and I had been friends after sharing a room in first year at university. I'd been a little annoyed about not having one to myself at first, but within days couldn't have imagined things any other way.

Allie was a cautious, studious type, someone to whom I wouldn't automatically have gravitated given that in those days my priority was finding a party and staying at it until I was only capable of crawling home. Yet from the moment we met, we clicked. We had nothing in common – partly because she'd grown up in Switzerland – but we had *such* a laugh. When I think about those days in our poky little room, with two beds, one sink and curtains that looked as though they must've been in the Domesday Book, that's what I think of: the two of us with tears of laughter spilling down our cheeks.

The swim was the fourth she'd entered and the first I'd gone to watch, partly because I was mildly intrigued by what sort of lunatics were motivated to do such a thing.

I was on the edge of the lake, cheering her on as noisily as I could, when I noticed the winner emerging from the water. You couldn't *not* notice him. He was improbably beautiful: all hard body, soft smile and general, Herculean gorgeousness.

It was an odd moment. It'd been years since I could recall fancying someone like that; so suddenly, so irrationally.

I was also thrown, I think, because in the years after Alex and I went our separate ways, I'd gravitated to scrawny blokes who smoked meaningfully and looked like they'd never seen daylight. Amateur psychologists might have made something of their passing resemblance to the object of my teenage affection – and his passing flirtation with Marlboros.

Yet here I was, at the edge of a lake, averting my eyes self-consciously from a man who was the opposite of all that. Someone athletic and muscular, with a six-pack so defined it should by rights have its own passport.

Anyway.

That, I'd thought, was that. A cloudburst of attraction lingering briefly in the air, before floating away, forgotten.

After the race, Allie and I hit the Swan Inn, along with other competitors. I was at the bar, waiting to be served, when I felt a tap on my shoulder. I span round, realised who it was and a pink glow bloomed on my neck.

'You owe me twenty pounds,' he said.

He might be a romantic these days and ask me to marry him (as a cynical joke, admittedly) twice a month, but the fact remains: they were Dan's first, profound words to me. *You owe me twenty pounds.*

'Sorry?' I replied, which I admit wasn't much of a comeback.

'Twenty pounds. But don't worry, I'd kind of written it off.' His lips softened into a smile. My knees gave way slightly.

'Sorry. You clearly don't recognise me.' It occurred to me when he said that, that he might be someone half-famous. Like an X *Factor* quarter-finalist from 2007, or a weather man who fills in at weekends on the local TV news.

'Well, no,' I confessed, feeling suddenly certain it was going to be the latter. He had the air of someone who knew his cumulonimbus from his cirrostratus, and I mean that only in a good way.

Ironically, I was the one whose appearance had changed most by then – my dreadlocks were long gone. He said later that he had only recognised me by the seashell tattoo on my shoulderblade, which he'd doodled on the edge of a contacts book he kept for years afterwards. That counts as possibly the only reason I've never regretted having that tattoo done.

We shook hands. It was the first time I felt his hand in mine and it was a window into his soul: warm, honest and strong. 'I'm Dan. We met years ago. Five, maybe six ... yes, it must've been six. You were in a bar in Liverpool and you were trying to get rid of your date. Then I bumped into you at the taxi rank.'

I looked at him blankly.

'I obviously made an impression. Well, I gave you twenty pounds for the taxi. And you said you'd phone to arrange to give it back to me.'

I blushed fervidly. 'Sorry, I just don't remember this. And I've only got a tenner, which I was about to spend on these drinks.'

'I don't really want it back,' he laughed. Then he paused, contemplating his next move. I wanted him to stay. Have a drink with me. Let me gaze into those eyes a moment or two longer.

'Nice seeing you again,' he said. And off he went, just like that, leaving my insides to collapse slightly at the sight of his back.

I've worked something out about myself over the years. When I decide I am interested in something, or someone, it starts out small, the grain of an idea, then it grows and grows until it's so all-consuming I can barely entertain another thought in my head.

On the drive home, I couldn't stop thinking about the guy at the lake. By the time I got back to my flat, he'd set up home in my head. The look of him. The smell of him. The everything of him.

I made dinner that evening replaying the award-winning script of what I should've said after he'd tapped me on the shoulder. Yet, it was only as I lay in bed the following morning, in the half-world between sleep and full consciousness, that I remembered what he was talking about.

I'd been seeing some horrible guy at the time – I couldn't recall his name, but I do recall he took me to an equally horrible pub.

Details of the evening started to appear in my head, like little spotlights illuminating one by one. I remembered the taxi rank. I remembered talking to Dan. Yet why hadn't I phoned him? I raced to my bedroom drawer and dug out my old diaries, then sat on the floor flicking through the pages.

Sunday, 14 January 2005 – 2.15 a.m.

Keg Dixon is yesterday's news. And so are my dreadlocks.

Earlier suspicions about Keg being a low-level arsehole were entirely confirmed on our fourth (and last) date tonight. Not sure what was worse: the fact that he 'forgot' his cash card and tried to pay for a round with a money-off coupon for ALDI – or his repeated assertion that I had 'blow-job lips,' which I was supposed to consider a compliment.

Anyway. I have met a *gorgeous* bloke. If it wasn't two in the morning and my brain was functioning slightly better, I'd use more impressive prose. But in the absence of any luciditiness (is that a word?) I will simply say this: He has GORGEOUS eyes. GORGEOUS hair. And has a GORGEOUS voice.

He's big, with proper biceps, so technically not my type at all.

I also think he might like me, even though am certain I'm not *his* type.

Am taking the dreadlocks out tomorrow, have decided for definite. Timing is sheer co-incidence, clearly – am not abandoning my quirky, unconventional identity just to try and pull Gorgeous Guy. Though if it works and I *do* pull him, then brilliant!

Anyway. Have Gorgeous Guy's number so will stick two fingers up to my copy of *The Rules* and phone him tomorrow p.m. Signing off now as v. tired and think I may have onset of hypothermia after standing in rain.

I turned the page onto the following morning.

Sunday, 14 January 2005 – 11.45 a.m.

> Worst Cold Ever. My nose is the same colour as my hair *AND THIS IS THE LEAST OF MY WORRIES!* Gorgeous Guy's number has rubbed off my hand, so cannot phone him.
>
> Is probably for the best. Thought I fancied him last night but in cold light of day, use of lip-liner in a potential boyfriend might be an issue for me. Hmm. Quirky, unconventional phase apparently *is* drawing to a conclusion.
>
> Still, lip-liner or not, he was lovely, am sure of it. Off now to weep a little. And blow nose a lot.

As the six-year-old words in my diary played on me the day after the swimming competition, I got a growing sense that – whatever the score was with the lip-liner – I'd let this guy slip through my fingers once. Now, fate had brought us together again.

It was time to make sure fate and I stayed friends.

Chapter 14

Dan

I wake forty minutes before I need to on an uninspiring Wednesday morning and lie watching rain snake down the windows as the soft skin of Gemma's cheek rubs against the bristles on my neck.

'I'm going to get us something nice for dinner tonight,' she murmurs.

I cuddle her into me. 'That'd be lovely.'

She looks up. 'We've got some important stuff to do afterwards, like deciding on a solicitor to appoint.'

I shuffle down to turn my attention to her lips, when someone takes what sounds like a lump hammer to the door. 'Don't be late for work, will you?' my mother shrieks.

'How does she think I've managed to get out of bed on time *all by myself* for the past twelve years?' I grouch.

Gemma remains diplomatically silent.

*

I'd known today was going to be challenging and it doesn't disappoint. By mid-afternoon, I've had five discussions with three people from an energy company who've cut off the gas supply to one of the properties a client of mine is in.

There is so much paperwork piling up on my desk that I could host the world junior papier-mâché championships and never run out of supplies.

And I've just returned from a visit that began when I discovered another client half-naked and carrying a two-litre bottle of cider outside his flat because, he claimed, he'd lost his key and his trousers had been stolen. By a police officer.

I'm finally back at the Old School House, key and trousers recovered – predictably, not from a police officer – and all I want to do is start attacking my correspondence, with as little distraction as possible.

'Big news on me and Jade,' Pete announces.

'Oh?' I ask, unsurprised that the *Daily Mail* aren't queuing up for an exclusive.

'I decided I need to be bolder, so asked her to go for a coffee at lunchtime tomorrow. Or maybe a sandwich. I said I'd pay.'

'Hey, Big Spender,' I smile. A text arrives from Gemma, checking again that I'm not going to be late. I optimistically reply saying I should be on time.

'I don't want to look too keen,' Pete continues. I decide not to tell him he couldn't look keener if he'd bought the ring, booked the venue and had tickets for the honeymoon on the Isle d'Amour, a luxury resort for the terminally soppy.

Later that afternoon, I leave the office for one of my first meetings with a new client, Sheila. I came across her two days ago when she emerged, bleary-eyed, into the living room of another service user during one of my visits.

She'd been sofa-surfing for a while, though trying to pin down her last fixed abode was like attempting to discover the whereabouts of Atlantis with a Boy Scout's compass. I discovered though, that she was forty-two, a sex worker, grandmother to a baby girl called Rose and that, despite a savage cough that rattled through her entire skeleton, she hadn't seen a doctor in five years.

It struck me when we first met that Sheila might have been pretty once.

These days, her intensely blue eyes are all that remain of her old looks, despite clear efforts to maintain her appearance, with make-up and curled hair. Both were fighting a losing battle against years of substance abuse – crack, I'd guessed (correctly as it turned out). It had permeated every part of her, leaving her face gaunt, her skin grey and her lips parched.

I pick her up at 3 p.m. from her friend's house and pile the bin bag full of clothes and pictures – her only belongings – into the boot of the Fanny Magnet. She follows me out and does a double-take.

'Is this your company car, lad?' she asks, clearly amused.

'You could say that.'

'If the fella sitting next to you got a BMW, I suggest you go and hand your notice in,' she cackles.

Sheila spends the journey in the back complaining about the lack of passenger seat and telling me about her new grand-daughter. Because, despite the fact that most of Sheila's life history is a dysfunctional mess, featuring an abusive father, neglectful mother, care homes, pimps and a litany of other pre-dictably nasty characters, she *has* managed to raise two sons. They're eighteen and twenty, never went into care like Sheila and, as far as I can tell, are fully functioning members of soci-ety. Baby Rose belongs to the twenty year old; her mother is a girl he's been with since school.

'Do you see a lot of them?' I ask.

'Every few months. They live down south these days. I've only met Rose once.' She looks at her hands. 'They despair of me, my boys. Not surprising, eh?'

The flat I've found her is in a tattier-than-I'd-like house in an area that's only leafy insomuch as nobody weeds their paths. But it's safe-ish, dry-ish and it's a home – something Sheila hasn't had in a long time.

It's obvious she's over the moon about it. Which is just one of the reasons I'm so annoyed when I discover that the land-lord has inadvertently given me the wrong key. And after learning on the phone that he's two hours away in Blackpool, my only option is for Sheila and me to reconvene in a café down the road until he can get it to us.

It's a busy place serving strong tea and heavily carbohydrated fare with prices scrawled on fluorescent cardboard stars. I buy Sheila a drink and a cake, which she proceeds not to touch.

The immediate priority when I take on a case like this is getting a roof over the client's head. But that's just the beginning: over the next few months, I'm going to help her become self-sufficient; set up her bills and a bank account, then show her how to look after them all herself.

She's eager and accommodating until I try to book a GP appointment, when she fixes her gaze on me and protests: 'I already know I've got *everything*!'

Then I raise the issue of her substance abuse and how we're going to tackle it. This is usually the thorniest of subjects and it's not hard to see why: the life of the average crack user tends to be more violent and unpleasant than most of us are used to. And nothing matches the ability of Class A drugs to neutralise that unpleasantness. It's little wonder most of them would rather *not* have someone like me banging on about giving it up.

This isn't just about a physical addiction though: most users are friends with other users. So those who do succeed are usually the ones prepared to turn their back on their social circle. And can you imagine saying goodbye to *all* of your friends?

Yet Sheila insists that's what she wants to do. She's hoping to check into the Kevin White Unit, a detoxification centre that she knows has helped several people she used to hang around with.

'We can't get you in there straight away, Sheila. To be considered for a referral, you'll need to demonstrate that you're committed by going to the weekly clinics and the GP when you're due.'

She takes a deep breath. 'I don't have to sit in a circle and say "My name's Sheila and I'm an addict", do I?'

I laugh. 'You'll have to go along to find out.'

It's gone seven by the time we finally get into the flat, and that's before I've shown her how everything works and settled her in. She steps into the living room silently as she takes in the fraying carpet and dodgy-looking patch in the corner. She swallows and looks at me, suddenly small.

'Lad.' I can tell she's about to get emotional. 'This is just . . . just brilliant.'

I get back to Buddington at gone nine o'clock. I enter the kitchen guiltily, clutching the only flowers I could find en route – from a Shell garage, which I am fairly sure negates all my theories about the power of floral gestures, and strays dangerously close to *Men Behaving Badly* territory. Gemma's obviously given up on me and gone to bed, and I wince when I find an unopened bottle of Prosecco and some M&S profiteroles in the fridge.

'That you, Dan?' Mum calls through from the living room. 'Come and have a little drink! I've just put *Glee* on – and made those caramelised nuts on the front of *BBC Good Food*. They're lovely once you've got them out of your teeth.'

I put my head through the door. 'I'll pass, Mum, if you don't mind. Tough day.'

'Gemma said the same. Do you know she'd got a nice dinner in? If it had been me I'd be *very* unhappy about you turning up at this time. So where've you been? And who've you been with?'

My mother's capacity for making me feel sixteen years old again is apparently infinite.

'I spent the evening with a prostitute,' I tell her.

'Don't be facetious, Daniel.'

'I've been *working*,' I clarify.

'Until this hour?'

'Yes, I'm afraid so. It's all part and parcel of the job sometimes, Mum.' I wonder why I thought, even for a second, she'd try and be understanding.

Instead, she lets out a short, high-pitched *hm* sound. 'I suggest you start asking them to pay you a bit more.'

'I'm due a pay rise at the next review,' I reply, not telling her that the last time I had one, it wouldn't have covered the cost of a modest night out.

'Hm,' she says again. 'So this is the norm, is it? Working this late?'

My blood suddenly feels several degrees hotter. 'Mum, what does it matter to you?'

She frowns. 'This is my roof you're sleeping under, young man. Of course it matters to me.'

124

At which point I make my excuses and leave this odd *Freaky Friday*-style vortex.

Upstairs, I push open the door to our bedroom to find Gemma lying on her side, her back to me. I tiptoe closer and see that she's reading.

'Hi,' I whisper, kissing her on her head.

'Hi,' she says, without moving.

I walk round the bed and produce the flowers. She examines the five wilting, psychedelically-coloured horticultural aberrations and looks underwhelmed.

'They're ... gorgeous,' she forces herself to say.

'You're a terrible liar.' She laughs. 'Sorry I missed dinner – and the house update,' I continue. 'And I'm sorry the best flowers I could get hold of look like they've been in a hit and run.'

'It's the thought that counts. I think.' She rolls onto her back and smiles. 'What was it this time? Squatters in your client's flat or an alcoholic who'd fallen off the wagon?'

'Neither. Just something I had to do. Budge up,' I say, sitting on the edge of the bed as she shifts over and I run my fingers through her hair. I feel dramatically better.

'It was only an M&S meal anyway,' she sighs. 'I probably made it sound fancier than it was. Although I did get Prosecco.'

'What about the budget?'

'It was half-price. Anyway, I found a solicitor.'

'Oh, brilliant.'

'And phoned the mortgage company to tell them we want to proceed.'

'Sorry it's all landed on you.'

'It's probably easier if one of us takes charge,' she says tiredly. 'We'll know where we are then.'

I pull off my shoes, socks and jeans, then slide into bed as the scent of bubble bath on Gemma's skin fills my head with primal thoughts. My eyes drop to her lip-balmed mouth and I have an urgent desire to kiss her. Her eyes dilate as I edge forward ... and am rewarded with a loud, uncompromising SQUEAK.

She lets out a long breath and gestures to the living room below. 'Has your mum gone to bed yet?'

A blast of camp-tastic music sears through the ceiling.

'No, she's watching her *Glee* box set. Hopefully she won't be long. We could, you know ... resume matters when she's asleep.'

Gemma smiles and snuggles into my arms, where I hold her. And hold her. For two long, tortured hours, I hold her.

When my mother finally turns *Glee* off and plods upstairs, Gemma is fast asleep, her mouth slightly open. And it's looking very likely that she wouldn't stir if Jamie Dornan bounced in here on a space-hopper and suggested a game of Spin the Bottle.

Chapter 15

Gemma

Dan and I visit Pebble Cottage again on Sunday, despite my failure to work out where we're getting the extra £4k – and the fact that we don't have an appointment. Rich has threatened to take out a restraining order if I don't stop phoning to check that no other interested parties have been allowed to view it since our offer was accepted.

We pull up in my car and step out silently. Even before I peek through the window, I notice features I hadn't spotted earlier: the little shelf below each windowframe perfect for a lavender box; the original tiles on the front step, patterned like a silk scarf. Even though there's no furniture now, everything about the place feels like home, from the location to the size, to the old-fashioned fireplace in the living room.

Dan squeezes my hand and I experience a wave of unease

about his enthusiasm for this whole thing. Particularly now the mutual tolerance between him and his mum is wearing thinner than her Threshers' loyalty card.

And, although I'd never say it, I'm starting to find her fairly difficult to live with myself. It's not just the fact that she has absolutely NO filter, or that she is *always* right about everything, or that she can be so overbearing that we never get a moment to ourselves.

Being alone with her is akin to locking yourself into an interrogation room: I'm bombarded with questions about Dan, his job, his financial situation, his health – all the usual stuff mums are interested in, but which Dan prefers to keep on a need-to-know basis. Which leaves me with the uncomfortable feeling that in answering her, even vaguely, I'm somehow betraying him.

'I can't wait to be in there, can you?' I ask Dan.

He glances down at me. 'I can't wait to be in anywhere but my mum's.'

I frown. 'You don't mean that, do you? Not after we've had an offer accepted and it's all happening. This is the only house for us as far as I'm concerned, and—'

'Gemma,' he interrupts, 'we're going to do everything in our power to get this house, okay? *I* will do everything in my power to get it. But don't ever forget that you and I would live happily ever after, whether it was here or somewhere else.'

I nod as he kisses me. 'I agree completely. But it won't be somewhere else. It'll be here. Just so you know.'

He laughs. 'Yes, I think I've got that message, loud and clear.'

A few days later, I'm daydreaming about our Happily Ever After – in Pebble Cottage and nowhere else – as I'm on my way to the filming of an advert I was involved in scripting. I pull up in an overpriced car park in Manchester and head towards the Northern Quarter.

Its bars and cafés are as bustling as ever on a sunny Friday afternoon, with outdoor seats at a premium and the weekend crying out to start early.

As I walk through a cloud of coffee-shop aromas, I picture my future with the man I love. My head is filled with visions of nights in front of our beautiful fireplace and Sunday mornings in our tastefully furnished bedroom.

But as my eyes drift to a small round table in one of a dozen pavement cafés, all those thoughts – and any others – vanish from my head.

I stand and stare, feeling winded, unable to believe what – or rather *whom* – I'm seeing, for the first time in twelve years.

Alex Monroe. The one-time love of my life.

It's difficult to describe my physical state as I attempt to look unfazed, holding my breath and hardly able to feel my legs, even if they're still technically walking. I slow down to make certain it's him, the confirmation of which makes my heart pound harder and faster than can possibly be good for anyone's health.

Eventually, as I'm about twenty feet away, my legs refuse to go any further and I stand watching as he reads a newspaper, like he always did, even when we were seventeen. He doesn't look twelve years older, at least not in a bad way. The soft features of his younger face have become more mature, more angular, altogether more impressive.

I take a small step without knowing whether I'm going to politely cough and ask if he remembers me, or throw myself into his arms with tears in my eyes.

However, when I've caught my breath long enough to start to approach, a woman – slim, blonde, intelligent-looking – appears at his side and places two drinks on the table, before sitting down next to him.

He is immediately deep in conversation. And in that split second I find myself desperate to know whether they're *together*, even though there are a dozen more pertinent questions, not least what the hell is he doing in the UK? He smiles and runs his hand through his thick blond hair, a gesture so painfully familiar to me, yet one I'd entirely forgotten about until this moment.

And it's that, accompanied by my cascades of adrenalin, that makes me realise I don't want to be here. The thought of seeing him after all this time and being introduced to a girlfriend, fiancée, *wife* . . . I instinctively feel repulsed by the thought.

He glances in my direction. And suddenly, only drastic measures are open to me. Namely, I have to hide.

Unfortunately, I am not in the dense jungle of the Amazon Basin with as much vegetation and camouflage that a girl could hope for. I am in central Manchester in strappy sandals, and the only thing I can find in the way of cover is a large specials board.

I dive behind it and crouch, panting, as if on the run from an armed gunman whose house I've burned down, dog I've run over, and whose grammar I corrected on Facebook.

'You okay?' A waitress with short spiky hair and a friendly, if mildly condescending smile bends down to talk to me.

'I'm just . . . I'm hiding from someone, that's all,' I breathe. Even as I say it, I know I'm being ridiculous.

She frowns and straightens up. 'Okay. Only, you've rubbed off half our specials there.'

I pull the back of my black top so I can examine it, realising I now have part of the line *king prawn, lime & ginger skewers* smudged backwards on me in chalk.

'Oh God, sorry.' I glance around the board again and see Alex still there, still talking.

I force the uncharitable thoughts tumbling through my head about his female companion to stop. Had I expected him to spend the last twelve years pining for me, for God's sake?

'Go out the back way, if you like,' the waitress suggests.

I hesitate. 'Would you mind?'

131

'Course not,' she grins, as I stand up and let her bundle me through the restaurant. Fellow diners look on as I optimistically wonder if they think I'm some sort of political fugitive – frantic but noble.

When we reach the door, the waitress grabs me by the arm and looks intently in my eyes. 'Word of advice,' she whispers. 'I got caught shoplifting when I was fourteen and got away with it. At your age, you wouldn't stand a chance.'

Chapter 16

That night, more than any other, I want Dan's arms around me.
I can't explain why, beyond an instinctive need to sink into him,
breathe him in and remind myself why I'm so lucky to have him.

Just him.

His text arrives as I'm turning into the gates of Buddington.

So sorry Gemma – something's come up at work.
Back as soon as I can.

I sigh and throw the phone onto the passenger seat. It beeps
again.

I love you xxxxx

I open the door with the key Belinda gave me, even though
it still feels like I'm breaking and entering, and am assaulted
by a barrage of music from the conservatory.

There, I discover Belinda and her friends in an array of high-visibility Lycra, having a dance lesson from an older, significantly sprightlier man.

'It's my daughter-in-law!' exclaims Belinda as the others take the opportunity to pause and catch their breath. 'Come and join us, Gemma – just get your shoes and socks off. Bobby's run us ragged!'

I attempt to suppress any visible alarm. 'It looks brilliant, Belinda, but I'm shattered after work. I'm just going to have a bath and something to eat. Sorry to be boring.'

The music that pounds through the ceiling is an eclectic and extremely noisy mix of disco classics. I run a bath and slip in, watching the surface of the water pound to each Chaka Khan track as if Godzilla is en route to tear the roof off. Even with my headphones on the highest setting, it fails to drown out six women squawking, *'I'm ev'ry womannn!'*

I close my eyes and try to clear my head – of everything. But all I can think about is seeing Alex today. About whether he saw me. And about why I couldn't bring myself to go and say hello.

Pressure builds in my brain, in direct contravention of the state of relaxation I'm attempting to achieve. Eventually, I pull myself out of the bath, climb into my dressing gown and head to the bedroom to flick through a copy of *Marie Claire* magazine. I'm unable to take in a word of it.

I consider going to make my dinner now, throwing myself

at the mercy of Belinda and her friends. But I'm feeling so rattled by what happened today that I haven't got the energy to face them or anyone else. Except perhaps one person.

I pick up my phone and text Dan, asking him if he'll be long.

Twenty minutes later, he hasn't responded. And I'm still trapped in this room with an empty stomach and tortured brain. Quite suddenly, the music stops. I give it a minute or two, then creep to the door and prise it open in time to make out that they're leaving to go for drinks.

The door slams. Footsteps crunch on the gravel. Car engines fire up, then fade away as they disappear up the drive. The house is still, silent – until another text arrives.

Gemma, so sorry. Eat without me, please & I'll sort myself out x

I fling myself onto the bed as a mental image of Alex forces its way into my head again. He's bulked out since we were teenagers, that slightly reedy frame no longer so skinny. I wonder if he realises how much better he looks? I hope so, as he was always mildly self-conscious about his body, though I could never work out why. I thought he was gorgeous until the day we kissed each other goodbye.

I shake the thought from my mind as I listen carefully for evidence of anybody else in the house. Then I creep to the top of the stairs and eventually realise I have Buddington all to myself.

When I get to the kitchen I take out a fork and plink it through the film on one of the ready meals I'd stocked up on yesterday. Then I place it in the microwave and wander round the room, idly picking up knick-knacks and examining them in a bid to divert my thoughts. I run my finger across the polka-dot spoon rest, then pick up the fridge magnet from Sorrento. My eyes drift slackly across to a drawer, which I open.

'Gemma?'

'ARGHH!'

I slam shut the drawer, before I spin round to be confronted by Belinda. She raises both eyebrows. 'I only wondered if you wanted a G&T.'

'Oh. Oh,' I repeat. I glance at my curry. It feels rude not to. 'Why not? It's definitely past Wine o'clock, isn't it?'

'Wine o'clock? Gemma, this is Pissed o'clock.' She holds up her drink. 'If I'm on my sixth you can join me for your first. They're not recreational in my case. I need a few to loosen up the joints before a dance lesson. My Moonwalk's shocking otherwise.'

She pours me a G&T – with a healthy measure of G – and I take a sip. As my chest warms, this strikes me as a better alternative to sitting upstairs, with nothing to distract me except the memory of a boy I – mostly – stopped thinking about years ago.

*

As the evening unfolds, one G&T becomes four – and it's not just the joints that loosen up. Belinda's stories about Dan are impossible to resist, even if he'd burst a blood vessel if he could hear. She's like a walking version of *Heat* magazine, she's so indiscreet. Hours pass in minutes as the gin disappears and I gain a growing sense of being very, very drunk. And if I'm drunk, Belinda is positively plastered, something that became abundantly clear when she picked up a pair of tongs and plinked a used tea-bag into her drink instead of a slice of lemon.

'Dja-ya know, half of the stuff I wrote – about men, I mean – the publishers wouldn't even put in the book.'

'Really? Why?'

She sloshes back her gin. 'Despite the title, which my editor Angela insisted on, they wanted my book to be mainshtream. I wasn't supposed to be some hairy-armpitted radical feminist,' she slurs. 'I was supposed to be *Everywoman*. The woman in the street. Of which a very large majority have been badly treated by men.'

'You really think it's a majority?'

She nearly spits out her drink. '*Of course*. The things the average man is capable of don't bear thinking about. They're *animals*. ALL of them.'

My skin prickles. Dan isn't an animal, I'm certain of that. And Alex wasn't either. Both are nothing but lovely. 'I'm not sure I completely buy that, I must admit,' I say. 'Yes, there are idiots, but there are lots of good ones. I happen to love men, generally.'

'You'll learn,' she snorts.

'Don't get me wrong, Belinda. I'm not some simpleton who believes in fairytales. I don't even particularly want to get married myself.'

She swallows another large mouthful. 'Dan mentioned that. Why not?'

'Oh, a variety of reasons,' I say vaguely, though in truth I never could pin down my unease about it, beyond the fact that my (still married) parents haven't been the greatest advert.

'The thing I find difficult to get my head around,' I continue, 'is how you can align your views with having a son. *He's* a man.'

'Nobody's perfect,' she laughs. 'Besides, although I will always love him – hell, I'd jump in front of a bus for him – he's been no angel either, you know. He's his father's son, after all. He's changed his ways since he met you, but who's to say that'll last forever?'

Indignation ripples through me as I pour another drink, feeling as though I need something fortifying. 'You mean you think he'll treat *me* badly? Do the dirty on *me*?'

'Oh look, I've got high hopes for you two. But it's not beyond the realms, is it? Sorry, Gemma,' she shrugs, looking far from it. 'But that's what men do. It's that simple.'

I feel a surge of defiance. I'm aware that this is partly due to the booze, and partly because I feel so weird after today. But fundamentally, Dan is my boyfriend and I love him – and the idea that I have to defend him against his own mother is, frankly, awful.

I tell myself to get a grip and put a lid on it, so instead of spurting out something I might regret, I stand up and mutter something about needing the loo. I get into the hall and dig out my phone, before dialling Dan's number, hearing it go to voicemail, and leaving a message.

'Dan, are you on your way home yet?' I hiss in hushed, drunken tones. 'Your mother is . . . well, it's all jusht getting out of hand. She's talking all this nonshense about . . . look, it doeshn't matter.' To my alarm I note that I'm also slurring quite badly and entirely failing to get to my point. I compose myself. 'If I'm honest, Dan, there was one moment when I felt like strangling your mother tonight. And unless you get home soon, I couldn't rule it out.'

And then I look up and see Belinda standing at the doorway with an expression like the mother in Stephen King's *Carrie*, just before she stabbed her in the shoulder.

Chapter 17

Dan

I have spent this evening in A&E with a seventy-nine-year-old lady called Jennifer, with whom I've been working for three months after her husband, a retired rail worker, died suddenly last year.

He'd looked after all their bills, so when she was left alone – grief-stricken and with no children to help her – she'd struggled to stay on top of them. For six months before she was referred to the Chapterhouse Centre, she'd been living on a friend's sofa. Recently, after I'd found accommodation of her own for her, she'd been making good progress. Until tonight.

The accident had happened after Jennifer tried to make herself some proper, deep-fried chips – the ones her husband liked – but had fallen asleep in the living room and forgotten they were on the stove.

I arrived to find her in an ambulance and the house virtually destroyed. Thankfully, doctors think she's going to be all right, but it's fair to say it's been a long night for all of us. All I want to do is jump in the car, fling on some tunes, fantasise that I'm in a Lamborghini and go home to kiss my girlfriend.

I turn on the phone and listen to Gemma's message. She is angry, upset and so far from sober that her impassioned speech sounds like she's simultaneously attempting to gargle with Listerine. By the time it ends, with Gemma threatening to inflict GBH on my mother, I am seriously concerned that the scene at home may resemble a Mexican street brawl.

I leap in the Fanny Magnet, fire her up and put my foot down.

Clearly, there would be some benefits to them not being Great Mates. I find the idea instinctively repellent anyway, perhaps because of the treasure-trove of mortifying information my mother delights in holding about me.

But they're outweighed by the alternative horror of being stuck between the two women in my life, fighting a battle that would overwhelm a crack unit of UN peacekeeping forces.

As I head towards the Mersey Tunnel, I add as much throttle as I can. It's like trying to win the Grand Prix in a compact roadsweeper. I'm in the tunnel for a quarter of a mile before I reach a trail of red tail-lights ahead and realise that there's been a crash. My phone rings and I put it on speaker. It's Pete.

'I'm just phoning because I knew you'd want to hear how my coffee with Jade went.'

'I've thought of little else,' I reply. 'Go on – did it go well?'

'Depends on your definition of "well". I didn't fart, fall over or throw up on myself with nerves, so that was a plus. And the coffee was good. Also, I did ask Jade on a date . . .'

The response is painfully predictable. 'She said no?' I venture.

'No, she said yes.'

My eyebrows jolt in surprise. 'Really?'

'Yes. It was excruciating,' he sighs. 'I said to her, as plainly as I could, "Why don't we go out for a drink one night?" And she said: "Great idea. Who else shall we get to come?" So I said, "How about just you and me?" At which point she howled with laughter, slapped me on the shoulder and said, "Oh Pete, you are funny! People would get the wrong impression".'

'What did you say?'

'It got complicated after that. I said: "What if the wrong impression was the right impression? And, you know, you and me were just out out. *Together*, you and me. And that *was* how it was".'

'Even I'm a bit lost . . .'

'Then the pensioner next to us spilled his Americano on me and we had to leave. I've reeked like the skip outside Starbucks all day.'

The traffic starts to move as I make my excuses and end the call, before continuing with my journey out of the tunnel and onto the M53.

I've gone about half a mile when I become aware of a flashing blue light in the rearview mirror. Incredulous, since I was only going about four miles an hour over the speed limit – though not through lack of trying – I pull in and attempt to generate my most amenable expression.

I catch a glance of myself in the mirror and see that this makes me look shiftier than a man wearing a brown mac and carrying a box labelled *ACME Dynamite*.

I open the door.

It's fair to say that nothing could have prepared me for the chain of events that follow. I have one leg out of the car when the air explodes into a thunderstorm of improbable action movie sounds – and three more cars screech up behind the others.

With my heart thrashing against my ribcage, I shield my eyes from their headlights and step forwards. I am rewarded by a Blitzkrieg of shouting and as I focus in disbelief past the blue lights, register a line of armed police officers.

They are all pointing their guns in my direction. AT ME. I cannot recall a moment when I have come so dangerously close to relinquishing the grip on my key bodily functions.

The next few minutes are a terrifying, bewildering blur. I have never been the subject of a siege by an Armed Response

Unit before, and can safely admit it's not something I'd be keen on being involved in again.

I am handcuffed and thrown into a police van, protesting with such spontaneous and befuddled outrage that even *I'm* not convinced I'm innocent of whatever it is they think I've done.

I'm told that, no, I'm not allowed to get my phone to stop my girlfriend and mother from killing each other, because it and everything else in the Fanny Magnet is required for a forensic examination.

And in the course of the next two hours, most of which are spent at a police station, several facts become apparent.

One: the Fanny Magnet was involved in a shooting the day before I took ownership of it.

Two: every shred of documentation I have for it is so fake that by rights I should only have had to hand over Monopoly money for it.

Three: I'm not allowed to drive it home.

Four: it takes two hours of my reasoned arguments (and a moment or two of pathetic pleading) to convince them that I have a rock solid alibi and couldn't fit the description of the perpetrator, who is 5 foot 4 and ginger with one finger missing from his left hand, less.

Then I *am* free to go home, but not in the Fanny Magnet because it's required as evidence. Indefinitely.

I walk out of the police station, spot a taxi in the distance and hold out my hand. Its driver pulls in too fast and sends a tidal wave of sludge over me. Then he looks me up and down, decides I'm too disgusting to let into his cab, and drives off.

I stand, exhausted, drenched and looking like I've completed a Tough Mudder course through a Bangkok sewer. A taxi cannot be seen for miles. I wonder how tonight could possibly get any better.

Chapter 18

Gemma

When Belinda overhears me threatening to strangle her, I begin mounting a defence which I hope sounds dignified but in fact comes out all wobbly-lipped and blubbing, as if I've lost my teddy.

Retreating to the sitting room, I weakly announce that I'm going to leave. Then she announces that *she's* going to leave. As she storms past and opens the door – yanking the handle off in the process – it strikes me that Belinda is significantly better at being in a huff than I am or could ever dream of being.

Then she stops. She turns round. Her shoulders slump and she plods in a slack-kneed, proto-Neanderthal stoop towards the sofa. She takes a deep breath to compose herself, then goes to sit down on the arm but misses by a centimetre and tumbles, arse first, onto the floor.

My first instinct is to dive over and help, but I stop myself as she sits up and tries to focus. I brace myself for what's coming next.

'I'm sorry, Gemma.'

'The thing is, Belinda,' I protest, then stop. 'What did you say?'

'I said I'm sorry. And I mean it.' She lowers her eyes and I go over to help her onto the sofa.

'It's okay,' I mumble. 'This whole thing got out of hand. When I said I – look, it just slipped out of my mouth. Totally stupid of me. So I'm sorry too.'

'I shouldn't have said those things about you and Daniel.' She lifts up the bottle of gin glumly. 'I've always been a terrible bruiser after I've had a few.'

'Shall I make us a cup of tea?' I offer.

She nods. 'That'd be nice.'

I head to the kitchen and flick on the kettle, wondering if she might have passed out by the time I get back with the tea pot and mugs. On the contrary, she's piling her hair up into a chignon and looks unsettlingly composed. I pour the tea and sit down.

'Can I say something, Belinda?' I ask, though I know I may be letting myself in for trouble. 'Don't you ever have any nagging doubts about parts of these theories? After all these years?'

'I do have moments, Gemma. Mainly after I've watched

Dirty Dancing – Mum and I love it,' she smirks. 'Then I remind myself that that's fiction. Reality is a harsher demon.'

'The break-up with Dan's dad must've hit you hard.'

'I adored him when we first met – and the feeling was mutual. I found a letter once that he'd written in the early days, full of lovely words about how he'd dream about the sound of my voice. Unlike later, when I'm sure he had nightmares about it.' She looks down at her mug. 'When I found out about all the affairs two years later – a month after Dan was born – it was terrible. I felt like an idiot. Yet I clung to the marriage, closed my eyes to what was plain to everyone else. Do you know what I did after I'd found out, Gemma?'

'Put ricin in his Scotch?'

She smiles briefly. 'When I was at my lowest point – and knew all about the deception, the adultery – I said I'd forgive him and take him back. Only he didn't want to come back.'

'Oh Belinda . . .'

'The rejection was the worst part of it.'

I wonder what Dan would think, if he could hear this. I'm very glad he can't.

'But that, as you know, wasn't the end of the story,' she goes on. 'I spent months wallowing in misery and loneliness, on my own with a small baby. Then I said to myself: "Enough's enough." That's when I rewrote the book.'

'Did you always know it would sell so well?'

'Oh, God no. My views were unpalatable to a lot of people.

But it struck a chord with so many who'd had similar experiences to mine. For years, women had been sold the old chestnut that "you have to work at a marriage". Compromise is one thing, but often, when their man went off with someone else, women were blaming themselves – convincing themselves that *they* hadn't worked hard enough.' She takes a sip of tea. 'So often, that just wasn't the case. I genuinely believe that we're conditioned by society – and Patrick Swayze and Jennifer Grey – to believe that romantic love will last forever. But it rarely does.'

I bite my lip. 'Belinda, you speak a lot of sense. I loved reading your books – it's obvious why they were so successful. They really do make you think. But, even after all the thinking, I remain one of the fools. I think lasting love *does* exist. I'm obviously a hopeless romantic.'

'Well, I won't hold it against you,' she winks. 'Part of me wishes I could join you.'

'What do you mean?' I ask.

'Oh, now that was *my* throwaway line. Don't ever repeat it.' She hesitates. 'I don't ever want another relationship, obviously. But there have been times over the years when I've, you know, dated. I always thought that was fine as long as it never went any further than a bit of fun. I kind of miss it,' she says.

'Belinda.' I lean forward in my seat. 'You're a gorgeous woman. You should do some dating again.'

She rolls her eyes. 'Oh, come off it, I'm sixty next year. The days when I'd jump on the back of someone's motorbike and go to the flicks are long gone. The only men I meet these days couldn't even get on a motorbike without taking their anti-inflammatories first.'

I hear the door slam and realise it must be Dan – finally.

'But thank you,' whispers Belinda, at the very moment that he bursts through the door.

He stands breathless and bedraggled, his coat splattered in mud, and glances between the two of us, confusion all over his face. 'What's going on?'

'Nothing,' we say in unison.

'I think it's time I turned in,' I add, standing up. 'Good night, Belinda. And thanks for the drinks.'

'My pleasure,' she smiles.

When Dan and I are outside the door, he grabs me by the hand. 'What's happening?'

'Sorry about the message – it's nothing to worry about,' I say, as he drips muddy water on my foot. And then I look up. 'What took you so long anyway?'

Chapter 19

Dan

Over the next week, the reality of buying a house starts to kick in. Gemma seems to be constantly surrounded by stacks of paperwork, and that's before we get onto her collection of home décor magazines, which are now so copious I'm convinced we could actually *build* a house with them.

'What's all this?' I ask as I walk into our room on Saturday morning when she's midway through some sort of colour-coding process. Gemma is a big fan of colour-coding.

I sometimes think my girlfriend could not be more efficient if she were German, had alloy wheels and did over 300 miles to the gallon.

'This blue pile is anything to do with the mortgage. The pink pile is the solicitor. Green is the estate agents, and this is miscellaneous – cushion colours and that kind of thing.'

'The miscellaneous pile is the biggest.'

'Cushion colours are important,' she grins. I think she's only half-joking. 'Pull up a bean bag. I need to go through some things with you. We absolutely have to finish the mortgage forms today or we'll be going nowhere.'

I drag the bean bag along the floor and sit next to her as she hands me a stack of paper. 'I've filled out most of these already – you just need to do pages twenty to twenty-nine. Although read through what I've written, won't you? It's important that we do this together.'

'Couldn't agree more,' I reply, wondering what her reaction might be if I suggested doing this in front of *Match of the Day*. Then I register her expression – single-minded, focused, somewhere between Miss Moneypenny and The Terminator – and decide against it.

I pick up a pen and start reading the form when I get a waft of her perfume. I glance over at her and am hit by one of the miniature thunderbolts I still get all the time. 'You are ridiculously gorgeous,' I hear myself say.

She looks up and the hint of a smile appears at her lips. 'So are you,' she whispers.

I'm forced to respond to an urge to lean in and kiss her. The kiss deepens as I pull her into me and murmur, 'Mum's out.'

She shifts closer and kisses me again, saying huskily, 'Is she?'

I abandon page 21 of the form, moving my lips to her neck. 'The bed could squeak as much as it wants. Nobody would hear.'

She freezes and pulls back. Then she pecks me on the cheek, as if she's just given me 50p for an ice cream and told me to be on my way.

'Fine,' she says, not sounding massively overwhelmed with lust.

I narrow my eyes. 'That isn't quite the response I was hoping for.'

'Dan, you know I'd love nothing more than to get naked with you,' she says, about as seductively as you'd expect someone to discuss their tax return.

'Glad to hear it.'

'In fact, I will.'

'Excellent!' I start unbuttoning my shirt.

'But first you have to tell me your monthly outgoings.'

'*What?*'

She rustles the form in my face. 'The mortgage company need to know.'

'Bastards,' I reply. She raises an eyebrow. 'Fine. Fire away.'

She clears her throat and picks up a pencil. 'Credit cards?'

'What about them?'

'Have you got one?'

I hesitate, considering my options. There are several alternatives to the truth, but sadly, I know she would see through all of them. 'Yes,' I say casually.

Her jaw drops. '*Have* you? You never told me that.'

'A man's got to have some secrets,' I grin, before straightening my face, it being abundantly obvious that joking about this is not appreciated. 'Why are you looking at me as if I've just confessed to selling my grandmother to pay for a week in Zante?'

'I . . .' She shakes her head. 'Sorry, go on.'

'There's nothing else to say,' I tell her. 'I got it a few years ago so I could buy some things for the flat, that's all.'

She looks at me as if this is something she patently should know about, an opinion I refuse to indulge. 'Amount owing?'

I feel a prickle on the back of my neck. 'Why do they want to know that?'

'They just have to, that's all,' she says quietly. She's trying not to show it, but frustration appears on her brow. 'They're asking, so we have to tell them. At least, we do if we want a mortgage.'

I think carefully before opening my mouth again. 'Couple of hundred.'

She looks at me with eyes that could get her a job at Guantanamo Bay. 'You'll need to be more specific.'

'I'd have to check.'

'Okay.' I don't move. 'Well, can you do so? Now, I mean.'

I have a horrible feeling this isn't going to end well. Still, I walk to the big cardboard box marked *Important Stuff* that contains bank statements, bills and anything else that might come in handy one day. In sharp contrast to everything on my bedroom floor, this is not colour-coded. In fact, it is not codified,

catalogued or filed in any way: it is the organisational equiv-
alent of one of those large South American landfill sites, the
ones where entire communities had lived for generations without anybody actually realising.

Gemma does not need to know this.

I open the first file, look inside, see an unopened pay slip
from 2009 on the top and close it again. 'I'll have to dig it out
another time,' I declare. 'With the move, my filing system
needs a bit of a . . . reappraisal.'

She's having none of it. 'Dan. Just tell me. How much do
you owe on that credit card?'

'Is this really necess—'

'Yes, *if we want a mortgage!*'

I hold my breath and spit it out in one go. 'Two thousand
three hundred and forty-seven pounds.'

'WHAT?'

I seriously resent the tone of her voice. 'I'm paying it back,'
I retaliate.

She puts the papers down. 'Dan, this could affect our mortgage application.' The voice she uses isn't even one of
annoyance. It's as if she's hurt. I hate that voice, I really do. 'I
had no idea you owed all that.'

I can't help thinking I preferred it that way.

The next hour and a half is spent with a full-scale evalua-
tion of my financial situation in which I'm forced to confess
every hire-purchase agreement I've ever taken out and every

bank charge I've ever been thumped with – not to mention the life insurance, savings and investments I've failed to acquire.

'Should I even ask about a pension?' Gemma says, semi-apologetically, as we reach the final page.

'There's no pension, Gemma,' I say, through gritted teeth. 'I work in a job that just about allows me to put food on the table at the end of every month.' I say this with what I hope is the air of a solid working man's dignity, as if I spend my days down a coal-mine in order to feed my twelve kids and still leave a little for the wife to pop in her petticoat pocket.

She goes to say something then stops herself. 'I know,' she concedes. 'Right. You just need to read this through now and then sign at the bottom.'

I flick through the pages and reach the one that lists, finally, our incomes. And there it is, for all to see: the fact that my girlfriend earns more than me.

If I were a better man, I'd say this was the twenty-first century and it doesn't matter. And of course it doesn't. As she's said previously, on many occasions, my qualifications could've got me a job earning several times more than my current salary. I only don't earn as much because I chose to do something worthy with my life. But, right now, worthy sucks.

'Sorry if this has been painful,' she adds, taking my hand. And as she looks in my eyes, I feel stupid and sulky and regret showing it.

'Don't be silly.'

'At least you've not had to go out and buy yet another new car, I suppose,' she says.

This is true. Though Mum must think I was born yesterday if I fell for the idea that it was 'sheer coincidence' that she'd chosen now to buy herself a new VW Golf, on top of the Porsche.

She knows there is no way I'd have accepted a car as a gift. And although I still feel very uncomfortable – because we all know that's exactly what it is, temporary or not – I can't deny it's got me out of a hole.

Gemma puts down the papers and places her hands on either side of my face. Then she kisses me and everything feels a bit better. A bit warmer. A bit nicer altogether.

'How about some squeaking?' she whispers, sliding her hand around my neck and wriggling into me.

'I'd love to squeak with you.'

'DANNY!'

I leap back from Gemma and look her in the eyes as she says, 'I thought your mum was out?'

'She is. It's Grandma,' I say, grabbing a cushion to cover my crotch as I limp towards the door.

'Oh God, I forgot – her curtain rail needs fixing, the one in the living room. Your mum was going to call someone out but I told her that'd be silly when you like doing that sort of stuff,' Gemma says in a rush.

Gemma knows full well that this is stretching the definition of 'like' beyond all recognition. Equally, to deny it would be to undermine my sense of manhood.

'I'll go and look for a screwdriver,' I mutter.

Grandma's skin smells of chlorine when I reach her annexe with the most pathetic excuse for a toolkit I've ever seen from Mum's garage.

'Nice swim?' I ask.

'Lovely, thanks. I didn't think DIY was your cup of tea.'

'Now I'm getting a new house I thought I'd practise on yours first,' I tell her. 'Don't blame me if I demolish the place, will you?'

'Oh, don't do that, Danny,' she says. 'I'd have to move into the main house – and I don't think my stomach's up to your mum's cooking.'

I examine the curtain rail and am relieved to see that it looks fairly straightforward. She takes a tea pot over to her table and sits down. 'Why don't you come and have a cuppa first? The curtain rail can wait.'

I sit down next to her and take a bite out of a biscuit as she sips her tea and breaks into a cough. 'You okay?' I ask.

She nods. 'Been a bit under the weather lately. I'm sure it's nothing.' She reaches over and curls her fingers through the handle of her tea cup, raising it to her mouth again. 'Hey, do you know what I was thinking about earlier? Do you remember that time when you were a little boy and your grandad and I took you swimming in Bala Lake in Wales?'

Everyone has a stand-out childhood memory, one that flickers to the front of your brain when asked to *think happy thoughts*.

'Oh yes. Grandad kept dunking me in.'

She laughs, her eyes smiling. 'He was a bugger, wasn't he? You were only about eight but he didn't let up. Poor little thing.'

'I don't think it did me any harm.'

She lowers her blue eyes. 'You know, I must've been swimming thousands of times; I couldn't count how many. But that day was my favourite.'

'Mine too, Grandma.'

'I think about it all the time, the three of us splashing into the water. My man on one side, my lovely grandson on the other.'

She pauses for a moment, soaking in the memory. 'I do miss him. He'd be so proud of you. The way you help people. The fine young man you've turned into. The special woman you've chosen to be with.'

'We should go back to Bala Lake one day, you and me.'

She shakes her head. 'You must go with Gemma. I should be giving all this sort of thing up really. Your mum's right – I'm an old, infirm woman.'

'Grandma,' I remind her, 'you've been saying that since you were forty-five.'

Chapter 20

Gemma

Since the day I saw Alex in Manchester, he's repeatedly slipped into my thoughts, uninvited. It's inevitable really, given how large he once loomed in my life, even if I keep reminding myself that it was a hell of a long time ago.

I was fifteen when we first met and the most socially artless, introverted teenager you could come across. I blushed when spoken to – not just by boys, but anyone: teachers, shop assistants, even the postman could elicit a mild reddening and he was about sixty-three and had a glass eye with a chip in it.

In my head, I felt sure this wasn't the Real Me. The person I hoped deep down would be actually quite funny and sort of cool – someone who could conjure up a razor-sharp reply to anything. And though these qualities still elude me more than

I'd like, it took meeting Alex to make me realise that someone vaguely *all right* might exist within me.

Our paths crossed at a party held by my friend Selena's older cousin after her mum and dad had gone to Spain for the week. It qualified as the most devastatingly boring party in the history of teenage parties.

There were about sixteen guests. Selena's cousin was in a state of high neurosis about spillages on the living-room carpet and her dad's stereo getting scratched. Nobody smoked, nobody took drugs, nobody made a sex tape on the bathroom floor. We all just sat around making polite conversation as we sipped the 'Bastard Sangria' Selena's cousin claimed would get us rolling drunk, but which tasted suspiciously like Vimto. I'd been to wilder parties that involved playing Pass the Parcel.

Despite this, I was still uncomfortable about the prospect of having to talk to someone other than Selena. I could feel my blood pressure rise every time she went to the bathroom and left me alone. So when Alex – with his skinny black jeans and easy smile – struck up conversation, I should've gone into meltdown. Except, oddly, fortuitously, I managed to hold it together.

'Wild party, eh?' he leaned in and whispered.

'Hope no one calls the police,' I replied, suppressing a smile.

'Yep, if it's raided they might seize all those bottles of Tango in the kitchen.'

He was flirtatious, cool and way too confident for someone

his age. He smelled of peppermint and fresh tobacco and soap, which was the most exotic combination I'd ever come across.

Yet, somehow, despite being instantly dazzled by him, I felt strangely at ease. He had this kind of magic that made the person I wanted to be appear out of nowhere. And he seemed to like her.

His father was a civil engineer who'd worked all over the world, latterly in San Francisco, where Alex had lived for two years. Now he was back in England and here to stay.

I remember the moment my dad came to collect me that night, when I ran back inside to get my coat and Alex grabbed me by the arm and pulled me into the kitchen. I thought he was going to kiss me. I thought I would die on the spot. Instead, he thrust a piece of paper into my hand and said, quite simply, 'Phone me.'

Our love affair exploded after that. We spent every free moment together, revising in the park when it was sunny, whiling away hours in my bedroom as – to my shame – my friends became strangers.

I lost my virginity with him at 9.30 one morning after his parents had gone to work. We'd planned it in advance, down to the bus I'd take to get to his place. In the event, it wasn't heavy with passion and lust – we were both too nervous – but it was gentle, loving and absolutely perfect. That moment, that rite of passage, would be ours forever, no matter what happened afterwards.

In the year and a half we were together, that peculiar intensity of first love never dwindled. I'd have done absolutely anything for him. And I know he felt the same about me.

So when he came to my house on a dark February night, held my hand and told me about his father's new job in Kenya – the one that meant he'd be moving 4,000 miles away – I honestly felt like my world had come to an end.

I grieved for him after he went, there's no other way to describe it. In fact, I rather dramatically convinced myself that this was worse than a death because it was long, drawn-out and devoid of any prospect of closure.

We stayed in touch for six months or so and I emailed every day. But with only an internet café in Nairobi at his disposal, his responses were intermittent, no matter how long – and loving – they were when they arrived.

It couldn't have gone on. It would've been madness. But I can honestly say that telling him on the phone we needed to end it constituted one of the hardest things I'd ever done.

I've told myself over the years that, had Alex and I not been ripped apart while still in the throes of young love, we'd have drifted apart anyway. Logic tells me that's true. And so does experience. Everyone else I know is *not* still with their teenage boyfriend, no matter how strongly they once felt.

Besides all that, had our love story not been ill-fated, I wouldn't have met Dan, wouldn't have had the happiest four years of my life and wouldn't be about to buy a beautiful house with him.

All things happen for a reason, as they say. And that's not something I'm ever going to forget.

I head to work the following day determined to focus on the campaign presentation for the Bang condom ad, even if I'm far from confident about it.

The only positive thing I can say about the three options we'll be presenting tomorrow is that none feature the Archbishop of Canterbury. I can't put my finger on why they don't work for me – not the 'sexy' one at an office party, nor the 'outrageous' one involving animated blob-shaped characters having a threesome – except to say this: they're all trying way too hard.

I make a mental note to ask Sadie if she thinks we should persuade Sebastian to rethink this, when she bursts through the door, stumbles to her desk and throws herself down.

'Oh. My. God.' My eyes widen. 'Oh. My. Bloody. God. Help me, Gemma. God help me . . .'

I frown. 'What's the matter?'

'Shhh!' Her eyes dart around. 'Ladies!'

She coughs, announces loudly that she's going to powder her nose, as if she's Veronica Lake and it's 1942, and disappears through the double doors, but not before throwing me another meaningful look, apparently designed to indicate that I should follow. When I get there, she is squatting to peer under the space below each cubicle door.

'What on earth are you doing?' I ask incredulously. 'Nobody's here. Calm down. It can't be that bad.'

'It is.'

'Have you killed somebody?'

'No.'

'Then it's not that bad.'

'You won't think that when you know what it is.'

I cross my arms and lean on the sink. 'Hit me with it.'

She bites her hand, splutters out the next words, as if she's trying to spit out a slug. 'I've totalled Sebastian's car.'

'What?'

She nods. 'I was reversing mine in the car park and I honestly don't know what happened except that I heard this hideous scraping sound and at first I thought, Shit, I've hit a bollard!' She hasn't paused for breath yet. 'So I started moving to try and get away from it, but it wouldn't budge. So I moved the other way, and the sound got worse, then I realised it wasn't a bollard – it was Sebastian's car. Only, the more I tried to move, the deeper I seemed to scrape into it and . . . oh God, it looks like something off *Scrapheap Challenge!*'

I listen silently, processing this garbled information, and come to the conclusion that this does sound bad. Very bad.

'It doesn't sound *too* disastrous,' I manage. It's very clear I am no Alastair Campbell.

'Of course it does!'

'What I mean is, you can't have been going at high speed. If it's just one of the panels, he can get that fixed.' I remind myself of how old his car looked. And how expensive. 'His insurance will cover it,' I babble, failing in the battle between optimism and delusion. 'Or yours. You'd lose your No Claims and everything, but—'

'I can't tell him it was me!'

'But . . . you've got to, Sadie.'

'Gemma,' she growls, 'insurance or not, he loves that car. I bet he goes to bed wanking about that car. If he finds out it's me, my career will be over.'

'You are exaggerating,' I insist flimsily. 'Let me go out and have a look at it. I bet it's not as terrible as you think.'

'Don't go out there! If people see you they'll put two and two together and know that I'm responsible.'

Something occurs to me. 'Isn't your car dented?'

'There are no dents, but I've got red paint all over my bumper. I've had to drive it down the road and dump it behind a bush in a lay-by. Oh God, this is like a scene in *The Fugitive*.'

'Except he was innocent,' I blurt out.

She starts whimpering.

'Look, this is going to be fine,' I reassure her. 'I'll go and check out his car subtly. Then I'll come back and we can talk it over.' And I'll hopefully persuade her to come clean.

I slip out of the ladies as Sadie makes her way back to her

desk, glancing round anxiously. I take the front staircase into the car park and the double doors open. It's one of those hazy mornings, hot and heavy, that gives the climbing flowers an over-sweet fragrance, almost like marijuana.

'Gemma!'

I spin round to see Sebastian jogging up behind me. 'Oh ... hello, Sebastian. Just getting something from my car.'

'Me too,' he grins. 'Forgot my SAD lamp.'

'Your what?'

'My SAD lamp. I get Seasonal Affective Disorder. I'm in bits without it.'

I decide not to point out that it's May. 'I just forgot my lunch,' I mutter, wondering why I'm sharing this.

'What have you got?' he asks.

'Hmm?'

'For your packed lunch?'

My mind goes entirely blank. 'Spam.'

He looks me up and down. 'Ah. Okay. Don't have too much though. All that processed meat'll kill you.'

'It's a salad,' I add, my subconscious clearly very bothered about ensuring Sebastian knows I'm a five-a-day girl. 'A Spam salad.'

'Right.' He frowns. 'You haven't got any keys.'

'Hmm?'

'Keys. How are you going to open your car without any keys?'

I look at my hands. 'Oh. Bugg— damn! You're right. Duh!' I hit my head on my hand in the manner of Homer Simpson after he's dropped a doughnut in his Duff beer.

And it's at that point that Conrad Bexton, one of our sales managers, fires up his people-carrier and drives away, revealing Sebastian's car.

The gash in its side is like the open wound in a slaughtered dolphin: large, gaping, if not fatal then near enough. There are shards of paint from Sadie's car all over it. It's difficult to see how it could be worse if she'd parked a tank in front of it and pressed a big red button that said *Destroy*.

I am suddenly devoid of ideas for small talk: not Spam, not SAD lamps, not a damn thing.

'Well,' Sebastian grins, oblivious. 'See you at the meeting.'

'Yes. Better go and get those keys!' I turn and walk away from him and have my foot on the first step at the exact moment that the damage becomes apparent.

'JESUS FUCKING CHRIST!'

I turn round briefly, long enough to see him falling to his knees and banging his head against the tarmac.

Chapter 21

Gemma

I get no sense out of Sadie for the rest of the day, such is the magnitude of her meltdown. The worst moment is during a meeting with one of our new clients, an organic food company called Good Honest Soup. She sits, mute, for almost two hours until Sebastian, whose mood is so foul you can almost smell it, asks her acidly if she'd care to contribute to the discussion. At which point she offers the client some biscuits.

I work late that evening and drive home, trying and failing to think of a solution to her mess. At least it keeps my mind off other matters. When I arrive at Buddington, Dan is at the kitchen table, scowling at Belinda's laptop, as she stands over his shoulder with her arms crossed. He'd told me he was planning to come home early after last week's *Fight Club* re-enactment, but I assured him that the whole thing had blown over as quickly as it started.

'Hi there.' I lean down to kiss him and he holds my face against his briefly, as if seeking momentary comfort in the midst of some ongoing horror. 'What are you up to?'

'Some IT for Mum,' he replies grimly.

'There!' she shrieks, pointing at the screen over his shoulder. 'That's it! That stupid message keeps appearing. I told you it was broken.'

He sighs. 'Mum, it's an update. It's nothing.'

'But I don't want an update. I never asked for an update.'

'You don't ask for them,' he replies patiently. 'They just appear.'

'Well, how dare they? It's my computer. I like it as it is. Tell it to go away,' she instructs, waving her hand about as if shooing away a mangy cat. Then she reaches over and prods a button.

'Mum. Just leave this to me,' Dan says calmly, as a little vein throbs on his neck. 'It's an update – it'll take about a minute, then the message will go away.'

'And it won't come back?'

'I can't promise that,' he sighs.

'I thought you said you could fix it.'

He spends the next hour trying to clean up the disaster zone that is Belinda's computer. He's always been good with this sort of stuff: patient, capable, enthusiastic about technology. She seems to think this makes him Mark Zuckerberg.

On the plus side, while Belinda is doing her best to make Dan's hair fall out prematurely, it gives me an excuse to offer to cook dinner. I'm no Nigella, but I can at least whip up a lasagne that doesn't dislodge any dentalwork.

'What are you two up to at the weekend?' Belinda asks.

'We'll be staying in,' I reply. 'The budget's very tight.'

Dan flashes me a look that says, 'she doesn't know the half of it.' I glance away, refusing to maintain eye-contact. Because the fact is, the extra £4,000 to which I've committed us is weighing increasingly heavily on my mind. I've spent the last three and a half weeks trying to think of a solution – and have singularly failed. Yet I stand by my assertion: in the scheme of things this is not a massive amount. Not the kind of amount you'd let ruin your only chance of living in the house of your dreams. I can't deny that the answer eludes me though.

'Doesn't sound much fun,' Belinda frowns. 'Why don't you let me pay for a night out?'

'That's really kind, but you're already doing enough by letting us stay here,' I insist. Dan looks at me gratefully as Belinda takes a slug of wine.

'Maybe I should have a party here then,' she says.

'Not on our account,' Dan says immediately.

'It's been ages since I threw one,' she goes on. 'My bashes

were legendary. Curiosity Killed the Cat on the stereo. Slippery Nipple in the punchbowl ... Hey, we could have one for Grandma's birthday! I've been wondering what to do.'

'I'm sure she'd prefer dinner somewhere,' Dan says.

'Oh no she wouldn't, not for her eightieth.' Belinda thinks for a minute. 'I've got an idea. I'll organise the party – you two can do a dance for her. You know, a *Strictly* type of dance. She'd *love* it. I can get Bobby to teach you. He can get you in the lake, just like in *Dirty Dancing*.'

Dan rolls his eyes and studies the computer screen, pretending not to hear.

Six weeks after I failed to get talking to Dan after the big Lake Windermere swim, I couldn't get him out of my mind. I could list a dozen things about him that I liked, but in truth none really explained why he'd made such a sweeping impression on me.

Then when Allie went to her second Lake District swim and said she'd seen him – and his club – again, I knew that the only chance I'd have of getting close to him was going to watch her at the next race. Only, there was a problem.

'This one doesn't start and finish next to a pub, so I have no idea how you're going to manufacture meeting him. It's only a small race, in Buttermere.'

'Maybe I could just come and say hello when he gets out of the water,' I mused.

'Yes, like his groupie . . .'

'Hmm. I take your point. What can I do to make this look natural?'

'Easy,' she replied. 'You can take part in the swim.'

I knew in the depths of my very being that it was a bad idea, for reasons that went beyond the fact that my wetsuit made me look like a massive black pudding.

I wasn't terrible in water – I'm not saying I still needed my rubber ring – but I was a long way from being a championship swimmer. I'd done a bit of wild swimming, if you can count a couple of practice sessions – both cut short by bad weather – and a university trip to Wales during which a few of us (after several Bacardi Breezers) stripped to our underwear and went for a dip. But my recent experience of swimming was confined to a sedate breaststroke in the pool of my gym, which I'd undertake in the manner of a blue-rinsed elderly lady who'd prefer to risk death by drowning than break into a front crawl and get her hair wet.

But I've always been an optimist. Even if on this occasion I was an optimist of the blind, stupid variety – one who shouldn't have believed a word of Allie's encouragement. In the light of what came next, it's a wonder we're still on speaking terms.

When we arrived at the race start, it was already overflowing with people.

'I thought it was a small event?'

'It's a little bigger than I'd thought, I must admit,' she replied shiftily.

I suddenly felt a bit ill. 'I should back out. This is not going to go well, I know it.'

'Oh, you'll be great! Think of how impressed your man will be.'

Impressing him seemed far-fetched, but equally, having come all this way, I didn't want him to think I was some sort of malingering spectator.

'Fine. But that's not why I'm doing it, just for the record.'

My overriding memory of that day was standing at the edge of the lake trembling as if I'd had both sets of fibulas surgically removed. I spotted Dan a little way down and my heart swooped as he noticed me and smiled.

'Isn't the atmosphere amazing?' Allie gushed.

I hadn't actually noticed the atmosphere. All I'd noticed was the massive stretch of opaque water. The fact that it wasn't turquoise with a neat black stripe down it like in David Lloyd. And that there were very probably *creatures* underneath. Real creatures. I had never hated nature more.

Meanwhile, the entrants were multiplying like the armies of Middle Earth, jostling and pushing in a manner that didn't bode well for the moment we plunged in the lake.

Then a whistle blew.

I could be romantic about my first lake race – tell you I

slipped in and was at one with the beauty of the mountains, the overarching sky, the warm camaraderie between competitors. I'd love to tell you about the music in my pulsating heart, the euphoria that engulfed me as I made it to the end, incandescent with sporting triumph.

But that would be bollocks.

While I could happily swim for twenty minutes in a nice pool, being in this cold, horrible, unchlorinated water was something quite different.

I told myself I just had to stay calm.

I told myself I just had to get to the other side.

I told myself I just had to *swim*.

But as I thrashed in the water, all I could think about was what was brushing my legs: the vegetation, the insects, the fish. Then I started to think bigger, more sinister. By the time I was halfway across, I wasn't worried about fish – I was thinking sharks, piranha, prehistoric plesiosaurs . . . all with their sights set on my juicy limbs.

Every time I quelled one of these lunatic thoughts, another popped in, until – convinced that the tail of a blue whale was about to rise up in front of me – I decided to flip over and try a backstroke instead. It had an instant and dramatic effect: namely, to make me hyperventilate and fling my arms and legs about as if I was attached to the jump leads for a 1978 Cortina.

But none of this compared with the indignity – and

horror – of the awareness that someone had grabbed my arm. I was being rescued.

I should've been grateful really.

But, delirious and virtually hallucinating from the volume of lake water I'd swallowed, all I could focus on was the reason I'd done this in the first place. I was meant to be dazzling someone with my best impression of *Action Girl*, a water-borne version of Lara Croft, all tough but sexy and infinitely capable.

Emerging from the lake under the arm of some big bearded bloke from St John's Ambulance was NOT part of the plan.

So I told the guy rescuing me, 'I'm fine, honestly – I might look like I don't know what I'm doing, but it's all part of a technique I've been mastering.'

At least, that's what I said in my head.

It came out like this:-

'Blgueerrurghhhh … (* GASP *) … bhleghobhhhrrrr (* GASP GASP *) BHAFOENOjonfon!!!!!.

I gulped in another mouthful of liquid – which couldn't have tasted worse if I'd swallowed a camel's fart – and gave up.

I knew he'd seen me. I was stumbling up the bank of the lake attempting to pull vegetation from between my teeth when I spotted him and realised he was looking at me. It struck me that he might have been amused, but he was actually something far worse: concerned.

He began heading towards me, but the thought of talking to him after my humiliation, particularly when my lips were now blue, was too much to bear. So I darted away to find Allie, who had our car key and access to towels and dry clothes.

I would discover later that she'd been looking for me too, after a fit of warped thinking had made her assume I'd finished before she did. But for now I was left to search, dejected and alone, having never felt a greater urge to cry in my life.

'The first time's always the worst.' I knew it was Dan before I even looked up, registered his heart-stopping handsomeness and wished I'd never come.

'Like losing your virginity?' I was relieved when he laughed because I regretted the words as soon as they left my mouth.

'Here,' he said, wrapping a clean dry towel around me. 'You look like you need to warm up.'

And how I felt right then was something I'll never forget: warm, safe and as though my limitless capacity for unintentional hilarity didn't matter a jot.

Chapter 22

Dan

We arrived at Mum's house nearly two months ago and haven't had a single night out since. There is, quite simply, no cash with which to do so – and in our frantic attempts to scrape together the extra £4k Gemma's committed us to, there isn't likely to be in the near future.

It's not like we spent every night living it up in piano bars and casinos before. But it's only when you've missed out on nights out with the boys, the girls and more importantly each other, that you realise how much they keep you going.

I am struck by the single, melancholic thought that I'd give my right lung for a night at the Royal Tandoori now; or to watch a movie at FACT, followed by a few beers in Bold Street. These simple pleasures are entirely out of reach.

Instead, my Saturday nights are spent in a Jim Royle slouch

on the sofa, listening to the three women in my life take bets on who'll win *Dancing with the Stars* while I shield my eyes from the phosphorescent glare of tans and teeth.

Gemma seemed at ease with this at first, but it's obvious even she's getting desperate for space now, for a glimmer of the Saturdays of yore.

With another weekend looming and nothing more than an extended *Take Me Out* on the horizon, I trudge to the photocopier in the Old School House and, when asked by Jade what we're up to on Saturday, can only grunt in despair.

'Get online and Google ideas for romantic evenings on a budget,' she suggests.

'Isn't that a Pot Noodle and a shag?' Pete offers, before looking around as if it wasn't him.

Jade taps at her computer. 'Here we go . . . "Stargazing: if it's cold outside, bring blankets and a Thermos and look for constellations." That sounds nice, doesn't it?'

'Love that kind of thing myself. Orion's belt and all that,' Pete mumbles, some way from sounding like Professor Brian Cox.

'"Alternatively,' Jade continues, 'clear your living-room floor, put on some music and dance. You can slow dance, or boogie, burlesque or even try some break-dancing moves, if you're feeling crazy!"' She grins. 'Are you feeling *kerrazy*, Dan?'

'More than I can say after living in my mother's house.'

The suggestions continue, encompassing the pedestrian (play board games), to the outlandish (roller skate round your garden to emulate Christmas ice-skating at Somerset House). However, a couple leap out.

I text Gemma.

You. Me. Saturday night. We're staying in and I'm getting rid of my mother. You in? x

She responds immediately.

Sounds good. But where will we dispose of the body? x

'Don't worry about me,' Mum insists as she hauls herself into a taxi clutching a bottle of Moët. 'Rita's hosting the book club tonight – they're always late so you've got the run of the house. And I've told Mother to turn her hearing aid down.' She gives a protracted wink before I shut the door.

Gemma drove Sadie to Pebble Cottage this afternoon to show her the place from the outside and analyse some crisis that, as far as I can tell, revolves around their boss coming to work in a Kia Picanto. By the time she returns at seven, I've got a risotto on the go, am in her favourite blue shirt, have splashed on some Christmas aftershave and have hit the button on the playlist to end all playlists. 'Winter Winds' by

Mumford & Sons. 'Sonnet' by The Verve. 'Tender' by Blur. 'Riptide' by Vance Joy. All classics, all sexy without being obvious, all offering a slim chance that she might stop thinking about fixed interest rates for a night.

I hear the front door open and go out to meet her in the hall.

'Hi there,' she murmurs, as I kiss her on the lips. 'I *like* that shirt.'

'I know,' I smirk. 'I could pretend I threw on the first thing I could find, but this is actually a flimsy ruse to try to work my way into your erogenous zones.'

She giggles. 'How long until dinner?'

'Ten minutes.'

She darts upstairs and returns twenty-five minutes later looking so devastatingly sexy that, for a moment, I can do nothing else but stand and stare at her. The slippers and sweatpants of the last few Saturdays are replaced by a flowery dress, hair done up like a funky version of Audrey Hepburn's, all loose and wispy. She glances at the table, which I've covered with candles in a shamelessly corny attempt to enhance the mood.

'This looks lovely,' she says.

'So do you.' I reach out to take her hand but she ducks away.

'Before we go any further, can you just sign here?' She waves a paper in my face. 'I've finally got it through from Annabel, the solicitor.'

I sign on the dotted line. 'What am I signing away exactly?'

'You know how in *Fifty Shades of Grey*, a contract is signed so that one party becomes a sex slave?'

'Oh yes?'

'This is nothing like that, just a contract to say we'll pay for the work they do.'

I place the paper on a work surface, out of sight. 'Right, now that's out of the way, can we resume our Romantic Night On A Budget? No distractions. No lunacy from my mother. Nothing but you and me.'

'Definitely,' she whispers.

As Gemma would say, it couldn't be more perfect.

Until the oven explodes.

Okay, it doesn't actually explode, but the crash from somewhere inside is genuinely cataclysmic. I dive to the oven and open the door, sweat bubbling on my brow as I'm hit by a blast of heat.

A string of expletives spring from my mouth as it becomes apparent that the dish into which I piled my tenderly-prepared, oven-baked risotto is not in fact ovenproof. It now consists of approximately four hundred pieces, while the risotto simmers obnoxiously on the bottom of the oven.

'Okay. Don't panic,' Gemma says, like she always does when she panics. Then she leaps over to help me try and scoop it up. Sadly, neither of us are bastions of cool-headed efficiency. We both look around frantically. We both grab a tea-towel. We both shove our hands in simultaneously to try to save the day, which has the converse effect of producing a cack-handed, Punch and Judy-style brawl. Which Gemma loses.

The shriek as her wrist plunges into thick, red-hot risotto is comparable to the mating call of a giant cockatoo, after six years in solitary confinement with only a battered copy of *Lady Chatterley's Lover* for company.

I drag her to the sink and thrust her arm under the tap. It takes several minutes before she stops screaming, jigging up and down, and contemplating amputation. 'You okay?' I ask.

She looks at her hand, under the gushing, freezing water and breathes out. 'Think so.'

She removes her hand. 'ARRRGGGHHH!'

'I'm going to have to take you to A&E,' I decide grimly as she thrusts it into the water again.

She pretends to weep. 'But I want my champagne . . .'

I kiss her head. 'I'll see if we've got a flask.'

The rest of the night is spent in the Countess of Chester Hospital's A&E department. I am stone cold sober. Gemma is stone cold sober (she gave up on the flask). Which, on a Saturday night, makes us a novelty. Added to that is the fact that my girlfriend does not fall into a category you might describe as Good With Pain.

I can't deny her arm looks very sore. Equally, her complaining is as relentless and unyielding as the talking clock. I am updated on average three times a minute as to the current state of play; whether the painkillers are working, or the ice pack melting.

I put my arm around her as she winces in another wave of agony and a text arrives from Mum:

MORE CHAMPAGNE IN FRIDGE IF U LIKE. NOT TOO MUCH 4 U THO – DN'T WANT PERFORMANCE ISSUES!

I stare into the middle distance as a merry band of hen-doers staggers into the waiting room, led by a bride-to-be, whose veil and L-plate are set off by an ankle dripping with blood.

'I was going to ask you to marry me tonight as well,' I say.

Gemma manages a smile and nudges me in the ribs. 'Bugger off,' she mumbles, snuggling up to me as I hold her ice pack against her arm and wonder when we're ever going to have a break.

Chapter 23

Gemma

It's a good thing I have such a high pain threshold or I'd find it difficult to talk about anything other than the agony I'm in. As it is, I maintain a stoic dignity throughout the evening, apart from to ask if anyone's got stronger painkillers. Like an epidural.

I wake the next morning, my arm still hurting but significantly better than it was. I'm feeling a bit low about things. Dan opens his eyes and kisses me.

'I know living with your mum was all my idea,' I tell him, 'but it's getting a bit much now, isn't it?'

He pushes himself up on his elbows. 'Don't be too down about last night. It was just . . . unfortunate.'

'It's not only that. I can see how stressed out the whole thing is making you.'

He frowns. 'Now you're making me feel guilty. Look, we've

stuck this out for two months – we can do a bit more. And as for Mum, I just need to be more tolerant. I mean, I love her to bits and I'm grateful for everything she's done for me. I just need to remind myself of that, next time she does the Hokey Cokey around the living room.'

I can't help but smile.

'Loath as I am to admit it,' he continues, 'you were right to suggest we move back. It was the only option. And it's going to be worth it.'

'Do you really think so?'

'I do,' he says, and for the first time since we got here, he seems to mean it.

I'm about to kiss him when my phone rings. I prop myself up and glance at the screen.

'Sorry, it's my mum,' I tell him. 'I'm going to take this, I haven't spoken to her since last week.' I press answer. 'Hi there.'

She answers in a low, secretive voice, as if she works for the French Resistance. 'Are you alone?'

'Just here with Dan, why?'

'Okay. Hmm. Don't worry,' she says. So obviously, I worry. I catch Dan's eye and shake my head as I get out of bed and wander onto the landing, before locking myself in the privacy of the main bathroom.

'I'm all ears,' I sigh.

'I've just had a phone call.' She hesitates. 'It was from *Alex*.'

I suddenly need to sit down. Unfortunately, the toilet seat

I'd registered as closed is anything but, and I plummet, bum first, into the pan, leaving my legs protruding like two chopsticks in a chicken chow mein.

'Gemma? Gemma, are you there?'

I clamber up with a dripping wet rear end, try to catch my breath and work out how to play this. 'Alex who?'

'Alex *Monroe*,' she says, clearly unable to believe I have a big enough social circle to include more than one person called Alex. 'Your *old boyfriend*.'

'Oh, how strange,' I say casually, my heart thundering. She doesn't respond. 'Well . . . how was he?'

'He seemed fine. Nice as ever. It just took me by surprise, that's all. I mean, doesn't it you? That he should phone up after all this time? I thought someone must've died.'

I wriggle out of my pyjama bottoms, grab a towel and wrap it round my waist. 'Did he say what he was phoning for?'

'Yes. He said he was back in the UK with work and wanted your phone number. He said he'd like to go for a coffee and "catch up".' The last two words are laden with meaning and disapproval.

I swallow. 'Did you give it to him?'

'No, I said I'd have to phone and ask your permission,' she replies indignantly. 'Because you were *buying a house with your boyfriend*.'

I am dying to know his reaction to that one, but restrain myself from asking. She offers nothing.

'I don't think you needed to make *that* big a deal of it,' I mumble. 'That makes it sound as if I'd have something to feel guilty about just by talking to him.'

'So you want me to give it to him,' she decides.

'Well, I don't mind either way,' I splutter. 'I mean, why would I mind? It's not like it's inappropriate. It'd only be inappropriate if there was anything still going on between us – and the fact is, I haven't seen him in years!'

'Okay. I'll give it to him then.'

My stomach lurches. 'Hang on, maybe you've got a point.'

'I thought so. Dan might get jealous.'

'He's not the jealous type. Besides, all we're talking about is a phone call.'

'He said coffee. And a *catch up*.' She might as well replace those words with 'oral sex in the back of a stretch limo'.

'Even that.'

'Do you really think that'd be appropriate, Gemma?' I can tell her lips are pursed without even seeing them.

'Oh Mum, I haven't seen him for years, it's not like I'm going to run off with him and leave Dan in the lurch.'

'So I should give it to him? He's phoning me back later today.'

My heart surges. 'I see.'

'So what's it to be, Gemma? Come on, I've got a bacon sandwich waiting for me here. Is it a yes or a no?'

Chapter 24

Dan

When Gemma returns from the bathroom, we head downstairs to find Mum at the kitchen table jabbing at her laptop like it's a wounded animal she's worried might leap up and bite her. I swear I think an Etch-A-Sketch would be too advanced for her.

'What happened to you two last night? Did you decide to go out on the raz, after all? I came back to a scene of devastation.'

Gemma fills her in and Mum's face crumples with disgust. 'Oh look, this is totally ridiculous,' she announces.

'What is?' I ask.

'Just let me give you the money for the deposit on your house!' she shrieks. 'You can stop saving. You can leave Buddington. You won't have to put up with *me* for a moment longer. You can simply go and buy your dream home, then live happily ever after. Which is how it should be.'

Gemma glances at me. 'Belinda, it's a lot of money.'

'Gemma, darling, if there's one good thing that came out of my craphole of a marriage, it was a book that made me some cash. And now there's more coming.' She gestures at the laptop. 'The publicity schedule is already going wild. I'm in New York at the end of the year, then London. Aside from that, I *want* to give you this money, as my gift.'

When Gemma turns to me, the hope in her eyes is almost – *almost* – enough to stop me doing what I know is my only option.

'Thank you, Mum. But I know I speak for both of us when I say we can't accept it.'

Gemma slides onto a chair, underlining the fact that I probably don't speak for both of us.

'We want to do this all on our own,' I state.

Mum rolls her eyes. 'But why?'

'You bought this house all by yourself, from your hard-earned cash. Dad did the same. I refuse to be some spoiled little rich kid who gets everything he wants because Mummy bought it for him.' Gemma looks away. 'That doesn't mean we don't appreciate the offer though,' I add.

Belinda looks me in the eyes. 'Don't you think you should consult Gemma before you make such a rash decision?'

Gemma's jaw starts moving up and down without any noise coming out of it. 'I ... I ... yes, it's very kind of you to offer, there's no doubt. Thing is, I can see where Dan's coming from, but—'

'There, you see? We're in total agreement,' I conclude.

Gemma clamps her teeth into her lip.

'Suit yourself.' Mum gives up. 'Right, I'm off to tennis. Have a good afternoon – and let me know if you change your minds.'

'We won't,' I assure her, as Mum grabs her sweater and skips out of the door.

I turn round as flames are licking up behind Gemma's eyeballs.

'Sometimes, Dan,' she says, 'I find you very, very hard to understand.'

Chapter 25

Gemma

I dream about Pebble Cottage that night. It's moving-in day.
The sun is iridescent, the air fragrant with bread from the
little bakery up the road, and the house everything we'd ever
wanted and more. The walls are newly-painted and although
we're scruffy and exhausted, happiness fizzes like lemonade
through our veins. I put my arms around Dan and start kissing him. And it's only as I pull away to look in his eyes, waves
of desire rising up in me, that I realise it isn't Dan at all.

It's Alex.

My eyes ping open and I sit up, my heart thudding. I reach
over and fumble for my phone. There are no missed calls,
despite the fact that Mum gave Alex my number nearly
twenty-four hours ago.

I don't know why the thought that he might be in touch at

any moment is so unsettling. It's not as though I still have feelings for him after all this time. Yet I can't deny that the possibility that I might hear his voice again at some point soon puts me on edge.

It's a feeling that grows throughout the whole of the following week, when I check my phone regularly. It remains resolutely silent.

Meanwhile, for a whole plethora of reasons, life in general is starting to feel like an uphill struggle.

I'm sure 99 per cent of it's due to the stress of the house purchase: the missing money, the feeling of being trapped at Buddington, the fact that there are arthritic molluscs that are more dynamic than our solicitor.

Everything we do is in sharp contrast to the way Belinda works: having decided she wants an extension to her swimming-pool room, she snaps her fingers and starts to make it happen. When I snap my fingers, I just break a nail.

Despite Dan's insistence that he is fine with being here now, the reality is that he's irritated by everything. His mother. His bedroom. Even being asked to fill out another form, which he can't do without peering at it suspiciously, as if it pries into his very soul, not his credit-card balance.

Meanwhile, he's working late more and more, which would be fine if Belinda hadn't roped me into being 'prepped' by Bobby the dance teacher for a big finale at Flossie's birthday party, while I look after all of the increasingly arduous admin for the house purchase.

The thing I'm struggling with the most though is the fact that he continues to turn down any financial help from Belinda, without any discussion with me. She wants to help us out, for the best of reasons – and her paying for the deposit would have solved all our problems. While I can understand his thinking, what's wrong with taking a *loan* – one we could pay back over a few years?

Despite all these thoughts, I hate the idea of any tension simmering between Dan and me. We've never had a relationship like that and, pressures or not, I don't want it to continue.

So I decide I'm somehow going to step up to the mark: to make a non-sugary gesture of affection to remind him exactly how much I love him.

I'm contemplating what to do as I open a letter from the mortgage company asking for one extra pay-slip from Dan, as proof of his income. He's out on a run, but I know where he keeps them. So instead of waiting and missing today's post, I head to our room, to his 'important stuff' box.

I take off the lid and feel my jaw drop as I'm confronted by an avalanche of paperwork, although to call it 'paperwork' gives the impression of some sort of order.

This is like a stack of Anaglypta wallpaper waiting to go to the tip after someone's entire hall, stairs and landing has been stripped.

'What are you doing?'

I spin round and see Dan at the door, still breathless from his run, his chest glistening with sweat.

'Just looking for another pay-slip – the mortgage company need it,' I reply, turning back to his box.

But he's suddenly next to me, snatching the pay-slip from my hand and slamming shut the lid so fast that it's impossible to conclude anything other than the fact that he's hiding something in there. I can't decide if it's a licence to kill, because he's actually a member of Her Majesty's Secret Service, or the Agent Provocateur Spring-Summer 2015 brochure.

'Dan, what's the matter?' I ask.

'Gemma,' his eyes are blazing 'do *not* go in there.'

I frown. 'Why not?'

'Because ... can't I have a single, tiny space that's private?'

'Dan, I'm sorry. But all I was doing is trying to get this house sale moving,' I say. 'I thought you weren't going to be back for ages and would've had to wait for Monday's post otherwise. I never imagined you'd have a problem with me going in there.'

He rubs his forehead. 'Fine. Then *I'm* sorry. But I'll get the pay-slip. Okay?' He touches my hand. 'I didn't mean to over-react.'

My eyes prick with tears as I squeeze him into me and wonder why things suddenly don't feel as easy as they always have. He lifts up my chin and kisses me on the lips, sending shivers across my skin. And it occurs to me, possibly for the first time, that all these issues and more could be dominating Dan's thoughts too.

Chapter 26

Dan

I wonder if some WD40 would stop that squeak on the bed?

Chapter 27

Dan

My first few dates with Gemma, and the subsequent weeks that do not cover me with glory, require context. In other words, don't judge me. (Only, I know you will. I do it myself.)

I was twenty-five. My modus operandi was to go out with a girl, enjoy myself, and move on. While I like to think there was more to me than some vacuous skirt-chaser, the reality was I loved the company of women – though mostly in the plural, rather than singular sense. And I didn't lose a moment's sleep about that.

Which might explain why, despite my certainty that the Mythical Perfect Woman would come along one day and blow all the others out of the water, this was not a lifestyle I was ready to give up in a hurry.

It is laughably obvious with hindsight that Gemma was her,

the Mythical Perfect Woman. But at the time I failed to see she was right in front of me, quietly blowing my mind.

I think part of me had assumed for so long that The One would come with flashing lights and a big warning sign when she appeared. But that wasn't how I fell in love with Gemma. I fell in love with her without even realising it.

That wasn't to say I wasn't fully aware of how much I *liked* her in that first week. I knew I liked her a lot.

I liked the way her hair swished when she walked through the door of the Shipping Forecast bar for our first date, which happened the very same night as the Buttermere swim. I liked the way that, even in denim and Converse she had this graceful way of holding herself, like Jackie Onassis or Grace Kelly. I liked her confidence. I liked her lips. I liked her taste in music and the fact that, the more she drank, the more convinced she became of her ace pool-playing abilities – something she might have pulled off had she not swaggered over to her cue and chalked up the wrong end.

We ended up in bed on the third date, and without going too far, I'll simply say this: it was unprecedented.

She was radiant, sensual, gorgeous, soft and skipped back and forth across a line between innocence and *on fire*. The taste of her stayed with me all the following day, her face flashing into my thoughts every time I moved.

So I saw her again the next day, and the day after that. We spent seven days going to museums, picnicking in the park, sitting in my flat watching *Casablanca* (the greatest movie of all time). I was the hero in an atrocious romcom movie and didn't mind one bit, nor indeed the fact that she effectively moved in for a week while my flatmate Jesse was away.

Then the inevitable boys' night happened.

I was still working for Emerson Lisbon then, where my former colleagues were all young, pumped, and liked their weekends so primed with Bacchanalian excess it made the average Roman orgy look like a vicarage tea party.

So when Chris Deayton, my old boss and mentor, phoned to remind me that he was picking me up at seven, I felt mildly guilty about wanting to go. Not that Gemma objected. I thought she'd mind more than she did. I kissed her and told her I'd phone the following day.

It was a great night, a messy night, one of those nights when it's just brilliant to be a man.

I recall little after about 1.30 a.m., but know it involved beer, Jäger Bombs, several women who seemed to think we were rockstars, and the loss of one of my shoes down a ventilation shaft in front of the Town Hall.

I woke up the next morning on Chris's living-room floor with lipstick on my shirt, vaguely remembering some History student in Concert Square dancing up to me. She'd been sweet and sexy, a Rachael Riley type, yet I'd given her the brush-off without a second thought.

And, as a hangover swam through my alcohol-riddled brain, I can't deny that part of that sat uneasily with me.

I thought of Gemma, the gorgeous, lovely Gemma with whom I'd spent almost every moment of the last week or so. And I thought of last night. The sheer joy of booze, friends and bad behaviour. When I thought of the two together, it became very apparent that they could not co-exist.

Chapter 28

Gemma

Fact one: Belinda has appointed James Shuttlemore as her architect. Fact two: she has the hots for him. As they sit in the kitchen discussing plans for the pool extension, it could not be more obvious if she was holding up a placard reading *PICK ME!*

I've been secretly enthralled by them this morning each time I've popped downstairs, by the way his eyes twinkle when she makes him laugh, which is surprisingly frequently, and not always for the wrong reasons. Unlike Belinda, James is a reserved sort, soft-spoken and efficient.

'Just getting a Diet Coke,' I cough as I enter. They slide away from each other, as if I've caught them discussing something significantly racier than the width of her ceiling beams.

I open the fridge and pull out a can, as Flossie walks in. 'Did I leave my iPad in here last night?' she asks.

'Yes, I've put it in the hall for you,' says Belinda.

Flossie freezes. 'Does that mean you had to . . . touch it?'

Belinda purses her lips. 'Don't worry, I didn't press any buttons. Stupid thing made a hell of a racket last time I made that mistake.'

'Are you going for a swim today, Flossie?' I ask.

'Probably. I do most days, though it's not the same when it's in a swimming pool. Nothing compares to real water.'

I scrunch up my nose.

'Not a fan?' she asks and raises her eyebrows.

'You could never describe me as a nature enthusiast, put it that way,' I say, and she laughs.

'Oh, Gemma,' Belinda begins, 'there are some of my Madeleines left in the fridge if you want a treat. Get some for James too.'

Flossie leans into me. 'For God's sake, don't let her feed him,' she whispers, before heading towards the hall.

'Oh . . . Dan and I finished those off last night. Sorry. They were absolutely delicious,' I say, slipping the last of Belinda's cakes, which resemble the artificial coals on a 1970s electric fire, into the bin. Flossie's right: one bite and James would run a mile – once he was out of Intensive Care.

'How are you settling in to the area, James?' I ask, opening my can.

'Very well. Buddington's just as I remember when I was little.'

'Had you lived in Manchester all your life? After you left here, I mean.'

'No, I'd been in Edinburgh for years. I moved up as a student, then got married there.' Belinda freezes. 'And divorced. We didn't have children but I decided to stay. I'd joined a tennis club by then,' he smiles.

'You should have a game with Belinda,' I suggest. 'She's a brilliant tennis player.'

Belinda flutters her eyelashes. 'Oh, I'm not quite Steffi Graf.'

James suppresses a smile. 'I'm not quite Andre Agassi.'

I almost wish I could stay and watch, but I have a pressing phone call to make after a letter arrived this morning announcing that the mortgage company have finally commissioned a survey. Sadly, it's for the wrong property. It's an administrative error, literally one digit wrong on the house number, but, clearly I am not interested in the potential for subsidence or rising damp in the place over the road.

Over the next half hour I become convinced that it would be easier to hack into the Pentagon than find an email address on the mortgage lender's website. So I phone again, and after negotiating the labyrinth of menu messages, I am rewarded by the piercing crackle of a canned version of Aerosmith's 'Love in an Elevator'. Then the line goes dead.

'*Bloody HELL!*' I want a glass of wine. It is 10.45 a.m.

I take several deep breaths and try again. Finally, after forty-five minutes and half a pedicure (I decided to multi-task), I reach the Golden Fleece, the Ark of the Covenant, a REAL PERSON.

'*You're-through-to-the-Lancashire-Building-Society-my-name's-Cheryl-can-I-take-your-name-and-account-number-please.*'

I glance down and realise in a panic that although I'm surrounded by a mountain of paperwork, the one on top doesn't reference my account number.

'Er . . . just a second.' I rustle through the letters and find my name and address on each, but no account number. 'Sorry about this.'

Cheryl sighs theatrically as I fling papers over my shoulder, desperately trying to locate what I need. 'If you just give me your name and address I'll see if the system can find you,' she suggests wearily.

Cheryl gives the impression that she spent last night on the lash and wishes she was at home watching the *Hollyoaks* omnibus and eating fried-egg sandwiches in bed.

'Do you want the address where I'm living or the address of the property I'm buying?'

'Let's try the place you're buying.'

'Pebble Cottage, which is at 43 Venbourne Road.'

'Forty-three Ven—'

'Except you have it on your system as thirty-three.'

'Right.'

'But that's not correct.'

'What isn't?'

'It's not number thirty-three. It's number *forty*-three. That's what I'm phoning about. A survey is due to take place on

Monday on number thirty-three. I need you to change it to the right number. Forty-three.'

My tone sounds like I'm telling her there's a bomb on a bus, but she's clearly failing to grasp the urgency of this matter. It soon becomes abundantly clear that this news has put Cheryl out *massively*. I spend the rest of the call either on hold, listening to a version of 'Congratulations' by Cliff Richard, followed by the same artist attempting 'Smack My Bitch Up' by The Prodigy, or waiting for Cheryl to tell me something other than 'the system's driving me mad today'.

Finally, she concludes: 'I've put a note on your account so it should be okay.'

'Great, so the survey will take place on the right house on Monday?'

'No, we'll have to cancel it and re-book another one.'

'But we've waited nearly two weeks.'

She doesn't respond.

'Okay,' I sigh. 'Let's re-book it then.'

'A different department handles that.'

'Can you put me through to them?'

''Fraid not,' she says unapologetically. 'They're not in until Monday.'

I end the call and close my eyes in an attempt to compose myself – when the phone rings. My first thought is that the mortgage company have had a burst of efficiency and are phoning me back.

Then I see it's a mobile number.

One I don't recognise.

My heart seems to stop entirely as another thought occurs to me.

This is Alex. I feel sure of it.

My head explodes with thoughts about what I'm going to say, what he's going to say, how I'm going to play this. But suddenly there's no other option but to take a deep breath and answer.

'Um . . . hello?'

There's a small silence, before the recorded message begins.

'Have you been mis-sold Payment Protection Insurance?'

I deflate visibly and end the call as my heartbeat subsides.

Gemma, it's *really* time to get a grip.

When I log onto our savings account on Monday morning I have a pleasant surprise. Dan and I have been living with such aggressive frugality, on top of the fact that we're now paying no rent or bills, that raking back a proportion of the missing £4k could be possible by the time we complete on the sale.

The thought buoys my mood as Sadie and I head to the canteen to prepare for our meeting later. She orders, while I find a seat by the window and spot Sebastian heading to his courtesy car, which he's been stuck with for weeks because getting the parts for a classic Jag is so difficult.

I couldn't claim that he's permanently grumpy since the crash. There have been moments when he's been perfectly civil, though I suspect he's distracted, like that feeling people get when they first wake up thinking everything's okay, then remember they've lost their job, family, house, and the cat's puked in their favourite slippers.

'I wish his old car would hurry up and come back from the garage,' Sadie mutters .

'Aren't you worried that he might find out it was you?' I ask.

'SHHH!' she hisses. 'There's no way he could find out, assuming *you* keep schtum. I feel so guilty though. I am going to burn in hell for this.' A flicker of panic crosses her face. 'Imagine if I lost my job, Gemma. The wedding budget is already out of control. How the hell am I going to pay for eighty sea bass fillets with an artichoke coulis if I'm on the dole?'

Our meeting takes place on the top floor, in the *Blue Sky Brain Laboratory*, where we'll be sharing the amendments to our soup campaign with Sebastian. Although the client hasn't seen the final version, they've loved every step so far – a water-colour animation telling a fictional, romanticised story about the soup being made by fairies, all set to a suitably indie sound-track with whimsical female vocals.

Sadie clicks on her laptop while Sebastian, who's been involved from the beginning, watches silently. A deepening crevice is appearing above his nose. As the commercial ends, an eerie silence descends on the room and thunderclouds like those in the final scene in *Ghostbusters* gather above.

'So,' I say, shuffling my pad, 'we'll be presenting this to the marketing team at Good Honest Soup next Wednesday, where we're hopeful of the go-ahead.'

Sebastian sighs despondently, as if he's on his twelfth marriage guidance session but can't get beyond thinking his wife has a fat arse.

'I don't know any more.' Sadie and I glance at each other. 'I know this is what they said they wanted, but I can't help thinking it's … wishy washy. Airy fairy. Flaccid. Damp. Altogether … *meh.*'

A bead of sweat travels down Sadie's brow. 'They *loved* the idea,' she breathes.

'I mean, soup fairies. *Seriously?* I'm wondering if we've got this right AT ALL.'

I swallow. 'Changing it dramatically would be difficult at this late stage.'

He shrugs. 'If it's not right, it's not right.'

'But, what if it *is* right?' I say, feeling mildly desperate. 'The client thinks so. Who are we to argue?'

His lip curls up. 'I just hate all this passive-aggressive tree-hugging shit with its flimsy watercolours. It's like, "Ooh, look at us aren't we organic and fluffy and not like one of those nasty corporate profiteering organisations who want to make *money*, God forbid!".'

I have a sudden and hideous feeling that this whim of Sebastian's is going to lead to a vast amount of trouble.

'Also,' he says, his nose scrunched up, 'it's not very . . . *sexy*, is it?'

'Well, it's soup,' I can't stop myself from pointing out. 'Sexy isn't normally associated with soup.'

'Then it should be up to us to make organic sexy,' he states. 'All I associate with this is some smelly, hairy-jumpered do-gooder who drinks twig tea.'

'Perhaps the soundtrack is the problem,' Sadie offers.

'Maybe. Try it with that Robin Thicke song instead. You know – the one with the boobs in the video. Spice it up a bit.'

I feel faint.

'Um, Sebastian,' I begin, 'I hope you don't mind me saying, but I think this is a strong campaign as it is. And I think they're going to love it. Robin Thicke . . . it's not them.'

Sadie glares at me, begging me to stop. But I can't. I won't. 'To try and persuade the client that we've produced something that's rubbish when, quite honestly, I think it's anything but – it doesn't make sense. Don't you agree, Sadie?'

'I can see both arguments really,' she murmurs. I narrow my eyes at her.

'I suppose we need to plough on with this,' our boss sighs. 'Reluctant as I am. Thank God we hit the jackpot with the Bang condom advert.'

Having persuaded Sebastian to have a radical re-think, we've ended up with a strong, funny ad showing a good-looking guy get to third base, before being repeatedly rejected by women who won't go further without protection.

'They liked it so much they've commissioned us to start work on a campaign for a *female* condom,' he continues. 'It's a niche market, but they think it could grow. They want us to work on that too before unveiling it in front of 150 staff and key stakeholders in a couple of months.'

'Great news,' I say.

'Brilliant!' adds Sadie.

'Glad you're enthusiastic. Perhaps *you* ought to present it.'

My ears start ringing and the room swims in and out psychedelically. 'Us?'

'Well, one of you. The CEO wants to say his bit so there'll be too many of you on stage otherwise. Gemma, you do it.'

He says this last sentence as if it's the most trifling matter in the world. In fact, he might as well have asked me to leap from the fifth floor of a burning building with a box of newborn kittens in my arms – and land on my feet.

'But I thought *you* presented these things,' I gulp.

'I would usually. But it'd be nice to give someone else a go for a change. If you're anything like me, you'll thoroughly enjoy the experience.'

The rest of the day is spent fighting off the thunderous palpitations every time I think about presenting to 150 people.

My only distraction involves trying to get through to the

mortgage company again about why we've heard nothing about the survey. A woman called Charmaine tells me that the surveyor arrived at the *correct* house on Monday only to find nobody was in and therefore they could not gain access.

'Of course nobody was in! I was told by your company that it was being booked for another time!' I squeal, loudly enough to persuade her to at least rearrange the survey for tomorrow. I'll believe it when I see it.

By the time I arrive home I'm feeling above-averagely disillusioned. Belinda, on the other hand, is pirouetting around the kitchen singing what she clearly believes are the lyrics to the Kings of Leon's biggest hit.

'OOOHHH! Dyslexics on Fiiirrre!'

'Hi, Belinda,' I call out. 'Good day?'

She spins round. 'Productive day. I've finished all my copy edits on the book. Plus,' her eyes dart away, 'I slipped in a game of tennis.'

I let out a small gasp, like I've dropped my lace handkerchief at the sight of someone riding past in a close-fitting pair of breeches. 'With James?'

A smile twitches at her lips. 'He's got a tremendous forehand.'

She has a 'will-we-won't-we' glint in her eyes, a feeling I remember well: the excitement, the fear, the trepidation and longing. Which was precisely how I felt when Dan and I got together, even if, after those initial few weeks, I became increasingly convinced that he and I would be a 'won't'.

Chapter 29

Gemma

Romantically-speaking, the years after Alex were not good to me. I couldn't muster up more than a sliver of enthusiasm for most of the men who fancied me. And the ones I did like (which is the strongest word I can bring myself to use) turned out to have the emotional maturity of a turnip; after an initial burst of enthusiasm, they went inexplicably cold.

But something about Dan told me there was no way he was going to follow that pattern. I was swept off my feet. All logic went skywards. And in a few short days – a little over a week – I let him peel away my tough-girl facade and see the real me.

I was certain I didn't have to hold back, or worry about seeming clingy when it was so obvious he wasn't going to mess me around.

So what did he go and do? He messed me around.

I hadn't worried too much when Dan didn't phone the morning after his big night out with his stockbroker colleagues. I assumed he'd simply been enjoying himself. But when the morning stretched into afternoon and evening, a familiar, neurotic knot began to form in my stomach.

I texted him the next day and heard nothing, until eventually, I received a lukewarm

Sorry I haven't been in touch. How are you? x

I replied that I was fine and asked when I would see him again – at which point he apparently disappeared from the face of the earth. He didn't return my texts. He just went silent. He was a ghost.

Sadie said I should phone him and demand a full and frank explanation. Allie said he was a toxic male and I should text him with a considered message, containing several four-letter words. In the end, I did neither. What I did was very hard. I wrote him a final text asking him never to contact me again, then pressed send. I felt empowered for about a minute, until I reminded myself that he was showing no sign of wanting to phone me anyway. I deleted his number from my phone. Then I cried. And cried a bit more.

After days of second-guessing what I did wrong (I slept with him too soon! I forgot to do my bikini line on date 4! I let him hear me singing 'Summer Nights' in the shower!) I told myself firmly: Gemma, you haven't done anything wrong. You need to forget him.

But that was easier said than done. For weeks, I walked around like a lost soul, comforted only by a playlist I could've called *Now That's What I Call Dumped – 25!*

Finally, after six weeks, he called.

I didn't return it.

He called again.

I didn't return it.

And as impossible as it felt, the harder he tried to get in touch with me, the harder I made it for him, because I knew in my bones that this was 'He's Just Not That Into You' behaviour if ever I'd seen it.

I'll give Dan this though, he persevered. The texts came thick and fast. There were flowers. He sang on my answer machine like in *When Harry Met Sally* because he knew that was my favourite film. He made me a mix tape – with 'Chasing Cars' by Snow Patrol, 'Something' by the Beatles and 'Cosmic Love' by Florence and the Machine. I hadn't even told him I loved it, but somehow he knew.

Then one Saturday, as I sat listening to it – because I couldn't not listen to it – a letter slipped through my door. I opened it with trembling hands and tight throat.

Gemma,

I've screwed up beyond words. I want to explain what happened but I can understand why you won't give me the airtime.

I know you don't want to hear from me again and I'll respect that. We can pretend it never happened. But I want you to know, for the record, that every moment I was with you, I felt sick with happiness, and I now feel sick with regret. I just realised that I am an idiot. Because it's taken until now to realise how much you burn me up, how much I love you. Yes, I'll repeat it: I love you.

I can think of nothing or nobody I could love more.

Except perhaps the idea of you and me.

Dan x

I sat in the hall of my flat and read and re-read the letter. I knew I didn't want to be without him, but giving him a second chance felt instinctively wrong. I decided to sleep on it. Except I didn't sleep. I tossed and turned all night, before waking early the next day to go to his flat, only to find that he wasn't there.

His friend Jesse suggested casually that I head to the enablement centre where Dan was working as a volunteer helping street sleepers.

The prospect, I can't deny it, filled me with trepidation. Yet I'd woken up deciding I couldn't leave it a moment longer before speaking to Dan – and that's what I was determined to do. Even if my determination began to fizzle out on the drive there.

I kept wondering if I was even allowed – as a fully paid-up Council Tax-payer with newly installed double glazing and gas central heating – to just march into a homeless shelter, uninvited.

I kept wondering what the clientele would be like, if they'd turn to look at me, like in *An American Werewolf in London*, before someone declared, *'She ain't from these parts.'*

It even crossed my mind whether I was wearing the right thing: the dual occasions of a surprise rendezvous with the man who'd wronged me and my very first visit to a homeless shelter presented quite the fashion conundrum.

In my defence, the only previous experience I'd had with homelessness was buying a few copies of the *Big Issue* and knowing all the words to 'Down and Out' in *Bugsy Malone*.

Yet when I arrived, clutching my bag tightly across my shoulder, the place was surprisingly unthreatening. Noisy, yes. Rough round the edges, definitely. But not threatening.

A cluster of young, hollow-eyed men in broken-soled trainers were taking part in a group guitar lesson, breaking into laughter when someone played a dud note. An elderly woman in a long, tattered coat was waiting to see a doctor as she chatted quietly to a girl who looked no more than eighteen.

The smell of a stew cooking in the kitchen wafted through the reception area and anyone who arrived was directed to the queue for the dining room by an administrator in her thirties, in jeans, suede boots and with an over-arching air of efficiency. 'Can I help?' she smiled.

'Um . . . I'm looking for Dan,' I mumbled.

'He's in with Jim. I don't think he'll be long if you want to wait for him.'

She directed me to a meeting room at the back of the building and I stood along the corridor, my hands clenched as I adopted the peculiar air of someone trying desperately not to stand out, but not wanting to fit in too much either.

Finally, the door opened. An elderly man in a three-piece suit emerged first, followed by Dan. Dan went to shake hands, but the man clutched hold of him and gazed into his eyes. Dan smiled. 'See you around, Jim,' he said, patting him on the arm.

Then he turned and looked at me, and I can honestly say I don't think I've ever seen so many emotions appear on one person's face all at the same time.

I'd been in some rough pubs in my time but few compared to this, the lurid blood-and-vomit stains on the carpet, the elaborately-tattooed barmaid, the thick fog of smoke in the door threshold. It wouldn't have surprised me if we'd had to duck under crime scene tape to enter.

But at least you could get a half of lager. Dan didn't say anything about what had happened between us at first, darting around the issue as I asked about Jim. The old man had been living on the streets of various UK cities for years, then in a hostel in Liverpool. As a nineteen year old, he'd been part of the small British contingent of soldiers fighting in Korea in 1951 and ended up as a prisoner of war. When he returned, despite getting married and starting a family, he was haunted by what he'd seen. He became dependent on alcohol, lost his job and family – and the rest was, rather depressing, history.

'What will happen to him?' I asked.

'We're going to find him a home. We're going to help him.'

And it was then, before he really explained anything about the last six lost weeks, that I looked into those eyes and decided I'd learned a valuable lesson, one I'll remember for the rest of my life. Some people deserve a second chance, no matter how long you've been apart.

Chapter 30

Dan

Gemma and I actually experience some between-the-sheets action tonight. Only, it's not between the sheets – we never get that far. It takes place when my mother, a force more omnipresent than God at the moment, darts to the shops to get some baking powder for a batch of rock scones, apparently unaware that she's already achieved the required consistency with everything she's cooked this year.

She is gone for nineteen and a half minutes, during which time we stumble up the stairs, rip off our clothes and have a frantic, Gangnam-style session, before washing, dressing and sprinting downstairs where we pretend to have been discussing mortgage rates.

'Is everything all right, Daniel?' Mum asks, peering at me.

Gemma scrutinises her magazine.

'Fine, why?'

'You're sweating.'

I swallow. 'I had to run to get something out of the car, that's all.'

She tuts. 'A young man like you should be fitter. You need to do more running.'

I look at Gemma who is gesturing at my crotch meaningfully. I follow her eyes to my zip, which is gaping open. I go to pull it up, but the damn thing is stuck, so I stumble out of the kitchen and upstairs to our room. My laundry is on the overdue side, but I know there's another pair of jeans I threw in the corner this morning that will do. Only when I look, they're not there. I lift up the bean bag and discover that it's not the only thing missing. The basket is empty. A thought punches me in the guts.

When I get downstairs, I try to be diplomatic. 'Mum?'

'Hmm?'

'I wondered where my laundry was?' Gemma throws me a warning glance, as if I have some sort of *tone*.

Mum looks up. 'It's my pleasure, darling.'

'Yes, I am grateful . . . but you don't need to do it for me. I'd probably prefer it if you didn't.'

She slowly turns around, a maleficent eyebrow cocked. 'Why not?'

'It's just the privacy thing again. That room is the only part of the house that's ours.'

'I think you'll find it's *not* technically yours,' she replies.

'And while we're on the subject, would you mind keeping it a bit tidier?'

I wonder for a moment if I've got batshit in my ears. 'You're asking me to tidy my room?'

'Sorry, Belinda,' Gemma steps in. 'It's my fault, I was in a rush before work this morning and—'

'No, it's not your fault, Gemma,' I contend. 'Mum, we've got all of our worldly belongings crammed into there so it's little wonder things look a bit—'

'I don't want to make a big deal out of it!' she interrupts. 'And Gemma, I'm not blaming you in the slightest. I know exactly what Daniel's like. He was the same aged fourteen. You should've seen the sort of thing I'd find under his bed in those days. There was one time when I actually found a—'

'OKAY! I'll tidy the room!' I decide this is a good moment to go and get my laundry. I enter the utility room and find it stacked up in a big pile.

For a micro-second I forget myself and am actually happy to see it there, all sweet-smelling and pressed – before practically slapping myself on the face. That way lies insanity; one minute I'll be enjoying having my laundry done, the next I'll be fifty years old and still here.

I'm about to pick up the pile and take it to my room when Gemma appears next to me, her complexion anaemic with shock.

'What's up?' I whisper.

'She's done mine too,' she breathes, looking over her shoulder. 'It's really kind of her – very sweet actually. But I don't want anyone handling my unwashed pants except me. It's not like I'm not grateful,' she continues, 'just a little uncomfortable and . . .' She picks up a shirt. 'Oh God.'

'What?'

'She's ironed my crinkle shirt.'

It's fair to say that 'crinkle shirt' has suddenly become something of a misnomer. It's smoother than Simon Cowell's forehead.

I start laughing. I'm afraid I can't help it. Then I notice something.

I move aside the T-shirt and pick up the jeans underneath. It isn't just the fact that she's put two massive creases down the front – the kind Des O'Connor might have had in his polyester slacks in 1972. I reach into the pocket and realise with a surge of dismay that she appears to have washed, tumble dried and then ironed my iPod Shuffle.

I pick it up between two fingers and examine the strange piece of modern art my plastic headphones appear to have moulded into. I put it in my ear and attempt to play it. To be fair to Apple, it tries its best to produce a sound, at least for a few seconds, before it makes the kind of noise you'd expect if you poured battery acid on a Dalek, then chucked it down a mountain.

I close my eyes momentarily. 'When's that survey due?'

'Any time now,' Gemma replies. 'I've phoned them every day except today – I've been too busy.'

'I'll phone them now then,' I offer.

'No, no, it's fine,' she insists. 'I know who to speak to.'

We head into the living room, where Gemma phones the mortgage company and I log onto Facebook. I'm scrolling through a succession of updates, dutifully 'liking' several new baby pictures, when a post appears that stops me in my tracks.

'What's the matter?' Gemma asks.

I glance back at the phone and decide to switch it off.

'Nothing. You seem to have been on hold for ages.'

'I could set up a dialogue with al-Qaeda faster than I could talk to Zoe in the New Lending Division,' she begins, before she suddenly gets through to a phone operator.

'The fact that we haven't got the survey yet is holding the whole thing up,' she tells the person. 'As you'll see from our notes, it was originally booked for … Oh. Oh really? That's brilliant! Is there any chance you could email it to me? Thank you so much!'

She ends the call. 'It's back.'

'And?'

'I don't know until I've seen it. They're sending it to my email address now.' Gemma looks mildly nauseous with excitement. 'You know what this means, don't you? If the survey says the house is structurally sound, it'll be all systems go on buying the place.'

And, more importantly, getting us both the hell out of here.

*

The survey is a disaster. Gemma reads it silently, in tortured contrast to her nervous babbling earlier, about how we mustn't worry if there's a *bit of damp*.

As we read through the document, including the bit that says it's worth £15,000 less than the price we've agreed, I become convinced that the only option is to walk away. Even if the buyers agreed to drop the price, who wants to be lumbered with a clusterfuck of problems that read like this:

The property may have had previous structural repair and there is evidence of distortion and cracking, especially to the rear elevation wall which could be ongoing. Dampness is affecting the ground-floor walls ... rot is affecting the skirting boards in the kitchen ... inadequate ventilation has allowed defects to occur ... defective mortar joints should be raked out and repointed ... defective cement work on the chimney pots ... disused flues to stacks should be capped and ventilated ... areas of cracked and weathered tiles and open jointed ridge tiles to the roof require overhauling and repair ... the electrical wiring may not comply with current standards as there are signs of some inadequate earthing and potentially dangerous fixtures and fittings ...

About the only positive thing the surveyor has found to say is under the section marked *Conservatories*, which reads: There is no conservatory.

After the first five pages my mind goes blank; I barely know what half of it means. All I know is that there are reams of this stuff, reinforcing the impression that this house isn't worthy of pissing in, never mind making, in Grandma's words, our new love shack.

I reach for Gemma's hand as a single tear slides down her cheek.

We hardly speak for the rest of the evening. There doesn't seem to be anything to say. Instead, we watch a DVD, head to bed and fall into a dark, uncomfortable sleep, from which I wake when someone wallops me on the shoulder.

'Oh sorry, did I wake you?' Gemma's face is two inches from mine.

'Yes,' I murmur, and roll over to go back to sleep.

'I can't sleep,' she tells me. 'I've been thinking about the house.'

I pretend not to hear.

'Dan, you know the survey . . .'

'Yes?'

She hesitates before speaking. 'I don't know what you think, but I'm still up for buying it.'

I sit up in bed and hope she's joking. 'WHAT?'

'I know the survey wasn't great—'

'Wasn't great? It couldn't have been worse if it'd been on a rusty skip on the edge of a subsiding cliff.'

'You're exaggerating. Look, I've been researching this since two a.m. – about what to do if the survey comes back worse than you were expecting. Listen to this.' She takes out her phone and starts reading from a website: '"As an interested buyer you do not have to walk away after a bad survey. One alternative is finding out how much repairs will cost. There may be things that can be easily fixed, without incurring high costs".'

She looks at me with big *Watership Down* eyes. I prepare myself for a torrent of emotional blackmail.

'It says here that surveyors go completely over the top to make sure no legal action is possible. They list every little defect and make it sound far worse than it is. Look at those people on *Grand Designs*,' she argues. 'You're always saying how much you'd love to do something like that. I can't believe we're going to be defeated by a bit of rot and rising damp.'

'And cracked rendering and a distorted threshold step. The other crucial fact is that getting that mortgage was dependent on the house being valued at what we agreed.'

'I agree we couldn't buy it for the original price and not do anything to fix it up. But what about if we got the buyers to drop the price to cover the cost of the repairs?'

'Rich said they weren't going to budge on the price.'

'That was before we had the survey. Even if this ended today and they tried to get new buyers, *their* survey would find the same problems. They're going to have to address it. '

She puts her arms around my neck. 'We're destined to live in that house, Dan. And the alternative is staying here and starting afresh.'

Suddenly, this doesn't feel like an argument I particularly want to win.

Chapter 31

Gemma

I refuse to panic about this survey. I refuse to believe that, when someone can restore St Paul's Cathedral, a few loose tiles and damp in Pebble Cottage are insurmountable.

But I'm equally aware that unless the buyers drop the price, there's no way we can continue with this purchase. So it's time to negotiate. Hard but fair, that's my approach. I just wish Rich would stop sucking his teeth.

'They said no way. Not a chance. You've agreed a price and they don't care what your man says.'

'But he's a qualified surveyor!' I argue.

'He could be a qualified orthodontist for all they care. They said there's no damp in the living room.'

'But he's got the readings!'

'Or rust in the gutters.'

'But he saw it with his own eyes!'

'And as for this potential issue with the electrics . . .'

'Well, if they're certain that's no problem, perhaps they could stick their fingers in a toaster and turn it on full, then see what happens,' I suggest.

He tuts. 'There's no need to be like that, Gemma. Look, I can totally see where you're coming from. But there are other buyers around the corner. I've got six people on a waiting list to see it.'

'What waiting list? You agreed not to show it to other people while it was under offer. This is *our* house, Rich.'

'It's not your house yet, Gemma. And it won't ever be unless you can come up with the asking price.'

'But Rich, even if I *wanted* to buy the house for £15,000 more than the surveyor says it's worth, the mortgage company won't give us enough money without the repairs being done. Plus,' I say, suddenly having a surge of confidence, 'all your other buyers are going to be in exactly the same position, aren't they?'

'No, actually. One is a retired couple who are downsizing so don't need a mortgage. Lovely lady. She fell in love with those eaves in the porch and—'

'Keep her away from MY eaves!' I shriek.

'Okay, okay! Look, I like you both and, hell yeah, I can totally see you both in that place. I'm certain you'd have more luck than Mr and Mrs Deaver and—'

'The sellers? Why haven't they had luck?'

'Oh— I shouldn't have said that.'

'Said what?'

He sighs. 'Between you and me, the reason they're selling is that they're getting divorced. It's messy. And bitter. This issue of the £15k is apparently the first thing they've agreed on in six months.'

It suddenly feels a bit odd to think that our lovely quaint cottage has been the scene of a marital breakdown.

'Look, I'm going to go and speak to the vendors again,' he informs me. 'How about we put this proposition to them: they get some quotes on the main elements of the work that need to be done. If they're acceptable, the work can be completed, you can send your surveyor back and see if you hit the jackpot on the valuation.'

I feel a bit breathless. This might put the final nail in the coffin of that early exchange I'd wanted, but at least it would put us back in the game. 'You'd do that, Rich?' I say, feeling a bit light-headed.

'For you, Gemma, I would.' He hesitates. 'Have you and Dan been an item for long? I only ask because if you ever fancy – you know, a bit of a dabble . . .'

'Goodbye, Rich,' I say, and put down the phone.

Rich doesn't phone for the rest of the day or the next day. During which time I whip myself into a frenzy of stress, determination and increasing certainty that, somehow, Pebble Cottage has to be ours.

My inability to relax isn't helped by the fact that our solicitor, having been on a break to the Costa del Sol for the past two months, has embarked on a flurry of letter-writing, which costs us money every time she hits so much as a full stop. Most infuriatingly, I receive three letters from her on one day, each on a different subject-matter and each one sentence long. Our bill, meanwhile, is ratcheting up like the cherries on a defective fruit machine.

The cost of the solicitor, the searches and the surveyor are not the only things that will all be for nothing if the buyers don't agree to do something with their house to satisfy the mortgage company.

In the sheer amount of time I've spent on this so far, I could've created a scale model of the Orient Express using only empty toilet rolls and used postage stamps.

Yet, when I sit and dissect the reasons I want this house so badly, it's about more than that. It's about the fireplace that I've always wanted, the fact that walking into that living room felt more right than anywhere I've been before. It's that I've spent weeks dreaming about Dan and me decorating the kitchen with those glorious Fired Earth tiles (the ones we can't afford), then spending lazy Sundays curled up in bed, reading the papers as the sunlight streams through the (apparently rotting) sash windows.

Then there's Dan. I can't allow him to live in this house with his mum a second longer than necessary. I always knew this had the potential to be bad, but I hadn't appreciated *how* bad. Before we got here, if you'd asked me to describe Dan's characteristics, I'd say he was unstoppably cheerful. Nothing gets to him. He doesn't bring his work home, he doesn't dwell on arguments. Yet, none of those seem to apply at the moment.

This is apparent when he returns from work on Monday night and enters the kitchen as Belinda hears the opening bars to 'Copacabana' on Radio 2 and decides to crank it up. She grabs him by the hands, shimmying wildly. 'Her name's CRAYOLA! She was a SHOW-GIRL!'

He smiles uneasily, disentangles himself and announces that he's going to get changed.

'You used to love dancing in the kitchen,' she pouts.

'When I was five, yes.'

'You weren't half as surly then,' she says, ruffling his hair as he ducks out of the way like a grumpy Boy Scout. 'It's like having your father around.'

And at that, to my astonishment, Dan walks out.

Belinda and I are so shocked that we look at each other, bewildered.

'What was all that about?' she asks.

I don't have a clue. 'Probably had a hard day at work?'

*

Dan is in our room with his back pressed against the Marisa Tomei poster. 'I didn't mean to storm off,' he says when I walk in.

'Is dancing to Copacabana that bad?' I ask incredulously.

'It wasn't that.' He takes a long, slow breath. 'Did I tell you Dad was coming home?'

'You mentioned he was thinking about it. Why – has he decided not to?'

'On the contrary.' He holds out his phone and shows me his Facebook news feed, which features a picture of his dad, tagged in a bar – in Manchester.

The facts take a moment to filter through my brain.

'He's been in the UK for a week and a half,' Dan says tightly. 'Half an hour's drive away. He mentioned weeks ago that he'd be here, and said he'd let me know when – but that was the last I heard from him. He didn't tell me he was here, that's how bothered he was about seeing his only son.'

I squeeze his hands and we sit on the edge of the bed. 'Oh Dan . . . I'm sorry.'

Dan rarely talks about his father, but when he does, it's clear that Scott's continued indifference bothers him more than the fact that he left in the first place.

Dan lies back on the bed and looks up at the ceiling. 'When I was little, I idolised him. I always assumed that because he was my dad, he was one of the good guys. An alternative never occurred to me.'

'When did that change?' I ask.

'It's hard to say. I remember once he told me he was going to take me to Alton Towers. I was about eight. I told Mum, I told my friends, everyone at school. I was so excited. Then on the morning he was due to pick me up, he never turned up. He just didn't come. I remember sitting on those stairs, insisting to Mum that he'd be there sooner or later. But he never came.'

'Oh Dan.'

'He phoned two days later to apologise and say that something had come up but he'd take me soon. We never went. And that happened time and time again. He'll have been with a woman,' he shrugs, trying to look nonchalant. 'God, I know it's hardly child abuse. I don't want to give you the impression I feel sorry for myself, because I don't. Honestly.'

'But the broken promises must've hurt. Especially when you were little.'

'You know what the most annoying thing is? It's the fact that when I looked and saw that Facebook update, I realised how much this sort of thing still gets to me. I'm like a pathetic child. There's still a part of me that wants his attention, his approval. Two things I should know by now I'll never get.'

The following day, I have a meeting with a client in Chester so Sebastian has agreed to let me drive there from home rather than going to the office first. It means that I get a mini-lie-in for the first time in ages, registering a sleepy kiss from Dan as he heads out before turning over for another ten minutes.

When I finally prise myself out of bed, do my ablutions, then go downstairs, Belinda is midway through a Skype chat with her longstanding American editor, Angela, who appears to be in full flow. 'We've got TV advertising, billboards and a major public transport campaign all launching in the week of publication. Our media team has everyone from Letterman to Ellen interested. You're red hot.' A look of surprise and mild delight appears at Belinda's lips as Angela continues. 'We want you to go in as heavy as you like with your message, Belinda. *That's* what's going to get the headlines for us. *The broad who told womanhood that men were surplus to requirements* – she's back and ballsier than EVER.'

When the Skype call ends, Belinda turns to me. 'It's all happening. I'm starting to feel a little nervous now.'

'Oh don't, you'll be amazing.'

My phone rings and it's Rich's number. The air vacuums out of the room as I answer it and dart into the hall.

'Gem. Rich. I have news-eroony.' He waits, like when they're announcing the results of *The Voice*.

'It's curtains, Gemma.'

My hopes and dreams seem to vanish in that small but fatal sentence. 'The sale's off?'

'No, I mean we need to talk about the curtains and carpets.

About whether you want them and if so, how much you're prepared to put your hand in your pocket for them.'

I pull myself together, and try to get my head around this. 'Surely the more pressing matter is the survey?'

'One's dependent on the other, Gem.'

'So if I buy their carpets and curtains they'll pay for the work to be done?'

'Ah, about that. They'll get some quotes – for the windows, the damp and the guttering – and are prepared to go halves on the cost,' he clarifies.

'Ok-ay.' I think about this. Going halves would be a fair solution. Sadly, there's just the small matter of us having no access to more cash to do so. Dan would think I was mad for even considering it when we're already over budget, but if the sellers *were* agreeable to it, I couldn't possibly let the opportunity pass us by. A question drifts into my head about whether I could just spare Dan the worry of all this and try to find the money for half the repairs myself.

'Well, I had hoped to buy my own carpets and curtains . . .' As I'm talking I wonder what the hell I'd thought I was going to buy them with. At least this way, we're saved the hassle and expense. 'Okay. I'll go halves, assuming the quotes are okay, on all the work necessary to meet our mortgage commitments. And for the curtains and carpets, we'll give them . . . £500.'

'Don't make me laugh!' he splutters. 'Sorry, Gem, but I'm going to have to play *serious* hard ball with you. I'm not known as one of the toughest negotiators in the business for nothing. You'll have to do better than that. Far, *far* better.'

'How much did you have in mind?'

He sucks his teeth again. 'Make it £510 and you've got a deal.'

I end the call, feeling like I got off fairly lightly on the curtains issue, so much so that when the phone rings again a second later, my first thought is that it's Rich to tell me the sellers haven't agreed to it.

But it's not Rich. I recognise who it is the second I hear his voice.

'Hello, Gemma. It's Alex.'

Chapter 32

Gemma

I feel more nervous than I did that first moment we spoke to each other when I was fifteen, something I can only put down to Selena's cousin's Bastard Sangria containing more alcohol than I'd thought.

'How are you?' he asks.

I'd tried and failed, over the last few weeks, to recall the exact sound of his voice. It's only now, when he speaks, that I realise how familiar it is, virtually identical to when he was a teenager except, perhaps, for a note of awkwardness.

Which both warms and surprises me. He is six months older than me and, when we were young, this seemed of huge significance: he was brimming with confidence. As far as my dad was concerned this made him 'cocky', but personally, I loved it. He was the opposite of me – and being his girl meant I felt like I could take on the world.

'I'm good. Really good – thank you,' I manage. 'It's lovely to hear from you.'

He laughs. 'Well, you are probably wondering why, after ... I don't know, twelve years ... the guy you used to listen to Nirvana with in your little bedroom is phoning you up, out of the blue.'

My heart flutters in my chest. 'That question had crossed my mind, yes.'

'I'm not sure how much your mum told you, but I've moved back to the UK, to Manchester. I've got a job here.'

'Oh God,' I blurt out. 'I mean ... wow. What is it you do?'

'I followed in Dad's footsteps and became a civil engineer,' he explains. 'I thought I'd seen you in the Northern Quarter a few weeks ago. Well, I wasn't sure – it might have been someone else.' I decide to say nothing. 'Anyway, it got me thinking about how nice it'd be to see what you were up to these days. You don't mind me phoning, do you?'

'Of course not. It's really ... actually, it's amazing to hear from you,' I say, unable to stop the truth spilling out of my mouth. 'I've wondered over the years what became of you.'

'Well, I looked you up on Facebook once – but you're not on it, are you?'

'I am actually, but my privacy settings mean I'm not easily found,' I confess.

'Woman of mystery,' he teases. 'Very you, Gems – I like it.'

Until this moment, I'd completely forgotten he called me Gems, especially when he was in a flirtatious mood. The thought makes my insides fizz.

'So . . .' my head spins as I attempt to think of an appropriate topic for small talk, 'are you married?' Oh no! I wince, realising I'm giving the impression I've spent twelve years pining by my window in the hope that he'll ride up on a stallion and sweep me off for a small but intimate ceremony at Gretna Green.

He seems unfazed.

'No. No significant others, I'm afraid.' I wonder for a moment who the blonde was, but he doesn't offer the information and I decide I've pried enough already.

Yet the conversation, from there, seems to feel a bit easier. I tell him about Dan and the house and my job. He tells me about Cape Town – where he's lived for the last eight years – his job, and family, who are still in Kenya.

We speak for about ten minutes, though it could be more or less. I'm just starting to feel the tension in my shoulders let up when he asks a question I knew was coming, but it still doesn't stop my pulse from trebling in speed.

'Listen, would you like to grab a coffee at some point? I don't know many people here and it'd just be great to say hello.' I find myself smiling. Then he adds, 'I'd love to meet Dan too.'

I am instantly silenced by this suggestion. Because, casual as it clearly is to Alex, the thought is horrifying to me.

Dan might be aware that I had a serious boyfriend when I was a teenager, but he certainly doesn't know *how* serious – and I've never had the heart to correct him when he's talked about mutual 'first love', as if it applies to me as well as him.

The thought of the two of them sitting together is enough to bring me out in a queasy sweat.

And it's this train of thought that leads me to the next question: should I meet Alex at all? Wouldn't it just be simpler to have this phone call and leave things be.

'Sorry – if that's difficult, don't worry,' Alex says, filling the silence.

'Oh, it's not difficult,' I leap in. It would only be difficult if I had lingering feelings for Alex, and after twelve years, that would be ridiculous.

I want to tell him that, to spell it out. But I know I'd be protesting too much.

'What do you say then?' he asks. And suddenly, saying no to the coffee doesn't feel like an option.

Chapter 33

Dan

I try to phone Sheila ahead of our meeting to check that she's remembered it, but I know the likelihood of her answering is minimal. She treats her phone like a box of Milk Tray: to be dipped into only when she fancies it.

When I arrive at her house, she opens the door and gasps, 'Were you due today, lad? Don't get me wrong, it's nice to see you, but I'd have tidied up first.'

She explodes into a savage cough and sucks on her inhaler as she shows me into the living room. It's spotless. She's become proud of the place, judging by the pink curtains and sparkly cushions that have appeared over the last few weeks. Photos of her sons and granddaughter line up along her mantelpiece and her shoes – all skyscraper high in retina-burning colours – are lined up neatly along the hearth.

She's a model client in most ways, even if one element of her recovery isn't quite happening.

She sits on the sofa and pulls a blanket over her legs while we discuss the usual pleasantries – what she's reading (the Mothercare brochure), whether she's seen baby Rose recently (sadly not), and if I've seen the bloody price of an electric breast pump (something I can't say with any conviction that I have).

She is gripped by coughing fits throughout, so I wait until she's finished before I casually raise the subject I really want to talk about.

'Did you go to your Addaction meeting last week?' I don't look up, just flick through my notes.

I've become aware that she's missed several doctor's appointments and, although she began attending her sessions at the drugs counselling service, they've tailed off dramatically. This is far from uncommon, even with someone as apparently determined as Sheila.

'Erm . . . I might have. I'm not sure.' I look up at her. She pulls the blanket over her bony shoulders and refuses to make eye-contact. 'I remember – I got up to go, but I got to the bus stop and realised I didn't have any money. So I came back home and looked, but by the time I found some, it was too late.'

'Sheila.' I lean forward. 'Do you still want a referral to the Kevin White Unit?'

'You know I do!' she protests, launching into another ferocious cough.

'Then you have to go to these sessions. I'd be happy to go with you.'

'I'd never miss them normally,' she goes on, deaf to my offer. 'People who do that are a disgrace. It's no wonder the country is in such a state, all these time-wasters making appointments and then not bothering. Terrible.'

I nod. 'So are you going this week?'

'Definitely. I've just had loads on, that's all,' she responds, as if she's Sheryl Sandberg. 'I promise I'll go to the one on Friday.'

'Thursday.'

'Sorry, Thursday. Don't worry, lad. I won't let you down.'

When I return to the office, I have a mountain of work to tackle, but Pete is intent on quizzing me about the intricacies of his love-life as if I'm a cross between Frasier Crane and a fourteen-year-old girl on a sleepover.

'I'm starting to wonder if I've taken the wrong approach,' he muses, polishing off a Gregg's sausage roll. It's not his first. 'Casually mentioning going out could be too ambiguous.'

'Hmm . . . I don't know, Pete.'

'So if I phone her, then there's no way she could interpret that other than me actually, you know, making *an advance*.'

'Hmm.'

Pete gives up. 'When are you going to be in this new house then?'

'Who knows? I'll be honest, I was amazed they agreed to budge on the survey. I thought they were going to tell us to get stuffed.'

'So the sellers are paying for *all* the work to be done? You don't have to contribute anything to it?'

'Nope. All Gemma had to agree to was £510 for the carpets and curtains.'

'She must be one hell of a negotiator.'

'You could never accuse Gemma of a lack of determination.' I pick up the phone, when Pete interrupts.

'You know, part of me wonders if she *does* know.'

'Who?'

'Jade.'

'Know what?'

He looks at me like I'm failing to keep up with some crucial twist in the world's most compelling soap opera. 'My true feelings.'

'It's a possibility you need to consider, Pete. I mean, the amount of coffee you've taken her for . . .'

'What's that got to do with anything?'

I put down the phone. 'Man plus woman plus romantic little coffee shop – it can only mean one thing.'

'What's that?'

I grin. 'Lust is in the air, my friend.'

Chapter 34

Gemma

I've arranged to meet Alex for coffee in an Icelandic-themed café-bar in Manchester called Löngun, a name I discovered to my alarm afterwards translates as 'desire'. It could have been worse, I suppose. At least it wasn't the Italian for 'come-hither eyes' or Swedish for 'sex on legs'.

Plus, the good things I'd heard about it seem warranted. It's cool without being full of itself, with books slotted neatly into geometric shelves, the air thick with the scent of espresso and a nice selection of artisan sandwiches on the menu.

Not that I'm interested in the sandwiches. I haven't eaten properly since last night, unless you count two bites of the near-calcified toast Belinda thoughtfully made me for breakfast.

He's already there when I arrive. I knew he would be

because he was always early, for absolutely everything. As I push open the door, he looks up and smiles. The familiarity of the gesture makes me relax, but it's a momentary sensation that disintegrates entirely when he kisses me on the cheek and warmth spreads right through to my fingertips.

'Gems. You look spectacular. Nothing less.'

'If you say so,' I mutter, reddening.

'I do.'

I sit down and, hyper-aware that he's looking at me – just *looking* – I start to talk. And talk. And talk a bit more.

'So, this is a nice place, isn't it? I know Liverpool a lot better than Manchester to be honest, apart from the Northern Quarter, which I like a lot. It's a great city – you'll love it, I'm sure. Not that I'm here all the time – just occasionally with work. What made you choose a job in Manchester? I'd always assumed you'd go off travelling the world somewhere and never come back to the UK again.'

I become aware halfway through this soliloquy that the *just looking* is still happening, so I continue for as long as I possibly can before coming up for air.

'Gemma.' He smiles. 'Let me get you a drink, then I'll fill you in – on everything.'

'Oh! Sorry!' I glance at the menu I appear to be clutching. 'I'll have a cappuccino. But I'll get it, don't worry.' I grab my purse, but he puts his hand on mine. 'It's fine, let me.'

I look down, momentarily stunned by the feel of his

fingertips on my skin. He withdraws his hand. 'I insist,' I say firmly, clambering up to head to the bar.

Only as I try to catch my breath and order the coffee, I realise that I used my last cash in the car park. Obviously, there is no way I'm going to go and bum some off Alex, not in the opening moments of a reunion (though to call it that makes me wince). So I hand over the first bit of plastic in my purse, my credit card.

'Sorry, there's a £5 minimum charge on all cards,' the assistant tells me.

'Oh … okay, I'll take a cake as well,' I reply reluctantly, eating being the last thing on my mind.

We then go through the charade of him cutting a piece of lemon drizzle cake the size of a house brick, before he announces that their card machine is on the blink and he'll have to bring it back to me at my table once the payment has gone through.

I return to Alex and place the plate in front of him casually. 'Would you like some cake?'

He laughs, his eyes sparkling as he catches mine. 'Go on then, I'll share it with you.'

'Oh, I don't want any,' I fluster.

He smirks and holds my gaze. 'What made you think *I* would?' And for some reason, that mischievous look on his face makes me laugh too.

'Maybe you just looked like a man in the mood for some sponge cake,' I smile.

He picks up a fork. 'Right then. You obviously haven't forgotten that I *never* say no to cake.'

Actually, I had forgotten. But now he mentions it, the first summer when we were together, we'd always end up in the little patisserie over the road from where he lived, working our way through their jewel-coloured pastries. If he'd continued with this daily sugar rush, you'd never know it. I'd be a stone and a half heavier if I had – which is another one to add to the list of *good* things that came of our break-up.

'In answer to your question, the move here wasn't really planned,' he tells me. 'I'd worked on big building projects all over South Africa for a while, but I fancied a change of scene. Then this came up – the chance to work on a project in Manchester. It's a six-month contract and they made me an offer I couldn't refuse.'

He nestles his fork into the cake, cuts off a piece and, distractingly, brings it to his lips. I tear my eyes away and decide to keep talking. 'It must feel strange being back in the UK.'

'A lot's changed in twelve years, but people are the same the world over – I've learned that much. Nice to see a familiar face though.'

I realise I'm smiling again. 'How long have you been here?'

'Just under two months. Still re-acclimatising really.'

Having been a maelstrom of nerves before I arrived, this whole encounter suddenly feels astonishingly enjoyable.

I wouldn't say it's as if we've never been apart – there are moments when I feel like I don't know him at all. But at other times, especially when we reminisce, it's like putting on your most treasured pair of shoes and becoming aware that they still fit and have the ability to make your heart soar.

He's still got that open, easy personality and mildly flirtatious sense of humour. He looks, essentially, like a grown-up version of himself, which I suppose is exactly what he is.

Yet this new history he's accumulated – with different people and places from mine – is one I can't get enough of. I tell him more about Dan and he tells me about his only other serious girlfriend, with whom he broke up two years ago. He's now single: the woman I saw him with in the Northern Quarter was just a colleague.

I suspect we could fill an entire afternoon catching up if I didn't have to get back to work.

'I'm seriously glad I tracked you down, Gems,' he concludes when I tell him I have to leave.

I nod. 'Me too, Alex.'

Then he puts his hand on my elbow and leans in to kiss me on the cheek again. The smell of him floods my senses.

I pull away sharply.

'Next time, we should meet after work,' he declares. 'Then we'd have all night to talk this rubbish.'

He registers my expression and clearly regrets opening his mouth. 'Sorry . . . that was the most presumptuous thing I've ever said.'

'Not at all,' I say, hating that I've embarrassed him. 'It's been fantastic to see you.'

'But getting together again is a no-no?'

I'm trying to think of a diplomatic response when the full implications of this hit me: that I might not see him again for another twelve years. Or indeed ever. And in that moment, I get a rush of that same, hideous feeling I had when I was standing at the airport as a teenage girl, saying goodbye to him for what I thought would be the last time.

'I understand totally,' he tells me. 'But just so you know, my intentions were entirely innocent. You and Dan are obviously made for each other and I wouldn't dream of—'

'Of course,' I interrupt. 'Of course you wouldn't. I feel stupid now.'

'Gems,' he says softly, reaching out for my hand. My heartbeat doubles in speed when he touches it. 'Don't feel stupid in front of me, please. I'd be mortified.' My eyes meet his and, for just a heartbeat, I can't tear them away. Then I snap out of it.

'Let me know if you change your mind, won't you?' he says.

I nod, but make it clear that my decision stands.

'Bye, Alex,' I whisper. And as I exit the coffee shop, my thundering heart makes one thing clear: I can never, ever meet up with him again.

When I get back to work, I bump into Sebastian in the car park. He's dressed in a suit the colour of chalk, with a blue polo neck. He looks like a cricket umpire at a Eurovision party.

'Heeeyyy!' he says, Arthur Fonzarelli-style, his smile so dazzling it makes my pupils twitch.

'Hello, Sebastian.'

He glances at my car. 'You know, in some ways I envy you, Gemma.'

'Oh?'

'There you are in your economical little vehicle which must've cost, what – a grand?'

'Yes, my boyfriend and I are buying a house so—'

'To make an insurance claim on *that* must be a doddle. I, on the other hand, am having NO END of trouble with my insurers. The excess is a fortune, my No Claims is in tatters and it'll still be three weeks before I get my car back. Whoever did this must have the morals of a sewer rat. '

I decide to change the subject. 'So has your contact at Bang said anything about me presenting the new condom campaigns?'

'If I ever find out who did it, I'm not sure I'll be able to restrain myself,' he snarls, ignoring me completely.

'Only, I'd been thinking about whether I'd be needed at all,' I say, ignoring *him* completely.

'I think this sort of thing should carry a prison sentence.'

'A voice-over might have a greater impact, unless of course you'd reconsider presenting it yourself?'

He looks at me and I finally appear to have got through to him.

'Hanging's too good for them,' he declares. 'Don't you agree?'

'Absolutely,' I mutter, and hurtle up the stairs as fast as I can.

When I reach my desk, Sadie is mid-confrontation with Jeremy, our favourite traffic manager. He's twenty-one, sweet, good-looking, and usually her top source of office gossip. For her to fall out with him would be like M pissing off the CIA.

'Sadie, my love. See reason, please,' he begs. 'This is a new client and we've got to cut them some slack. I know it's going to mean extra work on Thursday, but it has to be done.'

'We can't take on any more revisions!' she shrieks. 'If I have to do another revision I WILL GO POSTAL.'

He looks at her sympathetically. 'Don't do that, sweetheart. It'd be terrible for office morale,' he says, deciding to leave it there.

As he disappears, Sadie slumps into her seat. 'I can't cope with this.'

'We'll absorb it if we do a couple of late nights,' I reassure her.

She nods glumly. 'You're right. I need to focus. I just ... just ... I can't cope with the deception,' she hisses, leaning in with a trembling lip. 'I saw Sebastian this morning and I'm

253

starting to think he won't rest until the perpetrator is DEAD.'
I decide not to tell her about the hanging comment.

'You were so right. I should've owned up in the first place,'
she tells me, shaking her head dementedly. 'But I can't cough
to it now or he'll sack me.'

'Sadie, you're not going to be sacked. It was an accident.'

'The weeks of lying weren't.'

Which is, of course, true. 'Then maybe you should think
about coming clean,' I suggest.

She looks horrified. 'I screwed up mightily, Gemma,' she
says hoarsely, 'but if I want to keep my job – which I do – I
need Sebastian to never, ever know about this.'

'Know about *what?*' We look up to see Sebastian looming
over us, hands gripping the hips of his chalk-white trousers.

I recount the story to Dan the following day after we've driven
over to Liverpool for brunch in The Quarter, our favourite café
in our favourite part of a city we've both grown to love over
the years.

We'd dreamed of buying a house near here once, until it
became apparent that the smaller ones that we'd vaguely
hoped might be within our budget never came up for sale.

'How did Sadie get out of that one?' he asks.

'By the skin of her teeth. I leaped in and mumbled something about how we needed to finish off some amends we're
working on, and didn't want him to see until it was finished.'

After we've eaten, we stroll along the cobbles of Hope Street and I find myself holding Dan's hand just a little tighter than usual, kissing him a little longer as we reach the car. And reminding myself, with every word that comes from his mouth, just how much I love him.

Before we head back to Cheshire, we drive to Liverpool Watersports Centre and pull up in the car park, just as the sunshine that has dominated the morning starts to fizzle out. It's still a hive of activity. There are eight year olds having kayaking lessons, windsurfers heading across the dock and a girl heroically attempting to master water-skiing, but looking like she's slipped a disc while squatting to sit on a Portaloo.

'The shop's over here,' Dan tells me, as he marches up a walkway and pushes open the door. Inside is an Aladdin's Cave of watersports gear, with vividly coloured wetsuits, drysuits, sailing wear and any number of other items for which I won't even pretend I know the correct terminology. A peculiar sensation engulfs me.

I want to buy something.

ANYTHING.

I have absolutely no desire to get in any water, obviously. But I haven't indulged in any retail therapy for months, and suddenly have a burning need to do the one thing guaranteed to take my mind off things: shopping. I'm aching to purchase something so badly, it's as if my purse is incontinent.

As Dan looks around, I start eyeing up a snazzy yellow

Dinghy top, trying to work out any possible use I might have for it.

'Gemma, I think I've found one,' Dan says, holding up a wetsuit. I go over to take a look.

Flossie's eightieth birthday is in just over a month, and although most of the swimming she does is in the pool these days, she has been known to swim outdoors, as recently as last year. Personally, I'd have played it safe with a set of pearls or something, but then I've never had a grandmother quite like Flossie. I'm not sure anyone has.

'Mum's going over the top on the party organising,' Dan says as he takes the wetsuit to the counter and waits for an assistant. 'She's absolutely determined about us doing this dance for Grandma.'

'I think she probably would enjoy it,' I tell him.

He suppresses a smile. 'I had a horrible feeling you'd think it was a good idea.' He glances through the window as the sky turns even darker. 'Looks like we're not going to be able to eat outside tonight.'

I tut. 'It was gorgeous in Manchester yesterday too.'

'What were you doing in Manchester?' he asks.

It's a simple enough question. It should have a simple enough answer.

Yet, Dan can't fail to notice that blood drains from my face so fast I almost need to sit down. 'Hmm? Oh, just a meeting. Filming. A meeting and some filming,' I splutter, then I wonder why the hell I'm lying. 'I also met up with someone I used to know back home. He's been working abroad and is in Manchester temporarily so I thought I'd just say, you know . . . *hi*.'

'Oh right,' he shrugs, as – mercifully – an assistant approaches the desk to serve him.

I casually stroll away, pretending to look at some surfboards as I take deep breaths and try to stop my heart from exploding. And it's then that I feel my phone vibrate.

I pull it out of my bag and register Alex's name. The only option open to me is to dive to the exit like I'm trying to save a penalty.

I'm outside the shop when I answer, glancing through the window to check that Dan remains otherwise engaged.

'Hi,' I squeak.

'Hi,' he replies.

I hate myself for how happy I am to hear his voice, despite being near-paralysed with anxiety.

'Gems – I've been trying to get hold of you. I left a message.' I realise I must have had my phone on silent. 'You left your credit card at the bar yesterday.'

I close my eyes and try to breathe. 'Oh God, what an idiot.'

'He was very apologetic.'

'I mean *me*, not the assistant.'

'Ah,' he laughs. 'Look, I know what you said about not meeting, but I don't think I should put this in the post.'

'No,' I mumble, checking on Dan again as I feel sick with dizziness. 'I've got two cards, I can just use the other one for the moment. Then I can get my credit card from you next week.'

'Okay,' he replies.

'Okay,' I repeat.

There's a silence again, one that feels more awkward than when I was with him yesterday.

I glance up and see the assistant handing Dan the bag containing his wetsuit.

'I've got to go,' I say hurriedly. 'But I'll text you and arrange to get it. Thanks.'

'No problem,' he replies. 'And, Gems?'

'Yes?' I swallow, my heart ready to combust as Dan approaches the door.

'It was . . . spectacular to see you again. I loved it.'

'Me too,' I whisper, ending the call as the door opens and Dan walks towards me.

Chapter 35

Dan

As the house sale drags on, there are times when I have to think hard to recall why we're putting ourselves through this, especially when Gemma seems permanently on the verge of having kittens – generally stressed out and not really her usual self.

Then she arranges to drop into her friend Allie's new house in Hoylake – with a housewarming present that smashes our budget – a label you could apply to a box of PG Tips these days.

'What did you end up getting?' I ask as we pull in. 'Something from Poundland?'

'Picture frame from Utility,' she replies. 'It blew the budget but friendship is more important than some things. I did get some Tupperware from Poundland though. For *our* new place.'

'So we haven't got a sofa, a washing machine or indeed the

place itself yet, but at least we've sorted out something to keep our cheese in.'

I can honestly say that house envy – an affliction that grips Gemma regularly – is something it's never occurred to me to have. But even I feel slightly weak at the knees when we walk into Allie and her boyfriend Steve's place.

It's not huge, but it's the most supremely cool pad I have come across in quite some time.

The kitchen looks like George Lucas's take on a 1950s butcher's shop, with black tiles, stainless steel surfaces and the biggest bastard of a light you've ever seen.

The living room is white. All white. I'm talking furniture, carpets, the lot – it's so bloody white that I'm half expecting God to open the curtains and glide in. This is all offset by a wall of technology, with every piece of kit the fine men and women of Apple, Sonos and Sony could possibly conjure up in their beautifully geeky minds.

'You've got a white sofa,' I say, the same awe in my voice as when I first set eyes on a Game Boy, aged seven.

'Everyone comments on the sofa,' Allie laughs. 'I'm not sure if we're brave or just stupid.'

'You can get away with a white sofa when you haven't got kids,' Steve says. He's a graphic designer. Nice guy. Very hairy, like the fifth member of Mumford & Sons. 'You could have one in your new place.'

'We haven't got kids, but we've got *me*,' Gemma says.

'Anything white that I own draws red wine to it as if it's magnetic.'

I pretend to whisper conspiratorially to Allie, 'You know what a pisshead she is.'

Gemma gives me a prod. We stay for a coffee, then, before we return to Buddington Hall, decide to do a detour past Pebble Cottage.

As we pull up outside, a text arrives from Pete asking me to phone him for 'urgent advice', but as his definition of urgent differs from mine, I defer the call until I get home. Instead, I unplug my seat belt while two workmen carry a replacement skirting board through the door.

Although it's in a state of upheaval, I realise for the first time just how much I want this place.

I want to look as smug as Steve in front of his Bang & Olufsen speakers. I want an X-Box and a white sofa. Hell, I'll even take the Magimix and start baking cakepops if our place ends up looking as good as theirs.

I step out of the car to join Gemma, who's standing staring at the house. I uncross her arms and cuddle her into me. 'Won't be long.'

'I know,' she sighs. 'I just can't wait to be in that dining room, cracking open a few beers and surrounded by friends.'

I'm about to kiss her, when a workman stops and coughs 'politely', sounding like he's suffering from consumption. 'Can I help?'

'Oh no, it's okay,' Gemma says, sliding away from me. 'We're buying this place though.'

'Ah,' he grins. 'So you're the ones paying my wages.'

'Fortunately, the sellers are picking up the bill for all this,' I reply.

'Lucky you. Repairs on a house of this age can cost a bloody fortune.'

It's only the following day that what he said occurs to me again.

Our entire, already-optimistic budget-planning has focused on *buying* Pebble Cottage, then paying the mortgage and bills once we're in. We haven't put any thought into what would happen if any more of the 'original features' that the estate agent was wetting his pants over go belly up after six months. I've barely got the headspace to think about this as I'm walking into the Old School House.

'Dan!' Pete is legging it up the driveway, sweating like a Fray Bentos hot dog in a heatwave.

'What's up, my friend?'

He grabs me by the arm of my shirt and drags me back from the door. 'Didn't you get my text?'

It's only then that I remember him texting at all. 'Ah, sorry, mate. What's happened?'

'I've dropped a bollock. A massive one.'

'Now you're just showing off.' He sighs. 'Go on.'

'I need to talk. In private. This is a sensitive matter.'

'Let's go up to the office then.'

'I can't,' he says, with a constipated expression. 'That'd mean walking past Jade.'

'You're normally very keen to walk past Jade.'

'That was before The Colquitt Street Incident.'

He goes on to tell me a convoluted story about how he and Raj from the outreach team were in the city centre on Saturday night and they happened to bump into Jade and her friends. They went to Nolita Cantina, then Magnet, then a host of other places they were all too drunk to recall, at which point she said she was starving, so while her friends went home, he offered to buy her some chips.

'This is ever so romantic so far,' I say.

'Don't joke. She was really drunk.'

'How drunk?'

'She called me Paul twice.'

I stop myself from sniggering.

'I offered to take her home in a taxi, thinking I was being gallant. Then when we got to her house, she . . .' His voice trails off in an entirely uncharacteristic moment of coyness.

'What?'

'She tried to snog me.'

I slap him on the back. 'Well done!'

He purses his lips. 'Well, not really. The thing that was going through my mind was, "I know she's wasted. If I was a gent, I'd pull away and tell her I respected her too much".'

'Is that what you did?'

'No, I snogged her back.'

'That's beautiful, my friend. Well done.'

'*No*. Not well done,' he says grimly. '*She* pulled away a second later, saying: "What the hell am I doing?" And I apologised, so she said, "No, it's me. I have no idea why I'm kissing you as I don't fancy you IN THE SLIGHTEST. I think I'm making up for the fact that it's been six years since I had sex".'

'Hasn't she got a four-year-old daughter?' I ask.

'I didn't want to split hairs,' he replies. 'Anyway, it gets worse. She phoned me on Sunday morning – to apologise – and assure me once again that she has NO FEELINGS for me whatsoever.'

'Hmm. What did you say?'

'I said that's very reassuring. We haven't spoken since,' he says numbly. 'We've been avoiding each other all morning. The whole thing's a nightmare.'

I grab him by the arm. 'Where are we going?' he asks, as he starts sweating again.

'Just get it over with. Act normal. Say, "Hey, I hope things won't be awkward from now on," or something like that. It'll be fine. I'll be there for moral support.'

We head into the reception and spot her, ending a phone call. He tries to fly up the stairs.

'Jade, Pete's got something to say to you.'

I realise I run the risk of him trying to murder me with a

blunt pair of scissors when we get upstairs, but the man can't live like this.

He swallows. She swallows. The atmosphere is so tense you could bounce a ball of Edam off it.

'Have you got any staples?' he squawks.

'Yup,' she replies, throwing a box at him as she picks up the phone and turns away.

Chapter 36

Gemma

Two weeks after I met up with Alex in Manchester, I still haven't got my card back, despite his repeated attempts to arrange to get it to me.

I've been putting it off, pretending that I'm too busy at work right now to slip away like last time. Which obviously isn't the real reason. The real reason is far more complicated – and one I've been trying hard not to think about.

The point at which it becomes clear that I can procrastinate no longer occurs when he offers to drive over to Austin Blythe to give it to me there. The thought of him being anywhere near work – and the questions, explanations and introductions that would involve, especially to Sadie – is enough to make me aware that alternative action is required.

We arrange to meet in the car park of a country pub, the

Goshawk, about ten minutes' drive from work and on my way home. I warned him in advance that I won't be able to stop for a drink, to which he responded:

Understood, Gems. (Though I WILL try and twist your arm) x

That made me smile. Which made me hate myself.

When I arrive, all the outside tables are full and he's sitting on a swing in the little garden next to the pub. He's dressed in jeans and a crisp white shirt that's open at the collar. My pulse quickens at the sight of him and it occurs to me as he jumps off the swing that he's far closer to the definition of classically handsome these days, something that never could've been said of him as a teenager.

'One credit card,' he grins, producing it from his back pocket.

I take it from him sheepishly. 'Thank you.'

'I've obviously paid for a holiday to Barbados on it. Don't mind, do you, Gems?'

'You might get a holiday in Butlins with what's in my bank account, but that's it.' He laughs, prompting a reminder of how much I loved that sound once, how much I loved it when something *I'd* said made him do it.

'Thanks, Alex – for coming all this way,' I say.

'Oh, it wasn't far. Not really. Of course, it'd be worth my while if you'd stop for a drink . . .'

I glance at the tables. I really want to stay. 'There's not even anywhere to sit,' I argue feebly.

An elderly couple start gathering up their belongings to leave. The lady looks up and spots us. 'There's a free table here!' she yells, trying to attract our attention as if she's on a desert island and we're the first ship that's passed in six weeks. 'Come on – quick! I'll save it for you both.'

Alex pulls this funny, puppy dog expression and I shake my head. 'Don't give me that look,' I warn.

'QUICK!' she shrieks, as the entire beer garden turns to look. 'It won't be here forever. Come on – I've kept the seat warm.'

Alex nudges me. 'She's kept the seat warm – you can't resist that, surely, Gems? Come on, I'll buy.'

And although I hesitate for another second, I answer in the way I suspect I was always going to.

'Oh, I suppose one wouldn't do any harm.'

I enjoy it far too much. The wine. The sunshine. The everything.

The forty-five minutes I spend with him are both cosily familiar and strangely exhilarating. We talk, we giggle.

And he flirts. Which is the bit that puts me on edge, even if I know he can't help himself and I make absolutely certain not to rise to his compliments. By the time I tear myself away, resisting his suggestion of another drink, I have this strange, and mildly uncomfortable, end-of-date feeling.

Which he doesn't help by touching my hand as I go to open the car. 'Come on, Gems,' he grins. 'Meet me again – you know you want to.'

It's in his usual jokey style, but I feel a sudden need to get serious with him. 'I can't, Alex. I know how I'd feel if Dan was meeting an ex-girlfriend.'

It's only as I say the words out loud that I stop to think about them.

How *would* I feel if the shoe were on the other foot? If Dan was meeting some gorgeous woman, a woman he'd once been in love with?

It would kill me.

Alex takes a step back. 'Have it your way.' Then he holds up his hand and with a teasing smile simply says, 'See you around.'

When I arrive back at Buddington, Dan's in our room changing into a clean T-shirt after work. He doesn't ask why I'm late and this absence of suspicion only serves to fuel the guilt that started bubbling under my skin the second I left the pub.

'Hello you,' he says as I walk up to him and slide my arms around his waist. I don't answer at first, just hold him close and feel his skin against mine.

'Wow. That Old Spice must be doing the trick.'

Then he leans down and kisses me. I lose myself in the moment, relishing the future I'm going to have with him, once we're finally in Pebble Cottage. A future I'm determined will happen, whatever stupid nostalgic feelings Alex might have stirred up.

I take off my shoes and sit at the end of the bed as it strikes me that Dan seems a little distracted himself.

'Everything okay?' I ask, reaching out for his hand.

He sits down next to me. 'I keep thinking about the cost of Pebble Cottage,' he confesses. 'I'm worried about it, Gemma. About whether we can afford it once we're actually living there.'

The thought that Dan might be getting cold feet again is just too much for my poor, beleaguered brain to cope with.

'It'll be fine, Dan. I promise it will be.' And although I'm saying this as if I have a grasp on financial wizardry that would rival the BBC's chief economics reporter, the reality is that I simply do not want to even contemplate the idea of putting a halt to this now.

I want to be in that house as soon as possible, with the man I love more than any other. Dan.

He shrugs. 'Sorry. I'm sure you're right. Things are just getting to me a bit.'

'What things?' I ask.

'I still haven't heard from Dad,' he says, feigning indifference badly. 'He could be back in New York by now.'

'Have you tried phoning him?' I ask.

'Yes, and it went straight to messages. I'd already left one for him through his secretary, so I wasn't going to leave another. I have some pride.'

The following morning when Dan is on his run, his words come back to me.

There's no question that if his dad is thirty minutes' drive away, he should at least make time to go for a drink with him.

I do wonder though, privately, whether Dan himself should be a bit clearer with his dad about the fact that he wants to see him. For all his father knows, Dan might not give a toss. His sentence – *I do have some pride* – says it all: he wants his dad to come running after him.

Which of course, he ought to. But maintaining a stoic silence isn't going to make that happen. A wisp of an idea floats into my head, then it grows and grows until it's so irresistible the only option is to act before I overthink it.

I sit up on the bed and pull my laptop from my bag. Thanks to Linked-In, the email address is astonishingly easy to find. My finger hovers over the keyboard momentarily, before I brace myself and start typing a letter to a man to whom I'm long overdue an introduction.

Chapter 37

Dan

For the first time since I started working at the Chapterhouse Centre, I begin to think about what would've once been unthinkable: whether I should try to get a better paid job.

At the risk of sounding like I'm delivering a Miss World speech, I'd always wanted to *make a difference*, which is why I've always loved working here. But is making a difference worth it if it means I can't even scrape together enough to put a roof over the head of me and the woman I love? Is it worth the hassle, the hours and the distinctly unbrilliant wage-packet?

I tell myself as I glance in the recruitment agency window that I'm just looking. Window shopping does no harm.

By the time I leave twenty minutes later, I feel as if I'm walking out of a brothel: tingling from a dirty kind of pleasure, the knowledge that *I could if I really wanted*. Buy a nice car. Decent birthday presents for Gemma. Great nights out again.

God, I miss our nights out from when we lived in Liverpool – the days when I could just come home and, without reference to the budget, spend the next few hours taking Gemma out to every bar we could manage without falling over. I recall with a rising melancholy how long it's been since we indulged in that simple luxury.

I pull up the collar of my coat as I feel rain spitting against my face, then put my hands in my pockets and feel for my phone, rubbing its screen with my fingers as I contemplate making a call to someone I haven't spoken to in a long time.

When I get back to the Old School House, Jade is at her desk talking to Alana, another housing support officer. 'Is Pete in the office?' I ask.

Jade holds her breath. 'Think so.'

To say things have been difficult between the two of them since The Colquitt Street Incident barely covers it. Last week, when they found themselves in the hall together, they both rushed for the exits like the extras in *Snakes on a Plane*.

I'm about to turn to go up the stairs when something stops me. 'Have you got time for a cup of tea, Jade?'

She looks surprised. 'As long as you're making.'

The kitchen of the Old School House consists of a sink, a kettle, a toaster that sets your fingers on fire if you don't whip the bread out quickly enough, and a big table in the middle, surrounded by chairs. I make the tea in brown mugs and hand her one, with a Jammie Dodger, the provision of which constitutes the sum total of staff perks around here.

'I'm on a diet,' she tells me regretfully, her eyes burning so fiercely that the edges nearly turn brown.

Then she picks it up and shoves it in her mouth. 'These are okay as long as I log the points on my mobile,' she explains after she's finished, whipping out her phone and inputting data as if she's Dr Who's assistant. 'Bugger. I've only got enough left for a carrot soup for dinner now. Ah well. What can I do for you, lovely?'

I'm not really a fan of heart-to-hearts. If I'm honest, I'd prefer to borrow someone's dentures and chew a replica of *The Angel of the North* in the table leg than have a discussion about emotions with Jade. I suppress a fleeting notion that I could phone Gemma and get her to do this for me.

'There's no easy way of saying this, but it's about Pete,' I tell her.

Her eyes widen. *'What did he tell you I did?'*

'Nothing.' I regret this already.

'I thought I could count on him not to tell anyone,' she scowls.

'All he said was that there was a tricky moment when you met on your night out.'

'That's all?'

'Near enough, yes.'

She straightens her back. 'That sounds about right.'

'I think he feels *he's* to blame,' I add, hoping this makes him sound chivalrous, like Mr Darcy or someone, as opposed to a bloke who's had a fifteen-year love affair with doner kebabs and whose proudest achievement is completing the final level in *Call of Duty*.

'Really? I don't know why he'd think that,' she says, before adding, 'not that it was *me* who jumped on him or anything.'

'Of course not,' I reassure her. 'But the thing that strikes me is this: obviously there's been this ... *moment* ... between the two of you.'

'*Moment*, yes,' she repeats, deciding she likes the euphemism.

'And it feels awkward – that's natural. But it'd be a shame if you let this get in the way of your friendship. I know he values that more than anything else.'

I have used this 'shame to get in the way of a beautiful friendship' line many, many times before. This is the first time it's actually been true and not simply an easier way of saying, 'I want to run a billion miles away from you as fast as is humanly possible.'

She silently dissects this information, looking mildly disappointed at the idea that he's failed to be overcome with lust for her. 'Well, I must admit, I miss our coffees,' she decides eventually. 'And I miss him being my friend. There, I've said it.'

'You know what I'd do if I were you? Invite him for a coffee tomorrow and pretend none of this ever happened.'

'I'll think about it,' she concedes.

I sit back, satisfied in the knowledge that that's my emotional tête-à-tête done for this decade.

Chapter 38

Gemma

Jean-Paul Sartre said: 'Hell is other people'. But he was wrong. Hell is actually a public speaking course in a forgettable conference room in Haydock, in which I am standing before seven strangers to read out the words to 'Wee Willy Winkie'.

I've only reached the second line before my hands start leaking sweat, my throat constricts and I get tunnel vision each time I make eye-contact with Adrian, the boss of a company that sells vertical blinds for conservatories.

My arms are by my side because I mustn't fidget – fidgeting, according to my notes, seems to be akin to satanic worship, and I'm trying my utmost to do as the public-speaking tutor says. Project. Relax. Deliver the words *WITH FEELING*, which makes *me* feel like I'm being asked to do my third take in a porn film.

'Are the children in their bed, for it's past ten o'clock?' I conclude, as majestically as I can. I look up hopefully.

Adrian from the blinds company is fixing his comb-over. Jill, the ophthalmology manager next to him, is texting under her folder. The others are either looking out of the window, eyeing up the refreshments table or, in the case of Bob the NHS Manager, fast asleep.

'Hmm.' Our tutor, Rosie, rubs her chin, perplexed. 'Not quite got it, have you, Gemma?'

When Rosie introduced herself, I warmed to her immediately. She's a round-cheeked, ruddy-complexioned, twenty-first century version of Mrs Beeton, with a booming voice and hand gestures that make her look like she's conducting an 80-piece orchestra.

She told us we'd be safe with her, that she'd take me and the seven other hapless delegates under her wing. I had dreams of addressing the crowd like Hillary Clinton by the end of the day and so far we've been treated to a wealth of insider tips, including learning the first line of your speech by heart so you don't have to look down, to – her ultimate tip – checking your flies are closed before approaching a lectern.

To be fair to Rosie, everyone else has shown improvement.

But for some reason, while her words are going into my ears and I am completely au fait with the *theory*, none of it is translating into reality. Which, rounded cheeks or not, is pissing Rosie off no end.

'I'm sorry to sound exasperated, but everyone else has got

this,' she huffs. 'Do you remember what I said about delivering *with feeling*? That's the point of us using a nursery rhyme. Pretend you're saying this to a child. You've got to entertain them, beguile them. Don't worry about what anyone thinks. Sound like a loon, we won't care!'

I nod sullenly, despising myself and my abject failure to beguile anyone but the fly that keeps hovering around my ear. 'I'm so sorry. I don't know what's the matter with me.'

She purses her lips as if she'll let me off this once. 'How about we take it from the top?'

I'd hoped to be able to sit down and eat my caramel wafer biscuit in the corner actually. Instead I nod, pick up the words to 'Wee Willie Winkie' with trembling hands and remind myself that there are only seven people here. And it's only a nursery rhyme.

I clear my throat. I pretend I'm all alone, there's nobody else here, and all I've got to do is deliver these funny little words – *with feeling* – about a weird bloke in his pyjamas running round town and waking kids up. Easy.

I'm about to begin, when I have a small moment of inspiration. I think back to the panto my dad took me to see when I was about seven, *Jack and the Beanstalk*. I think of how over the top they all were, how animated. The inflection in certain words, the ups and downs of their voices. *That's* what she's talking about! That's how I'm going to give it all I've got!

'Wee Willy Winkie RUNS through the town.' Pause for

effect. 'UPSTAIRS! Downstairs. In his nightgown.' Breathe. 'RAPPING at the windows. CRYYYING through the locks! Are all the children in their beds? It's PAST eight O'CLOCK!'

I restrain myself from taking a bow and look up breathlessly. 'Better,' Rosie concedes flatly. 'Right, who's next?'

I sit down, deflated, as a text arrives. I'm supposed to have turned off my phone, but what the hell. If Jill the ophthalmology manager can get away with it, why shouldn't I? I surreptitiously pull the phone out of my bag and hold it by the side of my chair as I glance at it. It's from Alex.

I don't care what you're doing, your afternoon CANNOT be worse than mine. x

I compose a text back.

Public speaking course in a crap hotel. Bloke next to me has B.O., there's no aircon & tutor is a Nazi.

He texts back immediately.

You win x

I'm in the kitchen that night, practising what I've learned. It actually sounds better, astonishingly so. I prance round the room, employing the optimum number of hand gestures, doing my best to channel some stature. I make eye-contact with my reflection and begin a speech I fantasise would bring down the house.

'Baa Baa black sheep, have you any WOOL!'

'Have you been drinking, Gemma?' I rotate in shock. Belinda is in her silk dressing gown, an oversized roller propped on her fringe.

'No. I was practising—'

'You don't need to explain! Talking to yourself is usually the sign of someone highly creative.'

'Really?'

'Or clinically insane.'

'There's only one person around here in danger of fitting that description,' mutters Flossie, walking in. She's been for a swim in the pool and is wearing a huge, terry towelling robe and a cap on her head. 'How was your day at work, Gemma?'

'Oh, not bad, thank you, Flossie. I was on a public speaking course because I've got to deliver a big presentation in a few weeks. It's not really my cup of tea.'

'You're nervous?' she asks.

'Is it that obvious?'

'Just a guess,' she shrugs. 'Try not to be though. Work is important, obviously. But nothing's worth losing sleep over.'

Flossie stays to chat for a couple of minutes before heading back to her flat, at which point I casually ask Belinda about the reason behind her beautifying session.

'Are you going out tonight?'

'Um . . . yes. To Il Buco,' she says quietly.

'With James?'

She nods. 'He wants to get to grips with my trusses.'

'On a Friday night?'

'He's very dedicated.'

'Are you sure it isn't a . . . date?'

Her lips twitch as she is poised to deny it, then changes her mind. 'I don't know. Do you think it might be?' she asks, like a cheerleader who's been invited to the prom.

'Yes,' I say.

'Oh God,' she replies, her mind clearly going into overdrive.

'He's lovely, Belinda. I'm sure you'll have a whale of a time.' She looks uneasy. 'Is everything okay?'

'Of course. But it's *not* a date – honestly. Right, I'd better run. Give Dan a kiss for me, won't you?'

Belinda being out means that, for the first time in weeks, Dan and I have some romantic action that amounts to more than a fumbling quickie. It turns out it was about time, judging by the mild astonishment on his face afterwards. 'You were a bit . . . sprightly,' he comments as I snuggle into his arms, post-coitally fuzzy.

And although he's only joking I suddenly feel paranoid about whether he'll read something into the upsurge in my libido.

'I needed the exercise,' I reply. 'I wonder how long we've got before your mum comes home?'

'No idea,' Dan says, reaching over to open the door slightly so we can hear her come in. 'Where'd she go anyway?'

'Out with James. I must admit I was jealous – they were off to that new restaurant in Nantwich. It feels like we're never going to eat out again. Or drink out. Or just . . . GO out. God, I hate being broke.'

I pull a sulky face for comic effect. But Dan looks entirely serious as he lowers his eyes and says, 'Yes. Me too.'

That Saturday, Dan and I are finishing breakfast in the kitchen as one of Belinda's dance lessons is finishing in the conservatory. We're dragged in for an impromptu twenty-minute session ahead of Flossie's birthday party, and Dan does his best to pretend he doesn't enjoy it. He fails miserably at this charade, especially when Bobby suggests trying a lift and Dan has several hilarious (not) opportunities to pretend to drop me.

Afterwards, he goes for a swim while I dig out my interiors folders, deciding that another Saturday night in might be a good opportunity to finally grill my boyfriend about his opinion on the living-room décor.

Only he bursts through the door with other ideas. 'I've made a decision,' he announces. 'We're going out tonight.'

I open my mouth to argue. 'Don't argue,' he says. 'This is on me. And I won't take no for an answer.'

Chapter 39

Dan

Mum gives us a lift to Liverpool. I'd forgotten what she was like behind the wheel of a car until now. She leans forward in her seat, clutching the steering wheel like it's the reins of Santa's sleigh, employing her horn with wild abandon and hovering at clear junctions for minutes, before tootling across at the exact moment an articulated lorry thunders towards us.

When she drops us off on the Dock Road and we walk into the city centre, it's clear that Gemma is determined to understand how I can afford this night out. The money is playing on her mind more than anything else: more than any food she's about to eat or fun she might be about to have.

And it's the fact that we can't just enjoy a night on the tiles that makes me realise I've made the right decision, even if I'm not in a position to let Gemma into it yet.

I press my lips against her hand. 'Don't ask me about it again, Gemma. Let's just enjoy tonight, for old times' sake.'

'You make it sound like we don't have good times together now,' she responds defensively. 'We have a great relationship, don't we?'

I have no idea where this has come from, but I gave up trying to analyse these sorts of questions years ago. 'I just can't stomach another ready meal, that's all, Gemma. And it was that or my mum's Balti chicken roulade,' I grin.

I take her to the Salt House Bacaro, a buzzy little place in Castle Street, without a table to spare. We eat like kings, devouring ludicrous amounts of cheese and wine.

All that matters is that we have good, not-so-wholesome fun together. I want her to let down her hair, unfurrow that brow; I want to light up that face again and make her laugh until she can't move.

'How's Pete's love-life?' she asks, as a waitress removes our plates. 'I could never work out why he dumped Sarah. She was lovely.'

'She was horrendous,' I put her straight. 'Miss Piggy on acid.'

She tuts. 'You are vile.'

'Anyway, he's in love with Jade, he had to dump her.'

'Oh, still? God loves a trier, I suppose.'

Pete and Jade's trips to the coffee shop finally resumed this week after he built up the courage to ask her to come again. It's not entirely clear if it was his sparkling personality or the doughnuts that were the draw.

'Do you want a coffee?' I ask Gemma. And when she shakes her head, I say, 'Let's get out of here then. We're going on an adventure.'

It's a blistering summer's night, with a clear black sky, dredged with stars. I love walking through the city on nights like this. Past the hipsters spilling out of Camp & Furnace, students making the floors shake in Magnet, girls dressed like birds of paradise in the glare of Concert Square. The streets are incandescent, a playground for grown-ups.

I take Gemma's hand and we head up Hanover Street, dodging a couple locked in a kiss as I realise too late that we've slid into the throng of a hen party. My arse is smacked, and I'd obviously feel violated, if my girlfriend wasn't informed with a wink that she's a lucky lady.

She laughs and shouts, 'I know!' before teasing me: 'I take it you paid her for that?'

'I'm irresistible to all women, Gemma, I thought you knew. But, yeah, the fiver helped.'

We head towards our destination, the courtyard of Our Lady and St Nicholas Church, a secret corner that tonight belongs to us. I can hear Gemma breathing as we step into the garden, a lush green carpet flanked by extravagant architecture.

In the days when I worked in the city, I'd come here at lunchtime and laze in the sun with a cold beer from Ma Boyles Oyster Bar. It's great in the daytime, but its real magic is after dark, when it becomes a floodlit lagoon of calm.

Gemma lets go of my hand and walks towards the Blitz commemoration at the front of the church, the statue of a boy running up a spiral staircase, his mother reaching out.

She runs her fingers across its cast-iron curves as moonlight shimmers in her eyes. I urgently want to kiss her. But she drops her bag on the grass and flops down on her back. I lie next to her and reach for her hand as the sky swells above us.

'They do this in *Twilight*,' she tells me. 'I just realised and thought you must think I was being corny.'

'I've managed to never see *Twilight*,' I remind her. 'I still think you're corny though.'

I roll over on my side and kiss her, her face in my hands. We lie there until our clothes are damp and there are grass stains on our knees. And until the words I've said over and over, supposedly in jest, rise into my head again.

I know that if I say them, she'll grin and tell me to bugger off, a joke in which I've been complicit for years.

But tonight, I need to repeat them until the truth is unavoidably clear: Gemma, I want to marry you. And I'm for real.

Chapter 40

Gemma

I'm aware of my phone beeping in my back pocket but don't want to ruin the moment by reaching for it. Then a lightning bolt flashes through my mind: what if it's Alex again? If it is, and I don't delete it now, there's every chance that at the first moment I take my phone out, Dan will see his name.

Dan opens his mouth to say something and it beeps again. I cannot ignore it. 'Sorry!' I cry, sitting up so I'm out of his line of sight as I look at the phone.

It's from Belinda.

DNT NO WOT 2 DO!

I've noticed that she employs her own version of textspeak when communicating via mobile. I have no idea if she's trying to be down with the kids, but you'd need to be an Enigma-codebreaker to work out what she's on about. I scroll down.

THINK AM FALLING 4 JAMES. BUT CAN'T BCOS OF
BOOK! PUBLISHERS WILL HIT ROOF! ARRGH! ADVICE
REQUIRD PLS.

I look at it, wide-eyed.
'What is it?' Dan asks.
I'm about to respond, when another text arrives.

WD APPRECIATE YR DISCRETION. I.E. DO NT
DISCUSS WITH DAN.

'Sorry,' I tell him. 'It's just a minor emergency. Nothing important. Do you mind if I reply?'
He hesitates. 'Go ahead.'
I lean over and, making sure he's gazing at the stars and not my message box, start typing.

Are you with him now? If so, enjoy the evening then
consider your options tomorrow. Will have a proper
chat with you as soon as poss. X

I turn back to Dan.
'Right! I'm all yours,' I grin.

He looks at me oddly for a minute, as if he's got something he needs to get off his chest.

'What is it?' I ask.

'I . . . nothing,' he says finally, standing up and offering me his hand.

Our walking tour across the city continues, a Famous Five-style adventure that takes in cathedral graveyards, Liverpool One, Bold Street. We end up in Fleet Street, at Motel Bar, a quirky little place dotted with arty neon and Americana.

We buy scotch and soda and sit at the bar. 'I miss the city on nights like this,' I say, leaning woozily into his arms.

A few seconds later, he's looking at me strangely again.

'So when are you going to marry me?' he asks, draining his Scotch.

I laugh. 'You'd get a bloody big shock one day if I said, "Oh, okay, go on then".'

He looks strained as he replies, 'You're right, I probably would. How did that even become our standing joke anyway?'

'We were eating chips on the beach in Cornwall,' I remind him. 'I'd let you dip yours into my ketchup and you said, "I might have to ask you to marry me for that" or words to that effect.'

'I knew you were something special right from the beginning,' he jokes.

'No, you bloody didn't,' I contradict him. 'You disappeared out of my life for six whole weeks. You're lucky I'm still speaking to you at all, frankly.'

When she brings it up tonight, I deal with it in the same way as always. With the brutal honesty and regret I've felt ever since.

'It was the worst decision I ever made. And that's why I'm never going to let you out of my sight again.'

She looks at her drink. Then she raises her eyelashes and leans in to kiss me on the lips, drunkenly, softly. 'I know.'

Chapter 41

Dan

The morning after that big night out with the Emerson Lisbon gang, I woke up thinking of Gemma. I had fur on my tongue and dehydration in my bones and it was 11.15 a.m. and I was still moderately trashed. But! The existence of Gemma Johnston was going to make everything all right again.

I'd enjoyed the night before enormously. I can't deny I was concerned that getting serious with someone might change all this, because even though I'd only known her a few days, there was no doubt that that was happening. But overwhelmingly, I wanted to be with her, to feel her skin beneath my fingers, to bury my head into her neck.

I was poised to text her when the doorbell rang. I waited, hoping that Jesse would answer. It rang again. I dragged my corpse of a body out of bed, threw on my jeans and stumbled to the door.

There he was. The man whose absence had planted a chip on my shoulder the size of a container ship and who, despite my determination not to give a toss, I was queasily happy to see.

Dad was wearing a suit that no doubt cost more than I'd spent on my entire wardrobe. Yet the clothes and the man never looked as if they belonged together; it was like looking at a bin man driving a special edition Bugatti.

The five o'clock shadow and yard-brush hair never bothered the women who surrounded him; there were scores of them. I was constantly being told that he had 'something about him', that he had *charisma*, and if I'm honest with myself, I hung on his every word just as the others did.

'Son, how are you? Good night out? You look a bit chemically inconvenienced,' he grinned, throwing his arms around me.

He was inside my flat before I could work out how he'd got there.

'I didn't even know you were back, Dad.'

'It's a flying visit,' he replied, stretching out on the sofa. Even the way he sat reminded everyone how big his personality was: arms out, foot crossed over the knee, effectively claiming as much space as he could. 'I'm returning to New York tonight. Sorry I didn't give you any warning. Hope you haven't got a woman in here?' he glanced round the place.

I was suddenly glad Gemma wasn't present.

I took a hot, groggy shower while he disappeared into the kitchen and started cobbling together a fry-up with the provisions he'd brought with him (he'd always been a better cook than Mum). 'A man needs a full stomach before making any big decisions,' he said cryptically as I sat at the table and picked up my fork.

'What do you mean?'

'I'll come to that. Let's have some father and son time first.'

Half an hour passed before we got to the crux of the matter, underlining that he was in charge. Before then, he asked about my job, my volunteer work and Mum. Unlike her, he's always been disconcertingly relaxed on the subject of their marriage, which he discussed with the same happy-go-lucky shrug with which one might recall an ill-advised one-night stand. We talked about me mainly, a con trick he's always managed to pull off: for an ego-maniac he puts on a good show of being interested.

'Son, I'll get to the point,' he said finally. 'There's an opening at my firm in acquisitions. Well paid. Excellent prospects. Awesome boss,' he grinned. 'And that's before we get on to the office in downtown Manhattan.'

I looked at him blankly. 'And, of course, the once-in-a-lifetime opportunity to work with your old man.'

Comprehension slammed into my brain. 'You mean you want *me* to take this job?'

He smiled, then laughed. 'Why not? You've got an Economics degree. You're a smart kid.'

'But … I live here. I've got a job here. I've got the Chapterhouse Centre.'

'Which pays sod all.' He caught my expression. 'Not that it doesn't sound interesting. I mean, it does. I can see why someone like you might want to do it. You're a helper,' he said, as if this was an affliction on a par with a persistent fungal infection.

At this stage, he wasn't winning me over.

'Son, let me level with you.' He began clearing away the plates. 'I've been thinking lately about the fact that we haven't had much of a relationship.' He'd said this before, as if every so often guilt pronged at him, like he'd stood on a piece of Lego with no socks on. 'And I thought: I want to do something for Dan. I want to spend time with him. I don't want us to live these separate lives and—'

'You could just respond to some emails. You don't need to go as far as inviting me to work in New York.'

He sat down and leaned forward in the chair. 'A young guy like you and New York – you're made for each other. I'm actually jealous.' He appeared to mean it. And the flash of excitement in his eyes was infectious. 'You, me, Manhattan. If we can make it there, we can make it anywhere,' he trilled, laughing. 'Come on, Danny. What do you say?'

I protested, but the truth was if he'd asked me three weeks

earlier I wouldn't have hesitated. I'd been to New York once and, like every other twenty-something man, convinced myself it was my spiritual home.

Yet I did hesitate. Not because I thought then that I'd met the woman of my dreams and that I was destined to spend the rest of my life with her. At that stage, I couldn't have articulated that much.

I knew she was something special, but special enough to turn down an opportunity like this? I wasn't clever enough to realise that she was. After a long discussion, I told him I would think about it.

'Not too long. Your flight's the day after tomorrow.'

'I can't go the day after tomorrow. I've got a job. A flat. A ...' Did I have a girlfriend? I had no idea. Not that he'd have cared.

He threw an airline ticket on the table, grabbed his coat and left with three words lingering in the air, along with the aroma of leftover sausage fat: 'See you Stateside.'

I can't remember actively making the decision to go. It was as if I sleepwalked through the next forty-eight hours, propelled by Dad's insistence that I couldn't turn down an opportunity like this, which, on paper, was hard to argue with.

Jesse went apeshit when I said I was going, despite the fact that I promised to continue paying two months' rent. And Chris Deayton wasn't overly impressed when I handed in my notice at Emerson Lisbon either – though, as I'd predicted, I was put on immediate gardening leave so I was free to leave the country.

I drove my stuff to Mum's to face the inevitable fallout. Actually, that's not strictly fair. She recognised why I'd be tempted by New York, but worried about me putting so much at stake on one of my dad's whims, rightly, as it turned out.

More than anything though, was this: I kept thinking about Gemma. She'd texted a couple of times during the day and I'd been deliberately elusive. I had no idea how I was going to tell her. Doing it by text would've given me a prime slot in the wankers' hall of fame, no matter how short the time I'd known her.

I had to go round, explain face-to-face. Part of me, I think, wanted to take one look at her and decide I couldn't go through with it.

Once everything was ready, I got the bus to Lark Lane and went to her apartment for the first and last time. I stood outside this big old house and rang the bell to her ground-floor flat.

As I waited for a response, it began raining – that fine, misty rain that seeps into your core – as a realisation grew inside me.

I was making an almighty fuck-up.

Maybe.

The rain swelled and thunder cracked above. And, in the absence of being able to make a considered, intelligent decision – or any decision at all – I opted to do this the *Dice Man* way: if she opened the door now, I would stay and make a go of things with her.

I waited on the doorstep for an hour. But she never came.

Considering its size and location, everything about my dad's apartment, except the postcard view, was oddly uninspiring – like a corporate hotel that invests more in its trouser presses than creating an atmosphere.

He wasn't there when I arrived, but he'd arranged for a key to be left with the concierge. I dumped my bag in the spare room, climbed onto the bed and tried to sleep away my misery about what I'd left behind.

The clatter of a fumbled key woke me in the early hours, followed by shrieking laughter, smashing glasses and the vapid throb of music.

I tried to slide back to sleep, but was instead dragged out and paraded by my father in front of seven or eight of his friends. The women wore expensive clothes and had expensive faces. The men were chain-smoking, noisy wannabes who gazed at my dad like he was a cross between Vito Corleone and Santa.

Cringingly, Dad offered me cocaine. When I declined, he laughed, called me an old woman and told me to cheer up.

Obviously, it wasn't his fault I was uncheerupable, but he didn't particularly help that night by making it clear that I was failing on all counts. Failing to talk politics or take drugs with the grown-ups, failing to dazzle with my sparkling personality, a quality he valued above virtually everything.

The last thing I remember before escaping to bed was re-reading a text from Gemma saying she'd tried to phone me but couldn't get through. My head swam as I read it. I thought about phoning her. Yet, no matter how much I regretted my decision the second I got on the plane, I was here now – and besides, it was stupid o'clock in England. So instead, I sent a vague response and slipped into a disturbed sleep, plagued with nightmares and regrets. Which basically set the tone for the next six weeks.

I will fast forward the month of October because it can be summed up with the grim efficiency you might employ to recap a failed military operation. Dad and I fell out on day four when he took me to lunch with some fruitcake whose views were slightly to the right of Vlad the Impaler, but who also – apparently – was *Someone Important*.

I listened as he spouted his repellent views about blacks and gays and single mothers, while glugging 200-dollar wine. Then I expressed an alternative view. Fairly forcefully. I did so with a smile, in the pretence that this was 'healthy debate' but in truth I'd been itching to tear a strip or two off him and that's exactly what I did.

I was angry with the world, reeling from a text sent by

Gemma that morning saying she was deleting my number and never wanted to hear from me again. And I can't deny I took a perverse pleasure in Dad watching me do it, even (or perhaps especially) when he was slapped on the back and told, 'Not exactly a chip off the old block, is he?'

Dad went berserk when we returned to the office, but by then I was in combative mood. He yelled. I yelled back. None of it was pretty. His poor secretary (a surprisingly dumpy woman who he can only have employed to resist the temptation to sleep with) was so stressed you'd think she'd been plugged into a 100-amp fusebox and turned on full.

I apologised later that day and he accepted.

But it had lit the touch-paper to a dozen or more clashes, even when both of us were actively trying to make a go of things. My birthday, in week three of my stay, was a case in point. Dad had forgotten all about it, until he walked in from the office and saw the card from Mum.

He responded by writing me a cheque for $1,000, which was obviously totally over the top and – as I told him – unnecessary. He replied that it came with a condition: I couldn't spend it. I had to *invest* it – in any company I liked. He couldn't even just give me a birthday present without challenging me to prove myself.

I was tempted to invest the lot in the woman who wanted to market a brand of upmarket eyelash-curlers for dogs. Or the guy who'd written a pre-school book called *Billy the Badass,* about a convicted felon's adventures in an Alabama correctional facility.

But the ridiculous thing is, over the next few days, I put serious research into it. I didn't want a faceless multinational concern, I wanted something small, run by passionate people – the sort of thing I could really get behind. So I chose 45 Music, a hard-working independent record label that had signed a variety of up-and-coming bands, the sort of stuff I loved listening to.

While it wasn't quite *Billy the Badass*, there's little doubt I was basically giving it to them as a gift; there was no chance I'd get a return. But it felt like a sound decision, to give an honest break to a bunch of guys who genuinely deserved it.

Dad failed to share my enthusiasm. He put his head in his hands, shook it in despair and told me he might as well have just set fire to the money.

I won't go on about the profusion of other matters over which we fell out, except to say that the whole débâcle ended six weeks after I arrived when I announced, to everyone's abject relief, that I belonged in the UK.

Going back was bittersweet.

On the positive side, I landed a full-time job, one they actually paid me for, at the Chapterhouse Centre. I also persuaded Jesse to let me back, after his typically relaxed attitude to finding a replacement flatmate meant he'd never got round to doing so.

Despite all this, there was a Gemma-shaped hole in my life, one that ripped me in two every time I thought about her.

Occasionally, out of nowhere, I'll think about that time, when I nearly lost her, and the reminder of it grabs me by the throat. I've always felt ashamed of choosing my father over her. And even more ashamed that I wasn't big enough to find the words to phone and explain, even when I thought I'd never see her again.

My hangover is better than I deserve the following morning, though Gemma is making the sort of noises you'd hear in a vet's waiting room. I can only conclude she's suffering.

I blink open my eyes as I'm overcome by the effect this physical state has had on my sex-drive. There's no poetic way of saying this so I'll come straight out with it: I am raging.

I glance at Gemma and cuddle up to her, wondering optimistically if Mum might have gone out. My answer comes in the form of a rousing version of Maroon 5's 'Moves Like Jagger', as usual with her unique interpretation of the lyrics.

'*OOH I GOTTA MOVE MY JACKET, GOTTA MOVE MY JACKET ... I GOTTA MOO-OO-OO-OO-OO-OO-OO-OO, MOVE MY JACK-ET.*'

Gemma opens her eyes and smiles. 'You'd better go and have a cold shower.'

'I can't wait to get out of this place,' I sigh, pulling her into me. 'What's the latest on the repairs? Shall I phone Rich today?'

'I spoke to him on Friday,' she replies. 'They're almost done. The dampproofing's completed and they're just waiting for the plaster to dry before repainting it.'

'It should be all systems go then, shouldn't it? I mean, the budget is largely on track – with the exception of last night. Surely we should be in within a month?'

She suddenly looks a bit green.

'You okay?' I ask.

She sits up. 'I can't handle drinking any more, that's all.'

'You were an absolute disgrace,' I grin, leaning over to her and sinking into a kiss.

But after a moment, she pulls away and throws off the covers to get out of bed.

I study her for a second. 'You are still a hundred per cent certain about Pebble Cottage, aren't you?'

She freezes, just for a heartbeat, but long enough to make it look as though she has to think about her answer.

'Of course! It's the hangover making me feel funny, that's all.'

Then she grabs her dressing gown and dives out of the room before I get a chance to work out why I'm not sure I believe her.

Chapter 42

Gemma

I've never been a burying-my-head-in-the-sand sort. I've always prided myself on my pragmatism, my ability to grab an issue and grapple it to the ground through a combination of cognitive effort and colour-coded Post-it notes.

Yet my inner turmoil is at boiling point on two big issues I put behind me last night, thanks to the fuzzy optimism of freshly quaffed alcohol in my system.

One: Why Alex keeps pushing into my head, even when he's not texting me any longer, at least not as much as he was.

Two: How we're going to pay for half of the house repairs, an agreement I made privately with the vendors to spare Dan the worry.

Now that they're almost done, I literally have no plan of action except to watch the bills trickle in and secretly pay them with the money in our house fund which, short of a golden unicorn leading me to a pot of cash at the bottom of the rainbow, will leave a significant shortfall when the full amount is due on completion.

Of course, we still haven't exchanged contracts yet. It should happen in around a week, so I could technically still call a halt to this whole thing right now. But that doesn't feel like an option.

I've started to get this vague sense that Alex and our move to Pebble Cottage are interconnected.

That once we're in the house and our happy future is secured, I'll never even think about Alex again, just as I hadn't for twelve years previously. Not much, anyway.

As Dan heads out to the supermarket to replenish our multitude of Value foodstuffs, I log on to my emails and find myself re-reading the message I wrote to his dad the other day.

Last night, we found ourselves on the subject of his New York disaster, and it reminded me just how badly they'd got on with each other. I can't help thinking my email might have been another one of my bad ideas.

Dear Mr Bushnell,

My name is Gemma Johnston and I'm your son Dan's girlfriend. I'm sorry to contact you out of the blue but I wanted to introduce myself and also to congratulate you. You made one of the best men I've ever met in my life, an accolade I don't bestow lightly.

I know Dan has mentioned a few times how much he'd love it if he could introduce me to you next time you're in the UK. I have no idea when that might be, but if it's any time soon, then please drop me a line as it'd be a lovely surprise for Dan. I know how much he loves and admires you.

With my best wishes,

Gemma

At least he hasn't responded. If that remains the case, I can pretend it never happened.

I'm about to log off, when an email pings into onto the screen. It's from Alex.

Gems – how's it going? Forgive the intrusion, but given that we're no longer going to be seeing each other in the flesh, I wondered if you'd consider being Facebook friends instead? Or do you prefer to remain a woman of mystery? There's a link to my profile below if you feel inclined to find me. It's safe to say I'd *probably* respond positively to a friend request from you. But I'm guessing you already knew that ;-)

Alex x

I hold my breath and click on his profile. His settings are public – the direct opposite of mine – so all his pictures are there, for all to see. Or rather, *me* to see. I scroll through them with a pounding heart, filling in the gaps in my knowledge of him.

It's strange looking in on this other life: the house where he lived in Cape Town, the friends he had … and girlfriends too. Because, despite what he says about only having one other serious relationship, it's clear from the women who've tagged him that he hasn't exactly lived a life of monastic restraint.

The albums go back as far as 2007 and I'm pleased to see that he doesn't look good in *all* the pictures – in fact, there are a couple where he's quite obviously caught too much sun and his nose looks like one of Belinda's bacon rashers.

But there's one, buried somewhere in 2009, in which he's in the centre of a group of friends at what looks like a pool party. He's laughing and looking directly at the camera and, before I can even stop myself, a thought pops into my head about whether I can remember what it felt like to kiss him.

'Gemma!' There's a knock at the door.

I log off as quickly as I can, slamming shut my laptop and heading to the door.

When I open it, Belinda is scuttling towards her bedroom, beckoning me in. I dutifully head over. 'Got a min? Dan's out, isn't he?'

I remember her text last night and brace myself.

'Yes, but—'

She hauls me by the arm into her bedroom. I'm hit by that unravelling wonder primary school children get when they catch a glance inside the staff room. It is an exercise in taste, and with the exception of the odd Jo Malone candle and the vast four-poster, surprisingly minimalist.

'I'm sorry about the texts last night. I was feeling a bit lost,' she confesses. 'You haven't mentioned it to Dan, I hope?'

'No,' I promise.

'Or indeed anyone?'

'Not a soul.'

She descends with a forceful plonk on the wicker chair in front of her bay window. 'It goes without saying that I need to end this,' she sighs, circling her middle fingers on her temples until she looks poised to drill a hole in her head. 'I can't possibly publish a book rubbishing the fundamental idea that men and women are compatible at the same time that I embark on a relationship.'

'Is that what it is then, between you and James?'

She looks up. 'I know it looks like that. But despite how enjoyable it is, even I know that I've fallen foul of nature's cruellest psychological trick.'

'What do you mean?'

'I might think, in my weakest moments, that I have feelings for him. But the reality is more complex. Or more simple.'

'Which is?' I ask, bewildered.

'My hormones! They've gone off like an explosion in an HRT clinic. Once they settle down, there'll be nothing left.'

I hesitate, wondering how I should phrase the next sentence. 'What if your feelings for James were real?'

She looks at me as if she's about to put a dunce hat on me and send me to stand in the corner. 'I doubt it, Gemma. There's only one route open to me.'

'Which is?' I ask again.

She answers with a tremble in her voice. 'I need to put the brakes on this before it goes any further. I've got to get rid of him. Tell him that once the pool room's done, that's it.' She looks at her hands.

'Perhaps you can have a chat with your publishers, explain the situation . . .'

'It would be no good, Gemma,' she tells me. 'It's the book or him. And everything is telling me that my career has to come first. I'm going to have to arrange to meet him tomorrow on neutral territory, the Brown Cow or somewhere. Then I'm going to tell him that's it.'

I suddenly wish I could ask Dan's advice about this, rather than adding it to the heap of secrets I'm keeping from him.

She narrows her eyes. 'What is it?'

'Oh . . . nothing.'

'Are those repairs done yet?'

'Just about.' I try to maintain eye-contact with her momentarily – and before I know it she's virtually got me pinned down, with the same look in her eyes as Carrie from *Homeland* after refusing to take her pills.

'What's wrong, Gemma?'

'Nothing at all!' I leap up.

'Now look here. You might be able to pull the wool over Dan's eyes, but—'

'I'd never pull the wool over . . .' but my voice trails off as I realise this isn't a path I want to go down. I put my head in my hands.

'Tell me. I won't tell a soul.'

And so, unable to think of a way out of this, words start spilling out of my mouth. I'd be abysmal in any torture situation. I tell her that I'm worried to death about our financial situation generally. I tell her that I've secretly agreed to pay half of the repairs without having a clue how I'm going to cover the shortfall it leaves. And I tell her that we're racing towards completing on the house sale without any of this being resolved. I obviously keep quiet about Alex – I think that's quite enough to heap on her plate.

She listens silently, taking it all in. It feels strangely cathartic to tell her, but that doesn't change the basic, hideous facts of the matter.

'Here's the solution,' she says. 'Stop worrying.'

This doesn't sound like much of a solution. 'Well, it's a lot of money to us. Money I haven't got. I have no idea how I'm going to break this to Dan.'

'You don't need to break this to Dan. And you don't have to worry about a thing.' I look up. '*I'm* paying for the repairs.'

I shake my head. 'Dan would never accept it, Belinda. You know how strongly he feels about doing all this on our own. I didn't tell you about it because I wanted to get the money out of you. Although it's very good of you to offer. You've been nothing but generous.'

'Gemma,' she begins, 'it would be madness to refuse. Take it. It'll make all your problems go away.'

'But Dan's already refused the money for the deposit and—'

'You're not taking the money for the deposit, just the repairs. That's different.'

I try to think of a compelling argument to continue to say no. I hear the door slam and my heart constricts: Dan's home. I need to get out of here, fast.

'Just take it, Gemma,' she whispers. 'Go on. Say the word now and I'll transfer it into your account this afternoon. As simple as that.'

'Gemma?' Dan calls from downstairs, as blood thunders through my ears.

'Gemma?' repeats Belinda.

'Okay,' I splutter. I run to the door and turn back in time to see her smile. 'And thank you.'

'It's my pleasure. And it's our secret,' she adds, as I feel torn between relief and a new kind of worry.

Chapter 43

Dan

I don't know if it's the strain of the house move, or just living here, but a nagging question finally pushes to the front of my head: is Gemma up to something?

I have this instinctive sense that she's been meeting someone. The evidence isn't exactly conclusive: texts she rushes to open and the panic in her face when she said she'd been in Manchester the other week, something I wouldn't have given a second thought to otherwise.

Yet I trust her completely. Of course I do. So I tell myself to soldier on and forget these moments of doubt that creep up every so often. The same ones I got the first time I realised I never wanted to live without her.

*

The first time I proposed was in Cornwall and I'd have to admit that I hadn't put a vast amount of planning into it. We'd camped overnight in a tiny, moth-eaten tent on an unspoiled site near St Mawes, overlooking the crashing waves of the Roseland Peninsula.

We were at the end of the week and had run out of clothes, forgotten what a real bed felt like and, in my case, was so relaxed I could barely see myself in the mirror for facial hair.

'Don't you love being by the sea?' she said. 'Imagine living this close to it.'

'If I ever become mega-rich and successful, I'll buy you a house by the sea,' I promised.

'It wouldn't have to be the sea,' she shrugged. 'Just somewhere near a bit of water would do. How about one of those million-pound warehouse apartments in Liverpool with a balcony over the river?'

'Right. A dream home with a view, any view. I'll start saving now, shall I?'

When she laughed, a gust of wind blew hair across her cheeks and she shivered. I took her face in my cold hands and kissed her lips.

'I love you, Dan,' she whispered.

And suddenly, saying, 'I love you too,' didn't feel nearly enough to express what I felt. Nothing did. So it was then that the immortal words first slipped from my mouth, words I'd

never even thought about before but which at that moment –
and every day since – felt right.

'Marry me, Gemma.'

She didn't respond at all at first. Her eyes scanned mine,
reading my face as if trying to work out if I meant it. 'I . . . I . . .'
she stammered.

I can't think of a moment before or since when I've felt a
stronger desire to un-say something.

Not because I didn't mean it, but because I wanted her to
say yes so badly that I feared it would destroy me when she
didn't oblige. She was at least polite enough to decline with a
joke, one that stuck and has been repeated at least a hundred
times since.

I often wonder if I could twist her arm one day; in moments
of weakness or paralytic drunkenness I've come close to asking
her for real.

But I know it would only end in the same excruciating way
as in Cornwall, which is why I tend not to go there. So why
do I still keep the diamond ring I bought three weeks after that
day, hidden in the 'important stuff' box in my bedroom? The
ring that she came so close to finding when she was looking for
a pay-slip? Who knows. But it's the closest thing I've got to
proving the insanity of love.

Chapter 44

Gemma

The email lands as I pull up outside the village shop in Buddington following a difficult day after which, despite the budgetary implications, I need wine. I'm getting out of the car, idly flicking onto my phone, when the name Scott Bushnell appears and I scramble back into my seat, slam the door and start reading.

Gemma, what a lovely surprise to hear from you. Dan's told me a lot about you and you're right – a meet-up is long overdue. I'm back and forth to the UK at the moment as I'm in the process of securing a deal, so if you're free next Saturday I'd love to get together. I'll ask

my secretary to book something. Can you suggest
somewhere? I'll obviously come to you.

Kindest regards, Scott Bushnell

My emotions are at odds as I consider this. I'm nervous about
telling Dan about it, but also slightly surprised at how *nice*
Scott sounds. I know it's only a few paragraphs, but after
listening to Dan and Belinda, I'd imagined some sort of mega-
lomaniac.

It strikes me, self-indulgently perhaps, that maybe all he and
Dan needed to rekindle their relationship was someone reaching out to him. I suddenly feel quite optimistic as I put away
my phone and step out of the car again.

I can't tell you exactly what makes my eyes lift to the
entrance of the Brown Cow pub at the moment a couple fall
out of it.

It's only as giggles drift over the shrubbery and across the road,
that my eyes spring back and register that it's Belinda and James.
Judging by the fact that they're all over each other, her intention
to dump him doesn't appear to have quite gone according to plan.

I dart into the off-licence and emerge with the cheapest
bottle of plonk I can find, noting that the lovebirds are still
rooted to the spot. Every time he tries to say goodbye, she
drags him by the lapels and plasters her lips to him as if she's
trying to unblock a toilet with them.

It's only as I'm back in the car and have turned the ignition on that something else captures my attention: a bloke in a blue Mondeo parked on the opposite side of the road taking what must be the world's least interesting photos of the pub wall. Don't get me wrong, the Brown Cow is a nice-looking establishment; olde worlde and pretty, with roses climbing around the door. But he's at such an odd angle, the only thing he'd be able to get in the frame is half a window. And . . .

And Belinda and James.

I hold my breath as my brain attempts to process this information and work out if I've got it right. It's then that I spot the long lens firmly planted on the couple as they walk away. I process the scene – he must be a private detective.

I swing my car into the shop forecourt again and leap out as a red mist overcomes me. I'm across the road and knocking on the window unceremoniously before he gets a chance to move.

He winds down the window. 'Yes?'

I get straight to the point. 'Why are you taking pictures of that couple?'

He frowns. 'Well, they're in a public place, aren't they?'

'Yes, but . . .' Then it slots into place. He's not a private detective. He's a paparazzo.

'Delete those photos or I'll call the police,' I hear myself saying.

'I don't think so,' he says calmly.

'But—'

'Look, this is my livelihood. And I've done nothing wrong.'
My chest reddens. 'Technically, perhaps. But . . .'

'But what?' He looks in the direction of the pub again. 'Oh
God, they've gone now anyway,' he groans as he throws his car
into gear and drives off.

Chapter 45

Dan

I have my key in the front door when Gemma's car hurls down the driveway so fast she sends gravel machine-gunning across the lawn, nearly decapitating several pigeons.

'Come inside, I need to tell you something,' she announces, dragging me in. 'Your mum has been having a . . . *thing* with James.'

The name, clearly, is supposed to mean something.

'The architect!' she hisses.

'Oh.' I let this information sink in. 'Okay. Yes, I knew they'd been to dinner. But . . . a *thing?*'

'A relationship. Almost.'

'She doesn't do relationships,' I tell Gemma.

She raises her eyebrows in a *you-know-nothing* way.

'I'm serious,' I insist. 'I'm not saying she's been celibate forever. I know there have been flings.' The thought makes me want to bring up my lunch. 'None have ever turned into more than that. It'll be nothing.'

'Believe me, Dan, it's something. She's told me as much.'

I let this information filter into my brain and, despite my scepticism, surprise myself by how much I want it to be true. 'Well, if what you're saying is right, then that's great. Really great.'

'It would be, apart from the fact that she's been papped with him,' Gemma replies.

She proceeds to tell me about some bloke she saw taking photos of Mum and James stumbling out of the Brown Cow. It all sounds extremely unlikely. This is my mother and her neighbour we're talking about, not Kim and Kanye.

'Mum's not that famous. Not any more. You must have got the wrong end of the stick.'

The front door opens and Mum bursts in. She has lipstick on her chin, a ladder in her tights and looks as though she's spent the afternoon creating Neknomination videos. Her attempt to walk towards us in a straight line – resulting in a near-dislocation of her shoulder on the banister – confirms my suspicions that she is not sober.

'Belinda,' Gemma begins, 'I saw you and James in the village.'

Mum glares at her, then gestures in my direction with all the subtlety of an air-traffic controller.

'It's okay,' Gemma assures her. 'He knows.'

'Mum, it's fine,' I say. 'I'm glad you've found someone you like. I'm pleased for you.'

She tuts. 'That was what I was worried about. I didn't want you getting too attached to the idea, Dan, not when I've just dumped him.'

Gemma looks sceptical. 'You did it then?'

'I did, yes,' she replies, raising her hand to cover what – horrifyingly – looks like a love bite.

'So – it's over?' Gemma asks.

'Well . . .' she begins. 'Not exactly. We agreed to see each other again tomorrow. It felt so sudden, you see, saying goodbye just like that.'

'Belinda, it wasn't just you and James I saw in the village,' Gemma warns her. 'A photographer with a long lens was taking pictures of you. I think it was for the newspapers.'

My mother's reaction to this can only be compared to the red line in a cartoon thermometer, increasing in speed before it finally explodes out of the top.

'NO!'

Gemma nods.

'NOOO!'

'Belinda, I'm so sorry.'

'NOOO! NOOO! NOOO-OOO!'

'Oh God, will you all calm down,' I leap in, taking Mum by the arm as I lead her to the living room. 'I really wouldn't worry about it, Mum. I can't believe that this is going to qualify as news.'

Mum hesitates. 'Do you think?'

'I do. Look, go and run a bath. Relax a little.'

'But I need to get the dinner on. It's spinach-stuffed squid,' she slurs as I wonder if there is any food that sounds less appetising. 'I haven't even done the stuffing yet. The squids are lying in the fridge like six used condoms.'

Gemma and I finally persuade Mum to have a bath while we drive to get a takeaway so she doesn't have to stuff the squid until tomorrow.

'How come you didn't mention that Mum was getting serious with James?' I ask, as I climb into the passenger seat.

'She asked me not to say anything.'

I glance over at her. 'You've been keeping secrets with my mum? I can't tell you the alarm this causes in me,' I smirk.

'It's not like that,' she leaps in, the subtleties of my humour clearly lost.

'Hey, don't worry.' I reach over and clasp her hand. 'I'm just glad it's given her something to distract her energies away from hating Dad.'

She doesn't reply. 'What's up?' I ask.

'Your dad.'

'What about him?'

'Look, I don't know what you're going to think about this. I was in two minds at the very beginning, but it seemed like a good idea at the time. Only then I worried that what I've done was a massive mistake. But it was too late then.'

'Gemma,' I say. 'What *is* it that you've done?'

321

Chapter 46

Gemma

I heard from Rich this morning and the plan is that we will exchange contracts at some point in the next week.

Once that's happened, there is no going back. Pebble Cottage will be ours. For definite.

Which is one of the reasons why I decide, finally, to send Alex a Facebook friend request almost two weeks after he requested I do so. It suddenly struck me that not being Facebook friends felt like I was making far too big a statement about his significance in my life.

I mean, I'm Facebook friends with the office caretaker who retired two years ago, and my mother's second cousin Shirley who lives in Australia and whom I've never met. So why wouldn't I be Facebook friends with Alex unless for some reason I couldn't bear to have updates about what was going on in his life?

Besides, he's continued to text me intermittently and lately those texts have felt less flirtatious and more just friendly.

In the light of this, by continuing to tell him to back off, I'm starting to feel like some sort of egomaniac, as if in my swollen head he's pursuing me like I'm his fair maiden, resisting his advances.

The reality is that they're not advances at all – not for anything other than friendship anyway.

So I click on the button marked 'Send Friend Request' . . . and only then register something near the top of his profile. He was tagged at a restaurant last night by an attractive brunette, next to the words: 'Fourth date!'

I realise my eyes are wide open. Not because I'm surprised he's been dating, but I am mildly taken aback that it's the done thing these days to publicise such things on Facebook after only four dates. Still, she looks nice, I can't deny it: pretty, with hazel eyes and a creamy complexion. I bite my lip.

Obviously, I hope it goes somewhere. I want him to be happy and if it's not going to be with me, then—

What the HELL am I thinking?

Of course it's not going to be with me! Why on earth would it be with me, when I'm settled and about to buy a house with the most gorgeous and wonderful man I've ever met? Unquestionably.

I'm really starting to think there's something wrong with me.

*

Belinda is being interviewed by a journalist from the super-chic, super-stylish Italian version of *Tatler*.

I make this discovery while carrying a Tesco bag full of dirty laundry to the utility room, dressed in ten-year-old sweatpants with an arse so saggy you could bungee jump off a suspension bridge with it.

'I'm a family-orientated woman, as long as you don't consider the nuclear family to be the only relevant institution,' Belinda purrs. The journalist has glossy black hair, razor-sharp lip-liner and a stomach that's been honed to the consistency of an acrylic tennis court. At first glance, I put her at twenty-five, then add another two decades when I get closer.

'Let's move onto your style secrets,' she says.

'Well, I work out every day,' Belinda replies. 'I eat plenty of fresh, wholesome food – cooked by myself – and wash my hair in Stella Artois at least once a month.' She looks up and spots me. 'Here's my daughter-in-law! This is Gemma. We're very close.' She stands and thrusts her arm around my waist.

The journalist's eyes light up. 'Perhaps you'd like to take part in the photoshoot?'

'Oh, no. No, that's not a good idea.' I haven't washed my hair since the day before yesterday and there are only so many miracles dry shampoo can perform before it feels as though there's cement in your roots.

'Oh, go on!' Belinda hoots.

'I couldn't.'

She looks down and sees my bag of laundry. 'What's that?'

I clutch the bag tighter. 'I was putting a quick wash on.'

She places her hands on her hips and says reproachfully, 'You know I'm happy to do that for you both. You're too busy with your jobs.'

'No, honestly, Belinda, it's fine. In fact, I'd prefer it.'

'You're just saying that.' She grabs the edge of my bag.

'I'm not!' I squawk, as she grips on and tugs. I tug back.

'Gemma!' she scolds me. 'This is ridiculo—'

The bag splits entirely open and its contents are catapulted skywards, dirty pants flying around as if a bomb's gone off in a pervert's desk drawer. It all seems to happen in slow motion: confetti of M&S thongs cascading down in a breathtaking radius ... until a sock lands on the head of the lady from Italian *Tatler*.

She sits, blinking in disbelief and distaste. I can hardly blame her, although when I spot the knickers hanging precariously from the spout of the kettle, I can't help thinking she got off lightly.

An hour later, somehow, I am reclining by the swimming pool, dressed in a kaftan patterned with miniature pineapples and make-up so heavy I feel as if my face is melting.

'I really don't think I should be photographed like this,' I whinge. 'I haven't shaved my legs or done a pedicure for ages. I was planning to do one today.'

'Don't worry,' Belinda says dismissively. 'They'll Photoshop your nail polish on. That's right, isn't it?' She turns to the photographer. 'Photoshop?'

He nods.

'Becoming quite the techy these days, aren't I?' she grins.

Belinda is positioned on a recliner, while I am shunted above and instructed to pretend to give her a motherly shoulder massage. It all feels quite, quite wrong – and that's before Dan appears at the door and pulls a face like he's walked in on an orgy.

'What's going on?'

'I didn't realise you were home!' Belinda exclaims, delighted. 'Let's have a family shot.' She beckons him towards us.

'Oh, I don't think so, Mum,' Dan says softly, as terror blazes in his eyes. 'I'd love to, but I don't have time. Gemma . . . we're going to be late.'

I spot my opportunity and make my excuses.

I throw off the kaftan as soon as I get upstairs, leap in the shower and afterwards attempt to find something more suitable to wear. I'm not entirely sure what that is. I've never met a boyfriend's semi-absent father so am unclear about the etiquette.

I do know, however, that lunch is at the River restaurant in the Lowry Hotel in Manchester after his secretary phoned and asked us to move the venue to fit in with his meetings. Equally, I know that this is posh.

I've never been, but I peeked at the menu online while she

was on the phone and had to quell my palpitations at the prices. His secretary could sense my unease and said she was sure Mr Bushnell would foot the bill. I can't pretend I'm not mightily relieved about that.

The important thing though is that it's finally happening – I'm getting to meet him. And, after a bit of persuading, I can tell Dan's excited about the prospect.

'You look really gorgeous,' I say, tingling with nerves.

'Just fancied wearing a proper shirt for a change.' He's always feigned nonchalance badly.

I stand on my tiptoes and kiss him on the lips. 'Are you okay about this?' I ask.

He hesitates. 'I'm not worried about what he'll think of *you*. Only about what you'll think of *him*.' He begins tying a knot in his tie. 'I just hope he doesn't try and flirt with you. I may have to stab him with a dessert fork.'

'I'm intrigued about what I'll make of him after hearing all the stories.'

'It's possible what you've heard will have a converse effect. You'll get there and think: this guy's not a monster, he's good fun! Which he is. Despite everything, you'll find him entertaining. If he turns up.'

'His secretary said he wouldn't miss it for the world.'

When we're dressed and ready, we make our way downstairs and meet Belinda emerging from the pool room. 'I'd have sent a gift along, but Sainsbury's were all out of arsenic,' she says.

I laugh nervously. 'See you later, Belinda.'

'Bye, Mum,' Dan says, then he turns back and gives her a big, reassuring hug.

We arrive at the car park of the Lowry a minute after 1 p.m. and pull in between a Ferrari and a BMW. I'm relieved that the Fanny Magnet is still being held at Her Majesty's Pleasure. The hotel is of the large, glitzy variety, with a vast marble lobby that sweeps up a curved staircase onto a mezzanine area. Dan clutches my hand as we head up the steps into the bar and are greeted by an affable, softly spoken maître d'.

'Good afternoon, madam, sir.' He nods at us both. 'Do you have a reservation?'

'We're booked in under the name of Scott Bushnell,' I reply. 'He might already be here.'

The maître d's eyes flick over his file. 'Mr Bushnell isn't here yet, but I can take your coats and show you to your table. You can wait for him there, if you'd like?'

I glance at the door, hoping he arrives soon just to put Dan out of his misery.

The restaurant is bright and elegant, with pale stems of aga-panthus in oversized crystal vases, tables dressed with lush white linen. We are seated in the best booth, at the pinnacle of the room. I convince myself I'm entirely at home until I glance at the menu and am reminded that I should really be in the back washing dishes.

We order drinks and make enough small talk to distract us from the wait. Yet, as time ticks on and there's no sign of Dan's dad, my stomach begins to churn. I gave him my mobile number to text in case there was a hold-up, but it's remained resolutely silent.

A waiter appears to offer us something to eat and replenish our drinks. Twenty-five minutes pass and Dan is starting to get exasperated. He steps outside to try and call his dad, but returns a minute later saying his phone went straight to voicemail.

'Maybe I should try his office in New York,' I suggest, checking my phone again.

'There's no point – his PA won't be there on a Saturday.'

I release a long breath and refuse to say the words out loud, to acknowledge what I'm already suspecting: he's stood us up.

'Mr Blackwood.' Dan looks up as the maître d' addresses him. 'Your father has phoned to send his apologies. He's running late but is on his way. He's suggested that you order lunch and he'll join you as soon as he gets here. He added that he'd be picking up the bill.'

We exchange glances. 'Thanks,' Dan says, clearly relieved.

'Why didn't he just phone one of us?' I ask.

Dan looks at his phone. 'I've got a missed call. He clearly tried to. The reception's not great so he obviously didn't get through.'

We order a luscious lunch: hand-dived scallops and Parma ham & viejo goat's cheese, venison with chicory marmalade and Goosnargh duck breast.

'This could be the best-case scenario,' Dan says. 'We eat like kings and only have to put up with my dad for ten minutes at the end.'

'Sorry, but I'm looking forward to meeting him now,' I grin.

'I can't deny it – I'm looking forward to it too.'

We devour the first course, then the second and before we know it, the waiter is offering us dessert. My waves of unease return with a crash.

'This is getting ridiculous,' Dan mutters.

'Look, the fact that he's told the hotel that he's on his way must mean he'll be here sooner or later.'

A text pings on my phone. I take it out of my bag – two and a half hours after we got here. And I know that Dan can tell from my face what it says.

'He's not coming, is he?'

I swallow, barely able to believe how casually he conveyed the message:

Gemma, sincere apologies, but something came up
and we'll have to adjourn our meeting until another
time. Kind regards, Scott.

'I don't believe it.' Dan throws his napkin on the table.

'Neither do I,' I mumble. 'I'm so sorry. I shouldn't have doubted what you said about him.'

'And *I* shouldn't have thought for a second this would've turned out any other way.'

We stand up to leave and ask the maître d' for our coats. 'Certainly, sir. I will bring over the bill.'

We exchange glances. 'We thought Mr Bushnell was picking that up,' Dan says.

The maître d' looks embarrassed. 'He said to pass on the message to you that he would do so when he arrived. But given that he *hasn't* arrived – well, there is still the issue of the bill. I'm sorry, sir.' He's clearly sympathetic, but someone needs to pay.

'It's okay,' Dan sighs, taking out his wallet to cough up for the most expensive, delicious and disappointing lunch of our lives.

Outside, Dan is utterly deflated. And I feel terrible.

'I don't know what to say,' I tell Dan, as we head to the car. 'I thought I was doing the right thing. I should've kept out of it. It's all my fault.'

He takes a moment to respond to the last sentence. 'Gemma, this is not *your* fault. It's his.' He puts the keys in the ignition and starts the engine. 'He's spent a lifetime making me feel like that,' he says, putting the car in reverse. 'I couldn't bear it if he succeeded in doing it to you too.'

'I insist on paying you back for that lunch.'

'Don't be silly.'

'I'm not. The most frustrating thing is that he's sent you to this really expensive restaurant knowing you'd never be able to afford it. Did he do that on purpose?'

'I'm sure it wasn't calculated. He just can't remember what it's like to be broke.'

'Still, I insist on paying. You can't afford this.'

His jaw tenses. 'I can,' he replies, driving out of the car park.

'I know how much you earn, Dan,' I say, trying to be tactful. 'I also know that we're buying a house that's going to stretch you so far beyond your means it'll make your ears bleed. I'll put the cash in your account this afternoon.'

'The money will be fine,' he says shiftily. I realise that there's more to this than he's telling me.

'Have you robbed a bank or something?' I enquire.

He briefly catches my eye as we pull up at a set of lights. 'No. But I have got a new job.'

My mouth makes a shape as if I'm trying to swallow a doughnut whole. 'When were you going to tell me this?'

'I only found out yesterday.'

'Then why didn't you tell me yesterday?'

'I didn't have a chance.'

I shake my head incredulously. 'Well, what is it?'

'It's working for Emerson Lisbon.'

'Your *old* job?'

'It's a step up from that. I'd be starting on more than three times the salary I earn at the Chapterhouse Centre.'

I sit back and take in this information. It makes me catch my breath. 'Wow.'

'It's an amazing job. I'm lucky to have the opportunity, especially since I walked away once.' For some reason, I can't bring myself to answer. 'So the lunch is no big deal. In fact, the house will be no big deal. It's all affordable now.'

All I can feel is strangely, weirdly numb. 'The question is though, Dan: do you really *want* this job? You love it at the Chapterhouse Centre.'

'I'm not going to pretend it wasn't a difficult decision, Gemma. But I've made up my mind.'

Sometimes, when Dan says something, you just don't want to argue with him. So I don't. I shut up. And I sit silently, reminding myself that Belinda's donation and this new, if surprising news together mark the end of any doubt about whether we can afford Pebble Cottage.

Returning to his old job will give Dan a secure career path that a man of his intelligence and ability deserves.

But I can't ignore the fact that everything is starting to feel just a little bit wrong.

Chapter 47

Dan

I'm not saying I expected Gemma to react to my job news like the crowds greeted Walter Raleigh's return from the New World. But does it make me sound like a needy son-of-a-bitch to say I expected more than I got? I suppress my irritation as I walk through the city centre the following day, for a meeting at the Brownlow Group GP Practice, which provides medical help for many of our service users, and hear a voice calling my name.

'Dan!' It takes a moment for me to recognise its owner – and her familiar, expansive smile. Though when I first met Tracy Omubo two and a half years ago, when she was twenty-two, she had nothing to smile about. She bounds towards me, her long legs in faded jeans, a flowery rucksack thrown over one shoulder and silver bangles running up her arm. 'Dan, OHMYGODDD! It's been ages.'

'Wow ... Tracy.' I am genuinely astounded by her appearance. 'How are you?'

In the days when Tracy first appeared on my client list, she'd just escaped a violent two-year relationship with a bloke under whose influence she'd become an habitual heroin-user. The boyfriend, who'd hospitalised her several times (twice for suicide attempts) was hard to shake. But the drug was even harder.

Yet, somehow, through sheer, bloody-minded determination – and the same Addaction course I enrolled Sheila on – she kicked it. She was clean by the time I signed her off.

'What are you doing these days?' I ask.

She grins, her eyes glinting. 'I'm at college.'

'Seriously?'

'Yep. Who'd have thought *I'd* become a swot! I'm doing Business Studies, living in a flat just off Smithdown Road with three other girls. I love it.'

Tracy and I are heading in the same direction so we spend ten minutes catching up, until I arrive at my destination. 'This is me,' I say, nodding at the building.

She hesitates. 'It's so brilliant to see you, Dan.'

'You too, Tracy. I can't tell you how proud I am of you.'

She shrugs and smiles and suddenly looks awkward. 'I'll be honest, Dan. I don't know what I'd have done without you.'

I can't shake what Tracy said from my mind as I drive to the office, so much so that by the time I arrive I have to have a word with myself. This is just a job. There are dozens of brilliant people at the Chapterhouse Centre, all making a difference. And nobody can say I haven't done my bit, even if I hate the idea of unfinished business.

Like Sheila. I think she genuinely wants to kick her drug dependency. But after beginning with good intentions, her Addaction sessions tailed off in direct proportion to a particular group of 'friends' reappearing in her life, all of whom are users and fully intend to remain that way.

Deep down, Sheila knows that the key to breaking her cycle is in her own hands. But every time she stumbles, she takes it out on everyone else: Addaction, for holding their sessions a bus ride away; me, for not trying to slip her in the back door of the Kevin White Unit.

But I can't think about cases like hers. Someone else will step in and help her on her path. In the meantime, I need to focus on my own path. And, if I'm ever able to afford the kind of house that would make Gemma and me happy, this is what I've got to do.

Pete's out when I return to the office, so I pull up my chair and start writing my resignation letter. It's short and functional; there seems little point to an alternative.

The door bursts open as I'm printing it off. 'I feel liberated!' Pete declares, as if he's returned from a countryside ramble with no clothes on.

'Why?'

He flips himself into the chair. 'I feel good about myself, reinvigorated. Like a young man again.'

'Been rediscovering your porn collection?' I whip the letter off the printer and fold it up to put in an envelope.

'Crass.'

'So what is it?'

He puts his hands behind his head. 'I no longer have feelings for Jade.'

'I *see*.'

'Don't say it like that.'

'Like what?'

'Like you're Sherlock bloody Holmes uncovering a mystery. It's true. After what happened between us, I did a lot of thinking. I decided to take stock. We're better as friends.'

'But you've been telling me for years you're madly in love with her. Now you've walked in, taken one bite of a Jaffa cake and as far as you're concerned, that's it. This profound, all-consuming devotion I've had to listen to you bang on about has been switched off like the Blackpool lights after Christmas.'

'Good analogy. The difference is, they won't be coming back on next September. Or indeed any September. I'm moving on.'

'If you say so.'

'People do change, you know, Dan. It's all about adapting. I sat up the other night and said to myself: "Jade and I are never going to get together. Am I honestly saying that I can't be happy without her?" The answer is, *of course* I can. I mean, it's like this job. I love it, but if I had to leave for whatever reason, it wouldn't be the end of the world, would it?'

Chapter 48

Gemma

A text comes from Alex on Tuesday morning, just after I've arrived at work.

> I know the answer to this before I even try, but I'm
> going to do it anyway: I won the company raffle –
> dinner for two tonight at a Greek place in
> Manchester. Only I've got no one to go with * sob *
> Will you take pity on me, break the rules and come? x

I peer at the text. Company raffle? Who exactly has a company raffle? I have the same conversation with myself that I've had a lot lately – about whether this constitutes an advance of the non-friendly variety. And despite the cool response I attempt to compose, I secretly know that part of me wants it to be that.

> What about the lady on FB you've been dating? She
> looks LOVELY – take her. Do not blow it with her!

He replies:

> I tried her first but she's going out for her mum's birthday
> x p.s. I can think of no other circumstances in which it'd
> make a woman feel better to be second choice!

> You're right – I do feel oddly better. Still not coming
> though (sorry!) x

> You'd break a man's heart. If you change your mind,
> I'll be at Dimitri's at 8 p.m., alone and weeping into
> my taramasalata. x

I end the call and pick up the phone again, dialling another number altogether – that of Dan's dad, with whom I am appalled.

'Who *are* you trying to get through to?' Sadie asks as I sigh and pick up the receiver again.

'A tosser,' I mutter as the phone rings and, to my astonishment, someone answers.

'Hello? Mr Bushnell?' The line goes dead and I look at the receiver as if it's just farted on me. 'I don't believe this!'

Sadie shakes her head. 'It's a wonder he and Dan are from the same gene pool. Dan's so thoughtful and nice. Still, even accounting for that, you seem very worked up about this. Is everything all right?' The truth is, my head has felt as if it's on a boil wash all morning. 'Is the house sale getting to you?'

'Don't talk to me about the house sale,' I reply. 'We're meant to be exchanging contracts this week, so the deal is finally sealed – but for a reason I can't pin down, it hasn't happened.' Simultaneous pings alert us to a group email that's landed on her computer as well as mine.

Sadie opens it up. 'No team briefing this afternoon. YES! Hang on, where are you going?'

But I already have my coat on. 'Sorry, Sadie. I'll stay late and catch up, I promise.'

'Seriously, Gemma – where?'

'To see a man about a dog,' I reply, as she looks genuinely concerned that I'm off to buy a Chihuahua.

I'm glad I'm wearing heels today. The highest I own. They add to my sense of purpose as I arrive in the reception of the Chester Grosvenor, for if ever there was a day to dabble in power dressing, it's today.

I know that this is where Dan's dad is staying because his

PA mentioned it when she was talking to me. I have no idea if he's still here, or indeed if he remains on UK soil. But I'm about to find out.

'Can I help you?' The reception is manned by a demure, Scandinavian-looking blonde, who gives the impression that she bathes in ewe's milk and the honey of virgin bees every night.

I stand tall in my heels, feeling slightly faint at the pseudo-Bond Girl trick I'm about to attempt. 'One of your guests has been trying to get in touch with me. He's a business contact, but we keep missing each other. Could you see if he's in his room? His name is Scott Bushnell.'

Her expression is motionless. 'Is he expecting you?'

'Oh yes. Like I say, he needs to speak to me. If you could just call him.'

She reluctantly picks up the phone and dials a number, before waiting a moment. 'There's no answer, I'm sorry.'

The likelihood that he'd be at the hotel in the middle of the afternoon always was remote, but at least I know he's still in the UK. Problem is, I don't know what to do now. I was all fired up, ready for my showdown – I'd even rehearsed a speech – and now I've got nowhere to go. 'Thanks anyway.'

'Would you like to leave a message?'

'No, it's fine – oh!' I follow her gaze across the lobby to a man who looks as though he's been dressed by Armani and had his hair done by Ken Dodd. He's striding through the door with a phone plastered to his ear as the ice maiden attempts to catch his attention. He looks more than happy to end the call and give it to her.

'Um, Mr Bushnell, this lady wishes to talk with you. I believe you know each other?'

He turns and looks at me, blankly. I'm clearly entirely unrecognisable from the scores of pictures Dan's tagged me in on Facebook.

'I'm Gemma Johnston.' I shake his hand decisively before he can say anything. 'I wonder if you could spare a couple of minutes?'

He's nothing like I expected. I'd seen the pictures, of course – and heard the history – but somehow he's shorter, less impressive, nowhere near as formidable as I was led to believe.

'I have to be at a meeting three minutes ago, so I'm afraid I can't give you my undivided attention.'

'I just wanted a quick chat about lunch yesterday.'

'Didn't you get my message?' He looks alarmed.

'I got a text, but that was after we'd eaten, and—'

A crinkle appears above his nose. 'Something came up that I couldn't get out of. Look, I'm sorry. I'd like to get to know you better. I know how much you mean to Dan, and obviously you're a very successful and interesting person.' I narrow my eyes, wondering how he's managing to flatter me when

I'm so pissed off. It also strikes me that, contrary to Dan's prediction, he isn't flirting in the slightest. I lower my chin and sniff surreptitiously to check my deodorant hasn't worn off.

'I hope you don't mind me speaking bluntly, but—'

'I don't at all,' he says, holding up both hands like a 'stop' sign. 'But right now, I've got to be somewhere, then this afternoon I'm flying back to the States. So, whatever you want to get off your chest will need to wait. Sorry.' He walks in the direction of the lift and I scuttle after him.

'It's just that . . .'

I step into the lift and a sliver of panic appears on his face. 'You're not pregnant, are you?'

'No!' I reply.

'Getting married?'

'No.'

'About to go to prison?'

'No, nothing like that.' I am feeling ridiculous now. 'I just . . . you're acting like a man who isn't interested in his son. And I'm simply . . . well, I simply wanted to tell you that you *should* be interested in him.'

I'm suddenly both overwhelmed by how much I mean this – and by how much of an idiot I sound. I look up for reassurance, but he couldn't appear less impressed if I'd sung 'The Wheels on the Bus' and got the words wrong.

'Is this all?' He steps out of the lift and I make an unconscious decision to follow him.

'What do you mean, *is this all?*'

'You've come all the way here to stalk me long enough to give me a speech about my son. A son I knew a long time before you did.'

'I'm not stalking! And . . . well, the problem is that he's a son you don't know very well at all, as far as I can see.'

He glares at me with cold eyes as he stops in front of a door. 'Thanks for the pep talk. It was lovely to meet you.' He holds out his hand but I don't shake it.

'I'm not going anywhere.'

'Well, you're not coming in here.' He points to a sign that says *Gentlemen* and, with a thin smile, pushes open the door and disappears inside.

My heart is racing. My thinking isn't entirely straight. I barge in through the door.

'Actually, I am.' I find it impossible to announce this without accompanying it with a pantomime flounce, as if I'm dressed as Widow Twankey and have just caught Wishy Washy trying on my tights.

The two gentlemen at the urinals gasp in stupefaction, complain loudly, then zip up their flies rapidly enough to risk widespread trauma to the groin region.

'Is nothing sacred?' one asks.

'I'm sorry, but this is important. And I didn't look,' I reassure him as he pushes past to leave.

The door of a cubicle clicks closed. I sidle up to it.

'Look, this isn't my idea of a fun afternoon, but you're leaving me with no choice. Mr Bushnell, you left us alone at a restaurant, waiting for hours, before standing us up. That day meant so much to Dan. And me. He really thought this time that you weren't going to let him down.'

'I'm a busy man. He needs to learn to deal with it.'

'He *has* learned to deal with it. That's the problem. Why does it have to be that way? Why can't you just be places when you say you're going to be? Don't you feel any sense of responsibility towards him?'

'He's not four years old!'

'I'm told that things weren't much different when he was that age.' The toilet flushes, he comes out fastening his pants and marches past me to the sink to wash his hands. Next time Dan's scraping around for redeeming features in his father, good personal hygiene might be the best I can offer.

'Look, this isn't *Ally McBeal*,' he scowls. 'It's men only in here. Now get out before I call security.'

'Okay, I'm going.' I turn round, then spin back again. 'But you're missing out on so much, that's all I'm trying to say. Your son is a *wonderful* person. I know I'm biased, but he is.'

'He's fine, he's good – I know that. But not every father and son relationship is all fishing trips and Friday-night beers. He and I are different. He's ... not my cup of tea, I suppose.'

My jaw quivers. 'Not your cup of tea? He's your *son*.'

He marches past me, out into the corridor as a security

guard emerges from the lift. 'Is everything all right, sir?' he asks.

Scott knows this is his chance to get me out of his hair. Possibly arrested. Adrenalin jolts through me.

'Sure. It's fine,' he says calmly.

The security guard slinks back in the lift.

'Thank you,' I tell Scott.

He backs away. 'I've got to go.'

'One final thing: Dan wants to have a relationship with you,' I say simply. 'If you only took the time to get to know him, I really think you'd be proud.'

I walk off down the corridor then, a shiver of hope running down my spine. But when I reach the stairs door, I realise with a heavy heart that that seems to be the end of the matter.

Work is stupidly busy as we start on some ideas for a seafood company, while feedback comes in for our Good Honest Soup commercial, aired for the first time last night. It's all positive, made even better by the fact that we only have to deal with Sebastian once all afternoon, during which time he doesn't even mention his car.

'I think he could be getting over it,' Sadie decides optimistically as we head back to our desks after a late-afternoon meeting. 'It's nice to see him finally achieving some closure.'

As we approach our desks, I see that a bloke in overalls is on all fours under Sadie's, a toolkit next to him.

'Can we help you?' I ask.

He pops his head up. 'Essential maintenance work, love.'

Sadie and I exchange glances. '*Now?*' she enquires.

'Unless you want an electric shock through your high heels, yes, luv. And yours is next,' he tells me.

I look at my watch. 'This is no good,' I say. 'Look, I think we should ask Sebastian if we can both knock off early and finish this at home.'

'Good idea,' she says, then narrows her eyes. 'I hope you don't want me to do it?'

I roll my eyes. 'I'll go.'

When I reach his office and knock, there's no answer. Then a meeting-room door opposite opens and he pops out his head. 'Go in and take a seat,' he instructs. 'Won't be a minute!' and he dodges back inside again.

As I enter the office, the smell hits me instantly – and I recall it's the same one I picked up in the car park weeks ago. If I didn't know any better, I'd swear someone had been smoking pot in here.

Sebastian reappears. 'What can I do for you?' he grins, traversing the room.

I'm about to tell him about the electrical work when he stops dead, his gaze on the corner of his desk.

My eyes follow his, to a great, big *mutha* of a joint – I'm talking six inches, big enough to get an African elephant stoned. He swallows, eyeballs me and silently slides his hand across the desk, tucking his fingers around it and flicking it into his desk drawer. It occurs to me that I am supposed to pretend I haven't noticed. Which strikes me as a fairly sound tactic.

'There's someone doing maintenance work near our desks and we wondered if we could go and work from home instead?' I blurt out.

'Sure,' he replies. 'Close the door on your way out.'

When I open the door to Buddington, nobody's around, but I note that the door to the swimming pool is open and wonder if it's Flossie. Instead, Belinda is ploughing through the water in a frantic front crawl, goggles pulled tightly across her face like a Teenage Mutant Ninja Turtle. When she reaches the side, she looks up.

'Gemma! Come and have a swim!' I shake my head. I'm exhausted after today and still have work to do. 'Oh, go on,' she urges. 'I could do with a chat.'

I give in. 'Okay. A quick dip wouldn't do any harm.'

I dart upstairs, dump my bag and phone, then throw on my swimming costume and go downstairs to join her.

'I've heard nothing from this paparazzo you saw,' she tells me, slowing down to a breaststroke. 'The thought that I might get a call any day from one of the tabloids makes me feel green.'

'Surely you'd have heard by now if anything was going to appear,' I say.

'Maybe.'

'So what's the score with James?'

She stops at the edge and faces me. 'I . . . I haven't returned his calls.'

We spend the next half hour swimming, chatting and talking about Belinda's problems, as well as one or two of mine.

'When's this exchange going to happen then?' she asks me, as we get out of the pool.

'I honestly don't know, Belinda.'

'You must be absolutely desperate for it by now. At least when it happens you'll know for certain that you and Dan will have a future in that house,' she adds.

'Yes,' I agree.

'Is everything all right?' she asks.

'Of course,' and I turn away to pick up a towel before she can see the uncertainty in my eyes.

Chapter 49

Dan

When Rich introduces himself on the phone, I'd have to admit that a second passes when I struggle to place the name.

'Ah, the estate agent! Sorry. Had to think for a moment – it's normally Gemma who deals with you, isn't it?' I feel guilty as I say it, whether she's insisted on doing everything herself or not.

'True enough, my man. But at the moment your girlfriend is failing to return my calls. Wouldn't be the first time a woman's done that, I'll be honest.'

I laugh. 'What can I do for you, Richard?'

'It's Rich. Or 007, I answer to both. Right, I have two sets of bad news and one set of good.'

'Okay.'

'Well, the first bit of bad news is that there isn't really any good news. Just bad. There. It's out there. No point in me trying to dress it up.'

My chest tightens. 'Is the sale off?'

'God, no! That wouldn't be Bad, that'd be Really Bad. Big difference. No, this is just plain, common or garden B. A. D. Which is bad enough, don't you think?'

'I don't know what it is yet.'

'Aha! Course. Well, there's been a setback. The house Mrs Deaver is buying has fallen through. So she's not quite ready yet to exchange on yours.'

'I thought she'd already moved out? We were told there wasn't a chain.'

He sighs. 'Well, there wasn't in the sense that both parties had moved out. But now ... well, one of them is thinking about moving back in.'

'But that's our house. Or it's meant to be our house in *weeks*. How can she move back in when her stuff's in storage? Wouldn't it be easier for her to stay with her family, her parents or somebody?'

'She's been staying with a friend, but it was only supposed to be temporary – and her parents live in Australia. Besides, the house isn't yours yet.' I start rubbing my forehead. The thought of how disappointed Gemma's going to be makes me feel a bit sick. 'But it's close – it really is! Fear not. Do as Braveheart would.'

'Eh?'

'FREEEDOMMM!'

'What?'

'Enjoy it. Your freedom. You're about to get tied down with a mortgage for the next twenty-five *lonnng* years. You need to make the most of the months before that happens. Go out and get wasted. Get a few strippers in. Live like a single man while you still can.'

'What do you mean, months?'

'Did I say months? Oh, I'm sure it'll only be weeks.'

'But it *could* be months – is that what you're telling me?'

'It's a little unclear at the moment. Look, she's only *considering* moving back in. She's just asked me to let you know that this is why the exchange hasn't happened yet. I'm sure things will be back on track soon. *DON'T WORRY,*' he stresses, like some sage morning television agony aunt.

'Well, I am worried. My girlfriend happens to love this house and I happen to love her,' I blurt out. 'And if I don't move out of my mother's place soon I'll go out of my mind.'

'It's the repairs you're concerned about, isn't it?' he ventures. 'I know this puts you in a tricky situation. Because technically, if the vendor walked away from the deal, then all those repairs would've been on a house you don't own. And I can see why that might be a bummer.'

I frown. 'Why would that be an issue? I'm not following.'

'Well,' he laughs, 'any number of reasons – not least the thousands you've forked out for the repairs.'

A heartbeat passes. '*What?*'

'That'd tick anyone off. Paying half of the cost of damp-proofing a house you're never going to live in. Urgh! *Nightmare.*' I say nothing. 'But I'm sure it won't come to that. I'm sure the sale will all go through in the end.'

I let the words jostle round in my head until the pieces of the jigsaw puzzle finally come together. 'To confirm what you're saying . . . Gemma agreed to pay half the cost of those repairs?'

'Not *agreed* to – it's already been paid. She's paid it.'

'No,' I reply. 'That's not right. She hasn't.'

'Soldier, I'm telling you, it's true. I've got copies of the receipts in front of me.'

I confess I feel fairly bloody upset on the way home. I wouldn't say livid exactly, but as I weave through traffic on the M53, my mother's VW Golf virtually has multi-coloured smoke coming out of it, like one of the Red Arrows.

I'm just . . . just bewildered. And incredulous. And, not to sound too fluffy about this, *hurt* that the woman I thought I could trust above all others has been lying through her teeth to me.

I tell myself to calm down, that there must be an innocent explanation. But it escapes me. The closer I get to Buddington, the more the pressure in my head builds – and the more resentful I become about the horrifying set-up we've endured for the last few months.

A set-up that I resisted right at the beginning but that I did anyway, to make Gemma happy. I knew I'd hate it, but it's surpassed expectations.

The claustrophobia of living with my mother. The fact that we'd have more privacy shagging in the window of Primark on a Saturday afternoon. And that I haven't been able to go for so much as a pint with Pete without feeling guilty because it's three quid that should be in the house pot.

Now, as well as another massive cost emerging, instead of discussing it with me – because she knew I'd put the brakes on it – Gemma's gone behind my back and paid out thousands.

And where did it come from?

I have absolutely no idea. Why would I? I'm only her boyfriend!

A thought slams into my head. A memory of her reaction after my mother again offered to give us the money for the deposit . . .

She hasn't. She *couldn't*.

I grip the steering wheel and screech into the driveway, feeling my chest inflate.

I find Gemma in the kitchen with my mother, laughing over a glass of wine. 'Dan, come and join us,' Mum says. 'Gemma and I have just been for a swim.'

I look at this cosy scene, struggling to know how to handle this. 'You haven't been answering your phone,' I tell Gemma.

'Oh, sorry – I left it upstairs in the bedroom. What's the matter? Everything okay?'

'Not really.' I don't like the sound of my voice, but I can't just walk in here and pretend nothing's happened. 'Have you got a minute?'

She flashes a look at Mum – you'd think they were best mates these days – and follows me into the dining room.

There, I find myself crossing and uncrossing my arms, trying to find a way of standing that won't seem confrontational. But this is going to be a confrontation, there's no avoiding it.

'What's the matter, Dan?' She reaches out for my hand, but I move it out of the way. She swallows and looks at me as sweat appears on her brow. 'What is it?' she repeats.

'I got a call from the estate agent.'

Weirdly, she deflates momentarily, as if she's relieved about something. 'What did he want?'

'There's a hold-up on the house.'

'Oh God, I don't believe it. How long?'

'He doesn't know.'

She shakes her head. 'Oh well, as long as we get there in the end. This has been the day from hell.'

I can't think of anything to say now, so I spit the first angry, sarcastic words that come out of my mouth. 'Oh, *has it?*'

I regret this instantly, partly because I sound like a teenage girl after she's just been grounded. 'Sorry, I . . .' Then I stop apologising and remind myself what she's done. Or maybe she hasn't. Maybe there's an explanation. 'Gemma. I need to ask you something.'

She searches my eyes.

'Did you pay for half of the repairs on that house without telling me?'

A violent shade of red attacks her neck. 'I . . . I . . .' Then she says nothing. She just looks at the floor.

'I take it that's a yes,' I say. At this point, I just want her to tell me to shut up and stop being ridiculous, slap me on the face and gasp, 'How dare you, sir!'

But she sinks onto the edge of a chair, refusing to speak. I'm suddenly at a loss as to the right thing to say, so I stick to the default position – and launch into a good old-fashioned rant.

'Well, for a start, you've probably blown all that money, because there's every chance we might never get the house now. You've paid out thousands for a load of repairs on a property you may *never own*.' She gasps. 'Which leads me onto my second question. Did that money come from my mother?'

She rubs her forehead but again, doesn't answer.

That honour is left to my mum, who marches in through the door with a ridiculous swagger, like she's about to pull an Uzi out of her dressing gown and take out the lot of us. 'Yes, it did. And what exactly is the problem with that?'

I glare at her. 'The problem is that you knew I didn't want the money to come from anyone but Gemma and me.'

Gemma stands up and takes a deep breath. 'Dan. I'm really sorry.'

For a second she looks like she genuinely regrets it.

For a second I feel horrible for giving her a hard time.

I look at the tears welling up in her eyes and want to reach out for her, hold her and pretend none of this has happened.

Then she carries on talking and ruins everything.

'The fact was,' she begins, 'we couldn't afford this house, these repairs. Not without your mum's help. And that's all this was, Dan. *Help.* To get us on the ladder – to give us a step up and make sure that the upheaval of moving here for five months wasn't for nothing.'

'So, basically, you're saying you were right?'

She hesitates, unable to think of an answer. 'I wish it hadn't come to that, but I was desperate.'

'Desperate enough to lie to me? And do the one thing you knew I would never, ever, agree to? Like I say, Gemma, you don't sound very sorry.'

Her jaw twitches. 'You know what, you're right, Dan. At this moment in time, I'm not.'

We glare at each other, in this unflinching, unprecedented stand-off.

'You've marched in here throwing abuse when all anyone's tried to do is get us out of this house and into Pebble Cottage,' she argues. 'Don't you think that a more appropriate response – to your mother, at least – would be "thank you"?'

'But I never wanted the fucking money!' I fire back. 'I'd prefer to live on the streets than be sponging off my mother at the age of twenty-nine.'

'It's not sponging, potty mouth,' Mum leaps in. 'How ridiculous!'

'That *is* ridiculous,' Gemma snarls. 'You've been banging on for ages about being worried about affording it. Now you can.'

'Gemma, I jacked in my job and got a new one just to make sure we could afford it. Just to make *you* happy.'

She almost turns purple. 'You did that for me, did you? For *me*? I never asked you to leave your job. If you want my opinion, you've done the wrong thing. You'll be miserable outside of the Chapterhouse Centre.'

I clench my jaws together. 'Thanks for your support.'

'Support? I'll give you support . . . I've been doing every little thing to do with this house. The mortgage application, dealing with the estate agent. Every. Tiny. Little. Thing. I'm not even saying I *mind*. But a thank you might not go amiss – instead of this!'

'Gemma, it was you who insisted on dealing with everything yourself. YOU HAVEN'T LET ME DO A DAMN THING.'

She's not listening. 'And now here you are spouting off that I've made the wrong decision about the money. Well, I'VE SODDING WELL HAD IT!' she shrieks, banging her hand on the table, then wincing visibly. She marches out of the room, nursing her fist.

I march after her.

'I think you'll find *I'VE* SODDING WELL HAD IT!' I shout after her.

She turns and stares at me with a red, tear-stained face. Then she grabs her handbag and roots around in it for her car keys, a look of pure, unmitigated fury in her eyes.

'That's it. I'm going out,' she seethes, still scrabbling for the car keys.

'Fine,' I reply.

She continues scrabbling. And scrabbling a bit more, until she is virtually screaming at the bag in exasperation, as it refuses outright to give up the keys. Her failure to find them is no surprise, by the way: Gemma's handbag is the closest thing Planet Earth has to a Black Hole. Anything can get lost in there.

Eventually, she stops, a triumphant look on her face as she drags them out – along with three tampons that tumble to her feet. She hastily crouches down to pick them up, but this has definitely taken the sting out of her big exit.

Which might be why, to the surprise of everyone (including myself), I snigger.

This does nothing to instil a sense of harmony to this situation.

She looks up, fixing a Catwoman gaze on me as if her sole ambition in life right at this moment is to KICK MY ARSE.

'Don't say it,' she snarls.

'Say *what?*' I snarl back.

'Do *not* ask me if it's the "time of the month" – as if the only reason this is happening is because I'm hormonally-challenged.'

The thought hadn't even occurred to me. I know how much Gemma despises the implication that PMT can be responsible for less than reasonable behaviour.

Which is probably why I cock my head to one side. And I do my very worst.

'Well, is it? It'd explain a hell of a lot.'

If she *was* Catwoman, she'd pull out her whip and beat me into submission. As it is, she uses the only weapons at her disposal.

The Tampax start flying at me as if I am a human dartboard, one after the other. The first one hits me on the chest, but I'm too quick for the second, ducking nimbly out of the way. I'd be quite pleased with it actually, if the third one hadn't got me – square on the nose.

Then she storms to the door, without saying a thing, strides through it and slams it behind her, leaving it shaking.

I close my eyes, contemplating how much I've hated every minute of this. I can't claim I've never had an argument before, but when a woman aims three Tampax at your head and fires, you know things have reached a new low.

Chapter 50

Gemma

I sit outside Dimitri's in my car for a good ten minutes before I decide to get out. Trying to stop myself from shaking. Trying to cover my reddened nose with make-up. Trying to unpuff my eyes by putting the aircon vent on full blast and leaning into it (tip: this will never appear in the beauty pages of *Cosmo*).

I wouldn't say Greek food was my favourite, but Dimitri's is an institution; colourful, warm and overflowing with character. Besides, I'm not here for the food.

'Do you have a reservation, madam?' asks a waiter when I enter.

'No. Well . . . I'm meeting someone.'

I scan the restaurant, looking for Alex, but there's no sign of him. He obviously decided that dining alone wasn't an attractive option, after all. It's probably for the best, but a wave of disappointment hits me.

I'm unable to work out exactly why I'm here, after driving round aimlessly for half an hour, other than confusion, anger and a vague sense of wanting to stick two fingers up at Dan.

Do I really mean that?

At the end of the day, he's right that I lied to him, or at least didn't correct any of his wrong assumptions. But I took the money from Belinda in utter desperation and because it was the only thing that would get us out of a massive, Pebble Cottage-shaped hole.

The alternative would've been the one thing *he* found so abhorrent: staying with Belinda indefinitely. Add to that the fact that I spent the afternoon chasing Dan's father halfway across Chester to tell him what a magnificent human being his son was. To be rewarded for my efforts with a load of abuse from him hurts like hell. I didn't deserve that. The man who is meant to love me has made me feel like shit, there's no other way to describe it.

'What name are they booked under?' the waiter asks, looking at his folder.

'Alex Monroe. But don't worry . . .'

'He's outside,' he replies. 'Follow me.'

I clutch my bag as he leads me through the restaurant and out into a covered courtyard, where a dozen neatly-laid tables nestle between the lush greenery of oversized potted palms.

I spot Alex and feel my breath leave me.

Then I spot someone else.

Contrary to his last text, he is far from alone and weeping into his Taramasalata. He's with the woman from Facebook – and has probably already been tagged with the words 'Fifth date!'

I spin round to leave immediately, taking my red nose and puffy eyes with me. 'Gemma, wait!'

When I glance round, Alex is out of his seat and bounding in my direction. 'I hadn't dreamed you'd actually come,' he grins. 'Is everything okay?'

'Fine, yes,' I mutter, glancing round him. 'Sorry, Alex – I thought you'd be alone.'

'Francesca ended up having lunch with her mum instead, which is why she was free in the end.'

'You'd better get back to her. I'm so sorry.'

Even from a distance, Francesca is gorgeous, more so than in her Facebook picture. Her hair is long and sleek, her make-up flawless, her outfit so effortlessly chic it makes Alexa Chung look like the sort of woman who tries on six outfits in Debenhams before leaving empty-handed because they all make her bum look big.

Francesca also couldn't look more pissed off that another woman has gate-crashed her date if someone had snapped off the heels of her Manolos and used them as chopsticks.

'Don't be silly. Come and join us now you're here.'

'I couldn't, Alex. No. Absolutely not.'

'Stop protesting, Gems,' he says, steering me across the room. 'You know you want to. Besides, Francesca will love you.'

*

It is clear within ten seconds of sitting down that Francesca does not love me. Francesca hates me. Under the circumstances, I can hardly blame her.

'Do you remember that day we rode our bikes all the way into town – and got horribly lost?' Alex asks, his eyes glinting like they always do when he's reminiscing.

'How could I forget?' I mumble uneasily. Francesca looks away.

'We must've been gone for hours,' he tells her. It's the first time he's engaged her in conversation in ten minutes. 'I was starting to wonder if we'd need a helicopter rescue squad. Obviously, Gems knows that I always knew the way home really,' he grins at me.

'Yeah, right.' I find myself smirking, before I can stop it. Francesca grits her teeth – and I snap out of it.

'So . . . Francesca, are you a civil engineer too?' I ask, wanting, for some reason, to make friends with her.

'No, I'm in the architectural team,' she replies, as she takes a large, resentful mouthful of wine.

'That must be an interesting job?'

'Yes.'

'Are you from Manchester originally?' She doesn't sound it.

'No, Siena in Italy. My parents moved to London when I was three. I came here for work three years ago.'

'Ah,' I reply.

'Will you excuse me,' Francesca then announces, standing up and heading to the ladies.

I sit back, momentarily relieved. When she's out of earshot, I lean in to Alex. 'I feel uncomfortable here. I'm going to say goodbye to Francesca, then go.'

His face crumples. 'Oh, don't do that, Gems.'

'But, Alex, you're on a date. I feel like a gooseberry. I *am* a gooseberry.'

He leans in to whisper to me, 'You could never be a gooseberry. Not to me.'

'I'm not, I—'

'Stop,' he says quietly. He holds my gaze when he speaks. 'You're not the gooseberry. *You're* the one I want to be here with.'

I feel myself redden. 'Don't say that.'

'Why not? It's true.'

I stand up. 'I need to go.'

He stands up too and grabs my hand. But I don't pull away. I can't pull away. I like the feel of his touch too much to move. He steps forward so he's right next to me, brushes my hair away from my face. I like it all. Way too much.

The thought makes my eyes well up, for the second time this evening.

'Gems, what's the matter?' he asks, genuinely concerned.

'Alex, I've had a terrible night and I . . . I just don't know what to think about anything any more.'

'Why, what's happened?'

'Dan and I had a huge row,' I confess, dropping my head in

despair. Yet before I can argue, he's pulling me into his arms, stroking my hair.

I cannot fully describe the rollercoaster of conflicting emotions I go on as I sink into him, closing my eyes, listening to my racing heartbeat in my own ears.

Pain ... comfort ... desire ... guilt.

'I'm going to get rid of Francesca,' he murmurs.

'You can't do that,' I protest. But I know that the reality is, I want exactly that.

He looks deep into my eyes, clearly needing to get something off his chest. 'Gemma, you've had a row with Dan, so I want you to know right now that I'm *not* going to try and exploit that tonight.'

'I never thought ...' My voice trails off as I look down, embarrassed.

He picks up my hand again and threads his fingers through mine. 'I'm not going to do anything inappropriate, Gemma. Not when you're so obviously upset. I hope you know me well enough by now to know that I've got this terrible affliction – of wanting to do the honourable thing. But I can't deny it and I'm sure it's obvious anyway: I wish I was alone with you tonight. That's the truth.'

My heart is racing even faster now: the air between us feels thick with danger.

'I need to go, Alex,' I say eventually, letting go of his hand.

He nods and watches me gather my belongings with a troubled smile. 'I know, Gems.'

I look up at the door to see if Francesca is returning, but there's no sign of her. But it's still time to go. 'Bye,' I say, leaning in to kiss him on the cheek.

Only, this is no straightforward peck. As our skin touches, I realise he hasn't moved. And I haven't moved. We simply stand, with electricity firing through us, drinking each other in until the tension becomes too much to bear.

'Bye,' I say, pulling away and hastily heading for the door.

When I get home, Dan is in bed with his back to me. I don't know whether he's asleep, or lying awake, too furious to speak. I think about waking him up and trying to talk to him, but my head is already exploding.

So I climb into bed next to him and try to sleep. It proves a futile exercise; I spend all night drifting in and out of slumber, my eyes growing hot every time I wake.

Under any other circumstances, I'd be consumed with regret that I took that money when I knew how he felt about it. And consumed with hurt at his refusal to accept my apology or to try and see why I made what was unquestionably a mistake.

But at the moment, I'm consumed with neither.

I am consumed by one thing – one person. Alex. And how he made me feel tonight. How he still makes me feel every time I think about him: alive with desire, still tingling from his touch.

The next morning, Dan gets up at 6 a.m., showers, dresses and leaves the house. We have still not spoken to each other since last night. It's clear that something big has changed between us. And right now, I can't see any hope of it ever changing back.

I sniff tears back from my eyes yet again as Sebastian walks in, sits down and slams his folder on the table.

'No Sadie?'

'She's on her way,' I tell him, pulling myself together. 'Her meeting with British Upholsterers ran over.'

'Something the matter?' he asks.

'Oh, nothing. Just having a bit of a nightmare with the MOT on my car,' I lie, then wish I'd chosen a different subject to lie about.

'Don't talk to me about cars.' Thunderclouds gather on his forehead. 'I've just had to renew my insurance. You wouldn't believe the cost now I've lost my No Claims.'

I swallow. 'Oh.'

'I've had to cancel our family holiday to Disney World,' he continues.

'Oh my God. Really?'

'Somebody here is playing me for a fool. If I ever get hold of them . . . It's not just beyond the bounds of human decency, it's a disciplinary matter.'

'But accidents happen, don't they?' I mutter.

'It's not the accident that bothers me.' At that point, the door opens and Sadie walks in with a cheery smile. 'It's the *subterfuge*.'

There's something about the way he says it which, as I glance at my friend, makes me blush to the colour of Noddy's car. I look back at Sebastian, mid-rant, then focus on my pencil. Sebastian stops. He leans in and peers at me.

Sadie pours herself a coffee and sits down. 'Everything all right?'

I'm suddenly unable to answer.

Sebastian looks between the two of us and comprehension sweeps across his face. He sits back contemplatively as suspicion rises up in him.

'I think I'm right in saying that the culprit is right here in this room, aren't I?'

Sadie spits out her coffee, right across the table like a pump action water-pistol.

I look at her. She returns my stare, as if silently pleading, 'What the *hell* did you say?'

'Well? Are you going to cough to it?' Sebastian continues. 'Because the disciplinary hearing will look upon this even more dimly if you don't.'

I gaze fixedly at Sadie, willing her to say something, but she's not even being defiant. She's just lost, hopeless, unable to think of what to do.

'Okay,' says Sadie, crumpling in a heap. 'I . . .'

'Sadie, you don't need to do this,' Sebastian interrupts. 'I'd like Gemma to confess all by herself.'

I rear up. 'It wasn't me!' I bluster.

He shakes his head. 'Gemma, you're making this *so* much worse for yourself. Just come clean. Your face says it all. It's completely obvious.'

'Sebastian,' I beg. 'I'm serious, it wasn't me.'

He walks to the phone and picks it up.

'What are you doing?' asks Sadie.

'Calling security – to come and remove your pass, Gemma, and escort you from the building. You're suspended with immediate effect.'

My mouth drops and I look at Sadie. All I have to do is tell him it was her, then this is over. My job is safe.

Yet, I can't do it. I can't land her in it.

I stand up. 'It's okay, I'm going,' I say to him. 'It wasn't me though.'

'What possible reason can you give me that'd make me believe you?' he asks, through tight lips.

Sadie stands up. 'Sebastian, leave Gemma alone. She didn't do it.'

'I'm afraid I don't believe you.'

'Well, believe it,' Sadie says. 'It wasn't her. It was me.'

Chapter 51

Gemma

By the time I get home that night, I still have absolutely no idea what to say to Dan. It hasn't helped that Alex has texted me several times through the day, asking how I am and trying to persuade me to meet up with him again. I haven't responded yet, because the truth is I haven't got the headspace to work out what the hell I'm going to say or do. Tonight, tomorrow or, it's becoming increasingly clear, for the rest of my life.

When Dan opens the door, I stand up and immediately start talking. 'Dan, I think we need to have a discussion about—'

But he simply pulls me into his big arms as tears spill down my face. I feel a surge of emotion as I press myself into his chest, feeling his heartbeat run through me.

Eventually, he pulls back and looks at me through glazed eyes. 'I love you so much, Gemma, and I hate what happened last night. I'm really sorry.'

At that, I begin to sob, unable to control myself.

'Hey, what's the matter?' he whispers, wrapping himself around me again. I sniff, unable to get the words out.

'You shouldn't be apologising,' I manage to say. 'I'm the one who should be apologising.'

He brushes the hair out of my face and kisses my forehead. 'I think you'll find we both gave as good as we got.'

'I was wrong to have accepted the money from your mum. And to have kept it secret.'

He tenses momentarily. 'I know you thought you were doing the right thing. I shouldn't have been so uptight about the whole issue.'

Against all the odds, it has never felt better to be held by him. Or indeed anyone. I suddenly just want this whole thing to go away, along with Alex Monroe and the storm he's set off inside me.

Besides, I always have loved make-up sex. The emotion, the rawness, the urgent then gentle ebbs and flows, the feel of someone's lips against yours who yesterday made you fizz with anger, but right now you can't be without.

He brings his mouth to mine as his fingers caress the top button of my blouse and I push myself breathlessly against him.

'DANIEL! GEMMA!' Belinda's voice echoes up the stairs. 'THE HAM AND PINEAPPLE CURRY'S READY! GET IT WHILE IT'S HOT!'

Chapter 52

Dan

On the day before Grandma's eightieth birthday, I wake up and look at her present – the wetsuit Gemma and I bought her – and realise it's totally unsuitable. I need to get something different. That wetsuit has been bothering me for ages. Yes, she was swimming outdoors last year, but she's eighty, not eighteen. I've been in denial.

I intend to return the wetsuit at lunchtime but don't have time to do that, so go and buy its replacement instead – a Pandora bracelet, which as far as I can ascertain is a decent default gift to purchase for any female from the age of 0 upwards.

I'm walking out of the shop in Liverpool city centre, when my phone rings. It's Gemma. 'Hello you,' I say.

'Hi there,' she replies.

I can't fully convey how good it feels not to be fighting. To have put our conflagration behind us and – I hope – seen the back of the Tampax Ninja.

She made a mistake. I overreacted. We're over it. Or at least I am – I love her too much to want to dwell on it any further. But I can tell the whole thing has knocked her sideways, judging by how quiet she's been since it happened. She's barely even mentioned the house.

'Just thought I'd let you know I heard from Rich,' she says.

'Oh?'

'Mrs Deaver has decided that she doesn't want to hold up the sale any longer, so she's going to continue staying at her friend's house. We're back in business.' She sounds oddly flat.

'God almighty, could they mess us around any more? The woman's changed her mind so much she sounds virtually schizophrenic.'

'Well, don't slag her off too much. We're exchanging contracts on Monday.'

'Seriously?' I ask.

'Seriously,' she replies. But I can't help thinking she doesn't sound as happy as I might have expected.

One thing for which I have to give my mum credit is that she knows how to throw a party. By 9 p.m. Buddington Hall has been transformed into a Gatsby-style spectacular: there's a champagne fountain, fireworks and a spread that is not just magnificent, but also untouched by her own culinary hand. (With the exception of one dish – a 'Scotch Egg Trifle' which she describes as a 'savoury twist on a classic', like she's Heston Blumenthal's deranged cousin.)

Grandma is having a whale of a time. 'This must have cost a fortune,' she says, sipping champagne. 'You do realise that your mother is a lunatic.'

'I blame the parents.'

She grins. 'I would too.'

'So how does it feel to be eighty?' I suddenly wish I hadn't asked. Grandma's wearing make-up tonight and Mum bought her some new clothes last weekend. But she's looked inescapably frail again recently. Or perhaps, with her birthday approaching, I've only just started to notice.

'Well, I'd prefer to be twenty.' The lines above her lips fade into a wry smile. 'But it's not all bad. You weren't around then, for a start. And I've had a good innings, as they say.'

'You've still got plenty of time to score a few more runs yet. Are you dancing?' I ask.

'Are you asking?'

I take her by the hand into the hall and Grandma and I perform my best attempt at a waltz. It's based largely on instinct, tips thrust on me by Bobby and a vague recollection of what the conker-coloured blokes on *Strictly* do.

When the song finishes, she's slightly out of breath. 'I think you need to stick to someone who can keep up.' She nods at

Gemma, who's spent most of the evening in the corner with Sadie.

I made one attempt to strike up conversation, but Sadie responded with a tsunami of uncontrollable sobbing so I decided to 'give them some space' i.e. run a mile. But this could be a good excuse to tear my girlfriend away. I leave Grandma chatting to some friends from church and head over.

'Fancy a warm-up dance?' I ask.

'I can't. I'm not wearing the right shoes,' Gemma says, slowly enough to make it clear that she's already quite drunk. 'These ones slip off.'

'Perhaps we'd better call our big routine off then.'

'Not a chance. I've got another pair for that upstairs. Anyway,' she stands, grabs me by the arm and turns me away until we're out of earshot, 'I can't leave Sadie. It's terrible, Dan. She and Warren are thinking of calling off the wedding.'

'Why?'

'She's meant to be getting married in three months and now has no salary with which to pay for it. If she gets the sack, she'll be unemployable. Hey . . .'

'What?'

'I was just thinking, she could do with some advice from an objective source.' I look around the room. 'I mean you,' she replies.

'Me?'

Before I can object, I'm plonked unceremoniously next to

a weeping, hysterical car crash of a person – just the kind of guest you want at a party, obviously.

'Hi, Sadie. How are things?' I ask, employing an inane, smiley face in the vague hope that she might be compelled to follow suit.

'OHGODTHINGSAREAWFULI'VELOSTMYJOBAND EVERYTHING'STERRIBLEANDIDON'TKNOWWHAT TODO!'

Gemma nudges me.

'Really sorry to hear that, Sadie,' I cough.

'I was saying to Sadie,' Gemma begins, 'that she should see a lawyer to get some advice before she does anything.'

'Good idea,' I comment. 'I'd do that.'

'But that's going to cost a packet and it might be premature. So *then* I said, she should set up a meeting with Sebastian. Try and reason with him. Apologise.'

'That's a great idea,' I say heartily. 'I'd do that.'

'But that might make things worse because he was in such a foul mood.'

'Hmm.' I nod as if applying the kind of cognitive effort you'd put into trying to cure cancer.

'So that's the problem,' Gemma concludes. Then she looks at me, apparently expecting some pearl of wisdom. I mentally roll the dice.

'I'd go for option one,' I say decisively.

'The lawyer?' Sadie asks.

'Definitely.'

The two of them look at each other uneasily.

'I'll just go and apologise,' Sadie decides.

Gemma nods. 'Good idea.'

Pete is on fine, if supremely intoxicated, form. He's had at least six large glasses of my mother's Gin Blitz and is swaying so much all he needs is a lighter in the air and he could be at a Michael Bolton concert. 'Where are you having your leaving do?' he asks.

'I haven't put much thought into it.'

'Well, you better had – you're going in three weeks. You bastard.'

Pete wasn't impressed by the news that I've handed in my notice; he's taken it very personally, like a small puppy I've abandoned in the street, rather than a 14-stone grown man.

There's no going back though – my job is now a 'cost saving'. In these last austere few months, as soon as the council, who are responsible for half of the Chapterhouse Centre's funding, become aware of a vacant role, finding a replacement goes on hold. For months, or sometimes indefinitely. It's a way of shaving a salary off their extremely challenging budget without having to pay redundancy money. Which is little consolation for those who'll have to pick up my work, not to mention the service users.

I feel an urgent desire to move the conversation on.

'How are things with you and Jade?' I venture, picking the one subject I know will distract him.

'Great! Great!' he says, then he starts swaying again.

'What does that mean?'

'Well, I meant what I said. We're just good friends. And I'm fine with that. I'm back in the market.'

'What, dating again?'

'Not actually got that far, but I'm available. I'm ready, willing and waiting for the woman of my dreams to come and get me.' He grins. 'Anyone here single? What about that Sadie?'

'No, she's getting married. Or maybe not. The point is, forget Sadie. But there are loads of other single women.'

'Really?' His eyes light up.

I nod. 'Few of them are under fifty-five, but they're all single.'

He flashes me a look, then – to my alarm – starts scanning the room.

Before long, the party is in full swing and Mum is parading me around as if I'm her new poodle, in a series of encounters that go like this:

Mum: Jeremy! Have you met my son, Daniel? He's just got a new, high-flying job, he has a beautiful girlfriend, and he can speak Japanese.'

Me: I can't speak Japanese.

380

Mum: Why not? I bought you a CD last Christmas.

Or ...

Mum: Diana! Do you remember Daniel? You must! He peed in your paddling pool once.

Or ...

Mum: Elaine! How's Penelope? You must meet Daniel.

Me: Mum, we've met.

Mum: No, I don't think so.

Me: Um ... we have, Mum.

Mum: No, you're mistaken.

Elaine: He's not, Belinda.

Mum (remembering): Of course! You caught him and Penelope at it on her sixteenth birthday, didn't you? It could've been worse, darling. At least they confined themselves to the shed.

At ten o'clock, the moment arrives that my mother has been waiting for – her whole bloody life.

It's *Dirty Dancing* time.

Okay, I won't deny it. I kind of like dancing. And while I'm no Gene Kelly, I can bust a few moves better than the average straight bloke.

Still, we haven't exactly practised our moves relentlessly, or been in hard training for months. Though we did hit the lake a couple of weekends ago trying to emulate that scene where the hero (whatever his name is) lifts the girl (whatever her name is) above his head.

I spent most of the experience being hurled backwards with Gemma's crotch in my face – about as much of a turn-on as you'd expect when accompanied by pond water being flushed down my throat and out of my nose.

Gemma, having been mildly anxious about this dance earlier today, has relaxed after hitting the cocktail trolley. Unfortunately, she seems to have relaxed so much that she has also relinquished use of most of her motor skills. 'C'mere loverrrr boyyy,' she drawls down my ear, grabbing me by the tie. 'We're on.'

She drags me to the centre of the hall, gesturing to Sadie, who starts prodding at buttons on my mother's sound system, which was purchased in the mid-1990s and has a similar number of controls to an armoured personnel carrier. Eventually, Showaddywaddy are cut off in their prime. Everyone groans.

But when the opening bars of our song begin, they are recognised instantly and universally. The entire room stops and looks.

Gemma is in her swingy dress and she has never looked more gorgeous, nor more cross-eyed. Her head lolls from side to side, as she takes Bobby's instructions – to keep her neck loose – with spectacular literalism.

But she's always had more natural rhythm than me, so can get away with the added, gin-fuelled enthusiasm, while I opt for my usual policy: to do my bit, try not to drop her and hope that her twirly bits are distracting enough to get us by.

I'm quietly astounded that the first part of the dance goes okay. People are impressed with our co-ordination, and too polite to notice when she mutters, 'SHIT! I've got the wrong shoes on!'

Then it reaches the finale, the bit that was always a triumph of optimism over ability. Bobby had suggested we come up with a Plan B – a safe twirl that we could put into place if one of us was feeling nervous.

And while I'm not the nervous kind, I am currently sweating like a sex pest before a CRB check.

It's not that I'm not capable of holding her – it's that Gemma can barely see straight and I'm seriously concerned that if she attempts this lift, she'll fly directly into my hands and propel both of us into the downstairs loo.

So, as we're swinging our hips, I give her the wink, the gesture that's supposed to launch Plan B. But she just spins round, oblivious, with an elated grin on her face. I wink again. She fails to notice. 'Gemma, Plan B,' I hiss, but she's off improvising, lapping up the crowd.

'Gemma – PLAN B,' I repeat.

She spins round and looks appalled. 'No bloody way!'

'Yes – *way*.'

Her feet start tiptoeing backwards, preparing for her run-up, as it strikes me that I have no idea whether we're going for Plan A, B or bloody Z.

All I know is that my girlfriend is racing towards me as if she's been fired out of a cannon, and I have nowhere to go. So I hold my arms out, ready to do the full lift, only for her to collide into my chest, clearly expecting the twirl.

She is not impressed. 'That was rubbish.'

'I know,' I concede.

'Well, do something.'

'Something?'

'Anything.'

She throws open her arms and I oblige by bending down and picking her up to throw her over my shoulder. I am not in the best position to judge the resulting effect, but this is the only thing we've got that will save us from this dance turning into Gemma's worst, unspectacular flop.

And we *do* get a cheer from the crowd. I decide to make the most of it, so spin her round. And round. And round. I do realise I could be accused of a lack of diversity in this routine, but when something's going well, what's the point in stopping?

The *point* becomes apparent when I get to approximately the sixth spin and things start to fall apart, or rather off, beginning with Gemma's footwear.

Her high heel flies off her foot and hurtles across the room in the direction of the buffet table. I lower her to the ground, just in time to see the shoe land, with an unceremonious *splat*, right in the middle of my mother's Scotch Egg Trifle.

The room erupts in applause. And I couldn't think of a better finale if I'd planned it.

Chapter 53

Gemma

Despite entertaining the crowd (for all the wrong reasons) I am mildly mortified by the crescendo to our dnace, not at all reassured by those who subsequently thanked me for relieving them of their duty to sample Belinda's trifle.

'You're worrying too much,' Dan tells me, as we make a token effort to start cleaning up after the guests have gone.

'If you say so.'

He leans in and grabs me, sweeping me into a Mills & Boon cover clinch. 'Marry me, Gemma,' he declares theatrically. 'With your sparkly eyes and precision aim with a high heel, I can't spend a moment longer without you as my wife.'

And I can't help but laugh. 'You do realise I hate you sometimes.'

I loved the party tonight. Not just for the champagne and the dancing and because I've always loved a good do. But because, for one night, it made me forget about the turmoil that's been going on in my head. It made me forget about Alex – and focus solely on how much I love Dan.

But after the fireworks have faded, I can feel that clarity slipping away from me again.

I reach out to squeeze Dan's hand, when there's a bang from the direction of the pool room. He frowns. 'I thought all the guests had gone?'

'So did I. And your mum was quite emphatic about locking that up for the party while there was so much glass around.'

Dan puts down his bin bag and goes to investigate, while I follow. He has his hand on the door as a whoop echoes through the corridor, followed by a series of splashes. 'Oh my God!'

'What is it?'

As I turn the corner, he doesn't need to respond. There are two champagne bottles by the side of the pool. A pile of clothes. And Belinda and James, both in their birthday suits, getting it on in the Jacuzzi.

Dan looks as if someone's poured acid in his eyes.

The following morning when I wake up, Dan is fast asleep, snoozing in that way he does sometimes, with his lips slightly parted, blowing out a thin strip of air. I check my phone and see that a message arrived last night.

You've gone all quiet on me lately, Gems. Everything okay? xxxxx

I get heart palpitations as I close it down and look at Dan. Then I slip out of bed, pull on my dressing gown and tiptoe downstairs, making my way through dropped canapés and party poppers.

I put the kettle on and stand at the kitchen window, staring out with dry, confused eyes.

When I've made some tea, I head outside to breathe some fresh air into my lungs. I wander across the drive and onto the lawn, dewy grass between my bare toes. It's when I reach the lake that I see her.

Grandma is sitting on a rock, her feet dangling into the water beneath her long, flowing skirt. I walk over and cough.

'Hello, Gemma,' she smiles, shuffling up to make a space next to her.

'You didn't fancy a lie-in after last night?' I ask.

'I haven't been able to sleep past seven o'clock since I turned sixty, unlike the rest of them.' She gestures to the house. 'Talk about not knowing how to hold their booze. Oh, thank you for my present, by the way. Very thoughtful.'

'It was Dan's choice. Well, actually – it wasn't really his

choice. At least, not his first choice.' The words are out of my mouth before I can stop them.

'Oh?'

'Oh, nothing. We'd bought something else at first. But it wasn't suitable. At least, Dan didn't think so. Although he was in two minds about whether to take it back then.'

She looks puzzled, then says lightly, 'You've got to tell me what I'm missing out on!'

'It . . . it was a wetsuit.'

She opens her mouth to speak, then closes it.

'What is it?' I ask.

'Nothing. I love the bracelet, it's beautiful. Very kind. Lovely.'

'Then what?'

'It just makes me a little sad that I'm no longer up to a wetsuit.'

'Oh, it wasn't that,' I say awkwardly. 'It's not that you're not up to it . . .'

'Don't worry, I know Dan was just trying to do the right thing.' She leans into me and whispers conspiratorially, 'But I'd have *loved* it, all the same.'

I look into her milky blue eyes and, for a small moment, I can see her as a young woman again. There's no doubt about it, Flossie Blackwood has sucked out everything life has to give. I hope I can look back, aged eighty, and say the same.

I stand up and brush the grass off my pyjama bottoms. 'Flossie, will you wait here a minute?'

'I'm not going anywhere, lovely,' she replies.

I run back to the bedroom as fast as it's possible to do with a head that feels as though someone's put a pneumatic drill in my ear. 'Wake up, Dan,' I say, shaking him by the shoulders. 'We need to do something.'

He lets out a little groan and smiles. 'I know it's been a while since you got your leg over, Gemma, but it's not that urgent, is it?'

'Not *that*. It's Flossie. You need to dig out that wetsuit.'

Grandma turns round to look at us, squinting in the sunlight, as we march towards her. 'What are you two up to?' she asks as Dan produces the wetsuit from behind his back.

'We just thought we'd bring you your other present,' he says.

Her eyes widen as she holds out her hands, rubbing the fabric between her fingers. 'It's wonderful,' she smiles, her eyes glinting. 'Thank you, Danny.'

'I wasn't sure it was a good idea,' he says, sitting down next to her and giving her a kiss.

'I love it,' she replies. 'Thank you, both of you.' She looks up. 'In fact, I'm going to go and put it on. Fancy a dip, Danny?'

He grins. 'Why not? That'll clear the hangover, eh?'

He helps her up. 'Just a thought,' she says, an impish expression on her face. 'This is a *lovely* wetsuit. It seems wasted in our little lake ...'

*

As we leave for the hour-long drive to Bala Lake, Flossie is in such a good mood that she's close to singing 'I do like to be beside the seaside!' all the way there. The car is alive with laughter, even if there's also a flicker of anxiety on Dan's face.

When we arrive at the lake, we pull into a little car park next to the shore. The sun is hot enough to make the ground shimmer, and the only way to stop sweat bubbling on your brow is to open the door the second the engine stops. Dan helps Flossie out, before she carefully slips off the skirt over her wetsuit and I help her with her swimming cap, while Dan strips down to his trunks.

'This is where Grandma used to bring me with Grandad when I was a little boy,' he tells me.

'You were a lot smaller then,' she replies. 'I used to hold your hand and you'd go splashing in, dragging the two of us in until we fell flat into the water. You were a scamp.'

I can tell that Dan isn't worried any longer. He simply nods at his grandma as she clasps his hand and says, 'Come on then. What's stopping you?'

And although they don't run, there's a real spring in her step as they edge into the water, splashing and laughing just like they did all those years ago.

Chapter 54

Gemma

Today is the day we exchange contracts with the vendors of Pebble Cottage. Which means that, although we won't get the keys for at least another two weeks, as soon as the 'exchange' happens, the house is irreversibly destined to be ours – and our moving-in date is set in stone.

I feel breathless every time I think about it. And not in a good way.

For the first time ever, I am starting to admit to myself that I am not 100 per cent certain that any of this is what I want. Not when Alex made me feel how he did in Dimitri's. Not when my stomach continues to flip over every time another text lands, as it does this morning.

I miss hearing from you, Gems. A lot. I haven't won
the company raffle this time, but I seriously need to
see you. You and I have some things to talk about: will
you meet me for a drink on Friday? x

The exchange of contracts could happen at any time between 9 a.m. and 5 p.m. today. And, I can't deny it, the thought of it is making me feel mildly sick. As the hands on the office clock amble slowly round, I am entirely unable to focus on work. I check my phone every minute, then twice a minute. Then I set myself a rule that I can only check it every five minutes, which fails almost instantaneously.

Annabel the solicitor has said she'll call me as soon as the exchange has happened, yet I start wondering if she's forgotten about us. Or fallen ill. Or gone shoe shopping at lunchtime and stumbled across a particularly diverting sale in Kurt Geiger.

By 3 p.m., my internal pressure cooker is reaching the volcanic setting. I pick up the phone again and call the solicitor.

'Annabel, hi! Just wondered if there'd been any word at all?' I don't know why I feel the need to say this casually, as if it's as inconsequential as asking the sales assistant in Tesco if they'd run out of baked beans.

'I'm afraid not,' she says. 'It's not uncommon to go right to the wire, but I'm a bit miffed that their solicitor hasn't returned my calls.'

'He hasn't returned your calls?' My voice is wavering.

'Probably on the golf course. Or in the broom cupboard with one of the secretaries. It's like *Mad Men* over at Harveys. Only Tom Harvey looks more like Donald Duck than Don Draper. I'll chase them again in an hour if there's no word.'

I put down the phone and attempt to focus on the clock, but I'm now so firmly in that state between exhaustion and hyperactivity that it starts melting, as in a Salvador Dali painting.

Tick tock.

Tick. Tock.

TICKETY SODDING TOCK.

By 4.15 p.m. I've still heard nothing. Then my phone rings.

'No word?' asks Dan when I pick up.

I swallow. 'None.'

'What's Rich got to say for himself?'

'He hasn't returned my calls,' I reply.

'If only I worked a bit closer to their branch, I'd call in,' Dan says. 'He couldn't avoid me if I was there in person.'

I bite my pencil and look at the clock. Again, I get the sensation that the fate of Pebble Cottage and my stupid, confused feelings about two men are linked. As soon as our future is secured in the house, all will become clear and I'll stop torturing myself with these ridiculous pangs of nostalgia about Alex. 'You might not be able to make it, Dan,' I say. 'But I could.'

*

I power out of the car park, as Sebastian glares at me with gog-glebox eyes. I wind down the window. 'Impromptu meeting. Possible business lead. All good stuff,' I explain hurriedly. He pulls an expression as if I've asked him directions in Cantonese, as I thrust up the window and slam my foot on the accelerator.

Despite being a generally impatient person by nature, I am usually a calm and forgiving driver. I wave to people to say thank you; slow down to allow others to pull out of a space.

Today, I lean in to the wheel with an expression like the Tasmanian Devil.

It doesn't help that I am scuppered at every turn. I encounter a defective level crossing (with a green man that never disappears), three separate lollipop men (one of whom hands out a bounty of sweets to all twenty-odd crossing chil-dren), a police horse, several pensioners with a death wish and finally, roadworks (or rather, row upon row of cones which appear to have been stacked aimlessly along the road).

By the time I'm in Heswall, have driven round the block five times and parked the car illegally in a dubious-looking driveway, it is 4.55 p.m.

I peer through the window of the estate agents and see Rich leaning on the coffee machine chatting up the girl who does their photocopying. She's pretty, with a nose ring and hair the colour of vanilla ice cream. He looks up, sees me and leaps sev-eral centimetres off the floor in fright.

I point to him and mouth, 'I'd like to talk to you,' before marching to the glass door and pushing it open. The other staff stop what they're doing. Except, by the time I'm inside, Rich has disappeared. 'Where is he?' I demand.

The photocopying girl turns around and blinks, displaying the most perfect, if overdone, liquid eyeliner I've ever seen. 'He was here a second ago.'

'OOOHWWW!' shrieks another woman behind a desk, jumping up in alarm. 'What are you doing down there?'

Rich's head pops up sheepishly and he stands up to brush himself down. 'Just looking ... for this.' He holds up a bent paperclip. 'Ah, Gemma. Gem. Gem-Gem. What a lovely surprise!'

I cross my arms. 'Why have we not exchanged contracts today? My solicitor has been trying to get through to your client's lawyer all day, but nobody has returned her calls. Can you shed any light?'

He squirms. 'Ah. Hmm. Possibly. Hmm.'

'Go on then.'

'Hmm. Well, it's ... nothing's set in stone yet, but ... hmm ...'

'Rich. Tell me what's going on! Why has the deal not been done today, as planned?'

He swallows. 'The thing is, Gemma, it only happened this afternoon.'

'What happened this afternoon?'

He looks genuinely sorry. Or at least genuinely scared.

'The vendors let someone else go and view the house at lunchtime.'

I narrow my eyes.

'I'm really sorry, Gemma. But they've made the sellers of Pebble Cottage a higher offer.'

Chapter 55

Gemma

'Tossers,' Dan huffs down the phone.

'Bastards,' I agree.

'Time-wasting, moronic lowlifes.'

'I hope they . . . they go to a restaurant tonight and someone spits in their food,' I say.

'Is that the worst you can do?' Dan asks.

'No, the first thing I thought was so bad, I couldn't actually bring myself to say it.' I flick on my indicator as I sit at traffic lights, talking to Dan on my hands-free.

'So what now?' he sighs.

A deluge of possibilities scramble through my mind. 'We either walk away and write off the money we've spent on the house so far, or . . .' I gulp before completing the sentence. 'Or we match the new offer.'

'Well, we can't do that,' he says immediately.

I don't answer. He's right, of course, we can't.

'Look, we'll talk about this tonight, okay?' he suggests. 'I love you, Gemma.'

I choke up as I say the words back to him. 'I love you too,' I reply, as I pull up in front of Sadie's terraced house.

Sadie and Warren live in Aigburth in south Liverpool, which has made my round trip home stupidly long tonight. But not coming here wasn't an option, judging by how far into a black depression she's sinking. Although she's trying her best to stay positive, I have never felt sorrier for my friend than in the last few days. She's now resigned to losing her job and, judging by the number of bridal magazines in the recycling tray, her wedding isn't looking hopeful either.

'Before we get onto my woes, has your house exchange happened?' she asks, opening the door. 'Tell me some good news, please.'

It takes all my will not to burst into tears. 'We've been gazumped,' I reply, trying to keep my voice calm. 'At the last minute, someone's offered them more money. We've been told we need to increase the offer if we still want the house.'

'What sods. So are you increasing the offer?'

'We haven't got the money, Sadie,' I reply with a knot in my stomach.

'But haven't you paid for half of the work to be done on it?'

I nod. 'We could lose it all.'

'So that's it? No more house?'

The thought makes my blood run cold. 'That's not completely clear yet. The ball is in the owners' court now – they haven't accepted the other offer yet. They're thinking about it overnight.'

Sadie reaches out and holds my hand. 'Oh, Gemma.'

I feel my eyes get hot, before the words come tumbling out of my mouth faster than I can even think about them. 'This house purchase feels as though it's been doomed from the beginning. Every step has been torture. And ... and if I'm honest, it's taking its toll on Dan and me.'

'You and Dan?' She looks shocked. 'You're solid as a rock, you two.'

Once, I would've agreed with her. 'These last few months, I've been permanently stressed about the whole thing. We've been completely broke, Belinda is driving him insane, and ... I think it's brought out a side to our relationship I've never seen before. I hate it.'

I'm omitting a crucial piece of information, I'm well aware.

'You just need to talk to each other, be honest with one another. Have a chat with him tonight.'

'And I've been seeing Alex.'

She frowns. 'Who?'

I swallow. 'My old boyfriend.'

Her eyes nearly pop out of her head. I can do nothing but sit and fill her in – on everything.

'I take it Dan has no idea about any of this?' she asks.

'I don't think so.'

She clutches my hand. 'Are you seriously thinking that perhaps you should be with Alex instead of Dan?'

'No.' I lower my eyes.

'Are you *sure*?'

The answer is suddenly too difficult to say out loud. Because the truth is, I'm not sure about anything any more.

I'm on the way home, when I look at the text from Alex again, asking me to meet him on Friday. I close my eyes momentarily but all it does is make my head spin faster. I need, somehow, to get some clarity on this issue. And there's only one way to do it. I start typing.

Okay, Alex. Where would you like to meet?

That night, Dan and I share a limp ready meal and some lettuce donated by Belinda. We snuggle up together afterwards, and for a moment I forget everything other than how warm I feel in his arms.

'Listen,' he says. 'Why don't we go for a drink after work on Friday like we used to? We're going to know about the house one way or another tomorrow, so we can either celebrate, or commiserate. I'm just talking about the pub in the village – it'd be nice to have some proper time together.'

'I thought you had a team-building night on Friday?' I say,

trying to keep the panic out of my voice. 'Wasn't that what you said?'

'It's been cancelled,' he shrugs. 'Not a problem, is it?'

I stammer, 'N-not at all.'

'If you don't fancy it . . .'

'No, I do. I just – I'd . . . I had something on, that's all. I said I'd meet Sadie again. But I'll cancel her.'

'Don't do that. It wasn't a big deal.'

'This isn't either,' I insist, feeling myself redden.

'Gemma – go for your drink, your get-together, whatever it is. I'll see you when you get home. We can watch a DVD on your laptop in our room – go really wild.'

I nod, feeling guilt spread through my veins. And wondering how long I can go on like this.

Chapter 56

Dan

It's Tuesday night and I'm getting seriously concerned that Gemma is about to give herself a heart attack.

'Why do they need another week to "think about it"?' she says, slamming down on the bed. 'Part of me wishes they'd just said it's all off. I'm sick of it all.'

'You don't mean that,' I reply, sitting next to her as she unwrinkles her brow. 'Don't give up yet. Going with the new buyers would be a massive ball-ache for them. With us, the survey's out of the way and most of the legal work done. Our rivals might offer more cash, but if they go with them, they'd have to start the whole process from the beginning. And we all know how much fun that is.'

I go to reach out to her, but she rolls off the bed and stands up, oblivious. 'To top it off, the solicitor I've hardly been able to get hold of throughout is suddenly phoning me for an update. When I've got *nothing* to update her on.'

She puts her hands on her hips and leans back on the dressing table. 'Then there's the mortgage company, who are also stalking me. Apparently the offer they made us has a sell-by date; unless we draw the funds by the end of the month, we can't have them at all.'

She grabs her laptop and leaps on the bed again, opening up the Rightmove page for Pebble Cottage, presumably to torture herself. She starts scrolling through the pictures, and her eyes fill up. I put my arm round her and she sinks into me, sniffing back tears.

'Dan, I just have an instinctive feeling about this . . . that this sale is going to fall through.'

'Well, if it does, we will brush ourselves down and start again with somewhere else,' I whisper, kissing her on the head. Then I try to get her to smile, but it's obvious that nothing is going to make her do that right now.

Two days later, the sky is gorged with thunderclouds as I arrive at Sheila's house – and find her, in her words, *not in a good way*. She's weepy, she's missed a GP appointment this morning and, judging by her laboured slugs of breath, has at some point in the last twenty-four hours been smoking a not insubstantial amount of crack. She begins a long story about an argument with her son after he refused to bring baby Rose to Liverpool.

She's angry and upset. And one thing's clear: it's breaking her heart.

Without seeing a doctor to validate her benefits claims, Sheila's only source of legal income will come to a dead stop. So if she wants to keep this roof over her head, without having to hit the streets as a sex worker again, I need to get her to a GP, even if the idea terrifies her.

I decide to drive her to the enablement centre, where there's an open access clinic this morning, her shoulders trembling as she cries throughout the journey. When we arrive, two gentlemen with battling lager fumes are conducting a lively discussion in the doorway; others await their sole meal of the day inside, some chatting in groups, others alone and silent.

Some of the faces are new, others familiar, the long-term rough sleepers and hostel dwellers. Sheila stiffens as we shuffle past and her reaction, I'm fairly certain, isn't just about her fear of the doctor. She doesn't feel she belongs here.

The duty doctor can see her in fifteen minutes, so we head outside to wait. She drops her chin and refuses to make eye-contact with the old man in the tattered mac who stares at her. Her shoulders visibly relax when we're outside.

'You okay, Sheila?' I ask.

As she turns to look at me, she shakes her head, searching for words.

'I could've ended up like that.' Her voice sounds like there's glass in her throat today. 'That terrifies me, lad.'

'Sheila, you've come a long way – don't forget that.' My awareness that I sound like the script to a bad 80s soap opera doesn't stop this from being true. 'You're living independently. You've taken control of your life. *That* was the aim in all of this. I know things aren't perfect, but—'

'Lad, that's bullshit,' she interrupts. 'I'm *still using*. All those sessions you booked me in to – all those opportunities . . . I've thrown them away.' She begins to shake and slumps onto the step. With her shoulders hunched, she looks like a tiny, mal-nourished old lady, years older than the reality.

She looks up and sniffs back tears. 'I used to want to travel, you know. The girl I was best friends with at school became a hairdresser on a cruise ship. She had a hell of a life – went all over the place, and ended up living in Italy for ten years. She's back here now, runs her own salon, she's her own boss.'

She looks up, the rims of her eyes raw. 'I've never travelled anywhere. Until you came along I spent every day of my life from the age of fifteen giving blow jobs and trying to get through the day without a black eye.' Her jaw clenches. 'I never wanted to be this person, you know – I never wanted this life. I don't blame my boy. Why *would* he want his little girl near me? I wouldn't.'

I sit down next to her. 'Sheila, look up.' Reluctantly, she does so. 'I know how much you love that little girl – I knew it the day I met you. I remember you showing me the picture of her.' Her lip starts trembling again. 'How proud you were. How determined you were to turn your life around. And Sheila, you *have* done brilliantly. But you know what you've got to do to take the next step. There's an Addaction meeting today. I can take you there myself.'

When she looks up, her eyes are heavy with disbelief that after all the times she's failed to turn up, after all the opportunities she's stamped on, someone is still prepared to believe in her.

'It's up to you,' I go on. 'You can make that step again. But this time, make it count. It's up to you.'

A tear spills down her cheek. 'Thank you, Dan,' she says. It's not just the fact that it's the first time she's properly said thank you that strikes me: it's the first time she's ever used my name.

'So what do you reckon?' I sit back. 'Am I driving you there or what?'

She looks at me through her eyelashes. 'I'd like to, lad. If you don't mind.'

Alison, the administrator, pops her head through the door. 'Dan, the doctor's free.'

Sheila freezes, looking vastly less positive than ten seconds ago. 'Will you come with me?'

'Course I will,' I say, standing up.

But as we go to push open the door, a voice from the other side of the road calls my name. I turn around and hear one word slip out of my mouth. 'Dad?'

*

I can't fully compute the situation as I look at my father, then at Sheila. She brushes away tears and blinks.

'Aw, are you his dad?' She gets this gooey-eyed look on her face, as if she's just finished watching a box-set of *The Waltons*. 'Well, I take my hat off to you.'

Dad doesn't know how to answer that one and frankly neither do I.

'I'm serious,' she continues. 'To have brought up someone like this fella . . . you must be so proud. There is nothing this lad can't get done. Nothing at all. He's bent over backwards for me. I want to shake your hand.' She walks over and grabs Dad by the hand. He is dumbstruck.

'What are you doing here, Dad? I'm at work,' I tell him redundantly.

'I know,' he says, extracting himself from Sheila's grip. 'Your office told me where I'd find you. I hadn't realised I'd be interrupting . . . I'd wanted a chat before I flew home.'

'I didn't even know you were in the UK,' I point out. 'Again.'

'It's only a flying visit. I wanted to talk. That's all.'

Sheila's head is moving backwards and forwards during this conversation as if she's watching a lengthy rally at centre court in Wimbledon. When we stop, so does she, glancing once again at the door, where the doctor awaits her.

She suddenly looks broken and paralysed with fear – unlike my dad, who's popped over in his $3,000 suit, having finally decided he fancies a fatherly confab.

'Come on, Sheila, let's get you seen by this doctor.' I turn to Dad. 'Sorry, it'll have to be next time.'

I walk up into the centre feeling numb. I've spent so many years jumping when he asked me to, part of me thought I could never stop doing it. It's an oddly liberating sensation.

We're almost at the medical room, when Sheila turns on me.

'You can't leave your dad outside like that,' she hisses. 'Show some respect.'

I frown. 'Do you want me to come with you to this doctor or not?'

She doesn't answer at first. Then: 'Fine. But I'm not at all happy about it, just so you know. It's wrong.'

I'm only in with the doctor for a couple of minutes, when there's a knock on the door and I open it to see Alison. 'Dan, there's someone outside who says he's your dad. He's attracting a bit of attention.'

'Why?'

'Well, he's in a Bentley for a start.'

Dad and I find two seats in the corridor, which has become dramatically quiet after the announcement that lunch is served. He looks ill at ease here, but what he says surprises me.

'This is an impressive place.'

'We do our best,' I shrug.

'I mean it, Dan. These people, the life they're living ... well, it makes you think.' I get the impression it's been a while since Dad did much thinking, at least about anything like this. 'You know, your mother always said I was good with words. And she didn't mean it as a compliment.'

I snort.

'I don't feel very good with words at the moment,' he continues, 'but I'll have a go. I'm sorry about not turning up for the lunch. I was thoughtless and stupid, and all those things your girlfriend accused me of.'

'My girlfriend? When?'

'She came to see me – didn't she tell you? It doesn't matter anyway. The point is, I should've turned up. I can see you wanted me to meet her and – well, it *was* an important meeting I got caught up with, but that's not the point.'

I feel a kick in the guts that makes me determined to say something I've never had the balls to say before.

'No, Dad, that *isn't* the point. And I'm glad you're sorry about that – it's appreciated. But, you see, I *knew* it would happen. It's what you've always done. You did it when I was a kid and you're still doing it.'

He doesn't even try to argue.

'Oh look, it's not a problem,' I go on. 'I've learned to live with the fact that . . . well, that you don't find me very interesting. It's cool. We're fine.'

The hint of an expression crosses Dad's face. It could be regret, but no doubt I'm being optimistic.

He runs his hand over the stubble on his chin, concentrating hard. 'Dan, I've been a crap father. I can't deny it. But I want things to change between us.'

His words wash over me. I don't even want to hear his promises any more. 'Okay,' I say coolly. 'Then it's over to you.'

'What do you mean?'

'I mean … fine. I'm up for it. A shift in our relationship, whatever you want to call it. But next time – you're organising the lunch.'

He nods. 'I hear what you're saying. I do, son.' He realises there's nothing else to add. And I don't feel inclined to fill in the gaps. He stands up.

'I've got a plane to catch, but I'll be in touch, I prom—' But he doesn't finish the word. 'I'll be in touch.'

I walk him to the door.

'I liked Gemma, by the way.'

'Right,' I mumble.

'She's great. Balls of steel – and devious,' he smiles, 'but great.'

And he walks out of the door, leaving me thinking only of one of those words.

I tell Gemma about Dad's visit that night as she's pulling on her pyjamas.

'I can see why you'd be sceptical,' she says. 'And you're right to be. But you might be pleasantly surprised. I hope so anyway.' She leans over and kisses me on the lips.

'Did you see Grandma tonight?' I ask.

'Briefly when I got in from work. She was tired so was going for a lie-down.'

'Oh, really?'

'She did look a little peaky, to be honest,' she tells me. 'You should pop in before work tomorrow.'

'I will.'

She stands up and goes to the bathroom to brush her teeth. I've just opened my book when her phone rings. Sadie's name flashes up, so I hit answer. 'Hi Sadie, it's Dan. Gemma's just in the bathroom. Do you want me to go and get her?'

'Oh, don't worry about it, Dan. It's not important. Tell her we'll catch up at the weekend,' she says.

'You're seeing each other tomorrow night, aren't you?'

'Not as far as I know . . .' Her voice trails off. 'Oh. Possibly.' I can hear the cogs grinding in her brain. 'Yeah. Tomorrow.'

'She said you were meeting for a drink after work. Isn't that right?'

'Yeah. I'd just forgotten.' She could not sound more suspicious if she tried. 'I'd better go. See you,' she adds uneasily, before ending the call.

When Gemma returns, I can hear my heart thudding in my ears.

'That was Sadie for you,' I say, trying to look casual as I throw the phone onto the bed. 'She wanted a chat, but said

412

she'd catch up at the weekend. I think she'd forgotten you were going for a drink tomorrow.'

I look firmly at my book, but can't fail to notice, out of the corner of my eye, the look of horror on her face.

'Oh, her head's all over the place at the moment,' Gemma says. 'Thanks.'

She climbs into bed next to me, kisses me on the cheek and pulls the sheet over her.

And that's all it takes for me to know for certain. My girlfriend has been lying to me again.

Chapter 57

Gemma

He suspects. I can tell he suspects even before Sadie texts to warn me about their conversation and, yet again, I spend the night tossing and turning as I whip myself into a frenzy of anxiety.

When I wake the next morning after a fractured two hours' sleep, I creep silently to the bathroom, taking my phone with me. There, I compose a text:

> Alex, I can't meet you tonight. I'm really sorry to cancel at such late notice but something unavoidable came up. Gems.

I hit send, then delete the message from my outbox.

As I head back into the room, Dan's eyelashes are flickering open. I sit on the edge of the bed and press my lips against his warm forehead.

'Morning, sleepy head.'

'Morning,' he murmurs, slipping his arm around me. Then he stops, and the look in his eyes changes from blissful, slumbrous ignorance, to something else entirely.

'Have a great day. I'm going to head off,' I whisper, forcing a smile.

He nods. 'Good luck with your presentation.'

'Thanks – I'll need it. I love you,' I tell him.

He kisses me, but for the first time ever, he doesn't say anything in response.

I'm downstairs with my car keys in my hand and about to drive to work, when Belinda appears with her phone in her hand, her face drained of colour.

'Everything okay?' I ask.

'A journalist has just phoned.' Panic flickers in her eyes. 'The story's out about me and James.'

I don't get a chance to answer before she disappears into the living room.

'Belinda, I'm so sorry,' I say, following her. She perches on the edge of the sofa; her hands are shaking.

'I'm going to have to phone the publishers and tell them,' she frets. 'This is going to be awful.'

'It might not be as bad as you think,' I offer.

She looks at the phone and gulps. 'Sorry, I didn't mean to keep you. Have a good day, Gemma.'

I touch her on the arm. 'Good luck with your phone call.'

I walk out of the room as she straightens her back and begins dialling. Only when I have my hand on the front door do I realise that in my haste, I've managed to abandon my keys on the living-room table. I edge into the room, hoping to dart in and grab them without interrupting.

Belinda has her back to me and is facing the patio windows as she talks.

'I'm so sorry, Angela. It was stupid, I know.' I can hear Angela's response from the other side of the room and it's clear from her angry trill that she's *not* impressed. 'I know.' More trilling. 'I do know.' More and more trilling.

Then Belinda spots me in the patio windows' reflection and turns and glances at me.

'Is it over?' she repeats. 'Of *course* it is . . .' Then her voice trails off as we catch each other's eyes. She puts the phone back to her ear and clears her throat, before saying, 'Angela?' her jaw clenches. 'I know this isn't what you want to hear – but no. I lied. It's *not* over. And I don't want it to be either.'

The response from Alex comes not in the form of a text, but a phone call, which he makes as I'm pulling up into work. 'Hi,' I say, my heart fluttering in my throat.

'Hi,' he replies.

'Sorry about tonight,' I say, feeling the need to fill the silence.

'It's okay. But Gems . . . I'd hoped to have a chat. I need to get a few things off my chest. I hadn't wanted to do it over the phone.'

'That sounds serious,' I say lightly, as anxiety prickles on my neck.

'It is.' There's another silence. 'Gems, I think you already know what I'm about to say, but I'm going to say it anyway.'

'Don't,' I interrupt. 'Don't go on.' But he does.

'I've never stopped being in love with you. Not ever.'

My insides clench. 'Please, Alex—'

'I've got to tell you how I feel. It took longer than you could possibly imagine to get over losing you. I'm not saying I spent the last twelve years in mourning, but this is the truth: every woman I've ever met since has lived in your shadow. You're the only woman I've ever wanted.'

'Alex, we were just teenagers,' I protest. 'We're different people now.'

'That's just it, we're not. I've fallen in love with you again. You're all I can think about. I've never said this to anyone ever before – I've never been that kind of guy – but if I don't say it now, I'll regret it for the rest of my life.'

'Say what, Alex?'

He sighs. 'I want you to leave Dan.'

'Please don't say that.'

'I want you to be with me instead.' My heart constricts and a flood of tears spills down my cheeks as I listen silently. 'I'm well aware that that makes me a bastard,' he continues. 'But there's no point in me pretending any longer that I want things any other way.'

I can't bring myself to say anything. Anything at all.

'Meet me later,' he implores. 'And let's talk about this, face to face. Come on, Gems. It's the only way.'

Chapter 58

Dan

Is Gemma having an affair?

That's the question that burst into my head, the moment I opened my eyes this morning. I know things haven't been as easy between us as before we moved to Buddington. But did I think they'd got so bad that she'd run into the arms of someone else? I must admit, I didn't.

The possibility that she's sleeping with another man fills me with a jagged rage. It boils up in me in the shower as I'm getting ready for work and grips me by the throat as I'm pulling on my clothes.

And as I head downstairs minutes after she's left, it is still there, refusing to let me listen to the other possibility: that this might be innocent. It occurs to me that the only way I'd definitively find out the answer is by following her to wherever she's going tonight.

The thought is loathsome. But what the hell is the alternative?

I hear Mum on the phone in the living room, so leave without saying goodbye as Gemma's tail-lights turn out of the driveway.

I'm about to get into the car, when I'm reminded that Grandma wasn't feeling well. I'm late for work, but head to her annexe, where I find her sitting on the sofa in her dressing gown, watching the breakfast news.

I knock at the window and she looks up, startled, then gestures to me that she's coming to the door. She pushes herself up unsteadily and takes slow, deliberate steps to the door.

I'm shocked by how weak she looks, the grey undertones of her skin.

'Grandma, are you okay?' I hold her arm and help her back inside.

'Not feeling myself, I must admit. Come in. Let me make you a cuppa.'

'You should be over at Mum's,' I tell her. 'I think she should call a doctor.'

She sits down on the sofa, forgetting the tea. 'You're probably right.'

'I'll go and get her.'

'Danny?' I turn round again. 'Let's have that cuppa first. Flick the kettle on, won't you?'

I make the tea and bring it over on a tray, just as she likes it. Tea pot. Milk first. Three sugars. Grandma has never believed in depriving herself.

'I loved that day we went to the lake,' she says with a quivering smile.

'I'm glad. You're a madwoman though. You technically shouldn't be doing things like that at your age.'

'What's the point in sitting around all day? That's not living, is it?' she argues. 'Anyway, I wanted you to know how happy you've made me. Not only at the lake, but just by being here. You and Gemma. It's been wonderful.'

I fail to answer.

'What's the matter?' she asks.

'Nothing.' I look at my hands. 'Just . . .'

She rescues me from having to continue. 'It must've been hard for you two. I can see the pressure you've been under. You haven't had many breaks since you've tried to buy this house, have you?'

'Not really, Grandma. It's been strained lately, I must admit.'

'That's understandable.' She shakily brings the tea cup to her lips and takes a sip. 'Make sure you keep it in perspective though, won't you?'

I look up. 'What do you mean?'

'One of the benefits of old age is realising what really matters. Houses, surveys, the stresses you're under . . . they seem so crucial now, but they're all fleeting things. Love, on the other hand: that's important.'

I lower my eyes.

'Danny, what's the matter?'

Much as I love her, I don't want to have a heart-to-heart with Grandma about my fears that Gemma is having an affair.

'Don't worry, I don't want to pry,' she whispers. Then she reaches over and holds my hand, her papery fingers gripping around mine. 'But let me tell you this. You two belong together. I've never felt more certain. So make me a promise that you won't let her go. She's not perfect, Danny. Nobody is. But if you love somebody, you need to be gentle with them. Forgive each other. And never forget what's really important.'

Chapter 59

Gemma

I sit alone in the meeting room at work, rehearsing my presentation for this afternoon and making certain I'm strong on the bits that were written by Sebastian. I produce all the inflections Rosie told me to, and wind up sounding very much like I've got a screw loose.

But just as I reach my final slide, I slump in my chair and can't think about the presentation any longer.

All I can think about is Dan. Alex. Me.

I pick up my car keys and leave the building.

From the moment he came back into my life, there was only ever one man for me. I've had my second chance and I'm not about to blow it now. Because what I feel for him couldn't be clearer. And the thought of letting him slip away from me burns inside me like a firework, fierce and brilliant.

Love was easy when I was Alex's girlfriend, all those years ago. It was all-consuming and simple, and the world was a glorious place inside that little bubble where we lived.

With Dan, things have been difficult, complicated and far from black and white, at least in the last couple of months.

Alex wants me to make a decision.

But in truth it was made long ago.

And I'm furious with myself that there was ever any doubt of it. Though perhaps Belinda was right about one thing: our heart plays tricks on us sometimes. The key is recognising the tricks for what they are.

Alex has never looked more handsome as I push open the door of the same Icelandic coffee shop where we met, back in June. He's in civvies – jeans and a pale checked shirt that makes him look healthily tanned – and is chatting to a waitress as her eyes glint.

He glances up and stops talking. She looks over too, before moving quietly away. Then he stands and walks slowly forward, his face breaking into an enormous smile.

Chapter 60

Dan

Since the moment I made the decision not to follow Gemma, I've been trying to work out why, for whatever reason, I'm apparently not that kind of guy.

Though part of me wonders if I'm being that noble. Maybe I'm scared I'd get there, discover there *is* someone else, and be unable to face the consequences of that. Because infidelity is something I couldn't live with, I know that much.

So, effectively, it would mean no more me and Gemma. No more house. No more happy ending. And I can't face that. As appalled as I am at how infinitely and dangerously I love this woman, I don't want it to get to that point. I want her to change her mind. I want her to choose me, not him, whoever the fucking bastard is.

My alternative course of action – the one I decide to

pursue – is one I can't explain. In lots of ways, it defies logic. It only comes to me once I'm behind the wheel of the car, driving aimlessly with my temples throbbing. It's then that I realise, finally, that there's only one place to go.

Pebble Cottage looks sad and empty this lunchtime. The builders have gone and there are no vans outside, none of the bustle we've come to expect. There's a dent on the doorframe, a casualty of the equipment that's been hoisted in and out over the last few weeks. I stand in front of the house and think about Gemma and me. Our future.

Whatever she's done – or is doing – I just cannot imagine this place without her. As I look inside, a fantasy ignites in my brain and I picture us in there: her, me, maybe a baby toddling around. God . . . am I really thinking that? It appears that I am.

Does this make me a pathetic, deluded fool?

Possibly.

But more than anything, it makes me realise that I've taken way too much for granted. This is the woman I love, and I am gripped by a feeling that I can't just sit around whinging about her going off with someone else. I've got to fight for her.

I pull my collar against my neck and walk towards the beach, as the wind picks up.

There is, however, one problem with fighting for her. No matter how convinced Hollywood is that women love a good, old-fashioned punch-up, in my experience this is far from the case.

The one and only time I have come close to getting in a fight before today, it was with an 18-stone bloke over a parking space. He swore at Gemma. It was not acceptable. But she did not hold my coat and look on in admiration while I defended her honour. She just grabbed me by the shirt as if I'd taken leave of my senses and hissed, 'What are you *doing*?'

I clamber down onto a rock and sit with my legs dangling as I watch the ebb and flow of the tide, pondering one question.

How do I win back the heart of the woman who means everything to me?

I glance back in the direction of Pebble Cottage and draw in a lungful of air. I promised her a home with a view. It's time to deliver.

The stationery in Heswall's branch of Tesco isn't quite Liberty's finest, but it will have to do.

I find the nearest drinking establishment, a trendy cocktail place with a champagne bar on the other side of the village. It's warm and lively and I'm lucky to get a seat at the end of the bar, where I take pains to avert my eyes from the couple next to me, who are snogging so furiously they could've dived for pearls since they last drew breath.

I order a Coke, pull out my pen and begin writing. The

words emerge with surprising fluency for a man who never usually considers himself poetic, except when his back is against the wall.

Dear Mrs Deaver,

I realise that writing you a letter is unorthodox and that, technically, we're only meant to deal with one another via our estate agent. But I hope that when you hear what I've got to say, you'll understand why I wanted to make contact.

My girlfriend and I fell in love with Pebble Cottage the moment we walked into it. Not just for the usual reasons: location, nice fittings, good-sized kitchen, even though it has all of those things.

But because, quite simply, it felt right – no, perfect. Everything about it made us believe that we'd finally found our home, and after the number of viewings we'd endured, that was no mean feat. I hope you had some happy times there. Because it feels like a house that was loved and cared for – and that's exactly what we want to do with it too.

I know you've received a higher offer from another party, one we don't have the money to match.

I won't insult your intelligence by stressing that we're ready to buy now, risk-free, with all the surveys and legal work already completed. You know all that, and also that you would incur considerable expense and inconvenience if you were to start a sale – with different buyers – afresh. Despite that, Gemma and I take nothing for granted.

I wanted, simply, to give you an insight into what it would mean to us if Pebble Cottage became ours. Gemma in particular has dreamed about living in a house like yours for her entire life.

And while I wouldn't expect you to make a decision based solely on the pathetic (though genuine) pleas of a man you've never met, I wanted to let you know that the answer to that question – what it would mean to us – can be summed up in one word: everything. It would mean everything to us. I hope you give us a chance to make our dreams come true.

With my best wishes,

Daniel Blackwood

I fold up the note and check the time – it's almost 1.30 p.m. The estate agents might be closed for lunch, but I've got Rich's number and, although he hasn't answered one of my calls yet, I can only try. As I dial the number, a phone along the bar springs into life:

'*DIAMONDS ARE FOREVERRR!*'

I look over in time to see the male half of the snogging couple stick out his hand and grope around on the bar, refusing to unlock his tongue from the woman's tonsils. They finally prise themselves apart and he answers sounding so breathless you'd think he'd just completed a heptathlon.

'Hello, Rich,' I say.

'Sorry, but I'm at a conference in Slough at the moment,' he replies, as his female acquaintance puts her lips on his neck as if she's attempting to remove his Adam's apple via liposuction. 'High level – team-building stuff, you know.'

I put down the phone, stand up and go and move next to them.

'Hi, Rich,' I repeat. The girl removes her lips and looks up at me, clearly momentarily worried I might be her dad. She looks about twenty, with bleached blonde hair, a nose ring, and eyes made up like Bette Davis in *Whatever Happened to Baby Jane?*

'Wha . . .? I'm busy,' he says, straightening his tie.

'Your conference in Slough, I know. I won't keep you,' I grin, pulling up a chair. 'Don't mind if I join you, do you?'

He looks at the girl. 'Don't answer that,' I say, before he can speak. 'I need a favour.'

A sulky little frown appears on his face. 'What?'

'I need you to give this letter to the owners of Pebble Cottage.'

'What does it say? I can't accept bribes. I'll need to know the content.'

'It's easier if I read it to you.' I take out the letter as he rolls his eyes.

By the time I've finished, Rich appears to want to throw a

bag over my head and drown me in the River Dee for squandering his precious snogging time. 'I'll see what I can do.' He snatches the letter from me.

'That was just about the best thing I've ever heard.'

I look up and the girl's eyes are bright pink. 'Oh my GOD!' she sobs, grabbing the napkin and giving it the sort of blow that could dislodge brain cells. 'That's *so* romantic. Rich – we have to make sure they get this house.'

Rich looks alarmed. 'I can't. My client is the owner, not the buyers. I have to get the vendor the best deal they can. There's one and a half per cent at stake here. The point is,' he goes on hurriedly, 'this is totally unconventional.'

'And totally gorgeous,' she gushes. 'You believe in true love, don't you?'

Rich looks as though he's unsure what will explode first, his head or his trousers. 'My mum always said I was a "new man" but—'

'Rich, you're the man.' I stand up and slap him on the back, before turning to the girl, who's dragging Rich in the direction of the door, presumably to force him to spring into action. 'This is a good guy you've got here,' I tell her. 'You want to keep tight hold of him.' I wink in a manner I hope he might appreciate.

'I will,' she promises as Rich looks mildly astonished at this turn of events.

Chapter 61

Gemma

Alex can barely look at me. He knows what's coming and the only way he can deal with it is – mercifully – with his usual sense of humour.

'How about a piece of cake, Gems?'

'Not this time,' I say with an apologetic smile. 'But thank you.'

He glances at my face. 'Now I'm a born optimist, but I've got to be honest with you, Gems . . . I'm not getting vibes that this is going to be the big, romantic reunion I was hoping for.'

He's trying to sound joky, but his voice wavers.

And it's then that the words bubble to my lips that I've known since that day Dan and I met – for the second time – on the banks of Lake Windermere. I've felt it every day since. Sometimes quietly, obscured by day-to-day difficulties and distractions of the heart. Sometimes loud and clear. Which is how it is now. And how it always will be, deep down, no matter what difficulties and distractions the future holds.

I am now convinced, from the way the sellers have acted, that Pebble Cottage will very probably not end up being ours. A house I'd started to see as inextricably linked to my relationship with Dan. And that has given me a lot to think about.

I can come to terms with losing that house, with its feature fireplaces, original sandstone flagging and gorgeous oak panelled doors. But it's taken the prospect of losing that to make me realise that I can't live without Dan.

Telling my teenage love what I've decided to do is not an easy thing.

But my decision is unequivocal. What I want – or rather, *whom* I want – has never been clearer.

'I'm so sorry, Alex. But I'm in love with Dan. And I always will be.'

Chapter 62

Dan

As I march back to the car, my rage about the thought of Gemma seeing someone is replaced by something else entirely. Now, most of all, I find myself praying that she has an epiphany, realises I'm the only guy for her. I fantasise about her telling him she'll never see him again – because nobody could match my personality, my sense of humour, my massive ... okay, that might be pushing it.

Even if she tells him none of the above and just pities me too much to leave, I'll take it.

I'm near the car when my phone starts vibrating in my pocket. I close my eyes and pray that it's her. In fact, it's Mum. And when I answer the phone I can barely make out what she's saying.

'Dan!' she sobs as I remember that Gemma texted me earlier to say that the press were onto her and James.

'Oh, Mum, I'm sorry I didn't call you today. Gemma told me about the journalist and—'

'It's not that, Dan.' Her voice wavers. 'It's your grandma.'

'What about her?'

When she says the next words, I can feel the strength slipping away from my legs as I slump in the car.

'I'm at the hospital, Daniel. She's had a heart attack.'

Chapter 63

Gemma

I stand in front of 150 people, so terrified that I'm even unable to pick up my glass of water, without which I know I'll sound as though I've inhaled a bag of Hoover dust.

The words of Rosie, the public-speaking Nazi, pound through my head. Look confident. Project. Stand straight. Work the room. Work the room. WORK THE ROOM.

What the hell does 'work the room' mean anyway? I stand, mute, as people drift in after lunch – a lunch I've singularly failed to eat because my nerves were too busy ripping apart the lining of my stomach. I'm supposed to be doing as Rosie instructed – walking round, shaking hands, making friends with these people. In her words, 'Make sure there are no strangers – only friends!'

None of them look like friends. None at all.

Not the fat bloke with the moustache and pork-pie crumbs in his beard. Not the woman with the trowelled-on make-up and nails that could qualify for an architectural award.

None of them could look more like enemies if they wore Rambo headscarves and were toting AK-47s.

When they're all seated, Sebastian leaps on stage and gives a performance that is effusive, boundless, positively evangelical. And all he's doing is my introduction.

'Ladies and gentlemen, good afternoon,' he pronounces.

He is quintessential proof that it's not *what* you say it's *how* you say it that counts. Because, honestly, nothing that comes out of his mouth is anything other than garbage. But the audience are transfixed as he strides across the podium, charisma and charm almost bursting out of his chest.

'A wise man once said: "Advertising is the science of arresting human intelligence long enough to get money out of it".' He pauses for effect, and for the ripple of mirth to subside. 'Now I'd like to introduce one lady who plans to do *exactly* that. So, arrest your intelligence, guys and gals, and give a warm welcome to – Gemma Johnston!'

I straighten my back and focus. Then I reach my podium, feeling hot and cold at the same time, ready to embark on the presentation of my career . . . when a mobile phone rings.

The entire audience starts checking their bags and pockets, rustling round with phones as I try desperately – with sweat beading on my brow – not to be put off. My heart is kickboxing as my chest heaves up and down in panicked breaths and I pray that they'd all just stop and turn and look at me again. And more than anything, I wish whoever left their bloody phone on WOULD TURN THE DAMN THING OFF!

'Gemma, it's yours,' Sebastian announces.

Perspiring and scarlet, I scramble across the stage and down the steps to the bag I've left on a chair. But by some perverse twist of fate, it's stuck in the side pocket and, instead of neutralising the situation, I am left wrestling with my bag like I'm Crocodile Dundee, trying to get it out. The audience titters as I finally hit silent, try to stop hyperventilating, put it back in the bag that I then carry up on the stage, where it can do no more harm.

'Sorry about that,' I mutter, back at the podium. Only now I'm ready to begin, people have started chatting again; the silence Sebastian commanded has disintegrated and everyone is mid-conversation, except the bloke on the second row who's now picking bits of pork pie out of his teeth.

Sebastian repeats his call to order.

'Thanks, Sebastian,' I say smoothly, trying not to die on the spot as I prepare to read the bit of the speech he's written. 'I'm here to tell you about our vision for the future of female contraception. How to turn a woman on . . .'

My voice trails off as I become aware that something is vibrating, right on cue. Then I realise it's the phone in my bag. Only, nobody knows that. All the audience knows is that one minute I'm talking about getting hot and heavy – the next they're treated to a soundtrack that's very like a Rampant Rabbit turned on full.

'How to turn a woman on ...' I repeat, in the absence of any other ideas.

Only, now the bag has taken on a life of its own and is buzzing its way across the stage, edging towards me as if begging for attention.

'How to turn a woman ...'

The room erupts into laughter as I dive across the stage again, end the call and muster up a titter, as if the joke was fully intended. I register blankly that the phone call is from Rich as I shove my mobile firmly back into my jacket pocket, unable to start messing about to turn it off again.

Finally, the presentation begins and can be summed up thus: the most wretched fifteen minutes of my life.

This is partly because of the gems of wisdom Sebastian has forced me to come out with ('We ladies know just how bad fellas can be at remembering those rubber johnnies, don't we?') and partly because, every time my phone starts vibrating, I'm forced to raise my voice several notches, leaving the audience thinking I've got an elastic band round my vocal cords.

Relief ripples through me as I finally step down from the podium and sit trembling in the front row, listening to Sebastian as my reddened cheeks start to slowly extinguish.

And trying to work out how I can get my phone out of my pocket without anyone – particularly Sebastian – seeing.

He's midway through talking some bollocks about capturing the essence of liberation, when I become aware that everyone's staring at me. 'Isn't that right, Gemma?' I turn and look around to see if anyone else might go by the same name.

The answer appears to be no. So I take the only option that seems to be open to me, which is to concur with his point enthusiastically, only to realise as he moves onto his next slide that I've just agreed with the statement, 'women want to take control of their own vaginas'.

Refusing to dwell on the fact that Sebastian has just made 150 people – including six directors and the man with the pork pie in his beard – think about my vagina, I reach into my pocket for my phone, take it out surreptitiously and glance at the screen. I have four missed calls from Rich.

I slip out of my seat and run to the exit before anyone can argue. When I'm outside, I phone Rich's mobile.

'Jeeze Louise! Your Batphone has been red hot. Where've you been?'

'I'm in a presentation, what's the problem?'

'The problem is, my vendors want to talk to you direct after your fella wrote that letter to them.'

'What letter?'

'It doesn't matter, the point is, you need to speak to Mrs Deaver. Now. Directly. I've got her number. She hasn't told me what it's about – she wants to speak to you, apparently. But look, *if* things were to go your way, there is every chance you could exchange contracts and complete today.'

'Is that even do-able? It's 2.30 p.m.'

'The solicitors both say so. I took the liberty of phoning them after my conversation with Mrs Deaver, just to see – in principle, you know. Gemma, you need to get on that phone NOW.'

'I can't, I'm in a presentation,' I whisper hysterically. 'Get Dan to phone her.'

'I've been phoning *him* all afternoon and got no response. Look, it's up to you, but you have two and a half hours before everyone closes for business for the weekend. Do you really want to let this run onto next week and risk her changing her mind again?'

'I refuse to be backed into a corner on this,' I say weakly.

'Really, Gemma?' he asks furiously. 'When you're *this* close?' My stomach lurches. 'You could have the keys to this house by tonight. Think about it. In fact, *don't* think about it. Just phone her!'

My head swirls. 'Arrghhh! Oh God, okay. Give me the number.' I grab a pen from the hotel's reception and have started writing it down when someone grabs me by the arm. I spin round to see it's Sebastian.

'Gemma – it's part two. You're on. NOW!'

'Rich, I've got to go,' I say hopelessly. 'Please keep phoning

Dan. Tell him to talk to her and make the decision, whatever it is.'

'I've tried—' he begins, but I put down the phone and race back into the room, ready to face the enemy for the second time.

Chapter 64

Dan

I become aware that my back pocket is vibrating and only then register that the phone's been ringing for some time. I pull it out and spot Rich's number, before pressing 'off' and laying it on the hospital table.

Mum is beside the bed, her cheek resting on Grandma's hand, tears and disbelief in her eyes. Sunlight streams through the windows and casts light on Grandma's face. As she lies, still and silent, she looks like an angel, ethereal and otherworldly.

I put my hand on Mum's shoulder and she stirs and looks up at me, her lips trembling. I know I have to be the strong one today. When I was a kid, she used to say after Dad left: 'You're the man of the house now, Daniel.' And although Mum never really needed anyone to look after her, today, I need to step up to the mark.

Mum presses her lips against Grandma's fingers, then slowly stands as I cuddle her into me. She feels smaller than I'd ever thought of her, thin and birdlike. Or maybe it's just today's jolting reminder of how fragile life is, how precious and how short.

Mum tells me she's going to get a breath of fresh air, before leaving me alone with Grandma. I sit in silence next to the bed for a few moments before a dam bursts inside me and tears spill onto the bleached white bedsheet.

'I love you, Grandma.'

It feels good to utter the words, though they're followed by a punch of recognition that I wish I'd been able to say it one last time before this happened.

I run my hand gently over her hair. It's fluffy and fine, the texture of a baby's. And for some daft reason it makes me think about her pulling on that swimming cap and taking me by the hand as we went crashing through the waves, with Grandad when I was a little kid, then again just a few weeks ago.

If I'd known then that our Bala Lake swim would be the last time she'd get to do the thing she loved most … Actually, I don't know what I'd have done differently. Perhaps it was the most fitting finale to a lifetime of love for the water.

Of course, I always knew that she wouldn't be with us forever. But Grandma had this way of skipping through life in a manner that gave the impression that the day when she wouldn't be around any more would never come. Technically, she is still with us. But it really is technically – in a medically-induced coma, clinging onto life.

Mum was with her when it all happened; she'd called in just as Grandma said she could feel pressure in her chest. The heart attack happened afterwards, when they were in the ambulance. The paramedics sprang into life, and although their actions probably prevented her from dying instantly, the doctors have been clear that the Flossie we're left with will never be the same again.

Oxygen deprivation. They're the two words I keep hearing. That and the stark warning that it's unlikely Grandma will wake up. Her body might have made it through, but her spirit died in that ambulance.

It occurs to me that she might have been a little afraid of death as she grew older; perhaps that was why she went on about her age, underlining the frailties that those around her found difficult to recognise.

But if there's one truth about Flossie Blackwood, it's that she never let fear of anything stop her from living.

Chapter 65

Gemma

The rest of the presentation is no less ghastly than the start. An hour and a half of intense questioning from a group who, it emerges, have just been through a major cost-cutting exercise and aren't exactly keen on the idea of squandering resources on something as trifling as advertising.

I emerge from the auditorium sweating so much, it's a wonder I don't actually squelch when I reach the lift. And yet all I can think of is the call from Rich – whether he managed to get hold of Dan and – the real crux – whether we're actually going to own this house by the end of today.

I emerge from the lift onto the ground floor and am about to dart out of the hotel to make my one, crucial phone call, when Sebastian smacks me on the shoulder.

'So what do we think, kiddo? Triumph or damp squib?'

'Hmm . . . I thought it went okay,' I offer. 'Your speech was great, Sebastian.'

He grins. 'Thanks.' Then he frowns. 'Are you all right? You look a bit flushed.'

I'm about to protest that I'm fine, when I re-think it. 'I am feeling a bit light-headed, now you mention it. I'm just going to step outside.'

At which point I scuttle to the door, turn on my phone and discover . . . precisely nothing. I'd expected to have a barrage of phone calls from Dan and Rich at least, telling me what was going on.

I dial Rich's number but it goes straight to messages. I phone Dan's number and that goes straight to messages. I phone the estate agent's office and get through to Janine, the girl with the nose ring.

'Oh, hello, Ms Johnston. You are *so* lucky to have a boyfriend like Dan. That letter he wrote – how romantic! I'm going to start setting my sights higher. All it used to take was a bag of chips and a Lambrini and I was anyone's.' She giggles.

'Do you happen to know if Rich is there?'

'He's at a viewing. Should be back soon.'

'Okay. I don't suppose you know the outcome of his dealings with our owners? Did Dan get hold of her?'

She hesitates. 'I'm not supposed to say anything.'

'Oh please, come on! Put me out of my misery,' I beg.

'Well, I obviously don't know the official line. But I know what Mrs Deaver told Rich on the phone.'

'Which was?'

'That they couldn't possibly go with the higher offer after reading that.'

My knees almost buckle. 'So Dan *did* get hold of her?'

'Literally no idea. But I do know that they've said no to the people who put in the other offer.'

Dan doesn't phone me back, despite repeated calls and messages. I'm desperate to update him about the house, to share what Janine told me with him. But as the phone goes to messages yet again, I feel a surge of despair.

I think back to the suspicion in Dan's eyes this morning and am gripped by the possibility that he knows about Alex. That he's found out and that's why he won't speak to me.

I phone Annabel to see if she's heard from the Deavers' solicitors about exchanging contracts, but she says she's heard nothing yet.

'Don't worry though,' she reassures me. 'We seem to be all systems go, so all I need to do is pin down their solicitor. There's still an hour. It can be done.'

I continue trying to get hold of Rich, but he proves as elusive as Dan. And in the meantime I'm dragged back into the auditorium to be grilled by the lot from Bang, answering questions such as, 'Why can't we have a bunny like the one in the John Lewis advert?'

I tell myself not to get my hopes up about the idea of stepping over the threshold in a few hours. We've been messed around before and it's possible that Janine got this entirely wrong.

At the end, I dive out of the hotel and try Dan and Rich again, to no avail. The journey home is torture. I'm passing the village green of Thornton Hough when Rich finally, *finally* returns my calls.

My heart loops the loop as I pull in outside one of the Tudor facades and grab my phone.

Before he speaks, I gaze at two little boys on the lush lawn, giggling as they tumble over each other like baby lions play-fighting. I push my elbow onto the car window and feel the warmth of the sun on my skin as I'm filled by an overwhelm-ing sense of optimism.

'Gemma.'

'Rich.' I pause. 'Tell me you have good news. Did you manage to get hold of Dan?'

'Right, well, I'll come to that in a minute. Let me get straight to the point. That's what I've always prided myself on. None of that estate agency bullshit. I'm the Straight-Talking Kid.'

'Okay, good. So have we got the house?'

'Right.' He takes a deep breath. 'I think I need to fill you in on a little background first.'

'I thought you were getting straight to the point?'

'I am, I am. I mean, I will. But this is the point. Kind of.'

I decide it'll be quicker to humour him. 'Go on then.'

'Mrs Deaver wanted to speak to you direct, simply because Dan had gone to the trouble of addressing his letter to *her* direct. But she's now on a plane so can't do that.'

'Okay.'

'Right, well, she's asked me to do this instead. Mr and Mrs Deaver, as you know, were in the process of getting a divorce.'

'Yes?'

'And, well, as you know, another buyer came in and tried to gazump you.'

'Yes?'

'Well, I hand-delivered a copy of the letter to Mrs Deaver this afternoon. And Janine my assistant emailed another copy to Mr Deaver.'

'And . . .?'

'And after they read it, they said there was no way they could go with the other buyers.'

'That's what Janine told me,' I say with a jolt of elation.

'Right, well, basically they said they want to bring this whole thing to a conclusion as soon as possible.'

My jaw drops as I think about the implications of this. 'Rich, you don't know what this means to me,' I begin. 'I can't wait to tell Dan. Oh God, after all this – oh Rich! Thank you, thank you!'

'Gemma, STOP!' he interrupts.

'What's the matter? You've just said they've already told the other buyers to go and whistle.'

'They have. But – but I'm sorry to say . . .'

'*What?*' I ask sternly.

'Dan's letter – Mrs Deaver said it got them thinking. About true love, and commitment . . . and staying together. The upshot is, Gemma, they've decided to give their relationship another go.'

'Whaaaat?' I croak.

'I'm sorry, Gemma. I've been instructed to remove the house from the market. They're moving back in.'

I don't feel sad about losing Pebble Cottage. It's as if everything we've been through has stripped away its rosy glow and smeared it in something entirely less pleasant. I'm still angry about the money we've spent, the time we've wasted, the hopes and dreams that have been shattered, thanks to the emotional whims of a couple who clearly couldn't make a firm decision if their lives depended on it.

But most of all, I feel a deep sense of love for a man who did everything within his power to get that house for me, even if it didn't work out as he'd hoped.

I pull up the car into Buddington's drive and realise to my surprise that Dan's car is already here, prompting the question of why all my calls have gone unanswered.

I enter the house, with the letter he wrote – read out to me by Janine – still spinning around my head, and wondering how I'm going to break the news to him about Pebble Cottage. I head up to the bedroom, when I hear a noise from Belinda's room.

I follow the sound of soft sobbing and find the door ajar. I remember the call she made to the publishers this morning and feel a stab of pity.

'Belinda?' I say, as I find her stuffing clothes into an overnight bag.

Then she turns round and I get a proper look at her face. And I immediately know that this is about something far, far bigger.

Chapter 66

Dan

I'm sitting at the lakeside throwing stones into the water as they plink onto the surface like an un-tuned piano. Despite everything that's happening, my mind is surprisingly focused.

I feel a hand against my back and turn to see Gemma standing above me.

'Dan, it's raining,' she says quietly. 'Why don't you come inside?'

I nod and push myself up. She rests her head against my neck, and it's only as her hot tears touch my skin that I realise how cold I am.

'Grandma had a heart attack,' I whisper. She pulls back and nods, and can't answer in any other way than for her face to crumple up with emotion.

'Your mum told me what happened.' Looking at her unleashes something inside me and, in front of the woman I love, I weep the tears of a baby, tears of pure grief.

I don't know how long we stand in the rain. I just know that, against all the odds, having her hand in mine makes me feel better. It feels right. And I know that no matter what she's done, I *need* this woman in my life.

We crunch towards the house, hand in hand, and the words that have been spinning around my head for the last week come crashing out of my mouth. 'I know there's someone else.'

She stops dead and looks at me. 'What?'

'I'd suspected for a while, Gemma. Then Sadie blew your cover last night.'

Her eyes drift away from me, but then she grips my hand. 'Dan, there isn't anyone else,' she says emphatically. 'Not like that. Well, not—'

'Before you continue,' I interrupt. 'I want to say something.'

'But—'

'*Please.*' I leave her with no choice but to listen, even if she is shaking her head in protest.

'Gemma, there is literally nobody else I want. I'm done with playing the field. I'm done with being single. I don't want to be like my dad, with a succession of women on the go. When I met you, everything changed. You make me the man I want to be.' I say the next words from my heart.

'You're everything I ever wanted, Gemma. I'd do anything

not to lose you. So please, whoever he is . . . I suppose what I'm asking you to do is simply this: choose me.'

'Dan, I've already chosen you,' she whispers. 'But . . . I think I've got some explaining to do.'

Chapter 67

Gemma

The only thing left to do is to tell the truth. Nothing less will do, after all the trouble I've got myself into in the last few months.

So I tell Dan about Alex, about how I loved him once – or at least a version of me loved him. I tell him that I met up with him for coffee and that I replied to his texts. I tell him about meeting Alex in Dimitri's after our row ... and I tell him that I've seen him today too.

'Is this an affair you're confessing to, Gemma?' Dan asks, fear in his eyes.

'No, no. I suppose I'm confessing to ... being distracted by him. And flattered by him. I knew he had feelings for me and in the light of that, I should've cut all contact. But I didn't. And I'm so sorry for that.'

'But you never slept with him?'

'God, no.'

'Did you kiss him?'

'No.'

'And what happened when you saw him today?'

'I told him that I couldn't ever see him again and that I was totally in love with you and always will be.'

Dan hesitates for a moment, taking in this information as my heart seems to stop. When he speaks, his voice is choked. 'Well, what more could I ask for than that?'

He leans in and slowly sinks his lips into mine as a waterfall of relief rushes through me.

Then I remember that there's one piece of news I *haven't* broken to him. I pull away. 'We've lost the house, I'm afraid,' I sigh.

He blinks. 'Seriously? They've given it to the couple who offered more money?'

'No. They're getting back together. They're staying in the house. Thank you for writing that letter though.' I feel tears slipping down my face again as I clasp his hand. 'I don't deserve you.'

'Of course you do. Besides, it clearly didn't do a great deal of good. Bastards.' He forces a smile.

'Tossers.' I force a smile back.

He looks tenderly at me. 'At least we've got each other.'

I nod. 'And a roof over our heads. Your mum has always said we could stay as long as we wanted.'

'Which is very kind of her. But I'll be putting the call in to our old landlord first thing tomorrow.'

Chapter 68

Dan

Grandma has been in a coma, on a life-support machine, for four days and is showing no signs of improvement. Nobody has mentioned 'decisions' about the future, but given that recovery seems so unlikely, that will become inevitable.

The only thing to be said about the world around you going catastrophically wrong is that it at least crystallises what's important. Which is why I'm prepared to abandon any self-respect, get down on my knees and beg for my old job back at the Chapterhouse Centre until someone threatens me with a restraining order.

Pete and Jade are still holding their breath when I walk out of the chief executive's office.

'What did he say?' Pete asks.

'He said he *wants* me back.'

'I knew he'd jump at it!' Pete grins.

'Don't crack open the alcopops yet – it's out of his hands. He thinks my job is already gone, swallowed up by the council before I've even left the building.'

'God almighty, they were quick,' Pete mutters.

'That's how it works these days,' I say miserably. 'He's going to make some calls, but Jade – he's asked if you could dig out the relevant file and see what correspondence there's been about it so far.'

Jade doesn't move.

'What is it?'

'Well … you know your notice letter? The one I was meant to send to the council …' She reaches down, opens a drawer and pulls out an envelope. 'I was having a terrible week.' She shrugs mischievously. 'The whole thing totally slipped my mind.'

'But you never forget a thing,' Pete points out.

She winks at me. 'Silly me.'

I spend the next few days in a cloud of grief for Grandma, and gratitude that I've got Gemma, even if I singularly failed to secure her house with a view. Compared with the very human dramas we've endured over the last few weeks, that obviously pales into insignificance. Yet I can't deny there are moments, such as when we were looking at flats to rent last night so we can move back to the city, when I feel a sense of crushing disappointment about Pebble Cottage.

I'm dwelling on this issue as I'm walking through the hospital car park to visit Grandma – and Dad phones. 'Hello, son. I just wondered if there'd been any update on Flossie?'

He's been in touch every day since Grandma's heart attack and has been surprisingly good to talk to – less emotionally tangled up in it all than Mum, concerned but refreshingly calm. But there are still only so many times you can tell someone there's no improvement without it starting to get hideously depressing.

'No news, I'm afraid. The doctors seem to think that we've as good as lost her.'

'I'm really sorry, Dan.'

'Me too.' I reach the entrance to the hospital door and hover outside, gazing at a faded parking notice. 'I'd better run, Dad. I've just arrived for visiting hour and I can't take my phone in.'

'Okay. Oh, by the way – it's not your priority at the moment, clearly – but you remember that daft little music company you invested in when you were over here?'

'Hmm. The ultimate proof that I would never be the next Alan Sugar.'

'Actually, you might have had the last laugh on that one. It's just been sold for a princely sum.'

'Oh, right.' I can't muster enough enthusiasm to feel even moderately smug. 'Good for them. They were a nice bunch.'

'So nice they've made you a little earner.'

'What?'

'That money you invested in them. You're about to get it back . . . and a lot more besides.'

Gemma greets the news with such astonishment and incredulity I'm almost insulted. 'You? Invested in a company? A company that now owes you twenty grand?'

'Yes,' I shrug.

'When have you *ever* had any money to invest?'

It's a good point, I suppose. 'It was my birthday present from Dad.'

'Wow,' she mutters, sitting on the edge of the bed. 'What are you going to do with twenty grand?'

'I believe there are some good deals on second-hand Porsche Boxters these days . . . I'm joking.'

'Very funny.'

I clutch her hand. 'If you must know, I've been thinking. I know what the owners of Pebble Cottage said – but if we were to add £20k onto the price, surely they might be persuaded to let us have the house – and go and conduct their romantic renaissance somewhere else?'

Gemma pauses. 'God, I don't know. I'd kind of reconciled myself with the idea of *not* having Pebble Cottage. Painful as it is, I thought that was the end of it. Part of me felt relieved to have got off the rollercoaster.'

'It's within our reach again, Gemma. If we still want it.'

She bites her lip. 'Well, we could only ask. It's a straight-forward proposition. But this time *we* need to play hardball with *them*. Tell them that we need a decision within twenty-four hours or there's no deal.'

Chapter 69

Gemma

Six days have passed. SIX. I have never even met these people, yet I hate them with the burning, illogical passion reserved for the first boyfriend that ever cheats on you.

Despite the fact that we've got the cash, we've got the surveys, we've got the legal searches. We've got everything these bloody people could want. Yet they still need time to 'think about it'.

I sit next to Sadie in the HR room, and she glances at the doodles on my notepad.

'What's that?'

I look down, realise I've sketched a hangman frame, with two nooses. 'Nothing.' I tear off the top sheet and stuff it in my bag, looking at my watch. 'How long are they going to keep us waiting?'

The door swings open and Sebastian walks in with Babs Cartwright, who's head of our HR department. Babs is approaching retirement but is still a larger than life force in the company. Physically, she resembles a Beryl Cook lady, all formidable bosom and hairdo that looks like she's slept in rollers since 1984. Personality-wise, she's loud, outrageously flirtatious and has balls of reinforced steel.

They head for the desk in front of us.

'Would you like me to go first, Sebastian?' Babs asks, pouting her tangerine lips.

'By all means, I'll be right behind you,' he grins.

She giggles uproariously, then pulls herself together and contorts her face into a frown. 'Sadie, am I right in saying you've brought Gemma as your representative?'

'You are,' Sadie nods.

'Well,' Babs goes on, 'the matter we're here to discuss is a very serious one with very serious consequences. It is a grave, grave matter. It couldn't be more grave, or more serious, if—'

'I think she's got the picture,' Sebastian interrupts.

'We have reason to believe that on Tuesday, twenty-seventh May, you crashed your car into that of Mr Sebastian Boniface. Is this correct?'

'Yes, I've confessed to it,' Sadie says. 'Sebastian: I just want to express again how sorry I am and—'

'You went on to compound the issue by consistently lying about your involvement in the matter,' Babs continues.

465

'Repeatedly presenting untruths to a man who is your superior.'

Sadie lowers her head. If I could give her a hug right now, I would.

And it gets worse. For the next hour, Sadie is bombarded with her list of misdemeanours. Sebastian, it seems, has dragged up every tiny instance in which she failed to tell him about the car. Not to mention producing receipts, documentation and various other bits of paper proving how out of pocket he is – which, to be fair, is enough to make your eyes water.

Sadie's flimsy attempts to defend herself do nothing but irritate him and make him even more determined to get rid of her. It's such an obvious witch-hunt they might as well determine her guilt by throwing her in the swimming pool to see if she drowns.

After that one hour, she is broken, defeated. There's no question about it, she's going to lose her job.

We are finally asked to leave the room while Babs and Sebastian discuss the matter in detail.

I stand up and follow Sadie to the door when something compels me to stop and turn. 'May I add something, please?'

Babs looks at her watch. 'It's gone lunchtime.'

'This won't take a minute.' Recalling the words of the public-speaking instructor, I roll back my shoulders and project.

466

'I cannot leave this courtroom without saying a few words in defence of my friend and colleague.'

'You're not in a courtroom, Gemma,' Babs sighs.

'Oh . . . um. Well, you know what I mean.' I take a deep breath. 'Sadie has been a loyal employee of this company for six years, during which time I've worked closely with her. She is one of the most hard-working, dedicated and talented members of staff here. Without her, this company would be a far poorer place.'

Sebastian yawns. And it's that gesture that prompts a devious thought to bubble up in my head.

I glare at him. 'The thing is, Sebastian, it's not as if she's done something *really* bad. Such as taking drugs on the premises.'

Sebastian freezes and glances up, panic in his eyes.

'I know there's no *smoke* without fire,' I carry on. 'But anyone decent would defend Sadie. I *weed*. I mean . . . I would.'

Sebastian's jaw drops.

'If you're *ganja* fire her, then I think you'd be making a big mistake.' I glance between the two of them. 'A *joint* mistake. I think I'd put this issue back into the . . . *pot*. Especially if you are at all *spliff* on the matter.'

'Spliff?' Babs frowns, bewildered.

'Did I say *spliff*? I meant split, obviously.'

'Thank you, Gemma!' Sebastian shrieks. 'I think we're done now.'

467

When I'm in the corridor, Sadie turns to me. 'I really appreciate you saying all those things. I don't know what I'd do without you, Gemma.'

My phone beeps.

'You're going to be fine. One way or another,' I reassure her, looking at the message.

It's from Dan.

Rich has just phoned. Give me a ring as soon as you can. We have our answer on the house.

Chapter 70

Gemma

There's a pub in Liverpool's Georgian quarter that Dan and I used to go to all the time. It's called the Belvedere, is over 200 years old and, although tiny, is just about the most perfect city pub you could ever stumble across.

Dan is already there with Pete and Jade, when Sadie and I walk through the door. They're all talking over each other, laughing, and I feel a pang of nostalgia for the Friday nights of yore, before we only had someone else's house to go to and no money to spend.

'Tell me again the ins and outs of your sorry tale?' Pete asks.

Dan sighs. 'The owners of Pebble Cottage have decided not to sell, even in the light of our increased offer. Because they're no longer getting divorced.'

'And why are they no longer getting divorced?' Pete says.

Dan prevaricates. 'I'm sure it's for a variety of complex reasons.'

'But what did they say? Come on, spit it out.'

Dan flashes me a look. 'They said they read my letter and were miraculously reminded of the value of true love. It made them think, apparently.'

'So basically, the letter you wrote to them to persuade them to sell the house in fact persuaded them to keep it?'

'It would appear so. I'm so glad you're sympathetic,' Dan says. 'Gemma, Sadie – what are you drinking?'

'It's my round.' Pete leaps up. 'But don't start beating him up till I get back, will you, Gem?'

Jade shakes her head. 'I don't know why he thinks this is funny. You must be devastated, Gemma.'

I sit down and kiss Dan, then turn to Jade. 'Actually, I think it was fate. This whole process had become so messed up and tainted, that when I finally discovered today that there was absolutely no chance this house would be ours, I felt relieved.'

'I'm glad you've said that. Me too,' Dan confesses.

I glance at Sadie, who's suddenly gone quiet.

'You okay?' I whisper.

She nods. 'Planning on drowning my sorrows tonight.'

At which point, her phone starts ringing. She takes it out of her bag and breathes in. 'It's Sebastian.'

'Well, don't keep the man waiting,' I say gently.

She answers the phone and goes outside.

So we sit and drink and talk and indulge in well-needed light relief with friends who have the ability to make us laugh in even the direst of circumstances. And despite our despair about Grandma, the loss of the house we've battled to buy for six months, it reminds us more than anything, that if you're surrounded by the people you love, people who can dig out a glimmer of fun against all the odds, then you've got everything.

Sadie bursts through the door and runs over to us. 'Gemma! I'm back!'

'What?'

'He's given me my job back.'

I smile, relieved and happy that I've played a part, done my bit for Sadie. 'What did he say persuaded him?' I ask. Leading question, I know.

'Apparently, they've taken advice from some lawyers who said they hadn't kept the correct paperwork they'd need if ever they had to answer a case in front of a tribunal.' She grins. 'I was saved by red tape! Hallelujah!' She takes a slug of her drink. 'I'm sure your speech helped too, Gemma. Obviously.'

Several hours later, we emerge from the pub and weave through the moonlit city streets, the ones I've missed badly since living in Buddington.

We go across Hope Street, past the imposing splendour of Blackburne House and towards the cathedral, then make our way down a tiny back street dotted with old-fashioned street-lights. It contains a row of smart terraces, all with sunken gardens.

Dan suddenly grips my arm.

'What is it?' I ask.

'Look at that,' he says. I look up and see a For Sale sign, rising high above one of the properties. It's the type of house we'd originally wanted, months before we'd even looked at Pebble Cottage, but quickly realised would be way out of our price range.

I turn to Dan and say, 'Won't it be over our budget?'

He grins. 'I wasn't talking about that. Look.' He nods to the other end of the street and my eyes follow. Pete and Jade are snogging.

Chapter 71

Gemma

It is a week later when Flossie wakes up, on the first cold morning of September, when sunshine shears through the clouds and makes the whole world shimmer.

Belinda cries when she gets the call from the hospital, so hard and hysterically that at first we're all convinced that it's the news we've all been waiting for and dreading – that Grandma has died in the night.

In fact, she opened her eyes when a nurse switched on the television, and a clip from *Dirty Dancing* happened to be on *This Morning*, followed by a long discussion between Holly Willoughby and Phillip Schofield about whether or not it was the greatest romantic movie of all time.

Against all the odds, Flossie was up sipping tea later that

day, and will be allowed home soon. I don't think I've ever seen happiness shine so brightly in Dan's eyes before.

All in all, it feels like a fitting time to be moving out of Buddington Hall, even if it's a bit sad that we won't be here when Grandma comes back – though obviously we'll be visiting regularly.

I must admit, a part of me will miss living with Belinda, unlikely as that sounds. Okay, I'll be happy to give her culinary skills a wide berth, plus it'll be nice not to have to maintain a nun-like silence during every orgasm. But I've grown to enjoy having her as my 'mother-in-law', I can't deny it.

'Any more boxes for this car, Gemma?' James asks, brushing himself down. We're leaving the majority of our stuff in Belinda's garage until we actually own a house and are in a position to move in.

So for now, we are simply taking our absolutely-necessary belongings to the flat we're renting temporarily (we hope) for the next few weeks. Or probably months.

And because the Fanny Magnet has been returned by the police – and is now packed to the rafters with a duvet, our clothes and Dan's absolute essentials (which, annoyingly amount to about a tenth of mine), we've had to call in the cavalry, in the form of James and his Range Rover.

'Don't forget the Tripe Surprise I've made you!' Belinda hollers, marching down the steps and hurtling towards me with a casserole dish in her hand. I clearly hesitate: 'You don't look very enthusiastic, Gemma.'

'Sorry, I . . .'

She takes the lid off the casserole dish and shows me the contents: three ten-pound notes. 'I thought you'd prefer a takeaway. My treat.'

I laugh. 'That's really kind of you, Belinda. I'll bet it'll be strange being by yourself in the house, won't it?'

'Well, Mum might be able to come home by the end of the week and she's going to stay in the main house with me at the beginning – if I get my own way, at least. And I'm sure I'll have company in the meantime.' She glances at James, then winks at me as the paper boy rides down the drive and hands her a copy of *The Times*.

She unfolds it and glances at the blurb across the top. 'Ooh, look – I'm in the paper again!'

Belinda's publishing company weren't enormously understanding about what they considered to be catastrophic developments in her private life. Even if Belinda had agreed to back down and dump James, the story that one of the world's most notorious ball-breakers was *in love* was already out – courtesy of the photographer who caught them coming out of the village pub.

Their lawyers were called in, Belinda's lawyers were called in, and it was all heading towards something horribly messy, until someone at the publishing house made a suggestion:

that Belinda revise the book in the light of her recent experience.

It's now been re-branded – *They're NOT All Bastards* – and, while not entirely a climb-down (two words that CANNOT BE MENTIONED IN THIS HOUSEHOLD), it has been rewritten as a practical guide to sorting out the good men from the bad, to spotting the ones who are trouble, refusing to put up with any nonsense, and appreciating the good guys when they come along.

They've moved the publication date to Valentine's Day next year and it's being hotly tipped as one of the books of the year. It is *funny, caustic and wonderfully life-affirming* – at least that's what the publishers, who are *not* desperate, honestly, say. Belinda has dedicated it to her mother and father.

I don't know what makes me click onto my phone and look at Facebook, just before I get into the car. When I do, I find a message from Alex.

Gems. After much consideration, I thought it best for both of us if I un-friend you on Facebook. That is going to sound far more truculent than it's meant, but I hope you understand when I say I'd like to just remember the 16-year-old-you and the great times we had together, rather than sulk over the great times you go on to have with another man.

That said, I really – *honestly and genuinely* – hope you

and Dan are happy together and that you have a
wonderful life. You deserve it and, from what you've told
me, he does too. I'll never forget you, Gems. Even if lemon
drizzle cake will never taste quite as nice again. Alex xx

I click onto his profile and see that – sure enough, we're no longer friends. It's sad in some ways, but I can't help thinking he's right in this case: it's better to remember the past while you can still do so fondly.

I finally jump in the car, wave goodbye to Buddington and Belinda, and follow Dan to the city, to Liverpool.

Where, after months in the countryside, both of us are fairly certain we belong. When we'd first started house-hunting, there was absolutely nothing for sale in the part of the city centre we both love – the Georgian Quarter. Not that was within our budget anyway.

But after six months – during which our attention was focused solely on Pebble Cottage – that changed. The house we stumbled across on the night we fell out of the Belvedere pub is small but utterly perfect.

It is a stone's throw from Hope Street, walking distance from the Quarter (and the best breakfasts in town), and the air whispers with the music that spills from the windows of the Liverpool Institute for Performing Arts.

There is no sea view, of course, but there *is* a balcony on the top floor, big enough for Grandma's sweetheart seat and from which you can just about see the river. The living room is bright and quirky, with a high ceiling, generous windows and a Victorian fireplace, with a space above it large enough for the picture I've had blown up of Dan and Flossie running into the water in Bala Lake.

I'm not getting my hopes up. Honestly I'm not. We're at the very beginning of the house-buying process – again.

But there are times when I have to allow myself a ripple of optimism that fate might be on our side this time. Everything adds up, at least on paper: the extra £20,000 of Dan's means it is 100 per cent within our budget, particularly as the owners of Pebble Cottage had a pang of conscience and returned the money we paid for the repairs.

We put an offer in after two viewings and, although it was accepted, we have a long road ahead of us now – one in which nothing is guaranteed, as Dan and I know more than most. But what have you got if you haven't got hope?

In the meantime, the flat we're staying in is tiny, inexpensive, has all the atmosphere of a Travelodge. But as far as I'm concerned, it will do. Because it also contains Dan. And me. And nobody else.

When I arrive, he is waiting with two glasses of champagne. There are candles on the table.

'Why have you lit candles at 10.45 in the morning?'

'The booze is perfectly normal then?'

I take a sip of my champagne and he takes the glass off me

again, sliding his arms round my waist. Then he lifts up my chin and plants his lips softly on mine, reaffirming his status – officially – as the World's Best Kisser.

He leads me to the bedroom. 'What's going on?' I ask. 'Oh, I see.'

'Come on, it's been six months since we've been able to do this without the bed squeaking or my mother being downstairs. You in?'

'I'm in,' I giggle, as we tumble onto the bed. And then one thought shudders through my head: Dan Blackwood, I love you. And I'm going to give you the shock of your life.

Chapter 72

Dan

Sheila's son Mark has the same striking blue eyes as her, but that's where the similarities start and finish. He's approximately twice her size and with biceps like the inflatable rafts on a cargo ship, even if he keeps saying he's hardly made it to the gym since Rose was born.

'The lack of sleep's a killer,' he grins, rocking the pushchair back and forth. 'I used to spend Saturday nights clubbing. Now I can't make it through *Family Fortunes* without dropping off.'

'Oh, stop your moaning.' Sheila picks up the baby and snuggles her. 'She's my little angel.'

Mark has driven up from London with Rose so she can have one last cuddle with her before Sheila checks into the Kevin White Unit. She'll be there for several weeks, at which point he'll be coming back to pick her up – and has agreed that, at least for the first few weeks, she'll go and stay with him.

Only Sheila has it in her power to stay clean from then on, but this is a major step towards recovery and she's worked hard to try and set things up for when she returns, including tapping up an old schoolfriend for a part-time job in a hairdresser's.

As I help Sheila fill out the paperwork, wish her luck, and then walk out into the street, I feel genuinely optimistic. My mood continues all the way home, despite the fact that the bus breaks down and I get a call from work announcing that I've been nominated to attend a Health and Safety workshop next week.

When I enter the flat, Gemma is pacing up and down. She's wearing the red, screen-siren lipstick I know she puts on when she wants a confidence boost.

'Don't sit down,' she warns me. 'We're going out again.'

'To where? Can't we get something to eat first?' I open the kitchen cupboard and in the absence of any crisps, pull out some Crunchy Nut Cornflakes. She slams it shut and nearly negates the need for me to cut my fingernails for the next week.

'Not tonight. I thought we'd go for a walk.'

She takes my arm and we head downstairs and out into the street.

I have known my girlfriend long enough to spot when she is acting strangely. Equally, I have known her long enough to resist any temptation to point this out. So I decide to roll with it.

We dodge through Friday-night office workers, the throb of music bursting out of the bars. She leads me to the corner of Tithebarn Street, where the business district starts, and we walk in the direction of the river as office doors close and the world around us quietens.

'Don't get me wrong,' I tell her, as she breaks free and clatters ahead of me. 'I'm glad of this little diversion. But I'm also slightly surprised.'

'Why?' she asks, glancing back.

'Because you're not at home with your head in a pile of papers, phoning insurance companies and mortgage companies and shouting at estate agents.'

'What's the point in stressing about it? I refuse to let this wind me up again.'

The fresh air has clearly got to her.

We are rounding the corner to Our Lady and St Nicholas Church when the bells begin to ring – pealing out as they fill my ears and vibrate through my chest.

'They do this every Friday night,' Gemma shouts, as we approach the garden where we spent our one and only wild night of the last six months. 'I found out about it the other week. Don't they sound amazing?'

We descend into the garden as the river glitters on the horizon, golden sunlight streaming through the clouds. She takes my hand again and leads me into an oasis of roses and autumn flowers, a blaze of colour. And as we stand alone in this celestial place, the sun beating down upon Gemma's face, I lean in to kiss her – but she puts her hand on my chest and stops me.

'What's up?' I mouth.

She smiles. 'Nothing,' she mouths back.

Which clearly means *everything*. I've been caught out like this before.

I step back and hold up my arms, indicating my bewilderment in the only way I can due to the clamour of the bells.

'I HADN'T REALISED HOW LOUD IT'D BE!'

I can still only just hear her, despite the conversation taking place several decibels above our comfort zone. 'LET'S GO THEN,' I bawl.

But she shakes her head and looks at me in a way that says this has to be going somewhere. I cannot imagine where, but I stay put.

And then she shouts at the top of her voice, from the bottom of her lungs – four words:

'WILL YOU MARRY ME?'

The bells fall suddenly silent, as if they're too stunned to continue.

'What did you say?' I whisper.

She laughs joyfully. 'I said, will you marry me?'

The inside of my head does somersaults. 'Are you serious?'

She nods. 'I am.'

'But what changed your mind?' I ask dumbfounded.

She smiles and whispers, '*I just realised that I am an idiot. Because it's taken until now to realise how much you burn me up, how much I love you. I can think of nothing or nobody I could love more.* Someone wrote that to me in a letter once.'

'That's the corniest thing I've ever heard.'

'Don't you dare. It was written by the man I love. Although he still hasn't answered my question.'

I am light-headed when I reply, 'You know it's yes. It was always going to be yes.'

I take her in my arms under a luminous sky. And I realise that of all the things life may or may not throw at me, nothing will match this: loving her with every little bit of me.

Jane Costello

The Wish List

There are six months left of Emma Reiss's twenties ...
and she has some unfinished business.

Emma and her friends are about to turn thirty, and for Emma
it's a defining moment. Defined, that is, by her having achieved
none of
the things she'd imagined she would. Her career is all wrong,
her love life is a desert and that penthouse apartment
she pictured herself in simply never materialised.

Moreover, she's never jumped out of a plane, hasn't met the
man she's going to marry, has never slept under the stars, or
snogged anyone famous – just some of the aspirations on a list
she and her friends compiled fifteen years ago.

As an endless round of birthday parties sees Emma hurtle
towards
her own thirtieth, she sets about addressing these issues. But, as
she discovers with hilarious consequences, some of them
are trickier to tick off than she'd thought ...

'Close the doors, open a bottle of wine, get out the chocs and
enjoy this wonderfully witty read. Jane Costello at her best'
Milly Johnson

Paperback ISBN 978-0-85720-556-8
Ebook ISBN 978-0-85720-557-5

Jane Costello
The Time of Our Lives

It was supposed to be the holiday of a lifetime . . .

Imogen and her friends Meredith and Nicola have
had their fill of budget holidays, cattle-class flights
and 6 a.m. offensives for a space by the pool.

So when Meredith wins a VIP holiday at Barcelona's hippest
new hotel, they plan to sip champagne with the jet set, party
with the glitterati and switch off in unapologetic luxury.

But when the worst crisis of her working life erupts back home,
Imogen has to juggle her BlackBerry with a Manhattan, while
soothing a hysterical boss and hunting down an AWOL
assistant.

Between a robbery, a run-in with hotel security staff and an
encounter on a nudist beach that they'd all rather forget, the
friends stumble from one disaster to the next. At least Imogen
has a distraction in the form of the gorgeous guy who's always
in the right place at the very worst time. Until, that is, his
motives start to arouse a few suspicions.

Hilarious and heart-warming by turns, *The Time of Our Lives*
is Jane Costello at her romantic best.

Paperback ISBN 978-1-47112-923-0
Ebook ISBN 978-1-47112-925-4

CBS◉drama

Whether you love the 1980s glamour of *Knots Landing*,
the feisty exploits of BAFTA-winning *Clocking Off*, the courtroom
dilemmas of *Judge Judy* or the forensic challenges of the world's
most watched drama *CSI: Crime Scene Investigation*, CBS Drama is
bursting with colourful characters, compelling cliff-hangers,
love stories, break-ups and happy endings.

Winter's line-up includes Amanda Burton in popular British drama
Waterloo Road, new seasons of *Judge Judy*, big hair and bitch
fights in *Dallas*, and the trappings of wealth in *Beverly Hills 90210*.

Also at CBS Drama, you're just one 'like' closer to your
on screen heroes. Regular exclusive celebrity interviews and behind
the scenes news is hosted on Facebook and Twitter with recent
contributors including *Taxi's* Louie De Palma (Danny DeVito).

www.cbsdrama.co.uk

f facebook.com/cbsdrama

y twitter.com/cbsdrama

Sky: 149

Virgin: 197

Freesat: 134